THE
LAST
WIFE

Also by Karen Hamilton

The Perfect Girlfriend

THE LAST WIFE

KAREN HAMILTON

GRAYDON
HOUSE

GRAYDON
HOUSE®

Recycling programs
for this product may
not exist in your area.

ISBN-13: 978-1-525-80463-2

The Last Wife

Graydon House
22 Adelaide St. West, 40th Floor
Toronto, Ontario M5H 4E3, Canada
www.GraydonHouseBooks.com
www.BookClubbish.com

Printed in U.S.A.

For my family

THE LAST WIFE

PROLOGUE

Clients trust me because I blend in. It's a natural skill—my gift, if you like. I focus my lens and capture stories, like the ones unfolding tonight: natural and guarded expressions, self-conscious poses, joyous smiles, reluctant ones from a teenage bridesmaid, swathed in silver and bloodred. The groom is an old friend, yet I've only met his now-wife twice. She seems reserved, hard to get to know, but in their wedding album she'll glow. The camera does lie. My role is to take these lies and spin them into the perfect story.

I take a glass of champagne from a passing server. I needn't be totally on the ball during the latter half of the evening because by then, people naturally loosen up. I find that the purest details are revealed in the discreet pictures I snatch during the final hours, however innocuously an event starts. And besides, it seems this event is winding down.

The one downside of my job is the mixed bag of emotions evoked. I rarely take family photos anymore, so normally, I'm fine, but today, watching the wedding festivities, the longing for what I don't have has crept up on me. People think that envy is a bad thing, but in my opinion, envy is a positive emotion. It has always been the best indicator for me to realize what's wrong with my life. People say, "Follow your dreams," yet I'd say, "Follow what makes you sick with envy."

It's how I knew that I must stop deceiving myself and face up to how desperately I wanted to have a child. Delayed gratification is overrated.

I place my camera on a table as the tempo eases and sit down on a satin-draped chair. As I watch the bride sweep across the dance floor with her new husband, I think of Nina, and an overwhelming tide of grief floods through me. I picture her haunted expression when she elicited three final promises from me: two are easy to keep, one is not. Nonetheless, a vow is a vow. I will be creative and fulfill it. I have a bad—yet tempting—idea which occasionally beckons me toward a slippery slope.

I must do my best to avoid it because when Nina passed the baton to me, she thought I was someone she could trust. However, as my yearning grows, the crushing disappointment increases every month and the future I crave remains elusive. And she didn't know that I'd do anything to get what I want. Anything.

ONE

Ben isn't at home. I used to panic when that happened, assume that he was unconscious in a burning building, his oxygen tank depleted, his colleagues unable to reach him. All this, despite his assurance that they have safety checks in place to keep an eye out for each other. He's been stressed lately, blames it on work. He loves his job as a firefighter, but nearly lost one of his closest colleagues in a fire on the fourth floor of a block of flats recently when a load of wiring fell down and threatened to ensnare him.

No, the reality is that he is punishing me. He doesn't have a shift today. I understand his hurt, but it's hard to explain why I did what I did. For a start, I didn't think that people actually sent out printed wedding invitations anymore. If I'd known that the innocuous piece of silver card smothered in horseshoes and church bells would be the ignition for the worst argument we'd ever had, I wouldn't have opened it in his presence.

Marie Langham plus guest...

I don't know what annoyed Ben more, the fact that he wasn't deemed important enough to be named or that I said I was going alone.

"I'm working," I tried to explain. "The invitation is obviously a kind formality, a politeness."

"All this is easily rectifiable," he said. "If you wanted me there, you wouldn't have kept me in the dark. The date was blocked off as *work* months ago in our calendar."

True. But I couldn't admit it. He wouldn't appreciate being called a distraction.

Now, I have to make it up to him because it's the right time of the month. He hates what he refers to as enforced sex (too much pressure), and any obvious scene-setting like oyster-and-champagne dinners, new lingerie, an invitation to join me in the shower or even a simple suggestion that we just shag, all the standard methods annoy him. It's hard to believe that other couples have this problem, it makes me feel inadequate.

One of our cats bursts through the flap and aims for her bowl. I observe her munching, oblivious to my return home until this month's strategy presents itself to me: nonchalance. A part of Ben's stress is that he thinks I'm obsessed with having a baby. I told him to look up the true meaning of the word: an unhealthy interest in something. It's not an obsession to desire something perfectly normal.

I unpack, then luxuriate in a steaming bath filled with bubbles. I'm a real sucker for the sales promises: *relax and unwind* and *revitalize.* I hear the muffled sound of a key in the lock. It's Ben—who else would it be—yet I jump out and wrap a towel around me. He's not alone. I hear the voices of our neighbors, Rob and Mike. He's brought in reinforcements to maintain the barrier between us. There are two ways for me to play this and if you can't beat them…

I dress in jeans and a T-shirt, twist my hair up and grip it with a hair clip, wipe mascara smudges from beneath my eyes and head downstairs.

"You're back," says Ben by way of a greeting. "The guys have come over for a curry."

"Sounds perfect," I say, kissing him before hugging our friends hello.

I feel smug at the wrong-footed expression on Ben's face. He thought I'd be unable to hide my annoyance, that I'd pull him to one side and whisper, *"It's orange,"* (the color my fertility app suggests is the perfect time) or suggest that I cook instead so I can ensure he eats as organically as possible.

"Who's up for margaritas?" I say with an *I'm game for a big night* smile.

Ben's demeanor visibly softens. Result. I'm forgiven.

The whole evening is an effortless success.

Indifference and good, old-fashioned getting pissed works.

Ben snores after drinking, but I lie still, resisting the urge to prod him. There's no point in antagonizing him. It was actually my therapist who first planted the idea of playing it cool in my mind. Judy had implied (annoyingly, because I always want her to be on my side) that Ben's feelings mattered, too.

Last week's session began awkwardly as I struggled to find things to say, once again doubting the benefit of *talking things through*. Secrets develop out of necessity, and I'd already offloaded enough. Perhaps I'd simply run out of things to say or finally got bored of my own voice. But clearly not, because there I was, sitting opposite her. Again.

Fighting the urge to leave, I studied the titles on the bookshelf behind her.

"I hate silence."

It was the best I could come up with until a thread of thought tugged. Relief. I grasped and ran with it: a list of all Ben's good qualities and the positive aspects of our relationship.

I'm glad I persevered because I left the appointment buoyed up, full of hope. I imagine that if anyone ever found out that I was *seeing someone* they might assume it was because of Nina and her shock diagnosis the summer before last, but it was way before that. Not even Ben knows. I like keeping it to myself, a lost hour each week, tucked away on the other side of the New Forest.

Now that Nina has popped into my consciousness (and how can she not), I'll lie awake for even longer and my irritation with Ben will escalate until I'm forced to silence him. I get up, scrabble around for my clothes on the floor, put my underwear and T-shirt back on, drink the glass of water I had the foresight to place beside me, and go downstairs.

Wine and cocktail glasses scatter surfaces of the living area through to our galley kitchen. It looks like the aftermath of a party, not just four of us. I switch on the tap and down a pint of water. I diluted my cocktails, so I don't feel too bad, but I want to flush out as many toxins as I can. It can't do any harm to try.

This is a good opportunity to work as I've been so busy lately that I have a backlog. I clear a space at the dining table and open my laptop.

I love editing. There's something so indulgently omnipotent about the process because I get to choose what people retain as a memento of their special events. I try not to abuse their trust. I take my time, studying faces, expressions, colors, shadows, scanning for the unexpected to focus on. People think they can hide their feelings, but it's impossible, in my opinion, to succeed at it one hundred percent of the time. It takes practice. The way I do it is that I imagine that I'm being constantly filmed, which isn't difficult nowadays. It's hard enough to avoid surveillance, let alone everyone with their phones at the ready.

It's hard to concentrate. Distracted, I look back on old events. I can't help but zoom in on one person: Stuart. His pain is evident to me even when he's smiling because I'm privy to his vulnerabilities given that I am the closest friend of his deceased wife. He is much better looking on film than in reality. The urge to reminisce overwhelmingly takes hold as I browse through more of my collection. I have hundreds of photos of his and Nina's children because I find those harder to delete.

Friends sometimes mail me random shots or post them on social media. As a rule, I don't keep many of those because mine more than suffice, however one has slipped in. It's of me and Stuart, dancing at someone's thirtieth three years ago. Clearly, I couldn't have taken it, and although we look natural and relaxed, it's not a great shot. I can't think why I didn't discard it. I never mix my files up; it's disconcerting. I guess the stress of the past few years is bound to manifest in varying ways.

It's gone two by the time I return to bed. I know when I next open my eyes that it's morning because I never wake up late. I reach for Ben. My hand slides along the cool flatness of the sheet until I reach the edge of the bed. I sit up.

He was seemingly out cold a few hours ago, plus he doesn't have a shift today. He's not in the bathroom or downstairs, and his bike is missing from the hall. Dread, the anxious kind when truth is forcing its horrible reality into your consciousness, forms. He knows from all the advice that it's best if we try again this morning to maximize our chances.

I compose a message, then delete it. I can't think of the right words until I decide to keep it simple and unpressurized.

I love you xxx.

I press Send.

My phone rings, hope reignites; Ben isn't avoiding me, perhaps he's merely nipped out for croissants or milk.

It's not him.

"Hi, Stuart," I say.

"I hate to ask you but..."

He phrases it in the same way that Nina used to. Buried indignation rises, but I manage to suppress it because I already know that I'll do whatever favor he's going to ask me.

"Yes?"

"Someone tried to break in to the garage last night. There's a locksmith available at nine thirty." I note that his Australian accent sounds slightly more pronounced on the phone. "Any chance you could wait in after taking the kids to school? I'm unprepared for a meeting I can't cancel. I don't want to leave the garage door broken because it makes the interconnecting entrance to the house less secure."

"Didn't the security alarm go off?"

Nina insisted on having one installed earlier this year.

"I haven't got into the habit of setting it. It was something Nina usually did before we went to bed."

Fresh sadness hits me, as does guilt at my initial irritation.

"I'll be around ASAP."

I'm reminded of how much I enjoy being needed, although not taken for granted. There is a difference. Stuart and I have a clean slate. I must tread carefully, though, because by making myself so available to Nina and her family, it fueled my discontent in the first place.

TWO

There are moments when I genuinely forget until silence hits. Even then, it's not hard to imagine that Nina's nipped out for a sprig of rosemary, gone to chat with the holiday-cottage guests, or—later on—is upstairs resting. The locksmith was efficient and quick, he didn't even accept the coffee I offered him. He said that whoever had tried to break in couldn't have been that determined. The damage was minimal.

I never enter any rooms in her house (it's still her home to me) unless I have to, but today, it feels like there's something I need to get over with.

I go for it. I rush upstairs. My heart quickens, cringing at the thought of being caught out, despite having a plausible story at the ready. I push open the door to her room. Their bedroom. Now just Stuart's. Evidence is everywhere that he still sleeps here. I had wondered. Their place is so large, too large really, he could easily have moved. Yet, he hasn't.

There's something heart-wrenching about the way he's spread his belongings out, as if by doing so he'll disguise Nina's absence. The last time I was in here, Nina made me make promises. It gave me goose bumps: the intensity in her expression as she refused to break eye contact, the urgency of the way she grabbed my wrist as I stood up to leave.

"Please, Marie. No matter what, make sure everyone remembers the kind of person I truly was."

It was the first time she'd used the past tense. I think that's when it actually hit me, that's when I knew she was going to die, because if she believed it, then I must, too. There was no one else she could turn to, not really, because I was the only person who understood the intricacies of her life. Our friendship was forged when we were at primary school. Still, I wish I'd listened better even though it took all of my self-control to remain strong while I agreed to all she asked without pushing for a proper explanation.

I sit down on a white wicker chair in the corner, folding one of Stuart's ties over the armrest. It slithers to the floor. I used to pull this seat up, close to Nina's side of the bed. I read to her on the days she was too tired to talk properly. I thought Nina would prefer uplifting stories; however, she said it gave her strange comfort to experience fear in an alternative way to her reality, so we stuck to crime and horror.

I'm grateful for those peaceful memories. I tried not to overwhelm her because there were so many genuine offers of help, despite the feeling of shared helplessness. Nina absorbed all the love and care, meanwhile I tried not to betray my utter devastation and frustration at the unfairness of the situation.

"I think this time I'm pregnant," I say out loud. "It just feels… right."

If Nina really were here, I'd say more. Obviously. She was pleased when I met Ben, she'd offer good advice when it came to dealing with his aloofness. Her absence is stark. I lean down and pick up Stuart's tie from the floor. It's too…red. He has loads. Nina and Stuart had this thing where she'd buy him one every anniversary because she thought he looked handsome in a suit. I roll it up and push it into my jacket pocket. The past can hold people back; I'm here to help him heal. Christmas isn't far off and I feel a twinge of pleasure at now having a decent gift idea for Stuart.

Yet, all this is a delaying tactic because I'm not being decisive enough to do what I really came up here for, and I'll be frustrated if I don't. I can't waste any opportunity. I slide open Stuart's bedside drawers, check beneath the bed and open the wardrobe. After a quick scan of the bathroom, my heart rate slows. There's nothing incriminating. Which is good, because I feel slightly grubby at having poked around. But it's not as if I can ask him what I need to know outright, so for now, stealth is necessary.

As I walk down the stairs, my footsteps are muffled by thick carpet. Nina hated her feet getting cold. A large print, one of the first she completed at our art college, is framed in the middle of the wall, exactly halfway down. I briefly stop and study it, even though I could paint it myself from memory. It's alive, rich in primary colors.

Downstairs is child-friendly, no glass tables or sharp corners. Two giant bean bags, one green, one blue, take up space in the living room between the oval wooden coffee table and the TV. It's not quite to my taste, yet I've spent many happy evenings here watching movies with the kids (*Paddington* being the most popular choice lately) or discussing books with Nina's book group friends.

My favorite place, however, is the kitchen, with its black marble island, underfloor heating and built-in wine racks. Nina was a gadget person (I'm not sure what the purpose of some of them even are) but they look interior design–magazine chic.

The guest cottage to the rear of the back courtyard is designed to be a true haven. Nina came up with the idea to rent it out as a vacation rental when we first viewed this house. It's hard to think that was less than two years ago. Before…we all knew. There were no obvious signs; innocent times.

Stuart was doing well, there was no reason for them not to put in an offer for the spacious five-bedroom family home, complete with an acre of childhood-heaven-like grounds. It was very late in proceedings to put a halt to the buying and selling of their old and new homes—Nina didn't want to rent—so they went ahead. Denial? Maybe. Or perhaps it was a desire to inhabit the future family home, however briefly.

Nina had further plans: help organize family holidays, team up with a local horse-riding business and a nearby canoeing club, sell artwork (prints and pottery) at local markets. She was so utterly determined to be *there* for her children. Ever since Felix, her eldest—my godson—started primary school, she worked hard to ensure she could control her own working hours. Life is cruel.

However, my dreams aren't totally dissimilar to hers: I'd like to sell more prints. I could learn to enjoy horse riding, for the children's sake. There's no harm in being flexible, I will alter my future plans so they're more in tune with Nina's.

"Hello?"

I stop. Nina's mother is at the bottom of the stairs looking up.

My brain kicks in. "Hi, Deborah. Stuart asked me to take the children to school. Felix mentioned a cuddly toy he'd lost, I thought I'd search his room and leave it on his bed for when they get home."

"I got such a fright. Seeing you, walking down…"

Surely she must've seen my car? "Sorry. I didn't mean to give you a shock." Still, she stares. It gives me the creeps. "Shall I make you some tea?"

"What, here?" she says.

I push my hands into my pocket and grip the smoothness of Stuart's tie. "Um…"

"Which toy?" she says.

My mind races. "His lion," I say softly. Nina bought it for him on one of their last ever days out at a zoo. "Stuart also asked me to help out because they had an attempted break-in last night."

"Oh, my! Not again! Are the children all right?"

"Yes, everything's fine. I waited for the locksmith. All sorted. What do you mean, again?"

"Someone tried to break in eight or nine months ago."

"Stuart didn't mention it."

"Well, anyway, it was nice of you to help out. I'm going to check on the guest cottage, there are people arriving tomorrow for a long weekend."

"I can help," I say.

"You do enough."

"I don't mind."

She looks past me as though she expects Nina to follow me down. I take my hand out of my pocket and gently walk past her. She turns to follow me, and as she does so, I see her place her hand in the small of her back and wince slightly.

I stop.

"I promised Nina I wouldn't let you do too much," I say, truthfully. "Please let me help."

She nods her acquiescence.

I unlock the back door. We walk down the steps and cross the courtyard. To the right are empty stables. Two metal pails, left by the previous owners, hang off a white-painted side wall. Déjà vu hits.

Nina and I looked around here together when it first came on the market. Stuart was away somewhere—Glasgow, I think—at the time, and Nina had such a strong feeling that this would be The Place that she hadn't wanted to postpone a viewing. Nina asked me to keep it to ourselves though; she knew I wouldn't mind lying by omission. This meant that after they'd moved in, I had to ensure my surprise and awe appeared genuine. It wasn't hard; it is impressive.

Deborah and I walk side by side along the paved path edged with rose bushes that leads to the guest property. There's always a disconcerting moment as I push open the cottage door. Are the previous guests still here? What odd items will we discover they've left behind?

"Hello?" I call out as we open the front door.

The sound of the back door slamming shut makes us both jump.

Silence.

There is no sign of anyone as I check the back door. It's unlocked. I relax as I glance around because the cleaning company have definitely been and gone, I can tell by residual smell of furniture polish and bleach. The door must've been left open by the cleaners. In fairness, a rare oversight.

While Deborah fills a vase with carnations, which she takes out of a basket I hadn't noticed she was carrying, I flick through the guest book, skim-reading multiple paragraphs of compliments. *Clean, stunning location, wonderful attention to detail, comfortable.* I make a note to add the latest testimonial to the website.

"I'll make us some tea," I say. "I'll clean up afterward," I add before she can object.

I drop Stuart's tie into the bin, along with the tea bags and mini-cartons of long-life milk. Although it's only little by little, I've removed yet another unnecessary reminder for Stuart. It's rewarding. This is just one example of the many small but effective ways I can help.

I make Deborah's tea extra milky, exactly how she likes it.

"Thanks," she says as I hand her a mug decorated with poppies.

"Shall we sit down?" I say, pointing to the sofa.

"No, we shouldn't. We'll leave creases. I'd rather stand to be honest."

Grief makes me want to control things, makes me furious, makes me want to *live*. I mute my irritation; standing it is then. She sips her tea with obvious non-enjoyment.

As I struggle to think of something neutral to say (a contrast to our relationship pre–Nina's diagnosis), I compare my own surroundings with these luxurious ones. Our semi is nice enough, there's nothing wrong with it, but it's new and the walls are thin. It has a temporary feel to it as if the big bad wolf could blow the house down with one breath. Here, the old stone walls give off an air of permanence and security. I would feel happy and safe if I lived in a place with history. I've suggested to Ben a few times that we move; it's time to bring the subject up again.

It's the word *Stuart* that jolts me back into the moment.

"Pardon?"

"His parents have offered to come and stay," Deborah says. "I think it would be a good idea, it would give him the support he needs from the people best able to provide it."

"Oh," I say.

He hasn't mentioned this to me.

"People mean well, I've seen the steady stream of…" she pauses "…*women*—mostly—knocking at the door with a shepherd's pie, a casserole, a lasagna, books or an offer of this, that and the other, but that's not what he needs. He's a grown man, and it's best if he concentrates on the children for now, without distractions."

"People want to be kind and help. As you say, Deborah, he's a grown man."

However, she's not wrong. Still, I have the situation in hand. I wish I could tell her that. It's not something she needs to worry herself with.

"Stuart loved Nina, no, he adored her," I continue. "He isn't going to lightly replace her with some random woman in the near future just because she can cook," I say with what I hope is a reassuring smile.

It doesn't work. She washes up the mugs, wiping them dry with kitchen paper so as not to dirty a tea towel, while I remove the bag from the trash, tie a knot at the top and replace it with a new one.

"I'm pregnant," I blurt out.

I want to give her something else to focus on, I want to draw her back into my confidence, to trust me again. It's not a complete lie because you can do tests so early nowadays, my news is only a week or so premature.

It works. I can physically sense her warming toward me again now that she's got proof that I don't have designs on her son-in-law (technically, is he still)? She smiles and comes over to give me a hug.

"That's wonderful news!"

"It's very early days," I say. "So it's vital to keep it to yourself."

Deborah locks up while I dump the trash bag in the outside bin.

She asks all the questions I've been dying for people to ask me as we amble back to the house: due dates, scans, boy or girl preference, plans for work afterward. It feels good until she changes the subject to her disappointment in the latest gardeners Stuart has employed. Time to say goodbye.

I reverse. Bumping over the cattle grid, I exit the village as I head back to my own responsibilities and worries. Red, yellow, orange and brown leaves scatter the lane. I love the colors at this time of year. Smoke wafts from a cottage chimney, reminding me of my childhood home because Mum lit fires early on in the season. I loved going stick-gathering with her in the woods. A yearning to visit her as soon as possible forms; it's been too long.

As I slow down to avoid a trio of ponies huddled together, a horrible thought forms: Deborah will go upstairs and spend time in the children's room. I know she will, she always does. Felix's lion isn't on his bed. Lies work better when I go easy on the details, stick to my own tried and tested rules. It would be careless not to keep her on my side if I'm to figure things out in a way that works best for me.

I'll bake a Victoria sponge with the children on Sunday

and use some of her homemade raspberry jam. Ben will be at work, and Stuart has never turned down an offer of child-entertainment assistance. We'll drop it round to Deborah's afterward as a surprise. She can't fail to be softened by the gesture.

And, thinking about it, how can Deborah realistically react if I say that I (or she) was mistaken about a mere toy lion? There's not much she can do or say. It's not as if she can accuse me outright of being a liar, not without proper proof. Anyway, it's because of Nina—her daughter—that I was forced to make something up.

I must relax and quit the overthinking. Stress isn't good for a baby.

THREE

Parts of Nina's life became off-limits after Felix was born. She hung out with people from baby groups (as I referred to them), and these strangers offered her something I couldn't. I understood that, yet I envied her reaching a life-altering milestone, having her focus shifted away. I despised my petty reactions—why couldn't I be genuinely happy for her like a normal friend—still, I responded by going out, making new friends, posting my happy, child-free life on social media. Nina was too busy, too distracted, too in love with her baby to care.

It was then that I contacted a therapist because I wanted to hand over all the negative emotions to someone else to take care of. It didn't work like that. I wasn't brave enough to reveal the real, messy stuff, and when my counselor pushed, I moved on to a new one. Judy is my third. (I've never told her that). She lets me meander, set my own pace, and sometimes I dislike her because she lets me get away with it.

I did admit to something once: when Nina's tiredness *truly* kicked in after Emily's birth, as she naturally relied on me more by accepting my offers of help, our friendship equilibrium was restored. Because Nina's plight made me feel better about myself, I was frightened about what kind of a person that made me. My then-therapist helped me to accept that I wasn't a monster.

However, something I've come to learn about therapy is that therapists can only work with what their clients reveal. I framed it so it sounded as if Nina had asked me for help even though I'd been waiting a while for the right moment to step in. I knew from books and online forums that she'd find it tough at times.

I was happy to babysit, to give her and Stuart time to go out alone. I felt at home in their place, with the children snuggled on either side of me on the sofa, cocooned and safe. Some weekends, they'd go to an art exhibition or horse riding. Stuart loved taking her to his yacht club, even though Nina hated sailing, so they'd eat seafood and socialize on the terrace instead. While they were out, it gave me time to bond—properly—with Felix, despite not having been around as much as I'd have liked to have been during his formative years. It's regrettable (for all our sakes) that Nina was too overcautious when he was little. She'd hover around when I picked him up, roll her eyes if I dared to offer gentle suggestions to help them both get some more sleep.

Several months into her illness, when Nina asked me to host her popular village book group (of which she was the founding member), was a pivotal moment: I'd been fully let back in. I was good enough. Nina's other life automatically demystified as her friends became mine, too. I loved being included in the organizing of school events, fund-raising, barbecues, picnics, parties. I had different spreadsheets, more messages and emails than I could sometimes keep track of. Even my phone rang more; it was no longer used primarily for work. I was *there* for my oldest friend. When Stuart confessed how grateful they both were, dramatic as it may sound, I felt like my true purpose had been restored.

Tonight is important: it's the first meeting of Nina's book club since she's been gone. We agreed to take a six-month break, to mourn privately. She did make us all promise to keep it going.

"I want things to carry on, otherwise what was the point in anything?" I wasn't sure what Stuart's reaction was going to be when I asked if we could host it at his, but he was up for it.

"It's the evenings when I'm never quite sure what to do with myself," he'd said. "It will be a welcome distraction."

I hope he didn't think that I meant him to join in? We're a tight-knit bunch, his presence might upset the balance, despite his link to the group. As I rehearse a tactful letdown should the need arise, Stuart emerges downstairs. He surveys my careful preparations: black-and-white skeleton cakes, ghoul-shaped crisps to go with the dips and orange napkins. He helps himself to a carrot stick. The crunching grates; I hate the sound of people eating.

"Wine?" I say.

"God, yes," he says. "Emily just asked about Nina. It stabs every single bloody time. I know it's good that she feels able to ask questions, but it's so utterly heartbreaking, and there's nothing I can do. Nothing! I'm her father, I'm supposed to be able to make anything and everything better."

"It's bloody unfair," I say as I hand him a glass. "I remember after the funeral I was shocked to emerge from the relative darkness of the church into the daylight and see life going on as normal for everyone else. It made me so angry."

There's really nothing else remotely comforting I can think of to say that hasn't been uttered so many times. I'm an arm-patting, "there, there" type of person, not a natural hugger. A change of subject is my preferred method of grief and anger management.

"I'm going to leave the door unlocked like Nina used to, so the doorbell doesn't disturb the children," I say.

"Yeah, fine."

There's a brief silence before he joins in with my avoidance.

"What's the book?" he asks, taking a large sip of a French Malbec.

The aroma hits. I'd love one, but I genuinely do believe that I'm pregnant, despite four tests telling me I'm not. It's still too early to be accurate, so it was a complete waste of money and energy—as Ben didn't hesitate to tell me—but I couldn't help myself.

"A ghost novel," I reply.

Guilt hits at my insensitivity, before reason takes over. *Of course* Stuart doesn't think of Nina as a ghost. How ridiculous. I'm doing the exact thing he hates: people behaving abnormally around him. Not for the first time I notice that he touches his beard more when he's feeling awkward.

"Sounds seasonal," he says.

Silence hangs until I realize that this is the perfect opportunity to broach a delicate subject. Nina's promises have been unsettling me more than usual lately because I'm now her sole voice. My latest fear is that her words will distort and mist further over time and the importance of her promises will fade when more immediate priorities automatically take precedence. Some gentle but legitimate detective work is required.

Every time I mull things over, the more obvious it becomes that Nina was too overly concerned about her future reputation for someone in her situation. She was trying to tell me something without spelling it out. I'm not too worried—there can't be anything bad to unearth—she's hardly likely to have been the local drug dealer or involved in some elaborate scam. Still, theories worm away at my consciousness, along with the frustration that I missed my cues to delve deeper when I had the opportunity.

"I've been thinking of the best ways I could help out more. I'm happy to do even more of the admin and everything else in relation to the running of the guesthouse," I continue, pleased at how natural I sound. "Deborah does her best, but she doesn't update the website or reply to comments," I say.

"The trouble is, she enjoys it. It gives her a purpose."

"Understandably, but I promised Nina I'd do everything I could. I'll act carefully, make sure she doesn't feel like I'm treading on her toes."

Before he can respond, there's a distant thud coming from upstairs.

"Shall I go and check on them?" I say. "It's probably one of Emily's books."

He smiles. "Yeah, probably. She has a pile even bigger than her mother's was. Go ahead, shout if you need me."

He turns around and walks off in the direction of his study, shutting the door behind him. He really isn't himself. Stuart has excellent manners and is a good host, he'd never usually have a drink without offering me one, but still, it saves me having to pour it down the sink when no one is looking.

Upstairs, I peek into Felix's room first. His Batman bedside light shines yellow. He's asleep. A snow globe is lying on the carpet beside his bed, thankfully intact. Nina gave it to him to shake and watch the flakes settle if he ever needed a calming prop.

I sit beside him and stroke his hair like I watched Nina do so many times; he can't have been asleep long. The burst of love I feel for my godson is overwhelming. I can't imagine loving my own child more than this. I gently rub my stomach. It's not flat—it never has been—but already it feels rounder. (Rationally, I know it's not.)

"Night night, lovely boy," I whisper.

I kiss his forehead before I stand up and switch off the light. He likes sleeping in the dark, but Nina always insisted that he didn't. When I gently mentioned that perhaps it wasn't a good idea to pass on her own fears, she'd turned on me.

"What would you know, Marie?"

That stung because I know a lot, actually.

The doorbell chimes. It plays out an unnecessary, long-winded tune, which I'll suggest to Stuart he change. I open

Emily's door, all appears calm. I blow Emily a kiss and rush downstairs. Stuart has beaten me to it.

"Hi, Tamsin," I say to Felix's best friend's mum.

We hug. It's quite a huggy group. I've got used to it.

"Sorry," I mouth to Stuart. "You go back to whatever you were doing."

He obeys.

"Come in," I say to Tamsin, leaving the door on the latch and leading her toward the living room. "Help yourself to wine. I'll be through in a minute with some snacks."

I pick up a bowl of crisps and other nibbles before I join her.

"How are you?" I say.

"All right," she replies.

She looks around. Cobwebs drape over the mantelpiece, pumpkins grin in front of the fireplace and ghostly images stare from the large mirror hanging above. "You've done an amazing job in here, it looks so…welcomingly scary."

"Thanks."

"I can't believe she's not here. Was it strange getting ready without her? I feel like I'm being…*unfaithful* somehow." She takes a large sip of prosecco. "I was sure Stuart would rather we all met at mine or down at the pub."

"I'm used to being here," I say. "Nina and I were friends for so long that even when she met Stuart, nothing much changed. We almost became a threesome, although not in *that* way obviously," I add. "I find Stuart easy to talk to. He's a good listener."

Tamsin is looking at me as though she has something to say, although I can't guess what. Nina *would* approve of tonight; it was her baby.

"Hello?" says a voice—Sharon (mother of a friend of Emily's) walks in, followed by several women: mums at school, friends and neighbors, Miriam, Abigail, and a man, Greg, who lives on the other side of the village. As the room fills, I sense a danger of the evening becoming too somber because no one wants to be the first to seem too lively. In hostess mode, I do my best to lift the mood, but my repeat reassurances that "it's what Nina would've wanted" and that "Stuart has no issues with it" frustrate me.

"Between us," I say. "I think he likes the company. Especially after all the burglaries around here lately."

"What burglaries? I haven't heard of any!"

I feel my cheeks burn as I clock Tamsin's widened eyes. I feel mean—she lives at the more deserted end of the village. I shouldn't have exaggerated like that. Nothing was even stolen from Stuart's house or garage.

"Clearly, I'm mistaken, sorry, ignore me." Time to change the subject. "Who would like to go first and share their initial thoughts?" I say, choosing the kind of words Nina would use.

I feel like an overworked, underappreciated manager trying to bring staff to order. I don't want to give that impression, but what is the point in having a book club if you don't discuss it? Yes, it's incredibly sad that Nina's gone, but *I'm* here and I'm doing my best, just as I promised.

It's obvious who has read the novel and who is winging it. I make mental notes because they've had *six* months. Maybe I'll subtly suggest to repeat offenders that this may not be quite the group they're looking for. I promised to take care of things for Nina. It's a big responsibility. Ruining anything she set up would be a sad failure.

Deflated that the evening has not been the success I'd hoped for, I nearly cave when Tamsin offers me a glass of red as we both tidy up after the others leave.

"No, thanks," I say, drawing steeply on diminishing will-power.

"Ah," she says with a wink. "Any news to share?"

The problem with lies is that it's easier to stick to a thread. I nod. The moment I do, a memory flashes: Nina had confided that she found Tamsin overly inquisitive.

"Oh, huge congratulations!" she says, throwing her arms around me.

I stiffen. Heat flames my cheeks for the second time this evening as regret at my big mouth hits.

"It's a secret," I say.

"What's a secret?" asks Stuart, standing at the study door.

My mind grasps for words but they're elusive.

"Marie's got some news—" says Tamsin.

I interrupt. "It's very early days and—"

"Well, very early congratulations then," he says with a smile.

He looks genuinely pleased, yet the thought of new life can't do anything but highlight his own loss.

"I don't know what came over me. Ben will be so cross if he finds out I've blabbed."

An understatement.

If he discovers my lie, he'll throw our past back in my face and I dread to think where that will leave us. Just a few more days and all this will right itself by becoming true. I'll stay calm and ride this out. It's not as if it's the first time I've been forced to do this.

FOUR

Humiliation intertwines with grief, rage, disappointment, despair. I can no longer pretend. It has been another week of negative results. When it feels physically impossible to cry anymore, I chuck the white plastic stick into the bin with the others, tie up the bag and transfer it to the outside garbage.

Ben will go mad if he finds them.

Or, maybe he won't.

It's only seven in the morning, but fuck it, I pour a Baileys into a coffee and stir. I check the kitchen clock. Ben's due home from work in less than an hour. I need to think.

When I told him my period was late yesterday, his reaction was to warn me *again* about gun-jumping. I tried to believe it was because he was trying to protect me from more disappointment. But...I can sense lies. I'm good at detecting the telltale signs. More often than not, it's concealed in the barely perceptible shift of a gaze.

Ben's eyes betrayed relief. He does not want to have a baby with me anymore; he just hasn't got round to telling me. I down the contents of my mug and make myself another.

By the time Ben's key turns in the lock, I've come up with a plan: avoidance. Plus, a mental pact not to lie in future (at least not big ones), and I'll do all the things Ben's asked me to, like spend less time at Stuart's, talk about things other than Nina or our future baby, be more *fun*. I figure that if I weather this particular relationship storm, things will naturally settle down. My dad always says that. Most of the time, it's true.

"Hi," I say.

We hug, but don't kiss.

"Everything okay?" he asks.

There's no point in trying to hide my red eyes. I look like a frog. I shrug.

Ben knows what it means. He holds me tight and I give into grief again, my eyes shut tight, my face buried against his chest so I don't have to deal with his reaction.

There are practicalities to deal with in the aftermath of a big lie; enough of a reversal in order that I don't have to confess outright. There is an art to it: a mix of weaker lies, a dash of truth, a deflective comment, until I come up with something decent enough to let me off the hook. I enjoy it in a twisted way and almost take pride in my creativity. There's painful pleasure with the release of fear, the underlying panic at being caught out obliterated like a downpour after a dry spell.

I start with Deborah: a phone call. *My period came, a hint of an early miscarriage.*

Tamsin is next with a text outlining a similar fib.

I tell Stuart in person.

"I made a mistake."

"Sorry to hear that," he says. "Nina thought she was expecting twice before Emily came along."

Betrayal is a hard emotion to conceal because it twins with the physical symptoms of sickness. Sometimes, I used to think that I was being a bit paranoid or oversensitive when I felt left out of Nina's life. Each time I'm confronted with evidence that it wasn't my mind, it's bittersweet.

"I hope it happens for you soon," Stuart continues. "You're so great with children. Can I make you a coffee? Tea?"

"No, thanks, I'm on my way to work, a sixtieth birthday celebration," I say. "I just popped by to tell you and get it out of the way so that I can move on without any…" I struggle for the right word "…misunderstanding."

"I get it," he says. "I don't know if this is an appropriate time to mention this, but I was going to ask if you're up for a visit tomorrow lunchtime to the new pizza place on the high street? The children have been asking, and it would be great to have adult company. No pressure, though, only if you're feeling okay? Ben's welcome, too. All on me, of course."

I smile. "Ben is working. But I'd love to, thanks."

"It's a date," he says.

As I drive away, guilt hits at the broken pact with myself. Should I have told the truth, that I'm on my way to an appointment with my therapist? I've always kept it private. Maybe I should be more open with the people I trust, admit that I need help?

Yet, when it comes to doctors, dentists, fake work appointments, surely everyone fibs? It's not just me. Lies make life palatable. It's simply unavoidable at times. I do it to protect myself and others. Surely, it's not a bad thing to tell people what they want to hear? Sometimes, there's no choice.

Judy throws me.

"Why don't you just ask Ben if he still wants children rather than risk miscommunication with all this guesswork?"

"Because what do I do if I don't like the answer?"

"What do you think you should do?"

This is followed by the horrible silence which unnerves me so badly. Maybe it's time to move on from Judgmental Judy. Therapists are supposed to be impartial. Does craving a baby with a long-term partner make me a bad person? No, it does not. Ben will make a wonderful dad. On the whole, we're a great team and it's normal to have wobbles. A baby is a big commitment. It's good, in a way, that he's doubting himself. It means he's taking things seriously.

"The thing is," I say, choosing my words carefully, "Ben took some persuading."

The whole truth being that he thought it wasn't just about him, that it was primarily all about me and my desires.

"I feel like I could be just any man," he has said many times during our arguments. "As long as you get a baby, the father is irrelevant to you."

I've worked so bloody hard on our relationship to prove that isn't true. I've made so many compromises, told him whatever he wants to hear.

"Everything will be fine," I say out loud to Judy. "Once Ben made the decision to go ahead and start a family, he was committed. Ben is a man of his word."

I don't like the expression on her face.

I got it wrong. As I leave Judy's (five minutes early. I couldn't bear it any longer), I switch on my phone. Ben wants to talk.

In my experience, no one ever *wants to talk* about anything positive. I hate it when people do this, Ben knows that. Perhaps it's his way of letting me know quite how pissed off he is with me in general. My parents wanted to *talk* about "forming other friendships and not relying solely on Nina" and "the importance of telling the truth." Nina wanted to *talk* about lots of things, but I'm good at diverting conversations away from the unpleasant and back to neutral, less scary ground. It's where I feel safe.

I rehearse what I'm going to say to Ben: I've sensed he's had doubts, that I have them, too (I don't). That Nina's death has hit me so hard that I wake up feeling winded (true). However, the most effective thing will probably be if I tell him that I love him more than I've ever loved anyone.

"It's too late," according to Ben. "It sounds clichéd, but we've been drifting apart for a long time," he says. "It's easy to blame external things, like the amount of time you spent at Nina's, how low down your list of priorities I feel, but I know I'm not perfect either."

I sip the freshly ground coffee he made me before he instigated our *talk*. He's made it exactly the way I like it, full-fat milk, not too strong. I wonder if this is the last nice thing he'll ever do for me.

"I'm sorry if this sounds cruel, but I'm glad we couldn't conceive after all," he carries on. "It makes it easier for us to part amicably, without complications."

"Talk about kicking someone when they're down." I stop. There's a gentle art to applying emotional pressure. If I pile it on too heavily, too soon, he'll feel cornered. "A baby wouldn't be a complication," I say. "It would be an extension of our relationship. It would cement us, give us more common ground."

"I…" He stops. He turns away from me and looks out of the window before looking back again with an added air of determination about him. "This is hard, harder than I thought it would be to say, but I'm going to be honest. No more lies."

"Lies?"

Oh my God, please no. I know what he's going to say, it's so painfully obvious, I bet even Judy's guessed. I try to block out the words that will make me hate him, force me to agree to us splitting up, upend my whole life, my dreams.

The words, when he says them, are even worse than I feared. It's not just that he doesn't want a baby. He does want one. Just not with me. He's been seeing someone—no one I know apparently—and he's desperately sorry, didn't want me to find out from someone else (thoughtful of him) but…she's pregnant. Only just found out last night apparently! Unplanned, unfortunate, unexpected.

Un-fucking-fair more like! On and on the excuses, justifications and apologies stream from his mouth: a mess; he didn't mean to be weak and cruel; he should've addressed the issues between us earlier, blah blah blah.

None of this helps me because I can't fight something as catastrophic as this. Truth is a painful bastard. Lying to yourself is a much better option—it's the purest form of deception, the best protection there is.

"How long?"

"I told you. She's only just found out."

"How scary for you, potentially two pregnant women at the same time! You know very well that what I mean is how long have you been sleeping with her?"

"A couple of months."

Horrible realization hits hard, deep in my gut, that it means the problem must lie with me if Ben is capable of conceiving with someone else with such ease. I throw my coffee cup against the wall.

Ben flinches, but doesn't move. For a few seconds we both stare at the brown stain trickling down the white wall.

"Who is she?"

My mind scans all the possibilities I know. No one springs to mind.

"I told you. No one you know. A colleague. She moved here from France and—"

"How cozy. Get out!" I scream. "Get out!"

Which is exactly what he wants to do, but of course not what I genuinely mean.

I want him to stay, to put his arms around me and tell me that none of what he said is true.

Ben is the only man I've ever lived with. I dislike the thought of living alone. When my elder brother left the family home, it was the little, unexpected things that highlighted his absence: his trainers missing by the back door, his blue bike leaning unused against the garden fence, his not being around to take the piss out of me. The things that drove me mad about him were the things I missed the most after he had left with his backpack for "Asia, Africa, Europe—wherever I feel drawn to." He has yet to return to the real world, and I envy him. Sam chose freedom, leaving me with conformity.

Ben puts on his cycle helmet, clips the strap beneath his chin and walks out the front door. He must be going to see *her*.

It's a struggle to catch my breath. I have to push away the horrible, intrusive thoughts insisting that I deserve this karmic payback because of past bad decisions.

Ben is—was—my partner. I was drawn to him partly because he wasn't a natural risk-taker. He loves being a firefighter, but outside of work he is happy with weekends close to home, a pizza in front of the TV on a Saturday night, plus the odd trip to the cinema. We tend to go for long country walks in the forest, followed by a Sunday pub roast when he's not working. I wrongly assumed that he was a safe option.

Ben said he felt low down on my list of priorities. I hope I haven't thrown away my chance of becoming a mother. I tried everything possible to conceive. I was prepared to give anything a go because initial tests showed that there was nothing medically wrong. According to one of the fertility experts I consulted, I just needed to relax. Which was easy for her to say. I tried everything: herbs, hypnosis, yoga, reflexology, acupuncture, a healthy diet. The lack of control and disappointment chipped away at hope, month after month. I feel alone in my desperation.

From now on, I'm going to do things differently.

I dial Stuart's number.

He has the potential to offer something Ben has now denied me. Every sensible person has a backup plan.

FIVE

I've been blind. While focusing on my desires and disappointments, I've ignored the fact that the children need all the love and attention I can give them. One of the most heart-wrenching questions Felix asked me recently was if he was ever going to get a new mummy and if so, would she be nice to him? Good can come out of my heartache because I'll have more free time. We are in a horrible pizza place, the lights are too bright, the service is slow, the food uninspiring, yet I feel immense maternal pride as the waiter refers to my son and daughter. I belong.

It doesn't yet fill the hole left by Ben's betrayal—I feel sick at the thought of him with someone else—yet I can't deny that maybe...*maybe*...a part of me allowed it to happen. His actions mean that my hand has been forced and perhaps it's not such the terrible thing it initially appears.

Now that I can be more honest with myself, I can admit that I didn't ever feel totally secure in our relationship. Ben never truly forgave me for the pregnancy scare not long after we met on an online dating site. He said he did, but he was lying to himself. We'd already arranged to set up home together when I discovered that I wasn't expecting after all, and it resulted in a rushed overfamiliarity with our bad habits, rather than a more natural or romantic beginning. Even though I had good intentions (Ben is the overly indecisive type), I was aware that Nina and others would have negatively judged my methods, so I didn't share the whole story. But now, he's fulfilled a dream that was initially mine, not his.

"Fancy the park?" Stuart says the moment Felix and Em finish their ice creams.

I smile, pleased at our complicit desire to talk alone.

Stuart and I sit on a bench as the children pull themselves up a climbing frame.

"Careful," I shout out to Emily.

Nina came to the conclusion that it was best not to overprotect the children as they got older, to let them make mistakes, fall, hurt themselves. I disagree. I sense that Stuart feels the same; he is watching Em as she climbs higher and I can tell that he's ready to run if need be.

"Phew," I say as she descends before running off to the slide.

"I've thought about what you asked…" Stuart says.

I hold my breath.

"Perhaps it could work, but my parents' flights from Brisbane are booked. The guesthouse was deliberately kept free for them over the Christmas period. They *could* stay in the main house with me, but I'm not sure how my dad, in particular, will cope with the children's noise. How about you move into the guesthouse in January, depending on how it all works with future bookings?"

"There are none. I checked."

"Oh. Nina used to be quite on it when it came to marketing the place," he says.

"Nina passed on plenty of top tips. Bookings will pick up once I get more fully involved. Come spring and summer, we'll be turning people away."

"I wasn't suggesting that it was your fault."

"I know." I touch his arm reassuringly.

"Daddy, come over here! Spin the roundabout fast!" yells Emily, waving frantically from the middle of the park.

Stuart obediently ambles off in her direction.

I email Deborah, hinting that Stuart needs more help organizing Christmas, and offer suggestions, things that I don't want to get involved in, like ordering a turkey, providing up-to-date relatives' addresses for Christmas cards and choosing which charities she thinks Nina would've liked to support this year. It's a gentle nudge away from my chosen projects.

Another random parent has taken up spinning duties, so Stuart and I return to our bench. The cold seeps through my jeans. I couldn't think of practicalities, like gloves, when I left the house this morning so I blow into my cupped hands to warm them.

"A longer time frame gives you and Ben time to sort out practicalities, split your assets surely?"

"Our place is rented," I say, concentrating on my cold fingers. "We have separate bank accounts."

"Oh."

Stuart lives in a world where everyone owns a home.

"Ben and I... Well, it's bad. I didn't tell you everything. His new *girlfriend*, she's pregnant."

"What the...? That's shocking. Ben seemed like a straight-forward guy. I'm really sorry, Marie. That's...harsh."

"It is pretty crap."

We sit in silence.

"He even had the audacity to ask if he could keep our cats!" I start to laugh and find I can't stop. Stuart does, too, until we are both laughing so hard that I clutch my stomach. It's such a wonderful release.

"He doesn't love her," I continue, when I manage to catch my breath. "I know because he wants to continue to rent our place on his own while he considers all the best options. He's in shock."

"How about...?"

"Yes?" I jump in, praying that Stuart is going to suggest what I think he is.

"How about if you move into a spare room temporarily? It would help us both out, and when my parents leave, we have another chat?"

"If you're sure?"

"It seems like an obvious solution."

"What will people think?" I ask.

Stuart mulls it over.

It *is* a real concern because it's obvious what people, especially Deborah, will think. I need to play this carefully, Stuart is still protected by numbness, assumes that sympathy to his plight will remain. It won't. If he breaks "the rules," he will open himself up to local public dissection. Being under the spotlight is only welcome if it's positive attention.

As a teenager, I learned this the hard way. Thankfully it was during the years before social media. I don't think I could have coped with having a silly, tiny, white fib of mine publicly dissected. It was bad enough outside the humanities block at break time surrounded by nosy classmates. As they laughed and probed, I had a choice: to confess or brazen it out. I chose the latter. I stuck to the story and insisted that I had gone to a vague friend of a friend's party the previous weekend, even though I hadn't. Afterward Nina said to me privately that there was no point in lying. She was wrong. There's always a reason for lying.

"Well...there's nothing *to* think. We don't have anything to hide," Stuart says.

"That's true."

As I stand up, long-forgotten hope resurfaces. This is not *exactly* how I intended things to happen, but I'm going to make it work for everyone's sake.

"I think we should tell Deborah together," I suggest. "Reassure her that the arrangement is practical and workable, and that nothing will change."

"Good idea."

As I sip hot chocolate and watch Em pick the marshmallows out from hers with a teaspoon, I see an elderly couple glance over. They both smile at me. I smile back. Finally, I know what acceptance feels like. I've craved it for so long. Stuart and I are going to make a great team—I'll make sure of it. Before long, he'll struggle to cope without me.

I take out my camera and capture the moment. If it wasn't insensitive to do so, I would caption it in the memory album of Nina's life which I'm creating for Felix and Em with something along the lines of *Fresh Beginnings*.

Stuart and I smile at each other. Nina trusted that my loyalty to her was unshakeable, that I'd do whatever it took to fulfill her wishes. Gratitude was never her strongest point, but *this* has made everything I ever put myself through worthwhile. I briefly close my eyes and send her a silent thank-you.

Emily is staring at me when I open my eyes. She always was a tricky child. I felt betrayed when Nina had chosen a random woman from her prenatal group to be Em's godmother, but now, thanks to Ben and Stuart, I'm in a much stronger position to influence her behavior for the better. Nina was too soft on her. Seeing as I've just relearned the hard way that change is inevitable, I'll start as I mean to go on. It won't take me long to train Emily. She's old enough to learn decent manners.

I smile at her, but she doesn't reciprocate.

It stings.

I sip the dregs of my hot chocolate, even though it's gone cold, to distract myself, to stop my mouth twisting in displeasure.

I, more than anyone, can appreciate the benefits of playing the long game.

SIX

Trust someone to pour cold water over my happiness.

"It doesn't sound like a good idea to me at all, love," my dad says. "You wrecked your relationship with Ben over Nina and her family, and now you're stopping yourself moving on by letting yourself get sucked back in to Nina's affairs all over again."

He takes a sip from his pint of cider. He has one every Saturday lunchtime at his local. I joined him today because, usually, I love spending time with my father.

"Ben had an affair, Dad. Nina is no longer with us."

"I worry about you," he says. "Even now you put her above yourself. It's not right."

"I wish I hadn't said anything," I say, folding my arms, my teenage self resurfacing. "It's only for a few months, and it's good for me, Stuart and those poor children. It's only temporary while we all figure out a new normality."

He gives me a look. "Really?"

"Yes, really. I'll talk to Mum about it instead."

"How's work?"

His blatant change of subject says a lot, but I don't mind. I have a new therapist, a man this time, Christian, to share fresh stories with. It feels good, like crisp, blank stationery at the beginning of a September school term.

"Work is busy," I reply to Dad's question. "Lots of festive weddings and anniversaries."

I stopped photographing christenings and naming ceremonies over a year ago. Now that my family situation is different, maybe I'll be able to face capturing hope and innocent happiness again.

I leave him to his ritual. He likes to read the pub's free newspaper, picking out stories to get outraged by. I'll get a different reaction from my mother; his comments have touched a nerve.

I never used to enjoy talking to my mum much about personal things, but it's different now. From my eighteenth birthday onward, she impressed upon me the importance of not leaving it too late to have a baby because of her own struggles. Mum conceived me at forty-six, after a late miscarriage the previous year. Nina was nine months older than me. I sometimes imagined her to be the sister I never had.

Every time I see my mother, I hope (and pray) that *this* is the time that I can share the news of my pregnancy. I imagine her face lighting up. My failed relationship with Ben feels like a huge letdown on my part.

"Ben left me," I say, turning away from her and toward the window so that she can't see the tears forming.

I take a deep breath, pull myself together.

"But I'm fine. I'm moving in with Stuart temporarily to help him out. Dad's not impressed, just to warn you because he'll undoubtedly tell you. He actually took an extra-large gulp of his cider before he said I was going to get sucked into Nina's affairs all over again."

I make a face. My mum has always laughed at my expressions. "If the wind changes, your face will get stuck like that," she said the first time I ever did it.

"But I know what I'm doing," I continue quickly before she says anything I don't want to hear either.

Mum confided in me several times that aging was a shock to her. "My grandmother warned me that time passed quickly," she said. "But I never fully appreciated just how fast." I am reminded of those words every time I see her. I must seize my moment while I can.

Despite getting everything off my chest, I leave feeling strange. The first day in my new home was disorientating because I wasn't sure how to feel. Despite my familiarity with the house, I reexplored all the rooms with fresh, critical eyes now that it was my living space. It didn't take long to unpack. I scattered personal belongings—recipe books on the kitchen shelf, my favorite winter coat on the rack, towels in the linen cupboard—discreet, innocuous things. It's my home now, too.

I agreed to take over complete responsibility for Nina's business plans. Over time, I'll build on her dreams and expand to include more tailored holidays or short breaks. (My discussion with Stuart didn't go quite that far; I held back some of my ideas. I'm wary of coming across as too much. There's no point in overwhelming him at this early stage.) We've synced calendars; nothing that could lead to misunderstanding or resentment has been left open to interpretation. Yet, every time I push my key into the front door lock, I feel like an imposter. I need to be kinder to myself because I more than overcompensate for my presence.

It's on the school run that I encounter my first dose of reality—a hurdle in the form of Tamsin.

"So, you and Stuart," she gives me a not-so-subtle elbow nudge in the ribs.

I glare. "Me and Stuart what?"

"I'm only joking."

"It's a purely practical arrangement, it makes sense. We're putting the children's welfare first."

My voice sounds like a strict headteacher. I spot Emily emerge from her classroom. She is at the front of the line. I remove a fudge bar from my coat pocket and wave it at her. Nina preferred them to have treats on Fridays only so that "sugar after school didn't become a habit," but it's hard to stick to all the old rules. I'll ensure she cleans her teeth extra well tonight.

"By the way," Tamsin says. "I didn't think you'd mind, there's a new girl in my eldest son's class. They've moved over from Canada. I've invited her mother to join our book group, she seems keen to make friends."

I've really gone off Tamsin.

"Without discussing it with the group?" I say, bending down to hug Em before ripping open the plastic chocolate wrapper.

"It seemed a friendly thing to do. I thought that after what has happened, perhaps it would be a positive thing. I know no one can replace Nina, but there's an undeniable gap. A slight change could be just the thing we need."

"Nina set it up. She left me in charge."

I sound about five years old, but honestly! How dare Tamsin assume that she can do what she likes? Yet, I need to tread carefully. There's no benefit in pissing Tamsin off; I may need her on my side while the non-news about me and Stuart settles. Still, I can't resist reining her in, regaining some control.

"Do you know what, Tamsin, I'm sure the others will be happy enough. Perhaps you're right. One thing, I'd like to continue to hold it at..." I hesitate. What sounds best? My place? Nina's old house? I settle for "Stuart's. It *was* Nina's idea and it feels very important that I continue her traditions for the time being. I hope that makes sense?"

"Of course. Sorry, I should've checked. I get carried away sometimes."

"No harm done. See you at the next meeting."

I'm at work the following afternoon, figuring out the best angle to make the most of the fading daylight when loss, Ben and our nonexistent baby hits me. The bride's stomach shows a barely perceptible yet unmistakable swell of early pregnancy. I direct her and the groom to stand to the side of a pillar and request that she holds her bouquet a little lower as I focus and click.

I want to get this over and done with, to go home, cry in the bath, curl up on the sofa and watch whatever Saturday night TV is on. But I can't. If I go back before Felix and Em are in bed, I'll have to pretend to be happy. I don't want to lock myself in my room like a teenager.

Doubts at my impulsive decisions form. Perhaps I did swoop in to the rescue too soon? It was a fine line. Too long and it could've been too late. Even so, I could've held back, let Stuart feel his way in the dark for a while longer, make his own mistakes. I'm not a miracle-worker.

No, I decide, as reason takes hold. I had to let Ben go without a fight, there's no way I could possibly have ignored a baby with another woman. Our relationship wouldn't have stood a chance. He gave up on us, not vice versa. My conscience, on that front, is clear.

Back in my car I do something I've resisted until now: social media. I scroll through Ben's friends and followers to figure out who *she* is. He hasn't posted anything new since we split up and despite what he did, Ben isn't a cruel person. He wouldn't rub my face in it. There are two women who are the most likely candidates because they work for the fire service, but they don't share much, so unless I put more effort into my online digging to give my wound a good poke, I haven't learned anything useful.

I pull away from the five-star-hotel venue and turn right, opting for the long route. Without initially meaning to, I drive past my new therapist's house. In this low moment, I hope that by being in close proximity to him, it will be enough to calm my mind. It doesn't work. I consider people I could call to see if they fancy a drink and a chat, but most of my friends now were Nina's, too. However much of a positive spin I can put on my current living conditions, I cannot face their unspoken judgment. Neither can I tell them the complete truth. A promise is a promise. Nina trusted that I'd be discreet.

As I slide my key into the lock and push open the front door of my new home, all appears quiet, yet the inviting smell of food draws me in.

"Hi," says Stuart. "Have you eaten?"

"No," I say.

"Good. I've made a vegetable curry."

The fact that he's bothered to cook something vegetarian, (something that always frustrated Ben about me because he's such an avid meat-eater) makes me want to cry for a different reason. Pent-up pain dissolves as I sit opposite Stuart. Warm relaxation replaces stress. I *have* done the right thing, for both of us, for now. We can give each other what we crave: for me, it's a distraction while I build the foundations for a new life. For him, it's comfort.

It's something I share with Christian in my next therapy session, that it feels good to trust my own judgment after so long second-guessing myself. I'm going to give the process a proper chance this time. Christian appears wise; he's much older than Stuart with a long beard, kind eyes and lines that crisscross his forehead like he's heard a tale or two and is unshockable. We'll see.

Christian, however, has a different agenda.

"I'm interested in discussing some of the things you brought up in our introductory session."

I mentally rewind. I've got a good memory. I discovered from a fairly young age that it's best to remember what I've said and when. I'd been careful, kept the conversation bland. Perhaps that was the problem? I read online that people who insist they had happy childhoods—yet don't appear to remember them in much detail—often didn't. Denial isn't the case with me because mine was secure enough. Nonetheless, some of my teenage mistakes gave me vital life lessons, although it didn't feel like it at the time. Despite knowing this now, shame remains embedded in my psyche.

"Your friend Nina." He looks up from his notes at me through his glasses. "You said that you feel an overwhelming responsibility toward her family."

He places emphasis on the word *overwhelming* to guide my response.

"Wouldn't anyone?"

Christian doesn't reply.

"It's hard to explain. However, obviously I'm here and she's not. She trusted me to carry out her wishes."

"Her wishes?"

I'm unwilling to share too much, too soon. How do I know if I can trust him? That is the flaw with this type of thing. There are no testimonials, other clients remain a secret, time slots carefully managed to ensure we never meet. All I can do is tread carefully, use my instinct. Or park on his street at random times to suss out what kind of people his other clients are. But what would it tell me, really? I'd love Nina's opinion.

The now-familiar ache builds. I have no one to fill the gap.

"She trusted me to carry out her wishes. She was scared, she wanted to make sure that someone protected her family."

"Scared?"

"Well, you would be, wouldn't you?" I say.

"Different people react in different ways," he says. "And not always how you'd expect."

On his online bio it states that he spent many years volunteering at a hospice. It's partly why I chose him. I never really believed that Nina would actually die. Yet she did, and she's gone.

Ben has left me and I don't blame him. Some of the things he accused me of were true.

For the first time ever, I break down in front of a stranger.

It isn't cathartic, and I'm really pissed off at my weakness. All week it niggles at me, yet I feel compelled to stick with him for now. He managed to puncture me in a way that no one else has, and I feel a grudging respect for him. Perhaps I *am* getting better at judging people and situations.

Life does not work that way, however. There is never a constant upward spiral because when I walk into Nina's—no, *my*—living room to host the book group, full of burgeoning optimism that I'm on the right life track, sickening dread punches me in the gut. Because on the sofa—as if it's perfectly acceptable—sits a person I assumed I'd never have to face ever again.

SEVEN

Somehow, I snap into hostess mode.

"Camilla! What are you doing here?"

"Hello, Marie."

In the silent seconds that follow, I study her as if I'm about to take her photograph. She looks like she's come straight from work dressed in a pale pink trouser suit with a cream floral blouse. Her fair hair is curly, I've only ever known it straight, and she's wearing killer black heels. My hair is pulled back in a ponytail and I got splashed in the face when I bathed the children, so I wiped any remaining makeup off.

"You know each other?" Tamsin says. She almost sounds disappointed.

"We went to art college together before I moved to Toronto," says Camilla.

"Small world," says Tamsin.

"Not that small," I say. "What are you doing here? Why didn't you get in touch beforehand?"

"I didn't put two and two together."

"But surely Tamsin told you that this was Nina's book group?"

"Everything's been a bit of a whirlwind," she says.

"But you've had time to join a book club?"

"Tamsin was kind enough to offer."

"How long have you been back?" I ask.

I think she says "a few weeks," but it's hard to take in because my mind reels back to the last time I saw her and the relief I felt when she announced her move to Canada. I want to know why she's here, why now and why she didn't attend Nina's funeral, but I don't want to ask her outright. I'll dig in my own way. For now, she is safe, surrounded by a cluster of people—my friends—as introductions are made. I listen to everything she says.

I offer drinks before I get everyone talking about the book, but it's an act (a bloody good one, considering) because I can only think about Camilla. She has a daughter. She is a real mother. She really is back.

I feign tiredness to coax everyone to leave as early as possible. I need time alone to process what her return means to me and what impact it could have on my fresh start.

"Where's Stuart?" Camilla asks as I tug her jacket from a coatrack by the front door which I left ajar after the previous person left. "I'd like to say hello."

"Don't you have a babysitter to get back for?"

"Lulu is with my grandparents."

Camilla was practically brought up by them as both her parents worked away often. Behind us, Tamsin walks back and forth between the living area and the kitchen carrying glasses and bowls, even though I've said twice that there's no need.

"Stuart's exhausted, he's probably gone to bed," I lie—he's a night owl. "Besides, we have things to catch up on, too." I pull my phone out from my pocket and open our family calendar. "Let's see...Stuart and I are free on Saturday at three. How about you come round here with *Lulu*, did you say your daughter's name was? Felix and Emily would love to meet her."

"Yes. It's short for Louise. I'd rather—"

"Stuart and I would love to meet Louise, too." I lower my

voice. "It's early days still, things can be overwhelming. Saturday will hopefully be a better day."

"Sure. I understand." What else can she say?

"What's your number?" I ask, adding her to my contacts as she says it out loud.

It feels strange typing her name. It jolts me into remembering that she's the type of person with whom it pays to be firm. I pull the door open wider and shudder. I should put my car in the garage; the windscreen will be covered in ice by morning.

"Tamsin?" I call out.

She appears.

"Thanks for all your help," I say.

Despite the cold, I stand at the door watching as they head for their respective cars. I don't want them to feel comfortable enough to hang about and bond further by discussing my haste to get them to leave or my obvious protectiveness of Stuart. I wave as they pull away. By the time their lights disappear and I close the door, I'm shivering. I email Christian requesting an extra appointment with him tomorrow. He responds within minutes.

As luck would have it, I've had a late cancellation...

Did he really? I'm naturally suspicious. Perhaps I judge people by my own standards. I wasn't really expecting him to come to my aid, I just like the safety blanket of mentally having someone to fall back on. He has availability at eight thirty, which will be right in the middle of the get-them-to-school mayhem. Stuart will have to deal with it alone.

Despite a long bath and a chapter of a new novel (I always download the next book club choice immediately), I can't settle. It's not just Camilla I think about—who, annoyingly, I discovered, still isn't much into social media—it's Nina, Ben and even Stuart, who remains downstairs in the study. I didn't say good night, I can't face mentioning Camilla to him yet, so I left him a note on the kitchen table.

Didn't want to disturb you. I'll be out early in the morning so see you tomorrow night! Mx

"Have you ever tried journaling?" asks Christian.

I feel stupid for making an emergency appointment because clearly there's nothing wrong with me now; I was just unsettled at having been caught off guard in my own environment.

"Not really."

"Some find that it helps. Different things can help different people. Other clients have tried art therapy, meditation or they write down their dreams."

It sounds wishy-washy to me, but I don't wish to appear ungrateful, so I smile and nod as though I'm giving his ideas serious consideration. As a result, I feel compelled to talk about *something* to make this charade worthwhile for us both.

"I feel contaminated by Camilla's return. I don't like it. She's someone from the past I don't want around, especially not while I'm trying so hard to build a new life after Ben's betrayal."

"Contaminated?"

"It's hard to explain without making it sound too possessive or trite, but Nina and I were a definite duo. Friends came and went, as, of course, they naturally tend to, but we were always there for each other. Camilla shoehorned her way in to the friendship. She's a very forceful character. Nina, especially as we got older, liked to think of herself as a free spirit in a floaty, artistic, 'aren't I chill?' kind of a way, so she wasn't always great with boundaries. It was all 'easy come, easy go, the more the merrier.' Expect it wasn't merrier for me."

"In what way?"

"Nina and I went on holiday to Ibiza after we left college. Camilla was there, too, although she went out earlier because she got a summer job—a seedy one, in my personal opinion—and spent her time off with us. My boyfriend at the time, Charlie, flew out toward the end of our break."

I stop.

Christian doesn't respond or react.

Was that the holiday that did it? Melanoma. Nina was unlucky apparently. Her diagnosis was late; caught up in the demands of motherhood and real life, she'd neglected herself.

It is quiet. I don't know how long I've been sitting here, mute, reliving the past in my head, barely aware of Christian. I wonder how he does it, just sits there watching someone who isn't speaking? It's unnerving.

I lost a best friend once before, when I was young, Amelia. Her parents moved her to a new school because—apparently—I wouldn't "allow" her to be friends with anyone other than me.

Thankfully, Nina was moved to my class not long afterward. I studied her from the seat behind. I watched what she liked to do at break time, learned what her favorite subjects were (art, PE and drama). She had a packed lunch every Monday, so I did, too, otherwise we had to sit at different tables. I invited Nina to tea one Friday and persuaded my mother to buy all her favorite foods. From then on, Nina and I were inseparable.

"It was me who suggested Ibiza," I say out loud. "And me who insisted on staying on the beach all day. I tan easily. Nina never did."

"You sound like you blame yourself for a lot."

"Nina told me that the holiday ruined her life." When I tried to remind her of all the good times and how she wouldn't have met Stuart if we hadn't chosen that particular trip, or the bar where we first met him (true serendipity), or as a result of their meeting have had her beautiful children, she was dismissive.

I falter. I don't know why I'm talking about this, it's so long ago. It's Camilla, she's riled me.

I glance at the clock. Thank God we're nearly out of time because I know how it works. Christian will gently discourage me from getting into anything too upsetting at the eleventh hour. Because I know I won't have the opportunity to dig too deep, or elaborate, I take a breath and get something off my chest.

"The end of the holiday was truly dreadful, though. Perhaps it was inevitable that it eventually soured everything, in one way or another."

Delighted when the session is finally over, I leave the past behind with Christian, an exorcist with my ghosts.

The future—Felix and Emily—are what matters. I don't want to dwell on loss anymore, I've been surrounded by too much one way or another. I'm going to be brave and start putting pictures of family life on social media. I thought that it would be insensitive and too soon, but why should I hide my pride and joy? If I fade into the background, it's giving the impression that I have something to be ashamed of. Which I don't. Nina didn't hold back when it came to sharing things and she didn't ask me not to. I *should* celebrate their lives and achievements.

I stop at a supermarket, a more expensive one than my usual. As I push my cart around the aisles, I feel absurdly content. I'm going to cook us all a special family meal tonight. As I consider all the products Nina would've bought—she was big into brands—a thought occurs.

I replace "her" choices back on the shelves and instead, select all the ingredients I need for cottage pie, substituting the mince with a vegetarian alternative. No one will notice because I'll use one of Nina's recipes. I made it often enough when I babysat. While Nina got ready (she was rarely on time for anything), I'd take over in the kitchen. Stuart would sometimes assist, one of us would stir, one would chop, and we'd have shared at least one glass of red by the time Nina appeared.

I pick up a behavior chart and pop it in among the groceries before I head for the checkout. Hopefully, it will encourage Emily to become a nicer child. I'll continue to put these small, yet positive, changes in place. I love thinking like a mother: the children's welfare always at the forefront of my mind. It's no longer all about me, and that can only be a good thing.

My phone rings.

"Hi, Stuart."

"Felix is ill, he's got a temperature. I've picked him up from school, but he's really not well. I've got an emergency appointment at the doctor's. Are you okay to pick up Em?"

"Of course. Poor Felix, keep me updated."

I pay for my shopping, shove everything into bags and rush to the car.

Emily is unusually quiet. She helps me prepare dinner, I give her little jobs, which she usually enjoys, but she is half-hearted and abandons stirring the carrots and onions halfway through.

"When will Felix and Daddy be back?"

"Soon," I say.

"What if they don't come back?"

"They will, darling. I promise."

"I want my mummy."

I force back my tears and give Emily a hug, but she pulls away. She rushes upstairs. I follow quietly behind, uncertain what to do. Leave her for a few minutes or comfort her? I stand just outside her door. She is lying on her bed, facedown, sobbing.

I want Nina back, too, no longer for me, but for her daughter. What if I can't do this? There's so much to learn, so many things to get wrong. The vibrant undersea mural Nina painted on Em's wall is exquisite. I couldn't paint anything nearly as good. Self-doubt gnaws. It's not too late—yet—to gently back off, ease myself out, but the thought of venturing out again into the unknown, possibly throwing away my one chance at being a mother, is terrifying. Why risk it? I must consider the long-term.

Outside, I hear a car on the gravel. It must be Stuart and Felix, thankfully.

I rush downstairs and fling open the front door, but there is no one there and no car. Wishful thinking has played tricks on me. Except...I know what I heard.

It's as I shut the door that I see it: a blank white envelope. Assuming it's a random advertising ploy, I pick it up intending to place it straight in the recycling. Yet, curiosity takes hold. I open it. It's a photo of this house with Nina sitting on the stone steps leading up to the front door, both arms around younger versions of Felix and Emily. She's smiling, happy. For such an innocent picture, its delivery method turns it into something sinister, a seemingly unmistakable message to me that I don't belong.

I stand still, staring.

"Marie!" Emily's voice.

"I'm coming," I shout back automatically, folding the picture in two before shoving it into my jeans pocket.

I read Emily a story, but my mind most definitely is not on wizards or witches.

"They're home," I say to Emily when I hear the front door open.

She has stopped crying but has exhausted herself, so remains on her bed.

Stuart is carrying a sleeping Felix upstairs in his arms.

"It's just a viral infection," he says quietly. "He'll be fine. He needs to sleep it off, apparently."

I help slide off Felix's shoes and put him into his pajamas before Stuart goes and settles Em.

Stuart and I are both quiet over dinner. It's not the time to mention the photo. I'm horribly aware that if I wasn't around he'd give in to his grief. He's going through the motions of eating dinner, being civilized. I need to give him time alone. I wasn't privy to Stuart and Nina's final conversations and wishes, obviously. Stuart has seemed fine on the whole, yet this evening has been a wake-up call. There's so much to adjust to and it has made me reassess. Fresh determination to look out for and nurture Nina's family takes hold. It's reassuring to realize quite how much they all need me here.

"I overreacted," he says. "Nina was amazing with them when they were ill."

"So are you. We're both a bit shaken by this evening," I say. "But it will be okay."

Stuart gives me a weak smile. His face is pale and he looks like he needs a decent sleep.

"You go to bed," I offer. "I'll clear up down here."

"I think I'll take you up on that. Thank you."

As he stands up, I feel afraid of being left alone downstairs. The photo has shaken me because I don't know what I'm supposed to do about it, and I've got a horrible feeling that it's not going to be a one-off.

"I'll set the alarm," I say, before quickly adding, "Deborah told me that it wasn't the first time someone had tried to break in."

He throws me a look of...confusion? Mistrust?

Surely it's inevitable that I will take over even more of Nina's roles? I hope I haven't overdone it.

"The code is Nina's birthdate, but I haven't bothered with it much of late. It was Nina who decided she'd like the reassurance. Deborah is correct but the damage was minimal and nothing went missing."

"I'll leave it then," I say.

"Fine. Whatever."

"Call me if you're worried or need help in the night with Felix. I'm here for as long as you need me. I'm not going anywhere."

Every word is true. I promised Nina I'd look out for her family. No matter what, I'm here to stay. I'm becoming more convinced that it's what Nina would've wanted, even if some people won't see it that way.

I take the photo and pin it to the corkboard. It's now hidden behind the bin collection timetable until I decide what to do with it.

I check the doors are all locked, then do so once again before persuading myself that I'm overreacting. Anyone can tell that the photo is not the best quality and could well be from a clumsy well-wisher, assuming that Stuart and the children would appreciate the memory. If a mysterious someone really wanted to be threatening, they'd have written something, whether cryptic or openly threatening. It's what I would do.

The heart and soul has temporarily disappeared from this house, and I am the only person who can replace it. Nina had a black sense of humor, which only got darker as her illness took hold. Her own personal brand of gallows humor, as she would refer to it when I—or someone else—was shocked, unsure of how to react. She told me once that it was a good job she was on her way out as someone had it in for her. I didn't push her or take it seriously. I wish I had because what if someone *was* after her and now that person is after me instead?

The sense of unease that has been building all day is heightened as I head upstairs. A guilty conscience is relentlessly unsettling. I stop. Listen. Nothing.

I turn around and retrace my steps before jabbing the familiar digits of Nina's birthday into the keypad, changing my mind (again) and resetting the code to my own birthdate. The immediate reassurance it offers is gratifying, and some of the tension lifts as I creep to my room.

EIGHT

Nina and I slipped into our roles at school from a young age. We had a rhythm, a natural partnership. I did my homework in advance, she relied on me for all the times she "hadn't quite got round to doing hers." I was loyal. In return, she was there for me and shielded me when things felt too overwhelming.

One particular instance was during an English lesson when I'd been asked to analyze a passage out loud. I dreaded being picked. Only one sentence in, I froze. I couldn't do it. I looked up at Mrs. Palmer. Everyone was staring. I wanted to run out of the room, slam the door and hide. A nightmare come true: I was the sole focus of hostile amusement. I anticipated chants, some kind of fist thumping on the tables. Blood rushed to my face.

Nina's hand shot up to save me, but I could tell it was forced. She looked embarrassed. Of me.

I was asked to stay behind, which filled me with further panic. If I couldn't find Nina in the playground afterward, I'd have to eat my lunch alone, hang out in the loos or the library, acting busy, disguising my lack of friends.

Mrs. Palmer had kind eyes, but her tone had changed to the one people use when they've had enough. No matter how much encouragement she gave me, I didn't "get it." It wasn't that I didn't try, it was that I found lessons a struggle. I was never able to explain all my fears articulately enough. Not to anyone.

"Marie, I've been wondering, are things all right at home? Is there anything in particular troubling you? Are you still seeing the school counselor?" she said.

As if I would have spoken truthfully to, or trusted, the school counselor! There was nothing wrong with me. I was only referred to her because of a misunderstanding when the PE teacher had allegedly overheard me "telling a story" that couldn't possibly have been true and he "was concerned." I pointed out to the counselor, quite rightly, that all anyone had to do was listen in to any conversation at break time. Everyone exaggerated. Everyone wanted to be seen in the best light, to pretend that they'd gone somewhere exotic for the school holidays or that they'd been invited to the popular parties or some exciting event. And everyone also knew that the majority of us stayed at home most nights watching TV or being nagged to do our homework. Yet, unlike most people, I was forced into my exaggerations because my mother was at her happiest when I was safely at home.

When I shook my head in answer to all Mrs. Palmer's questions, she shared something that did actually resonate and eventually helped: no one surrounds themselves with clingy people. Apparently.

"It drives them away, Marie. Pretend you're okay no matter how much you have to fake it. Nina can't always be there for you. You have to learn to stand on your own two feet, however hard it is. You must learn to tough it out."

When I escaped, I found Nina had been waiting for me outside. I wanted to hug her with sheer relief. But I didn't. I put on a brave face—acted happy. The incident taught me to say only what people wanted to hear and hide my true self. I've often wondered if Deborah was behind it, if she'd been in to talk to

the teachers about Nina "being allowed to widen her friendship circle." I'll never know for sure.

When Stuart and the children appear for breakfast in the
morning, I head off for a shower, making sure I don't come
back down until they've all gone. I ignore the abandoned cereal
bowls and the scattering of Cheerios across the kitchen counter-
tops. I'm on a mission this morning to try to sort out some of
Nina's affairs. Not to mention that Christmas is six weeks away
and Stuart's parents' arrival is imminent. I'm nervous because
I want them to like me. We've only met once before, at Stuart
and Nina's wedding. I'm going to devote time to making them
welcome and plan interesting family days out, especially when
Stuart is working.

I lift the lid on Nina's old laptop. The battery is dead. I hunt
round in her kitchen drawers (which need a good clear-out as it's
where she stored *stuff*) but there's no sign of a charger. Annoyed
at the waste of my time, I step into Stuart's study and glance at
the shelves above his desk. Nothing. I yank open a drawer—he's
so much neater than Nina was—then another. The bottom one
contains a twisted mess of wiring. I put them on the floor and
sort through them, identifying one that will hopefully work.

It does. The laptop is slow to power up. I wipe the screen
with a tea towel as it's dusty. I switch the kettle on as I wait,
hoping that Nina would have had a good filing system on this.
She didn't. Just as I'm about to give up for the day and shut it
down, her old email address catches my eye. It is not her latest
personal one or the business one. She'd saved all her passwords
so it's easy enough to log in. I scroll… She'd last used it the
week before she passed away…and…one of the very last people
she contacted was Camilla.

I click open the mail and read. As the words sink in, sickening realization stabs.

My concentration is killed for the remainder of the day as I desperately search for something to explain what I've found. By school pickup time, I have still not succeeded.

"Marie? Are you all right?" asks Felix.

I stop. For a moment, I thought he said, "Mummy." I carry on heading in the direction of our home. I feel strange, like I'm having some sort of out-of-body experience, as if it's someone else walking down the lane, holding hands with the children. The conversations between Nina and Camilla are at the forefront of my consciousness. Someone told me once that if we all knew what our closest friends said about us behind our backs, we wouldn't be friends with them. It doesn't make sense that Nina entrusted me with her final wishes if it's true she didn't one hundred percent trust me with her fears and secrets.

The afternoon drags. I let the children watch TV and don't bother asking about homework or their day at school. I order in pizza.

Stuart puts the children to bed before hanging around in the kitchen, trying to chat while I attempt to cook, and I can't do it anymore. I can't act normally. I put down the knife I'm using to chop some red peppers.

"Did you see in the calendar that we have a surprise guest coming round on Saturday afternoon?"

"Kind of," he says. "I assumed it was Deborah."

"Well, no, funnily enough, it's Camilla! You know, Camilla Preston!"

I smile as though it's all fine.

"Camilla? The one who moved abroad?"

"Yes, the very same! She's back. She only turned up the other night at my book group! I was slightly caught off guard when I invited her round. I had no idea that she and Nina kept in touch."

"You and me both."

"Don't you think it's odd that she kept it a secret?"

"I guess."

"I wonder why she's moved back *now*?"

"Didn't she say?"

"We didn't get much of a chance to chat, so it felt polite to invite her and her daughter, Louise, back here. Although she calls her Lulu, such a typical Camilla thing to do."

"She has a daughter?"

"Yes, and she's already started at the same local school as Em and Felix. Camilla hasn't moved back half-heartedly. Book group, school, a home, a job, the whole lot."

I pick up the knife and carry on chopping.

"Strange timing," says Stuart. "And odd, surely, that she didn't get in touch beforehand? She just showed up? Did she know about Nina?"

"Seemed to." I pause. "Maybe she thought that catching me unawares would make me more amenable. Did you know she had a fling with Charlie?"

Sometimes, I get tired of hiding things.

"You mean *your* Charlie?"

"Yes, didn't Nina ever say?"

He shrugs. "It was ten or more years ago." He frowns, just slightly, as though he's digging as far back into his memory as he can. "I must've missed that part. I guess it got overshadowed in the aftermath."

Thankfully, Stuart did miss the embarrassing, horribly public, drunken argument Camilla and I had about it. Flashes of unwanted memory reappear. The urge to hit her. Humiliation. The ugly words coming out of my mouth that I knew I should stop, but somehow couldn't. Nina not backing me up. I appreciate that I'm older and wiser, but there's something about Stuart that always makes me want to present myself in the best possible light. He's right, though, about things becoming overshadowed in the aftermath of Charlie's horrific accident.

"I guess I should move on, the past is the past, forgive and forget and all that," I say.

I put down the knife. The red pepper is so finely chopped, it's practically mush. I throw him a questioning gaze, but he doesn't elaborate. His reply is not what I expect.

"Not necessarily. Forgiveness can be hard. And at times over-rated."

Still, I don't want to come across as overly bitter. Even though I do still blame Camilla for robbing me of my future with Char-lie. Her selfishness had long-reaching ramifications.

"Perhaps she wants to apologize for not making it back for Nina's funeral?"

"Who knows? Deborah provided the contact list. It was all a bit of a blur. Still is, if I'm honest."

I need to pry with a different approach. Stuart genuinely seems as surprised as me at Camilla's return.

"Nina's admin is in a bit of a mess."

"I didn't realize, otherwise I'd have done it myself. Sounds stressful, send anything that's a pain my way."

I'm not stressed, I'm seething, but there are no words, no decent ways of breaking the news to him that his perfect wife seems to have had secrets. It's not the right time—not yet—though temptation to blurt it out is festering. I can't give Stuart any reason to dislike me.

"No, it's fine, it's nothing I can't manage. I like a challenge and the children need as much of your attention as you can give them right now."

I invent a call I need to make as the urge to be alone for a few minutes, to try to grasp at memories, takes an overwhelm-ing hold.

Stuart barely acknowledges my excuse; he, too, seems lost in thought. Our dinner later than planned is a struggle. We both make an effort, but are careful with our words, flitting from one light meaningless conversational topic to another, as though each of us is afraid to drop our guard.

Grateful when I can finally slide beneath my duvet, I reach

for my usual savior—books, but after attempting two new, very different ones, I admit defeat. The words won't stick as I reread the opening sentences.

Long after midnight, I take up Christian's suggestion of journaling. I vent until gone 2:00 a.m. I hide the notebook beneath my pillow—for now—but it's an uncomfortable feeling having evidence of my thoughts and mixed feelings about Nina in a physical form. I tear out some of the pages and rewrite them in a more cryptic fashion. I hope this isn't homework, that Christian doesn't expect me to take my private ramblings along to our sessions. He and I won't last long if that's the case.

However, the exercise turns out to be useful because something becomes clear: the downside of loyalty is that it holds you back. Now that I'm free from some of its grip, I'm no longer restrained.

NINE

"When did you find out about Nina?"

We are strolling through our garden en masse. A walk seemed like the best way to ease the tension of the forced chitchat, not just among us three adults either. Stuart, in particular, seems slightly ill at ease and I assumed that the children would just get on and play but it seems shyness and age differences play a factor, too.

I've lent Camilla my wellies because she pitched up in high-heeled suede boots. Actually, the wellies were Nina's, but they're black and indistinguishable, so it's not as if it's obvious. They were new, she'd hardly worn them, and she's only one size bigger than me. I didn't mean to wear them, it felt weird at first, but I discovered—too late—that one of mine had a hole in the bottom before the school run one day. It was pouring, I had no choice but to borrow hers which had been abandoned in the garage. By the time I'd trudged to school and back I realized that there was nothing wrong in doing so. A boot is a boot, any weirdness relating to previous ownership is all in the mind.

"Not that long ago," Camilla replies.

I'm gently herding everyone toward the fence at the back which is easy to climb over so we can wander through the forest. I've promised Louise (I refuse to call her Lulu) that we'll probably see ponies. Stuart is slightly ahead of us with the children. Felix is waving a big stick in the air and every now and then Em screeches in fear of being whacked.

"Em, darling, just try to keep out of his way."

I'm a little frustrated that she hasn't figured this out for herself yet.

"Roughly how long ago?" I say, turning my attention back to Camilla.

I'm not letting her get away with such blatant evasiveness. The timing of her unexpected reappearance means she's going to have to put up with the inevitable curiosity.

"Maybe a few months or so. It was such a shock. I don't like to think about it."

"Why didn't you come to the funeral?"

"I didn't know then."

Liar. The on-and-off emails between her and Nina were written in the five months leading to her passing away.

"Really? No one told you? How did you find out?"

"Maybe it *was* a bit before. Like I say, I don't like to think about it. It all seemed to happen so quickly and it was...devastating."

"I see. No, I don't actually. I think it's odd."

"I'm sorry you find it odd. How *is* Stuart?"

"Coping," I say.

"And what's with you and him?"

"Nothing. I promised Nina I'd stick around, help ease them through the worst parts."

She stops.

"Marie, I know we didn't always see eye to eye but...is it a good idea? I must admit seeing you in the same house as him, in Nina's world, it's uncomfortable."

I focus ahead. Louise is a mini-Camilla, strikingly so. Long blond hair almost flows behind her as the younger two follow her, Pied Piper-like.

"I know what I'm doing." Her turn for an inquisition now. "Where's Camilla's father?"

"It's complicated."

"Things usually are," I say. "That's why it's best not to judge others' situations, in my opinion."

"You haven't changed, Marie," she says. "I suspect Nina knew you'd be amazing with the children, but she clearly didn't fully appreciate just how much you'd try to take over. It's about balance, surely? Stuart always was and still appears to be capable. What does Deborah think about the situation?"

"She's very happy with it," I lie.

Deborah said something very similar to Camilla. It's deeply insulting and disconcerting, like they're all conspiring against me. I think back to the conversations Nina and I had as we reach the edge of the forest. We talked a lot about Ben and how he'd make a good father. I wonder now, was Nina testing me to make sure that I really did love Ben before she made me promise to look out for her family? She had nothing to worry about at the time, I never used to think of Stuart in *that* way. He's...well, he's just Stuart. Admittedly, I didn't tell Nina about all the relationship cracks Ben and I experienced because I wanted our relationship to be more like hers. Sometimes, when I used to photograph weddings, I'd compare them to Nina and Stuart. They were my relationship barometer.

"I didn't know that you were the book group host or that it was Nina's old house. I was so grateful that Tamsin was friendly. I'd been worried about Lulu making friends, finding all the changes a struggle. I was going to get in touch with you eventually. I was waiting for the right time. I wasn't sure how you'd react toward me."

I don't believe her.

"Well, what a coincidence," I say. "You couldn't make it up."

Camilla freezes as a dog runs up to us, sniffing our feet.

"She's scared of them," I say, giving the owner an apologetic smile.

I wish I hadn't said that because by showing Camilla that I remember little details about her, it reinforces the facade that we are great buddies with a rich and warm shared history.

As the Jack Russell is called away, Camilla takes the opportunity to break away from me and catch up with Stuart. No matter, I fall into step alongside Louise, hoping she'll be a better source of information. But no, she is a closed book, just like her mother.

"Is your dad coming over any time soon?" I ask.

She shrugs.

"He must miss you."

She doesn't bite.

We walk for longer than I'd intended and get caught in heavy rain, mud making the journey back in the dying light tricky. We coax the younger children into bed after hot chocolates, another pizza dinner for them and a warm bath. While Louise is occupied watching a movie, Stuart, Camilla and I thaw properly over glasses of red wine.

"So, you became an architect…" says Stuart to Camilla.

The tone in which he says it is annoying because he sounds just a little too impressed. I don't understand it. Anyone can be an expert in their chosen field, it's how the world is. Designing houses and offices can't be that difficult once you've mastered the art.

"Has the transfer from Canada to here been plain sailing?" he continues.

I don't listen to her reply because dormant envy is worming its way into my consciousness. Two's company, three's a crowd. Stuart's fascination with Camilla not only irks, it feels disloyal now that he's aware of what she did. Old philosophies are usually the best, and right now, the whole "friends close, enemies closer" approach makes perfect sense.

"How about we meet up at the Christmas market and grab some lunch?" I say to Camilla. "I can invite some of my friends, it will help break the ice within a wider circle, give you a chance to meet others?"

Camilla looks as uninspired as I feel. She hesitates. "I'll check my calendar and let you know, thank you."

"Shall we order in a curry?" says Stuart. "I'm starving!"

"I'd better get Lulu home, thanks," says Camilla. "I'd love for us to keep in touch. I need some tax advice. Do you work solely from home or are you office-based, too?"

"Both," says Stuart. "I'll give you my card."

Great. Now, I need to keep an eye on Stuart's work calendar, too. Camilla is desperate to get Stuart on her own and I need to know why. It can't be anything favorable when it comes to me, or she'd be more upfront.

"Lulu!" Camilla calls out. "Come and say goodbye and thank you."

I let Stuart show them out, holding back so as not to appear possessive. It's hard, especially when I overhear Camilla telling Louise on the way out to "wait in the car please, darling."

I clear away the glasses and open the menu of Stuart's favorite takeout place on my phone. I order his usual—Madras—and an eggplant curry for me. While waiting for him to return (how long can it take to say goodbye, it's taking all of my self-control not to eavesdrop), it dawns on me that I really only have one choice.

Through therapy, I've learned to control the things I can and to try to accept the things I can't. (Well, kind of, it's not always that easy or simple, if I'm honest.) I've plenty of places left to dig. I'm in the perfect position to find out what Camilla is trying to hide from me, and in doing so, I'll find out exactly what Nina's emails really meant. If I'm to integrate into my new life,

I need to be aware of all the facts. Something about the way Camilla is behaving is off-kilter, and I will get to the bottom of it.

I rummage through my purse and pull out a coffee-chain loyalty card. It's the best I can come up with. I head for the front door.

Stuart and Camilla stop talking as soon as they see me approach them.

"Did you drop this?" I say to Camilla, handing her the card. She barely glances at it. "No."

The three of us stand still.

"Perhaps we can all go boating come spring?" says Stuart.

"Definitely," I say. "The kids would love it."

I smile my enthusiasm, too, even though it seems odd to be making spring plans before we've even celebrated Christmas. I've been missing an opportunity here, I realize. I love being out on the water. It's a hobby of Stuart's I can embrace. It will do us all good.

"Not for us, thanks," says Camilla.

"Oh?" says Stuart.

"Seasickness," she adds.

"You or Lulu?" he says.

"Both."

Times change. Some of our happiest moments in Ibiza were on Stuart's friend's speedboat.

"I'll call you," Camilla says to Stuart, touching his arm. "So nice to see you again. Nina would be proud of the way you're dealing with things."

Like she would know!

"Poor Louise must be absolutely freezing in the car!" I say.

There's something I'm not quite grasping. Some of what Nina confided to me toward the end didn't make total sense. I thought it did while I was emotionally caught up in the moment, but later—once it was too late—I realized that I hadn't really understood what she meant. (Kind of like being introduced to someone at a party, who tells you what they do for a living, which makes perfect sense at the time, but when you next meet them, it dawns that you really have no idea.) Perhaps Nina had known that Camilla was planning to move back and feared her intentions around Stuart? Leopards, spots and all that.

My mind shoots off in multiple directions. What did Nina say? Something about sometimes being friends with people through necessity rather than personal choice. Perhaps Camilla and Stuart had a history, too? Unlikely. Stuart wasn't Camilla's type. Then again, no one thought he was Nina's. Fresh determination bubbles. Camilla stole from me once in front of my very eyes; this time they're wide-open and watching, crocodile-like.

As Camilla's blurring red taillights fade into the darkness, I realize something important. Being here, it no longer feels solely about survival and loyalty; it's about entitlement.

TEN

Stuart's parents are not how I recall at all. If I had to describe Stuart in one word, the overriding one that springs to mind is *serious*. Kevin and Suzanne are friendly, fun and have such a brilliant sense of humor, I feel at immediate ease. The relief is immense. I realize that I've subconsciously been bracing myself to defend my role (yet again) and it's a luxury to relax and not watch every word, to not continually walk the tightrope between genuine grief and allowing life to move on with Nina still very much cemented in our collective memories.

Kevin and Suzanne naturally have questions, but—and this is the bit I've found the most surprising, although it's blindingly obvious—they didn't truly know Nina. Of course they didn't. The first time they met her was around the same time they met me at the wedding party Stuart and Nina held on a Brisbane beach. They flew out once for a few weeks after the births of both Felix and Em, but I wasn't invited to the house at the time. Other than that, Nina was almost a stranger to them.

The joyous possibility that this is an area that I can excel in, that I don't have to try to be as good or better than Nina, that I can actually be myself—on my own terms—is exhilarating. It opens my mind to fresh perspectives and possibilities.

From the outside looking in at Nina's life, everything was near-enough perfect. In my mind, even her relationship with her mother-in-law was sickly sweet. I pictured long Skype calls every Sunday evening, thoughtful, beautifully wrapped parcels traveling halfway across the world every Christmas and birthday. We mistakenly, I realize now, forced Nina to defend her decision to marry Stuart (everyone thought she was too young to get tied down, especially to someone dull and older) so maybe she rigidly stuck to the script of an idealized version of her own life.

Cracks I never imagined existed crisscross through my mental version of Nina. Maybe she realized that she wasn't as wonderful as she liked to portray and knew, deep down, that I was the person who could protect her family from any mistakes she'd made. I've never really got the true meaning of schadenfreude. Until now. By experiencing a delicious sliver of it, it forces painful acknowledgement that I'm flawed. It's not pleasant.

"Stuart and Nina's wedding day was everything I'd ever dreamed of," I say to Christian. I wonder how he can bear listening to all the random rubbish that people like me come out with: Stuart's parents' visit, my insecurities—all the while I try to hide my true feelings from him as I don't want to appear like some sort of monster. If I had the choice, *of course* I'd rather that Nina was alive, that Felix and Emily had their mother, that I was with Ben and we had our own baby. I couldn't have tried harder at times to make my relationship with him work; my conscience is clear on that one. But that's not how things have worked out, and I've been forced to be adaptable and open-minded. Life moves on whether any of us like it or not.

However, I will continue to ramble about the wedding because I feel embarrassed by my dramatic revelation at the end of our last session. It was unnecessary. If I'm not ready to talk about my feelings surrounding Charlie's tragic death and my shattered dreams, then I should leave well alone. I know this. I used to check in on social media for all my hospital and medical appointments, even if I was only having a blood test to check my hormone levels. At the time, I welcomed and enjoyed the attention and speculation. But some (okay, most) people got fed up after a while. Be open about the fact you'd like some sympathy, an online "friend" had messaged, or keep quiet.

"Nina and Stuart went all out with their arrangements. Stuart had lived in England for many years so there were friends and family to include on opposite sides of the world. They had a church ceremony followed by a hotel meal in London. Afterward, a group of us flew to Brisbane for a two-day celebration."

I describe everything to Christian: the beach (holiday-brochure perfect), the music (jazz—Stuart's choice), the food (lobster, oysters and giant prawns served in huge bowls of crushed ice). "Nina wanted everyone to be as happy as her."

"And were you?"

"What?" I say, slightly irritated at the interruption.

"Happy?"

I shrug. "I guess. I was happy for her. Perhaps not so much for me, but I suppose the benefit of Stuart being the type of person he is, I'd already sussed out that he wouldn't try to come between us." I pause. "That did make things easier because I was single at the time. I didn't meet Ben until a few years later on a dating site. I was very upfront about the kind of steady, reliable man I was looking for."

I smile to show that I'm only half joking and Christian gives a weak one back. Awkward silence threatens to invade what, until now, has been a bearable session, so I talk about what I want to, which is still the wedding.

"I offered to be their photographer, but Nina had wanted me to 'relax, for once, Marie.' I still took pictures, and mine were better, I'm not being conceited, they just were, but probably because I knew who and what was best to focus on. I'm at my happiest when I'm behind a camera. I feel like myself. When

Stuart and Nina traveled to the Whitsundays for their honeymoon, I hung about for a bit."

"Hung about for a bit?"

I mentally debate. The truth or not the truth? I had intended to take a trip, to go and explore, but when it came to it, I couldn't be bothered on my own. This left me at a loose end as I wasn't due to fly back to the UK for another three days.

I meet Christian halfway.

"It was hard to let go of her. I was so grateful that Nina was my friend, I never thought about myself and how maybe I deserved some input into our friendship, too. I just molded myself to be whatever Nina needed so that she'd let me stick by her side. So, I admit, her whirlwind marriage shook me a little."

Confession is uncomfortable; it reminds me of going to church. I didn't come here to talk about Nina or the wedding. I don't know why I do this to myself, why I come here and talk about such pointless stuff. I wish I could cut through the bullshit, say what I really came to therapy to share.

The undivided attention is alluring, however—when I can push from my mind the fact that I'm paying for it. Out of all my therapists, he's the most adept at making me feel like he cares. While it's intoxicating, it makes me shy further away from the truth. I don't want him to think badly of me, despite it being a waste of time, money, energy—everything—yet a buried part of my subconscious hopes that *he* can cure me. I want to feel normal. I want to feel, well, just *better*. I don't want to feel like me.

Yet, I seem unable to move on from Nina.

"I get the impression from Stuart that Nina valued me," I say. I don't want to come across as a complete leech.

"In what way?"

"He treats me as if he's fond of me. He trusts me with the children. He wouldn't do that if Nina had spoken badly of me."

"Why do you think she would have done that?"

"I found some correspondence when I was sorting out her

affairs," I say, trying to make it sound businesslike. "She'd been in contact with a friend and it's hard to put my finger on precisely what was wrong with their exchange, but it was odd. Their conversations appeared stilted. I'm really not being paranoid, honestly, but it also felt like they were discussing me in an unfavorable way."

"In what respect?"

"That's the puzzling thing, I don't really understand. Nina and I had disagreements, but not major ones."

That is true, but the unsaid and unacknowledged issues that nonetheless existed perhaps cast wider shadows than I'd ever fully appreciated.

Christian does his best to lift my mood, but I leave on a downer, my mind in overdrive, especially after he tells me that he's taking a fortnight's holiday next month. I appreciate that it's irrational, but it makes me feel like I'm not special or interesting enough, the fact that he needs a break. Maybe I do need to be more honest and discuss how devastated I was when Charlie died. But then again, what good can it do, really? It's not as if talking about him can bring him back.

Back home, I hesitate as I open the front door. I needn't have worried. A cozy, happy family scene awaits and one that I feel immediately welcomed into when Suzanne looks up. She beams as I enter.

"Lovely to see you, Marie! We're making Santa Claus–shaped gingerbread men. Come and try one!"

"Love to!"

Only Emily looks put out as I taste their creations. I need to work harder to win her round, make her trust me. Perhaps I've been too strict lately. The reward chart didn't go down well. I concentrate on giving her positive attention (like I've read in parenting books) by saying, "Well done, Emily," "Great job," and "Clever girl," as much as I can bear to.

Watching Stuart with his parents is eye-opening. He jokes

around. His mother play-hits his arm when he teases her, laughing. Ben always treated his mum and dad as if their visits were something to be endured rather than enjoyed. Suzanne cannot do enough for Stuart and it makes me wonder if it's because she rarely sees him or if it's because their relationship is naturally like that.

I want to get to know her, and therefore Stuart, better.

When Stuart and Kevin begin an involved conversation about whether it would be a waste of money to invest in repairs to Stuart's current boat or buy a newish one, I turn to Felix and Emily.

"Why don't you two go and watch a movie?" I say. "There are lots of new ones to choose from."

I've resorted to stockpiling them because being a full-time mother is harder than I'd anticipated. I've started to do things I used to judge Nina for, like relying on the TV when I'm desperate for privacy or to get things done.

"Suzanne, there's something I've been meaning to bring up. I haven't said anything to Stuart, so please don't think I'm being meddlesome—"

"Marie, my dear, you most certainly are not meddlesome. This is the most welcome we have ever felt in Stuart's home." She claps her hand to her mouth. "I mean..."

Loyalty dictates that I stand up for Nina, but pride at my warm hospitality feels good.

"It's okay. Nina was my closest friend. I know what she was like. She needed a lot of time on her own. She could be very private."

"Really?"

"Oh, I assumed that was what you meant."

"Oh, no, not at all. Nina was very hospitable and kind. No, I meant she had to work hard when we were here to hide her unhappiness. I got the impression that she and Stuart were having problems."

"Nina never said anything of the sort to me. Their marriage was as good as perfect." I pause. "I envied them at times, I admit."

Suzanne glances over at Kevin as if to check that he can't overhear before she says, "It's simply not possible that everything was fine all of the time. Believe me, it's not realistic."

"Perhaps. But because I knew her so well, I can picture what she'd do in certain situations. I'd have known if she was particularly unhappy. I'd have sensed it before she'd even confided in me."

"People hide things from those closest to them for many reasons," she says. "Shame, guilt, fear, a desire not to add to the problems of others."

"Suzanne, I don't know how to word this diplomatically, so I'm just going to come out with it. If Nina wasn't happy with Stuart, she wouldn't have stayed with him. She didn't feel bound by loyalty the way most of us do. Nina was...unique."

Selfish is the word I'd like to use.

I change the subject, concerned that *I've* just come across as disloyal.

"What I've been meaning to ask you is would you and Kevin prefer to be in the house? We can swap. Stuart thought that it may be nicer for you, but I'd hate to be in the way and—"

"Not at all. The whole arrangement suits us perfectly." She pauses. "We would've come sooner, you know. For the funeral or soon after, but Stuart thought it would be better now. That he'd need the support as time went on. He was in so much shock."

"We all were."

I excuse myself immediately after dinner. I run a bath. In the darkness, I watch the lavender-scented candle—my Christmas present to Nina last year—flicker. If Suzanne is right, if she has somehow picked up on something (as outsiders are prone to, seeing as they can home in on things that people who are too close can't), how come I didn't know she was *that* unhappy as opposed to having normal periods of discontent? Did Tamsin know anything?

Jealousy prods at my mind, clouding my thoughts and memories. Every avenue I explore draws a blank. I can't think of one thing—not one—that suggests Nina had made a mistake in marrying Stuart. Not even a hint, and obviously, after her diagnosis, our collective focus shifted toward getting her well. The water turns lukewarm, then cold, before I realize I'm shivering. My mind none the clearer, I get out, towel myself dry and blow out the candle.

Felix and Em's nativity the following early evening is perfect timing. It's nice to get out, to do something different. I spent ages making a narrator's costume for Felix. Emily is a shepherd, so it was easy enough to knock something together with a tea towel. They're not the best costumes by any means, but I was determined to give it a go. Nina obviously didn't know what they were going to be this year, but had wanted to contribute nonetheless, so she'd ordered an array of costumes online: Mary, Joseph, wise men, stars, camels, angels. When I took the slips out of their schoolbags and saw their parts, it was such a cruel and blatant reminder that Nina had tried so hard to see into the future. I considered speaking to their teachers to see if they'd switch their parts, but I dithered so much that I left it too late.

Deborah doesn't compliment the costumes. She sits next to Suzanne and only speaks to me when I address her. She reminds me so much of Nina in a mood. Same pursed mouth, same unforgiving stares. I concentrate ahead, smile and clap. Stuart bought me a ticket. He asked me to come. I have a right to be here.

I concentrate on taking the best photos I can, even though every few minutes, my vision blurs with tears. It's my responsibility now to record their childhood in any way I see best.

Nina's memory book won't be a one-off project for me. I'm determined to create optimistic, hopeful stories. I've got this.

I focus on the shiny happiness of it: the shimmering tinsel, the gold star, the funny lines, the younger children waving at their parents, donkeys ears falling off. But when they sing "Silent Night," the tears build up inside and I fear that I will sob out loud. I swallow, deliberately looking ahead so that I don't catch the expressions of anyone else, but especially Stuart and Deborah.

Afterward, I attempt to get Tamsin to one side to see if I can pin down a time for us to meet and chat, but she's "busy."

"Sure we can meet," she says, "but it will have to be in January. Work's manic."

"What are you doing next Wednesday evening?" I say.

"I'll have to get back to you."

Damn. People quite often get caught out when I attempt to tie them down by phrasing a question in that way. They aren't usually quick enough to come up with an excuse and end up admitting that they have nothing specific on. It allows me to get them to agree to a fixed date. It worked nearly every time with Nina.

I chat to Greg from our book group instead, who has come along as an unofficial photographer for the school website.

"Is it a hobby or are you hoping to develop your interest into something more?" I ask.

"I wouldn't say I'm a natural, but I'm improving all the time. Nina and I attended the same photography course."

"Oh. I just assumed that all her friends were made through connections to the school."

I didn't know Nina had taken a photography class. I hate things that may seem inconsequential to others, but to me, feel like deliberate snubs, as if Nina was deliberately hiding things from me on purpose. It's not as if I'd have enrolled at some ran-

dom photography class, too! Perhaps she kept it a secret because
it was something I was naturally better at.

Ben said I had a tendency to take things too personally. I do
try not to, but if I'm being honest, it's hard when you discover
that your supposed friend hid normal things from you for no
clear-cut reason.

"It's a small world around here," says Greg. "People tend to
be linked in some form or other. You'll be glad to move on."

"I promised Nina I'd stick around for as long as it took."

I pick up a glass of white wine and take a sip, but it's so bitter I wish I'd gone for the cordial instead.

"That's good of you. She must've thought highly of you."

Is he joking? Had he really missed how close we were? I've
been part of the book group for over a year now.

I opt for a simple response.

"Well, of course. There wasn't anything that Nina couldn't
ask of me."

"Anything?"

"Well…" I say, giving a half laugh, half smile. I bite into a
mince pie, unsure how else to respond.

Stuart heads over.

"We're ready to leave," he says. "If you are, too."

I nod. Greg and Stuart barely acknowledge one other apart
from a brief "hi" as I swallow my mouthful, before we say our
goodbyes.

"Deborah has left already," Stuart says as he helps me into
my coat. "I think she's upset with me."

"It's not you she's upset with, it's me," I say.

"I feel bad for her," he says. "Let's invite her round more or
take the children over there."

"It's probably best if you do that alone," I say. "For now."

I zip up my coat and wrap my scarf around my neck as I brace
myself for the cold.

Christmas lights seem to adorn nearly every house as they

light up our route home. The sky is clear and there's no wind. The village is film-set magical, and I half expect snow to complete the scene. Kevin and Suzanne walk ahead holding hands with the children. Feeling partly responsible for Deborah's early exit, I decide to try to lift the mood.

"I think they're looking forward to Christmas despite... Well, I know it won't be the same but... Sorry, what I'm trying to get across is that you've done a great job," I say.

Stuart looks pleased. "I've had a lot of help. But thank you. It's good to hear."

I smile.

"Why don't I put the children to bed?" I say. "Then you can walk your parents back to the guest cottage, have some time alone with them and maybe have a nightcap? I'm sure they'd appreciate it."

"Great idea, thanks," he says, walking ahead to catch up with them.

Felix and Em are tired and tetchy so it takes a while to persuade them to put on their pajamas and brush their teeth. I orchestrate it so they're both snuggled on either side of me on Stuart's bed for a joint bedtime story, to save having to do it separately. I suggested this routine to Nina many times, it's not always practical to read two separate stories, but she wouldn't have it.

"They need quality time," she'd said. "I like to give each of them at least some of my undivided attention every day."

I tuck them both in by pulling up their duvets and fitting them snugly around their shapes. I'm firm with Em when she wants to chatter.

"We can talk about the play more over breakfast tomorrow," I say. "You were wonderful."

I remind them both how proud we all are of their brilliant performances and switch off their lights.

I walk downstairs in my stockinged feet, which slide slightly on the wooden floor. I'm not used to wearing dresses, and it wasn't strictly necessary to make an effort for tonight, but when Suzanne mentioned that she was wearing a dress, I felt as though I should, too.

It's quiet without Stuart and his parents. I pour some red wine into a saucepan and add in some cinnamon, cloves, nutmeg and star anise. I stir, inhaling the aroma.

I'm not normally a huge fan of Christmas tunes, but the magic of tonight has wormed its way into my mood, and it's infectious. What Nina's death has taught me is that you have to enjoy the rare moments of calm. I feel so at home right now. Apparently, the grass isn't greener, but perhaps that's meant to be interpreted as a caution against general dissatisfaction, rather than a situation such as mine.

When the wine is warm enough, I ladle some into a large, thick glass. Steam forms at the sides. Nursing it, I decide to take it into the living room and choose a film. I should examine and back up the photos I took tonight as I want to create a gift out of the best ones for Kevin and Suzanne, but right now, I feel too chill.

The back door opens. Stuart steps inside, dragging the cold in with him.

I watch him take off his coat, boots and hat. "Mulled wine?"

"Perfect," he says. "It smells exactly the same as Nina used to make it."

It is her recipe, but I don't tell him that.

"I was going to watch a film, if that's okay?"

"You don't have to ask."

"I know, thanks. But…it feels polite to. Fancy joining me?"

He grins. "It depends what you like watching."

"The scarier the better," I say.

"Let's give it a go," he says.

We walk through to the living room and I let Stuart faff around with the controls. When we agree on what to watch—

a documentary on spies, Stuart's choice, but I'm prepared to try it—I dim the lights. As I do so, the doorbell rings. Stuart pauses our selection. The opening credits freeze, blurring the letters on the screen.

"Carol singers," says Stuart as he heads for the door, pulling his wallet from his back pocket.

I wait.

I don't hear any singing. Or voices. Perhaps Deborah has returned to check up on us?

Something doesn't feel right. As I stand up to investigate, Stuart returns. He doesn't look himself.

"What's wrong?"

"I'm not sure, it's odd. Nothing like this has ever happened before..."

He's clutching a card which I prize gently from his grip. It's not a Christmas card. It has a picture of a black heart on the cover. Inside:

Wishing you both a dreadful, shame-filled Christmas.

The words take a few moments to fully sink in.

"Very childish," I say, handing it back to Stuart. I feel queasy.

Stuart rips it in half, then into smaller pieces. "I'd chuck it in the fire if we had one going."

"Light one," I suggest.

I hesitate. I don't want to say what I'm going to out loud, but if I don't do it now, the moment will pass. Again.

"Nina thought someone was after her."

"What do you mean?"

"Just that."

"No way! Not to my knowledge. Why would that even be the case? She would not have hidden something like that from me. Besides, everyone loved Nina."

"That's what I thought."

"This ridiculous card delivery, it's about us being under the same roof. It's nothing to do with Nina."

"What about the attempted break-ins?"

"I don't think they're relevant. These things happen. No point in dwelling."

"When did Nina want the burglar alarm fitted?"

"Earlier this year."

I give him a dose of therapy-type silence to mull it over himself without me having to spell it out.

"It is a big house," he says. "She wanted her family to be as safe as possible. It's understandable."

True. Although, we're not that isolated compared to some New Forest properties.

"I'll go and get us more wine," I say.

As I pour, I feel shaken, but I shouldn't. I knew this would happen. I'd told myself to be prepared. I'm not even sure this is just about Nina, although she was popular and well-liked. It's about people not liking the thought that they too could be replaced. Even though I'm not Nina's replacement; I'm here on my own terms.

The smell of spices is too sickly now. I open a fresh bottle of red—a Châteauneuf—and pour two large glasses. Ben and I brought this over last New Year's, but Nina wasn't up to drinking so we all stuck to the one glass of champagne at midnight. I gulp my wine and top it up again before I head back to the living room.

Stuart is bent down in front of the fire, which looks like it is just about to take hold.

"If you want me to leave, I'll understand," I say to his back. "It wasn't my intention to cause trouble."

He doesn't turn round.

I regret my offer until he replies, "I don't want you to leave."

"It might get worse."

He stands up and turns round to face me. I hand him his wine.

He puts it down on the coffee table. I do the same. The fire crackles and makes me jump. The fairy lights on the tree flicker on and off. Stuart looks younger, less troubled…almost defiant.

He steps toward me. I have seconds to do the right thing, but I already know that I won't.

"I guess you're going to ask if we should give them something real to talk about?" I say.

"Something like that."

It's a joint decision. I can't say that either one of us moves first. We exchange a look, a silent agreement that this is what we both want. We kiss.

At first, I can't help but think of Ben, but Stuart is nicely different. When I start to undo his shirt buttons, he breaks away to lock the door. Although it's him who guides me to the sofa, it feels natural to fall down on to it, although it's been so long since I've been with anyone new, it reminds me of being a teenager. I half imagine I should listen out for some imaginary parents upstairs. It's impossible to switch off and when I hear a scuffling noise outside, I almost ask him to stop. But I don't, of course, because this is how things have to be.

It's awkward, yet enjoyably comforting, rather than all-consuming. I'm relieved when it's over, as if now that the inevitable has happened, we've no choice but to move on. I glance up at the mantelpiece and see Nina on her wedding day looking down at us. I pull down my dress, even more acutely aware of my surroundings. The Christmas tree lights flash red, green, white.

Stuart sits up, too, and we both reach for our wineglasses and sip. Neither of us says anything. There are no words. When I can't bear the silence any longer, I stand up and drop the ripped pieces of card into the dying fire. We both watch as the edges blacken and crumble.

ELEVEN

Red wine gives me the absolute worst bouts of paranoia, doubt and self-loathing. Only this time, I wish it was simply hangover-induced. It seemed like such an obvious solution last night, the right thing to do. Now, I fear that I've created a huge messy complication. It could be too much, too soon.

I open my eyes. Thank God I'm in my own room. Alone. I pick up my phone and check the time. Five a.m. I lie back down.

What have I done? It made sense at the time. I think of Nina and how she'd react if she were here. A knot of horrible, familiar rising anxiety presses against my chest. The physical pain is real. I sit up and lean over. I feel dizzy. I'm supposed to face the fear, to ride through the attack until it passes. It works for general fears, not real, self-induced, guilt-ridden ones. I place my right hand on my chest as I struggle to get a grip on my trepidation. I thought I could handle this.

I force myself to put my legs to the side of the bed, get up, shower, pull on some jeans, a thick sweater and get my sneakers out of my gym bag (the gym I rarely go to, but should). I head downstairs, deliberately not looking into the living room, and open the front door, embracing the blast of cold. I close the door gently behind me, stand still and breathe. I must remember to breathe.

I don't have the strength to run, so I brisk-walk. The downstairs lights in the guesthouse are on; Stuart's parents are early risers. I walk toward the darkness of the woods. I'm not sure why, but it feels like the only thing to do—to keep moving and hope that the fear of what may be in the darkness will help override my conflicting feelings. I rely on my phone's flashlight to see after I nearly trip over a root. I feel watched, as if Nina can see me, is judging me. My breathing is heavy and unnerving.

Behind me, I think about Stuart and the children. The warmth of the house. His tenderness. It has been a long time since I've felt cared for. Although it wasn't amazing (perhaps guilt held us both back a bit?), it forced me to wake up to how lonely I've been feeling for longer than I cared to admit to myself, even. Ben emotionally left me a long time ago, but I wasn't ready or didn't have the guts to deal with it.

By the time I decide I have no choice but to return, I've made up my mind. It takes two and Nina, well, surely she'd rather me than a stranger? I'm fond of Stuart—more so than I realized—and life *does* have a strange way of working out. I mustn't falter from what I believe to be the true and right thing to do.

I let myself in through the back door. Stuart and the children are up, but they're not alone. Camilla and Louise are sitting around the table with them, eating pancakes. Maple syrup, honey, lemons and sugar gather on the surface.

Who invited them over? Probably Suzanne. She's chatted to Camilla at the school gates, they've shared memories of Nina. I'm not impressed with the casual way Camilla acts like she's a part of the family. I appreciate she's a link to Nina, but still...

Suzanne is in front of a frying pan at the hob, clutching a spatula. She is wearing an apron that belongs to me. I don't like the overfamiliarity of it. I don't know why, but it feels wrong.

I wish I was brave enough to ask her to take it off, but obviously, I can't.

"Morning," I say in such a cheery voice that it doesn't even sound like mine.

"Morning," several voices chorus.

I avoid Stuart's gaze and he me. Big mistake. Camilla stares at me as if she can tell. It's a schoolgirl error to ignore the object of your affections. I make a cappuccino, taking my time over the frothing of the milk before I sit beside Stuart.

"I hope you or the children didn't hear me go out early this morning," I say. "I couldn't sleep, needed some fresh air."

"I didn't hear a thing," he says.

I turn my attention to the children. "You two were brilliant last night," I say.

"My play is next week with the older classes," says Louise.

"I'll come and watch if you like," I say.

"No need," says Camilla. "Two nativities a year is above and beyond."

"It's not a nativity," says Louise. "That's for the younger ones. Mine is a proper play."

"I'd really love to see it," I say.

"Very thoughtful of you." Suzanne beams over at me. "Marie, love, we were just talking about how it might be a good idea for Camilla to move into the guesthouse when we leave," she says. "It seems silly that she's paying a fortune in rent while she finds her feet back here and Lulu will be wonderful company for the children. Such a lovely girl, a natural with little ones."

Camilla does a commendable job of acting the innocent, her expression full of *oh, goodness, I don't want to be any trouble, I wasn't hinting*, yet she's clearly taken advantage of Suzanne's trusting nature, carefully worded a few hints and run with it while I've been briefly out of the picture.

Thankfully Stuart intervenes. "Mum, these are the types of issues that need more discussion."

Stuart hardly ever snaps.

Oh. It's about last night. He wants me out. If Camilla rents out the other place, it's harder for him to ask me to leave. I feel sick. From the corner of my eye—I daren't look—I sense rather than see Camilla's expression. She's playing a game. She knows exactly what she's doing.

I decide to back Stuart up, to make him realize that I'm sympathetic to the situation. "Although commune-living has its advantages, I'm not going to be here for much longer either. I guess we all need to find our way in the big, bad world."

Silence.

Suzanne leaps up and picks up plates and starts stacking the dishwasher. Stuart still hasn't made proper eye contact with me; it's irritating. He's the one who is going to give the game away, not me.

Camilla stands her ground. "Thanks, Suzanne, it was something I hadn't thought of, but it would help immensely. My move back here was fairly sudden and I'd forgotten how expensive the UK was. But I don't want to put you in an awkward position either, Stuart."

"Why don't we all have a chat after Christmas?" I say, keen to get back in Suzanne's good books, play Camilla at whatever her game is *and* try to give the impression to Stuart that I won't make life difficult if he's full of regret.

It's exhausting trying to please everyone all of the time.

Stuart looks tired. I guess he didn't sleep much either.

Camilla smiles at him.

Unease forms in the pit of my stomach as I await his reaction. It's not what I expect. He walks out of the kitchen as if he doesn't trust himself to react.

Hopeful that Camilla has caused enough ripples for one visit, I escape upstairs for my second shower of the day. Standing beneath the cascade, I turn the temperature up as hot as I can stand. My head clears.

Wrapping a towel around me, I'm too impatient to get dressed before I Google the fear of dogs: cynophobia. Camilla was badly bitten by a dog, not once but twice. The first time was when she was very young (but she said she still remembers the pain), the second time was when she was on holiday with her grandparents. Hospital visits were involved on both occasions.

Camilla will suddenly find being around here a whole lot less appealing. A dog really is for life, not just for Christmas. I scrap my idea of getting Stuart new ties because, of course, it's so *obvious* now that a pet is exactly what they all need for a fresh focus. It will help them heal.

More and more, I can see why Nina entrusted me to make the right choices for her family.

TWELVE

When I come downstairs, Stuart is alone. Everyone else is at the park.

"Apparently, I look like I could do with a break." He grins. Relief. He looks happier.

"I didn't sleep much either, as you've gathered by my early morning exit," I say.

I wait.

"Do you regret last night?" I can't help asking.

"No. Do you?"

"No."

"I feel guilty, but that has nothing to do with us."

I love that he's just said *us*. "Likewise." I pause, then say, "What about Camilla? We can't have her living in our garden. She'll be on to us in no time, and we need to take this—whatever this is—slowly."

I stop, praying that I haven't overstepped the mark, that Stuart is as keen as me to see how things cautiously, and secretly, develop between us.

"What's the story between her and Louise's father?" he asks.

"She hasn't said, but I get the impression it's not amicable.

She likes to keep her cards close to her chest." I don't elaborate. "If you feel you need to offer…" I add.

I let my words hang. I don't want to be the one to veto her move here.

"Nina would've wanted me to help her."

I knew Stuart would cave. He's too soft.

It turns out I'm not the only non-fan of Camilla.

"It's turning into a mini-bordello around here," says Deborah in a low voice.

She takes another sip of prosecco. Deborah rarely drinks. Her face is flushed, her eyes look a little…demonic. It's Christmas Eve lunchtime. Stuart's parents, Deborah, Camilla, the three children and myself are finishing off a parsnip soup and crusty bread made by Stuart.

"It will all come out in the wash," I say in response to Deborah's comment. "It's a saying of my mum's. I haven't said that in years."

Today is a farewell meal because Suzanne and Kevin are heading home the day after Boxing Day. Stuart and I have agreed that I will go to my parents' for a few days. "It's for the best, it's too soon," we keep saying to each other, but I'm not really sure what that means anymore. Nothing else has happened between us, not a hug, a look or a clandestine kiss. It's disconcerting.

We adjourn to the living room to exchange gifts and Stuart furnishes the adults with festive drinks.

My plan to adopt a dog is well under way. Apparently you can't go wrong with a golden retriever. There are a lot of administrative and practical hoops to jump through on the route to dog-ownership (which I agree with, I can think of many people I've met who should never be allowed to own a pet). I've already planned to take Felix and Emily dog-accessory shopping in the new year so even if their pet still isn't quite ready to be adopted, things will still be too far gone for Stuart to put the brakes on the idea.

"My main gift will be a late surprise," I announce. "Sadly, it wasn't able to be delivered in time for Christmas. But I do have some small things for you to unwrap now," I say as I watch Emily rip open the wrapping paper. Felix mimics Louise by neatly opening each end.

I've bought them children's cameras, plus an illustrated beginners' guide to photography. Louise has a similar but more advanced version. For Deborah, I've bought gift cards —again, you can't go wrong—and for Camilla, a memory album, not dissimilar to the one I'm creating to celebrate Nina's life.

Sifting through the photos of us brought up a proper mixed bag of memories. There are plenty to choose from: house parties, pubs, the beach, pools, bars, but the best are the Ibizan ones. The three of us on an aqua bus to Formentera, the sister island of Ibiza, clutching a mojito in front of a wooden beach kiosk, huge grins on our faces. Hanging out at Stuart's friend's villa, barbecues by the pool, boating. Charlie, Camilla, Nina, Stuart, me, various other friends, all of us so innocently happy, oblivious and blissfully unaware of what lay ahead.

Camilla makes a show of flicking through the pages, saying she's "touched," yet she appears anything but. She clutches it tightly like she can't wait to hurl it out a window. I deliberately included a few pictures of Charlie—it felt wrong to leave him out.

Stuart was a tricky one to buy for. After ditching the tie idea—he and I can start our own thing—this year (especially as we've gone for a horribly public group-present-sharing experience), I had to walk the fine line. He's got a voucher, too—a certificate for a valuable, rare wine of his choice which he can apparently keep in storage in some mysterious wine cellar or have delivered. Who knows if this wine even exists or not, or if it is indeed decent, but that is the joy of internet gift-buying. It makes it look as though I've tried.

Deborah knocks back the last of her Baileys, crocodile-like eyes glaring at me over the top of her glass.

She can doubt my motives all she likes, but they are pure. I have Stuart and the children's best interests at heart, I really do. Not one of them can prove otherwise.

After exchanging gifts with Suzanne and Kevin, I excuse myself. "I must pack."

There's only so much false cheer, I, and even Deborah, by the looks of it, can take. Nina would've hated this. I feel grubby and restless.

Finally, Stuart catches my eye. He even manages a genuine smile. It's a relief. It dies, however, when I return downstairs with my bags and spot Stuart and Camilla alone in the kitchen. Both their glasses are empty, yet they seem unaware, clutching them regardless while they talk. Camilla stops talking as I approach.

"Marie!" she says in a happy voice, which sounds like a warning to Stuart of my arrival.

There's nothing else I can do but smile. Graciously. It's bloody hard.

Most of her belongings have already been moved into the guesthouse by a removal company. Suzanne and Kevin said they didn't mind being surrounded by boxes for the last few days of their stay. (Camilla appears to have an awful lot of *stuff* for someone who moved to a different country at short notice.) She is spending two nights at her grandparents' before flying out to Toronto for the remainder of the holidays. Upon her return, she will be our (very) immediate neighbor. She didn't waste any time at all in making it happen. Neither would I if I had an underhanded agenda.

We all say our goodbyes, festive wishes and farewells among

hugs, kisses and promises. Actually, I don't mind being the first to leave, I realize, as I drive away. When I return, it will be for good. Unlike Camilla, my ties to this place are strong.

I check into a boutique hotel near my parents'. I'll go over and help cook Christmas lunch tomorrow, but I couldn't face three nights home alone with them. There's too much time to fill, too much…*expectation* for me to take on the role of two siblings. Rightly or wrongly, I feel like I need to make up for my brother's absence, smile in a jolly fashion when he Skypes from a beach or a mountain or a desert or wherever he can get Wi-Fi, when really, I'm jealous.

I shouldn't have lied to Stuart, but he'd have insisted I stay if my parents weren't expecting me. We both need space and it can't do any harm.

Perhaps *that's* something I should talk about with Christian. Why I chose to stay, not travel, to take over Nina's role so wholeheartedly. I loved Ibiza, but it's my one and only experience of traveling abroad. My parents were campers, great believers in the magic of the fresh British countryside.

With the TV on in the background, I sit cross-legged on the comfy bed and open my laptop. I've transferred everything over to mine from Nina's. I need to concentrate, to try to read between the lines and cross-reference to unpick what Nina was really trying to convey to Camilla. I've been putting off reading the words again because they sting, but now that Camilla is trying to worm her way into my life (or Stuart's—her motivation isn't obvious), I need to be in possession of all the facts. It's not a wise enough tactic to bank on the hope that a dog alone will be enough to scare her off.

The emails are dated earlier this year.

03/01 12:32

Hi Camilla,

Long time and all that! I don't know if you ever check this email address. If you don't, I'll have to find some other way to contact you. I'm not sure how to word this, I don't imagine that it's necessarily welcome to hear from me.

I thought about this a lot, whether or not to write, sleeping dogs and all that. I know our goodbye was supposed to be just that. But I'd like to make amends because I'm dying. Sorry to put it so bluntly, but I'm running out of time. I'm married (to Stuart still), two children aged seven and five. A boy and a girl, Felix and Emily. Marie said after I'd had Em that of course I'd have a boy first and a girl second, isn't that everyone's ideal? I never thought of it like that, and I don't know why I'm telling you this. Maybe I'll delete that part.

I stop reading at this point every time, wondering why she didn't delete it. Thinking about it again, perhaps it makes sense. Toward the end, Nina became even more brutally honest. Our conversations didn't dwell on trivialities. She got straight to the point, or so I thought.

I don't need to read on—I know what it says—but I do anyway. Every time I hope that something new will leap out at me, and I'll come up with a better interpretation.

There's not much about you online, other than you still live and work in Canada. Long shot, but any chance you'll be in the UK within the next few months? I'm not sure how long I have. I'm not up to traveling too far. All my time now will be spent with family. I know you'll understand why I needed to get in touch. I need to tie up all the loose ends, make amends and ensure that my conscience is completely clear. We must speak.

Much love, Nina xx

Forty-eight hours later...

Hi Nina,
I do check this mail. I've been expecting to hear from you sub-consciously, I think, and somehow, it almost wasn't a surprise to see your name in my inbox. I'm so, so, sorry to hear your news. How utterly devastating! My daughter, Louise, is eleven. My partner and I are on the verge of splitting up. I've been thinking about moving back to the UK for a while, strangely enough, but obviously it's a big decision to make. I'll do what I can.

I'd love to see you again. It was all a bit rushed, way too sudden toward the end. Please send pictures of your children, a pigeon pair, how lovely! How is Marie? Still the same? :)

(The smiley face really bugs me. What does it mean?)

Much love, hugs, kisses and millions of good wishes, Camilla xoxo

There isn't much I don't know about pregnancy, babies and young children. Technically, according to my many hours spent online figuring out how the hell to get pregnant and reading endless random pieces of information, a proper pigeon pair refers to boy-and-girl twins. An old belief was that pigeons sat on two eggs at a time, resulting in a male and a female. I have a strong, almost irrepressible urge to message Camilla and tell her that she was wrong.

But I know what it's really about because it's something that

I actually *have* managed to discuss in therapy. I was jealous that Nina had children with such ease when for me, it has been an ongoing struggle filled with disappointment. The fact that it clearly wasn't hard for Camilla either reignites fresh feelings of being the odd one out.

I read on.

I cannot tell you the relief that you may be coming over!!! We so need to talk, to catch up before it's too late. A great weight has been lifted. Marie is fine, she's been a good support (of course).

I've got important decisions to make and share with you. It's increasingly playing on my mind. Please try to get here asap. If my situation wasn't so dire, it would be different, but I'm tired. Some days are worse than others, and sometimes I have nightmares that I run out of time with so much left to say to so many people. I hope this is isn't oversharing, but then again, what the hell!! :)

Much love, Nina xx
P.S. I had a feeling you'd have a girl!

The next day:

Nina—hang in there. You've done the right thing reaching out to me personally. It's entirely normal that you're worried. Call me on the number below. Any time. Or give me your number. Let's have a general chat.
Love and hugs, Camilla xoxoxo

Why would you specify a *general* chat with someone who was terminally ill? It doesn't make sense.

After that, there was a six-week gap between emails. Which

means they only spoke on the phone or in person, leaving me with no possible way of finding out what was said or shared.

I'm glad we got to speak. It's not goodbye, it's farewell!
Nina xx

Did Camilla definitely visit during that time? I check my own diary to see how often I visited Nina during that period earlier this year. I covered a wedding on Valentine's Day and the two weekends on either side of it. Nina said that she and Stuart weren't going to do anything particularly special for Valentine's A) because Stuart doesn't agree with "being forced to be romantic" by card companies and B) because they had their date night every Tuesday (the day they first met in Ibiza), which they'd stuck to religiously for as long as I can recall. Valentine's Day this year was on a Wednesday. If Camilla visited during that time period, then it would make sense why she didn't come to the funeral. Two long-haul trips in short succession would probably have been impractical and expensive.

What *doesn't* make sense is that they met in secret, why Camilla kept her visit from the rest of us. Things I don't like to think about resurface. Seeing the words going back and forth between Nina and Camilla still have an incredible amount of power to wound. Heat warms my face as one such unsettling example plays out in my mind.

Nina couldn't sunbathe for a few days in Ibiza as she'd been badly burned the previous day. We hung around in the shade reading before setting off to have an early dinner at the bar where Camilla worked. As we arrived, Camilla stretched out her arms and enveloped Nina into a hug.

"Careful," I said. "Nina's in pain."

Camilla muttered something to Nina that sounded like, "Is she playing Mum again?"

I acted like I didn't hear, that I wasn't crushed. I didn't look at Nina to gauge her response. Maybe on a subconscious level, I was scared of what I'd see.

"I hate being the peacekeeper," Nina had said to me more than a few times.

The way she said it, it was as though it was my doing, however much I tried to get her to understand that I just wanted us both to be happy.

Instead, I tried to act cool and not look disapproving. Camilla's job involved writhing around in a barely there, see-through bikini in a giant champagne glass filled with water. After each twenty-minute stretch, the person taking over from her would climb up the adjacent makeshift, red-painted wooden steps and hand her a towel as they swapped places. In the chill-out zone on the terrace, masseurs offered head massages, and aromatherapists and fortune-tellers entertained in among the bar staff hard-selling two-for-one cocktails and shots.

It was me who initially spotted an impossible-to-miss Stuart—he was blatantly out of place with his sweater over his shoulders, the arms wrapped in a neat knot. His trainers were new; there was no attempt to scuff them up a bit and make them look a little worn. He was pristine and smiley with white teeth and clean trousers.

I was weaving my way back from the toilets and he stood there, looking so…taken aback (or was it disapproving?) that I took pity. We made eye contact. When I smiled, he smiled back. It transpired that he'd got the venue wrong; he was supposed to meet his friends at the place next door.

"The sunsets are better from here, anyway," I said. "Come and join us for a drink on the terrace."

I wasn't being totally selfless. When Nina and I had booked the holiday, I hadn't factored in my boyfriend, Charlie. He worked in a bar near our college. He'd been a bit distant lately and overly casual about his summer plans, but I nonetheless felt guilty when I realized that I couldn't afford two holidays, so Charlie had joined us for our final week.

Except, it didn't make things all right between me and Charlie again. The first few days were good, our brief time apart had helped, but by the third day, he was slipping away. I could sense it. He laughed more when Camilla was around, sat a little straighter, looked more…awake.

Words can be tailored to sound more palatable: actions are the biggest giveaways.

When Stuart sat down beside Nina, it was the most natural gesture. They hit it off from their first few sentences. Our holiday picked up after that. Stuart's friend had a villa with a pool, a sea view and a small speedboat moored nearby, and he introduced us all to a different world. Stuart's mate—Dan—was a jolly, sociable person who welcomed guests "as long as they restocked the bar and fridge."

Camilla packed in her temporary job and hung out with us instead. It was impossible not to be intoxicated by the glamour of it all.

And now, here I am—alone—in an anonymous hotel room on Christmas Eve. How things change. This does not feel like the best progress. I shut the laptop, place it on the bedside table, lie back and close my eyes.

I sit up and open my journal. At the back I list all the things that Nina shared about her relationship with Stuart, everything from the Tuesday date nights (those two words make me cringe, I wish someone would come up with a better description) to her love of buying him ties. His and her dreams, their plans. Stuart's love of sailing, jazz and decent red wine.

Camilla has no chance of wrecking our family situation, whatever her agenda is. She'll be gone within a month; I'll do whatever it takes to get rid of her, to win Deborah and everyone else round. Stuart and I need time alone without outside pressures so I can mold our fledgling relationship into what it needs to be.

I'm glad that the Christmas period will soon be over. The first of every significant date will be hard, and the festive season has been looming ominously since the first sign of tinsel and gifts in the shops. Clichéd as it may or may not be, a new year is a good time for change. I will tailor my interests and energy so it's as if I was always there. I accepted second best when Nina was alive, but there's no need to be sidelined anymore.

But still…why did Nina get back in contact with Camilla? What were they trying to hide from me? The answer, when it comes to me, is so bloody obvious, that rather than reveling in my cleverness, I'm annoyed at not having twigged immediately and heartsick at what it means.

THIRTEEN

My newfound knowledge is eating me up. I want to confront Camilla in person, hear the words from her directly, but I won't be able to until she's returned from Canada. Christmas is an effort as exhaustion hits. Feeling utterly disconnected from the rituals, I mentally tick off each one—presents, lunch (even though I have no appetite), crackers, paper hats, the Queen's speech, drinks with the neighbors, Boxing Day—everything a painfully slow countdown until I can escape the constraints of tradition to give myself space to think clearly, to rewind my memories, to piece it all together with the benefit of fresh knowledge. If my suspicion proves right—which I'm convinced it will—the past takes on a completely different meaning.

I keep busy, distracting myself with to-do lists and outings with the children. I post photos of our woodland walks, museum visits and horse rides on social media under delicately worded captions so they don't—hopefully—come across as too much.

Ben messages me not long after my latest post.

I know you don't want to hear it again, especially not from me, but please believe that I did love and care deeply for you. Don't let Stuart over-rely on you. Help out occasionally, but don't let him suck you into Nina's world again. I knew this would happen. You can be a support and a friend without sacrificing your dreams for a family of your own.

I hope you meet someone decent like you deserve. Please don't think I'm trying to be patronizing, but I couldn't not say anything.

Unexpected tears form as I unfriend him, but staying in touch—on social media—is clearly not healthy. Ben liked Stuart but felt that he was an opportunist.

"Aren't we all to varying degrees?" I said at the time, keen to rush to his defense.

"There's a difference between seizing opportunities and taking advantage," he replied.

I delete Ben's message. His supposed care and concern expired the moment he chose to be unfaithful. Quite why he thinks it's fine to give me advice when he is one of the reasons I'm in this situation, I don't know.

Yet I can't deny, his words resonate on some level. I like being needed.

On Stuart's birthday, the third of January, he is out for most of the afternoon visiting some important client. It's perfect timing as it gives me and the children a valuable few hours. When he returns, looking tired but no doubt expecting a homemade cake and a few balloons, Goldie (as Felix and Em have renamed her) has taken up residence in her new home.

He is genuinely shocked and keeps asking if "the dog" is really staying?

"It's a sweet gesture, Marie," he says when the children are distracted, getting her to chase them around the house. "I know you mean well, but I'm barely managing as it is. I just can't cope with any more responsibility right now. And you can't do this, you can't try to fix us with surprises as a fait accompli. Nina wouldn't have done something as momentous as adopting a rescue dog without consulting me. I feel hugely manipulated seeing as the children obviously adore her already. It's not as if you're going to be around forever."

That's what he thinks.

Despite my inner indignation, I assure him that I've thought of everything: training school (if need be, but apparently Goldie—formerly Lady—is "a dream"), vet's appointments, pet insurance and that I'm on hand to bear the bulk of the care. However, his harsh words sting, long after he's apologized and admitted that maybe it's a good thing after all. I try not to hold it against him; he is not yet in his right frame of mind. I am the one holding it all together. I am their rock.

Camilla is due home sometime today. I keep an eye out for a taxi. I intend to head over later and confront her with my discovery, hopefully while she's still jet-lagged and feeling a little overwhelmed in her new surroundings.

However, Stuart throws me.

"A friend of mine is going to pop in later for a drink."

"Oh," I say. "Sounds fun."

"I was wondering…" he says.

"Yes?"

"If you'd mind babysitting for a couple of hours so that we can nip to the pub?"

"Of course," I say. "I'm sure Goldie will keep me busy."

But I'm miffed, of course I am.

I go through the motions of lighting and blowing out candles, singing "Happy Birthday." Our hearts are not in it, but the children are putting their all into it, and that's what counts.

They smile, taking genuine pleasure in having made and decorated the cake themselves. It gives me hope that I'm doing something right.

When Stuart's friend arrives, I say hello and hang around for a while making polite chitchat. James makes a huge fuss of Goldie.

"I'd love a dog," he says. "But my wife isn't keen."

I'm secretly thrilled because it shows me in a good, tolerant and generous light.

"Can I get you both something to drink?" I say. "We're still trying to get through the Christmas champagne."

"No, thanks," says Stuart.

He doesn't waste any further time grabbing their coats, as if he doesn't get out immediately, the opportunity will be lost. However, he bends down to stroke Goldie before he leaves, and I am so relieved that I nearly cry. Honestly. I thought I'd made a huge error.

I hear the front door close.

Apart from Goldie, I am alone, which feels heightened by the party leftovers I've been left to clear up.

The house already feels colder, which I know can only be my imagination. Rising frustration that I can't go over to Camilla's, that I'm trapped because I'm responsible for the children and Goldie, increases my restlessness. I pour myself a glass of champagne—why not—and wander around, memories keeping me company.

I helped Nina write thank-you cards for her wedding gifts one evening.

"I'll feel bad if I don't do it soon. People chose specific gifts for a reason. They were kind enough to come to our wedding. The guilt will get to me."

We'd both laughed.

The guilt will get to you, was something our religious studies teacher used to say to us.

We had a fun evening making up gratitude paragraphs about vases, kitchen utensils and suchlike. It had given me hope that nothing would change between us. I'd been happy.

However, now the guilt is getting to me, in giant waves.

These are the type of complex feelings I should bring up in therapy. Not sit there yacking away telling stories and divulging unrelated snippets of my life.

I pour the remainder of my champagne down the sink. The acid is burning the back of my throat. I hope I'm not coming down with a cold; I can't afford to be ill. Maybe it's the thwarted desire to speak to Camilla that's causing the problem. I go upstairs and check on the children. I hesitate outside Stuart's room. There's no longer any point in searching for clues of potential fairy-tale, wicked stepmothers now that I'm here. I'm Nina's stand-in, the best protector of Felix and Emily. Another woman on the scene could change my relationship with them or muddy the waters.

I go to my own room and shut the door firmly, as if the gesture itself will prevent me from any temptation to pry.

I sit on my bed and take out my journal. The words don't come.

Instead, I take out Nina's paperwork and rework through the figures, making careful notes. Nina was siphoning off and hiding money in dribs and drabs. A few hundred here and there, but all differing amounts. The main pattern is that she did it regularly, once a week usually, starting several years after she began earning money from her various small businesses.

Annoyance builds. I wish Nina had opened up to me. We had opportunities, not just toward the end, but before that. We went to church together once because she said she didn't want to go alone. It wasn't during a service—the place was empty. We sat in silence, near the front, for a good ten minutes in the cool darkness. Neither one of us had prayed since school, so we couldn't bring ourselves to do it in front of one another. Silly, maybe, considering. Still, it was peaceful, until we were disturbed. The church door banged. Nina leaped up, as did I, but no one was there. It was odd, as we'd both heard footsteps.

"Do you believe in ghosts?"

"Yeah, headless ones running around with axes," I laughed to ease the mood.

How could I have been so bloody insensitive? A horrible thought: what if she was waiting for me to ask her something, to push her? What if I was too stupid, too self-absorbed, to read the signs? I trawl through all our last moments, desperately trying to think, to grab hold of something relevant. She was deliberately vague, perhaps trying to tell me something without having to spell it out.

"Promises aren't always easy to keep," she said when she impressed upon me the importance of keeping mine.

"Not for me," I assured her.

"I want people, especially the children, naturally, to remember me for who I am now, the person I became, not the self-centered one I was when I was younger."

"You've nothing to worry about there, then. As far as I'm aware, children don't think that their parents ever had a life before them."

I waited for her to smile her response, but one never came. I realize now—after talking things through with Christian—that I wanted to give her space. I couldn't imagine what she felt like, or what she was going through, so when she appeared wistful, I'd go silent and hope that by just being there for her, it would offer some comfort. Maybe that's why I didn't push for specifics. Who knows?

We each lit a candle and stood there watching the wax soften as I wished for her to live. I imagine she did the same.

"I'm sorry, Marie," she said.

"What for?"

The church door opened, and this time, we did see a man enter. The moment was lost.

The pain in my chest aches all the way up through to my jaw, and I give into the tears. She was apologizing for the secret she kept from me. And I didn't realize. Fresh anger reignites at Camilla. It was because of her that Nina was put in the position of having to withhold information, which clearly went against what she felt was the right thing to do.

It's gone midnight when I hear Stuart return home. Outside, the wind builds up. I can hear the branches of the New Forest trees swaying and the cries of night creatures. Foxes? Owls? Inside, quiet, apart from the odd creak. I hear him come upstairs, slightly louder than usual. His door shuts.

I creep downstairs to check on Goldie, who really is a chill dog. She opens her eyes but doesn't move from her bed in the corner. I made sure it wasn't too cold or too warm. I've been warned that there may be an adjustment period of up to three months while she susses things out and that she may sleep at lot at first because it was so noisy with all the dogs constantly barking at her previous home. Mainly, however, it's all about trust, love and routine. Sounds easy enough.

I turn on the kettle. Goldie seems fine with that. Phew. I open a cupboard and rummage through a pack of mixed herbal teas until I find a chamomile one, which promises me a good night's rest.

Stuart's wallet, house and car keys lie on the kitchen counter, a sign that he must've had a good few drinks. As I wait for the flavor to infuse, I open his wallet and flick through, craving some form of intimacy through a little more knowledge or insight into him. We haven't slept together again. It's concerning. We've fallen back into our friendship as if it never happened, and I'm at a bit of a loss as to how to steer us back in the right direction. A little knowledge can't harm.

The first thing I find is a picture of Nina on their honeymoon, which evokes mixed feelings. Envy, a little, of course, but it would also feel callous of him to discard any memories of her overly soon, so it also reinforces my belief that he is decent. There are the expected pictures of the children, including the most recent school pictures. A parking receipt for Heathrow airport: dated today for around the time Camilla and Louise were due home.

I pick up his keys, slide on Nina's wellies and go outside. I press the ignition switch on Stuart's Range Rover. His GPS only confirms what the ticket has already told me.

Why hide the fact he was picking Camilla up from the airport? I feel sick because there is only one reasonable explanation. Images of Stuart and the children forming a perfectly blended family with Camilla—not Nina, not me, but bloody Camilla, of all people—are a real kick to the stomach because I've realized that Louise is the daughter I should've had with Charlie.

FOURTEEN

Camilla doesn't even try to deny it. When she opens the front door to the cottage just before seven the following morning (I couldn't wait any later), she doesn't look surprised, almost as if she's been half expecting me.

"I'm not proud of myself," she says. "I didn't know I was pregnant for a surprisingly long time afterward. Denial, I guess. I went abroad for a fresh start. My paternal grandparents lived out there. I built a life. My parents died within a few months of each other not long after I moved away. I buried everything until Nina got in touch and—"

"Why keep your visit secret?"

"It wasn't *a secret* as such. Think about it rationally—Nina was desperately ill. Who she chose to connect and why I'm sure were deeply emotional, complicated decisions and wishes. Marie, Nina wasn't your responsibility. You shouldn't be here. You still have that tendency to overdo things."

"Stuart wants me here," I say.

Even as I say the words out loud, I don't know if they are true.

"Oh for God's sake, Marie. Get your own life. At college you stifled Nina. Even on holiday she wasn't even allowed to sunbathe on her own. There you were, getting her towels, telling her to wear a stronger sunscreen, buying her favorite things from the supermarket, fussing over her like a protective mother. It was suffocating."

"Because now you and Stuart want to make a go of it?" I say. "That's why he came and picked you up from the airport, that's why he agreed to you living here. That's why you came back. It's all very convenient."

"Of course not," she says. "He was visiting a client in Windsor. He offered me *and* Lulu a lift. Look, there's no great mystery. Nina only wanted to protect you. She said you struggled to move on from what happened to Charlie, that you were desperate for children. If it helps, Nina was really angry about me and Charlie. We fell out over it. That's why we lost touch for so long."

That Nina knew so much more than she ever admitted to, that she sat there and listened while I went over and over where it had all gone so wrong with Charlie, that I regretted accusing him of sleeping with Camilla, is yet another blow.

Renewed doubts about my loyalty to Nina and my being here, playing at happy families, take hold. Perhaps I was too much of a pushover in the past. I've had enough.

"And why should I believe anything you say? You lied to me, you and Charlie. You said that there was nothing going on behind my back, that I was being paranoid."

"I am sorry. I felt guilty—we both did."

"How long did it go on?"

"It was a few times."

"When?"

"Why do this? What will it achieve?" she says. "This, in all likelihood, is why Nina kept quiet. I can't undo anything I've done."

"I want to know."

"At the villa," she says. "Whenever we could."

I feel sick. The picture album I made her for Christmas. The photos were meant to taunt her, to remind her of our argument, but I didn't realize how horribly accurate I'd been.

"But still, why move back?" I say. "Why now?"

"There were lots of reasons. One being that my relationship had broken down. My ex and I were angry with each other. I needed a change of scene." She sighs. "Please listen to me, Marie. Nina was a good friend to you. I beg you to leave all this alone. Louise knows that she is the result of a holiday fling. I wish I'd done things differently."

I give her a dose of some Judy-and-Christian-type silence.

She caves, fills in the gap. "It's only now, as Louise gets older, that I realize the impact my silence may have on her," she says. "Naive, I know. Selfish, yes. Young and stupid? Very. Believe me, you can't say anything that will make me feel any worse."

I bet I can.

The remainder of the day I'm on autopilot: replying to clients, looking after Goldie, which takes up an extraordinary amount of time, tending to the never-ending household chores.

I went to a New Year's Eve house party at an old college friend's place this year because Stuart took the children round to Deborah's for a meal. It was unexpectedly good fun to be out, and it reminded me how much I've sacrificed for Nina's family by throwing myself so fully into the daily grind. My life isn't exactly how I pictured it. Yet, knowing what I know now, it helps. Anger is a powerful driving force. No more tiptoeing around guilt and loyalty; I need to move my relationship with Stuart on. As well as being a mother to Felix and Emily, I still crave a baby of my own.

I pour a large glass of champagne and drink half a glass. When Stuart comes downstairs, I hand him one.

"Happy late birthday," I say. "I thought it would be nice to have a celebratory meal, so we can catch up properly with no distractions."

"Thank you, Marie. The table looks lovely," he says.

"But?"

He looks uncomfortable. "Do you mind if I choose a different candle? That one was an anniversary gift."

All the signs are stacking up that tonight is too staged—it's just not going to work. If it means so much to him, if he can actually remember little things like this, why was it left in a drawer with all the others? Honestly, what does he expect? I nearly tell him about her wellies, how actually it makes no difference if you use stuff, but instead I summon up all my self-control and outwardly exude an air of patience.

"Choose whatever candle you like, I'm not that fussed. We don't even have to light one," I say. "By the way, I haven't cooked. I've ordered in from a decent restaurant."

"Perfect."

"Cheers!" I say to Stuart.

"Cheers!"

We are standing close to each other.

"You look nice," he says.

I smooth down my hair. "Thanks, so do you."

"I—" we both say at the same time. We laugh. It breaks the ice.

"I was going to invite Camilla, too, but she said she'd caught up with you on the drive back from Heathrow," I say.

He doesn't hesitate in his response. "Fair enough."

"I didn't realize you were collecting her and Louise from the airport."

"It was a last-minute arrangement," he says. "I was in the area, remembered that she was due back and thought that I may as well."

"Oh."

"I guess I forgot to mention it, what with the surprise arrival of Goldie."

The doorbell rings: our delivery. We both stand up. I let him go.

As I'm about to spoon our Japanese fusion dishes onto plates, Stuart comes up behind me and puts his arms around my waist.

"I'm sorry, I know I've been a bit off. It was hard for me. It was like admitting Nina was gone all over again. It felt unfaithful somehow."

Relief floods. "I understand. It's strange for me, too. I'm happy to take things slowly. I know it's hard for you and you have to put the children first."

"Camilla suggested that I hire a part-time nanny. She felt that it might be fairer on you so that you can be more flexible with your working hours. Perhaps she has a point? I know you've turned down weekend weddings because of social commitments involving me and the children."

Anger surges. "Oh come on, Stuart! Since when has Camilla cared about my welfare? What the children definitely do not need is a stranger giving them orders in their own home, of all places. What they need is love, security and consistency. I'm here. I know I'm not Nina, but I'm not trying to be. I'm me."

"I agree, but when she said it, I can't deny it touched a nerve. It made me feel freshly concerned that maybe I've been selfish by relying on you so heavily. Long-term, I have to do what's best for the family."

I'm what's best. Stuart has to understand that.

It's two thirty before I'm tired enough to sleep, but the bed is empty. I check the bathroom. I wonder if one of the children has woken up, but I'm kidding myself. He's gone back to "their" room.

I open the door. Stuart's asleep. I slide in next to him and pull the duvet over. It's cold, I lie rigid, unsure what to do. What am I doing here, really? Sleep feels impossible. He doesn't snore like Ben. A fondness toward him comes over me. I toss around until he half wakes up.

"Nina?" He sits up.

"No, it's me."

He reaches for his phone to check the time before he looks around the room in the semidarkness as though he can't work things out or isn't sure who I am. I refuse to feel like an intruder.

"It's strange to think of us like this," I say. "Lie back down."

He does. Thankfully. He closes his eyes.

I trace my finger gently over his lips. "We didn't plan this," I say. "We're not bad people."

"I feel like we're having an affair," he says.

"It won't always be like this."

"How do you know?"

"I just do. This has happened to other people. It's normal to feel confused, up and down."

"Maybe," he says.

"Did you and Nina talk about…" I want to say *moving on*, but it doesn't sound right. I opt for "…the future?"

He seems to be coming around more, adjusting to a more wakeful reality. He gets what I'm trying to say.

"Kind of. She said as long as it was with someone who accepted and loved the children, then that was the most important thing. She wanted me to be happy."

"I'm not sure I could've done that in her position," I admit. "She wouldn't have necessarily wanted it to be me, though," I say, choosing my words carefully.

"Nina wondered if you were settling for Ben," he says.

"Is this your way of changing the subject?"

He laughs. "Maybe."

"Nina never said that to me. I thought she liked him."

"She did like him. I did, too. I think she was worried that he didn't want children as much as you did."

"Sometimes I think I never really knew Nina at all," I say.

Up until now, I've gone along with the narrative that Nina was an angel, that she could do no wrong, that she was a great friend. But…perhaps it would genuinely help Stuart if, over time, I drip-feed in some more truthful elements about her. Doubt may speed up his healing, allow his guilt to diminish. Naturally, he'll be more drawn to our new life because he won't feel so duty-bound to her.

"But…" I say.

He sits up.

"She kept secrets from me, too."

He bites. "Like?"

"Like she knew that Charlie was Louise's father."

"No way?"

I'm pleased that he sounds shocked. "Yes way."

"How do you know?"

"Camilla and I had a little heart-to-heart this morning," I say.

"And she just came out and told you?"

"No. I worked it out."

I realize I haven't told him about the emails or that I've been doing some digging. I'll hold back a little longer, until I'm sure that there really isn't anything developing between him and Camilla. Today has left me reeling and a bit jaded with human nature. I need to know everything that Camilla and Nina discussed, everything that Nina kept hidden from me.

"Did Camilla confess to anything else interesting?" Stuart says.

"Like what?"

He shrugs. "Like…I don't know."

"Let's make a pact to always tell each other the truth," I say.

"Ben did me a favor," he says. "You've been amazing, Marie. Truly. I'm glad you're here."

He reaches for his phone and glances at the time. "It's late. I'm going to feel like shit tomorrow."

I try not to take it personally.

He gets up and heads for the bathroom, quietly shutting the door behind him. We're too new for a casual open-door intimacy. His phone screen dims, the room goes black. I reach over and tap his phone, the screen relights. It's then that I notice that it's still unlocked.

It's a flash decision, I can't resist. I scroll: call lists, messages, nothing too interesting. Some from me—I clearly keep in touch with him more than I realize. Notes. Stuart is a list-keeper.

The toilet flushes. I reach for my own phone and snap pictures of the top few notes and place his phone back down, sliding mine under my pillow.

When he emerges, he doesn't seem to clock that his screen is still light enough for him to see his way back to bed. As he lies next to me, it dims again.

We hold each other tightly in the darkness. It's nice. Well, as long as I can keep mentally blocking out Nina. I must keep reminding myself that I'm not just any other woman or girlfriend. I'm the best possible option there is, whichever way you look at it.

When he's asleep, I lock myself in the bathroom with my phone. Stuart's notes are odd, but in fairness, so are mine. They're a hodgepodge of random things I need to remember and I even make a note of my dreams sometimes so I've got something to say when Christian occasionally asks me about them.

The latest note is a flight number, date and time. Oh my God, he looked up Camilla's flight in advance. Did he really even have a meeting in Windsor? He's never gone there before to my knowledge.

My heart starts to beat a little faster.

The next is a reminder to buy mouthwash.

The one after that is harder to decipher.

Veg recipes, dog treats, work-related interest, thank-you gift from F&E. Stability.

It's only when I start to shiver that I realize I'm cold and how long I've been sitting on the edge of the bath trying to make sense of things.

As I climb back into bed, I feel nauseous. But as I'm finally drifting off, I hear a cry. I sit up. Stuart doesn't stir, even when I switch on my bedside light.

I pull on my dressing gown and open our bedroom door fully. Emily's light is on. She's sitting up in bed, tears streaming down her face. "Emily, darling, what's wrong?"

"I dreamed about Mummy."

I hug her. I don't know what else to do or say for the best. She breaks away and hands me a mini photo album. "Mummy gave me this to me for when I'm sad."

I flick through all the pictures of Nina and Emily.

"It's beautiful," I say, forcing back tears as I hand it back. "Shall I put it under your pillow or somewhere else safe?"

"Under my pillow is good," she says, settling back down and closing her eyes.

I wait until I think she's asleep. As I stand up, her eyes open.

"Mummy had a secret place where she kept things for when I'm older. And for Felix, too."

"Did she? Where?"

My voice must sound too keen because she looks at me suspiciously, reminding me of Deborah.

"Umm..."

I wait.

She closes her eyes.

"Em?" I say, a lot more gently this time.

"She climbed up the ladder to the loft a lot before she got really tired," she says.

I wait a few minutes longer, but she drifts off.

Back in my own bed, listening to Stuart breathing, my mind is full of questions and memories of Nina, as are my disturbed dreams when I finally manage to sleep.

★ ★ ★

Despite promising to be truthful with Stuart (can I even trust him to be honest, too?), I can't bring myself to tell him when I discover the next day that I'm pregnant. It's too late to take things slowly. This changes everything.

FIFTEEN

The last thing I feel like doing is hosting the book club meeting, but I can't think of a good enough reason to cancel after the song and dance I made about continuing to host it. Everything, except my future child, feels less significant and unimportant. Not wishing to repeat my earlier mistake under Tamsin's watchful gaze, or Camilla's for that matter, I clutch a glass of white wine heavily diluted with sparkling water.

The book talk is a blur. Time drags. Greg arrives late, interrupting the flow. It veers us off track. The conversation turns to the local council's planning permission procedures and policies. I used to be good at listening when I first joined the group. I'd make an effort to remember things about people, so I could fit in better. Now…there's just too much else creeping through my mind.

I haven't read the book (I do feel slightly bad about it, but I skimmed through some online reviews to get a flavor), so I nod and agree with whoever is speaking at the time. Apparently lots of people lie about the books they've read and the films they've watched. Clearly, I am not alone. I smile; I engage.

It's not hard because there are the usual reactions: Greg likes endings tied up neatly with the villain getting their comeuppance and being carted off to prison as he insists that it is the only one-size-fits-all way to deal with society's ills. Miriam thinks the book was too long. Abigail never likes to disagree with anyone so "loves everyone's choices" and Tamsin is the only one, to my mind, who ever offers a balanced opinion.

Camilla leaves early, having brought Louise with her because she didn't want to leave her alone in the guesthouse. This gives me a much-needed opportunity to catch Tamsin before she leaves.

"Stay for another drink," I say. "I've got something I'd like to ask you."

"I'm intrigued," Tamsin laughs. "You normally can't wait to get rid of me."

I laugh as if it's not true, but we both know it is.

I get straight to the point.

"What was Nina like before she became ill? Did she seem happy?"

Tamsin's expression doesn't give anything away. "In what way?"

"In any way. Did she ever seem...I don't know...preoccupied? Upset? I'm talking about a few years ago. Not recently."

"Nothing jumps out. She was fortunate. Obviously, I'm talking about before..."

"That's what I thought. It's just that I've got the impression lately that maybe she wasn't that happy."

"Does it matter now?"

"Yes and no."

"Why don't you talk to Greg?" says Tamsin. "They used to break off from the group from time to time, have private chats."

"Greg? I never noticed."

"Back when the group started, they appeared really close friends."

"They did a photography course together once, he told me."

"Maybe that was it then," she says, not sounding particularly interested.

The more I think about it, Greg is quiet and not someone I would've thought Nina would be friends with. But then, I don't know—do I—because, as I'm starting to discover, I didn't know Nina as well as I had presumed.

"You do know he's a private investigator?" Tamsin adds.

"Is he? He merely told me he was a keen photographer."

Tamsin smiles. "Well, yes, he is. But he works part-time in varying other jobs from what I understand. He may even do some work as a security guard from time to time."

"He does blend in well."

"Just like you, Marie. Sometimes it's as if you've always been here."

"I'm not sure how to answer that," I say.

"Can I be blunt?"

What choice do I have?

"Go on."

"People are talking. Maybe it's judgmental, maybe it's wrong, but it's hard for people to accept."

"Accept what?"

I'm getting into uncomfortable territory. I can't outright deny any longer that there's anything going on between me and Stuart because soon it will be blatantly obvious.

"You. Here. It's too soon."

It flits through my mind that Tamsin may be the nasty card and photo sender. She doesn't look like one, but then who does? Greg? Sharon? Abigail? Deborah? Camilla? Someone at school? Ben? No, not Ben, he has well and truly moved on.

Tamsin is staring at me, waiting for a response. I refocus.

"When *would* be a good time? Nina asked me to look out for the children. Stuart is grateful for the help."

"I'm just telling you how it is. Nina had a lot of friends."

"Thanks for letting me know, Tamsin. I do appreciate it. I'll bear everything you've said in mind." I'm dying to ask—is it me they're judging or both of us? But I don't want to hear the answer out loud. "Did Nina ever talk to you about…afterward?"

"Afterward?"

She knows what I mean, she's trying to force me to spell things out.

"About her fears. Stuart moving on. Someone else playing a mother role in her children's life?"

Tamsin hesitates. I mentally brace myself, fully prepared to hear something I don't like, but then I realize that she's pausing because she doesn't want to admit she wasn't quite the confidante she likes to think she is. If Nina didn't trust her, she wouldn't have told her anything. Nina took issue with people who couldn't keep secrets.

"Not really, but I did get the impression that she would have liked it to be someone with children the same age as hers. She thought they'd get it, really understand."

"Oh."

"There is one more thing, while we're on the subject…"

I brace myself. Again.

"I think it would help if you let go a bit. Everyone loves the book group, but your insistence on hosting it here and nowhere else, it's causing tensions."

"Seems there's a lot going on that I don't know about."

If I didn't have my baby to think about, it would be a real wrench but…I'll let this particular project go. However, it's the only thing I *am* going to let go. Everything else is mine. If I'm going to hang on to it, then I need to be more proactive. It's not just about me anymore. I have my child's future to consider.

The next morning I wait a few minutes until after Stuart has left for work, in case he's forgotten something (not that I can imagine him doing so), before I climb up into the loft. I tread carefully up the ladder as if I'm old. The thought of falling down and hurting my baby fills me with dread. Right now, he or she is the size of a poppy seed.

I struggle to find a light switch, even though light seems to force its way through various gaps. Once I manage to find it (it was a pull-down cord), I take in the area, aware that the smell, a mixture of cardboard, damp—maybe, or just sheer mustiness—is mildly suffocating.

There are ten or so cardboard boxes all neatly labeled: Clothes, Makeup, Shoes, Accessories. Stuart seems to have kept everything. I use a key to slice open several boxes, photographing them with my phone first so I can buy the same type of tape to reseal them. I'm safe for a while. I've never seen Stuart come up here. He's packed away his pain, hidden until such time as he feels ready to truly let go.

The first four boxes are labeled Children's Books (why haven't they been kept out in easier reach for Felix and Em?). There are her favorites among old school exam books, but also plenty of nonfiction: healthy food and cookbooks, art, pregnancy, child-care ones, all subjects that have been a part of her life journey. But there are also others I didn't know she was interested in: crime and punishment, prisoner rehabilitation. I take out a few, including one of the better-looking pregnancy ones.

A loud thud on the roof makes me jump. A bird? It scratches. My peace shattered, I stifle the urge to climb down to the comfort and familiarity of downstairs as I hear indistinguishable, muffled noises from the house below. I reassure myself that everything sounds different when it's approached from a fresh angle.

The boxes containing photos—temporarily freezing time—and paintings are naturally the hardest to deal with. Young versions of Nina, pictures I've never seen, fill albums and shoeboxes. There must be other copies. I'm sure Deborah would want these. It annoys me that they aren't being properly looked after, the thoughtless stuffing away of all these memories. I vow to sort them myself at some point as I select five to add to my own collection. They all include me, along with Nina, at various stages of our childhood: I'm closely at her side while she's blowing out nine candles; I'm sitting next to her at a pantomime—*Aladdin*; we're side by side at the beach, both holding matching chocolate ice creams.

There are ones from Ibiza, too, which is a surprise. I didn't know she'd had this many printed. I'd asked her for access to her photos sometime during the months after Charlie died. I wanted some good memories as a memento. She'd been reluctant at the time, however much I tried to reassure her that it wouldn't upset me, quite the opposite. I understood that she was trying to protect me, but it wasn't helping. So, I insisted.

There is one of Charlie that I love (even though Nina and Camilla are on either side of him), smiling, looking happy and carefree. It's how I remember him when we first met. I don't recall taking it. I asked Nina for this particular picture, but she'd insisted that I crop her out because she didn't "look good." It's true to be fair, it's not the best one of her. But still, memories are memories. I smile. She is wearing sneakers. I remember how cross she was when she had to take them out of her backpack and wear them while we were still partying because she'd snapped the kitten heel of one of her new leopard print shoes. (Camilla and I had both told her that she shouldn't wear heels, but she wouldn't listen.) One of Nina's things was that she was proud of the fact that could walk in heels anywhere. She was stubborn.

I help myself to a few more pictures. I want Nina's memory album to be rich in memories from all periods of her life.

Nina's paintings are disordered. When Emily mentioned that Nina had a secret place where she kept things, I imagined that Nina would've earmarked certain prints for her children. It seems I'm wrong, given the level of disorganization contained within all the boxes. I don't have time to go through them all, but I come across two that are undeniably representations of me. I can interpret Nina's style, probably even better than my own. In the image, my fringe drapes in front of my face, it's solid, looks greasy and is hiding my right eye. But the exposed eye is creepy, watching, painted shades of green.

I feel compelled to cut open more boxes, to steal knowledge. Clothes: coats, scarves, belts. As I delve deeper, reckless indulgence takes over and I tip the boxes upside down. Nina's old belongings litter the ground. It makes sifting through easier, although I feel desperate at my lack of findings. I hadn't appreciated how much hope I'd pinned on finding something, just like in a novel or a film, which would illuminate all of Nina's old world.

I shove as much as I can back in, but the stuff is in the wrong boxes and it won't all fit back in the same way. The cardboard lids won't flatten properly and random items poke out, one of which is a turquoise scarf. Nina loved it and it seems a shame to leave it up here. I add it to my pile of things. My back aches. I'll have to return soon and clean up the mess.

To prevent the risk of falling, I drop the books, scarf and photos down onto the carpet below so that I will be able to grip the metal ladder with both hands. The books thump, one after the other. Goldie's muffled bark sparks a pang of guilt; I've neglected her this morning.

I glance around one more time before I switch off the light and climb carefully back down, sealing the hatch behind me.

Goldie's barks are still muffled as I walk downstairs, the kitchen door is shut. I never close it.

Icy fear grips.

"Hello?"

The door to Stuart's study opens, but it isn't him. It's Camilla.

"What are you doing?"

"Stuart said I could borrow a heater from his study. There's something wrong with the central heating in the cottage. It's freezing in there. My hands and feet are like ice."

"So you let yourself in? How?"

"I rang the doorbell. No one answered. I phoned Stuart, he told me to use the spare key if you were out."

"What spare key?"

"The one he keeps hidden by the back door."

"Where?"

As we walk into the kitchen, she stays behind me as Goldie rushes up to greet us. I place the photos on the kitchen table and put the books on top of them. I open the back door. Camilla points out a large stone by the metal boot-scraper as she leaves, handing the key back to me as I hold out my right hand in readiness to accept it.

For goodness' sake. I'm shocked at Stuart's carelessness. Any old burglar with a spot of imagination and a dollop of determination and desperation could find it in seconds. Or anyone else with malicious intentions. I chuck the key into a kitchen drawer; it's safer inside than out.

I put on my coat and wrap Nina's turquoise scarf around my neck. It is warm and comforting.

I stroke Goldie.

"Sorry, gorgeous girl. Let's go for a walk."

She is gracious and forgiving. If only people around here will be like that when they find out about me and Stuart. As I open the door and step outside into the cold air, I'm apprehensive about what lies ahead. Unseen horrible, future judgment almost feels tangible, like an imminent, unavoidable thunderstorm.

Stuart and I coexist in pleasant, respectful politeness. Fleeting random moments present themselves, when I could open up a conversation with him about his decision to collect Camilla and Louise from the airport. But I hesitate each time, and the opportunity dissipates with a change of topic or a child's interruption. I remind myself that I had no right to read his notes anyway, that there was nothing incriminating to worry about. But I can't help feeling that there is.

★ ★ ★

As I tuck the children into bed that evening, it strikes me as weird that Nina and I are interlinked, yet again. Her children will be related to mine. Our lives remain entwined.

I make my way downstairs when they've drifted off, ready to break the news to Stuart. But he is not alone.

Camilla is with him in the kitchen. They both have their backs to me, but Stuart is nodding as Camilla speaks.

"It seemed the best thing to do," she says. "It's what she would've wanted."

I hesitate.

Are they talking about me? Judging me as a mother?

They must sense me as they both turn around.

Seeing the two of them looking so cozy yanks back memories of Nina and Camilla. Talking. Shutting me out. It physically hurts, so much so that I clutch my stomach. I have a genuine moment's panic before I reassure myself there's nothing wrong with the baby.

"Are you all right?" says Stuart.

"Can I have a word please, *Stuart*?"

"Sure thing," he says. "Are the kids all right?"

"Yes."

"I'll come back another time when it's more convenient," says Camilla with her irritating, oh-so-understanding smile.

Stuart sees her to the back door. He stands and waves as she heads back to our bloody guesthouse where she has seriously outstayed her welcome.

I feel strangely close to tears, like a child who has to share their favorite toy with another child—a sibling or cousin—who they didn't even invite around to their home.

Stuart surprises me. He hugs me, pulling me in close and it feels the most natural it ever has between us.

"I'm pregnant," I say.

He releases me. "What did you say?"

I repeat myself.

What I'm growing to appreciate about Stuart is that he's a fully rounded, responsible adult. Not that (I hope) I've set my sights too low. He doesn't immediately react with any negative clichés or assume that it's my problem which he'll try to wriggle out of. He doesn't ask if it's his or insult my intelligence by asking if I'm sure. He trusts that I wouldn't drop such a bombshell without being certain.

Nonetheless, he's silent and stares at me for a few seconds.

"Take your time," I say. "It was a shock for me, too. A pleasant one, of course, especially given my history, but clearly not how either one of us would have planned it and it's awful timing."

"Yes, I am shocked. I don't know what to say right now but… life *is* precious. We've both learned that."

He pulls me close, hugs me tightly.

We both stand still; it's the closest I've ever felt to him.

Behind his back, the door opens.

"Only me, I forgot my phone." Camilla's voice.

She stops. Her expression can only be described as murderous.

"You two?" she says. "Of course, stupid me."

Stuart releases me and swings round.

"Oh my God." Camilla looks straight at him. "You've made a big mistake. Marie always wanted Nina's life. You promised there was nothing between you, that she'd move on. Have you no respect for Nina's—your *wife's*—memory?"

"Of course I have!"

"Oh, Stuart, for God's sake, open your eyes! Next you'll say that life goes on," says Camilla. She strides toward the back door. "When we all know that it doesn't." She opens the door. "No wonder you didn't want me round here," she says directly to me. "That's why you bought a dog. Don't kid yourself, Stuart, that it was anything to do with helping your precious family heal. Marie is the ultimate smiling assassin, she plays the *wronged girl next door* card to a T!"

"Camilla, please come and sit down—"

She slams the back door without hearing the rest of Stuart's sentence.

He paces the kitchen.

Despite the moment, real joy at becoming pregnant, after all the heartache and disappointment, finally takes hold. Finally I can tell my mother, make her happy again. I can't wait to see her face. I'm so relieved that Stuart seems cautiously pleased.

"I can't believe that I'm going to be a father again."

Again. Such a small, insignificant word, yet it needles me. The stark reminder that he's had this kind of conversation before, but with Nina.

I notice that Stuart has gone silent.

Now the news is sinking in, he's fully realizing the enormity of our situation.

"What's wrong?" I say.

"I'm going after Camilla," he says. "I need to talk to her."

"Why?" I say. "You've done more than enough for her. We don't owe her anything."

"I want her to keep quiet. You and me, we can tell people when we're ready. She's becoming a loose cannon. I'll calm her down."

"There's nothing really to tell," I say. "She only saw a hug. She doesn't know about the pregnancy."

It does not change Stuart's mind. He leaves, shutting the door firmly behind him.

Sickness unfurls. His desperation to speak to her doesn't make sense.

I check the children are both asleep. I won't be long.

I follow in Stuart's footsteps, taking care in the dark as I don't want a flashlight to give me away.

The lights are on, but the curtains are drawn. The front door is shut. My heart is beating so hard it hurts. I circle the house, but there's nothing to see. There's only one thing I can do if I want to find out the truth, put my mind at rest. I take out my keys to the cottage. I slide them into the lock and push the door open.

SIXTEEN

A scream. Louise is downstairs on the sofa, her big brown eyes wide, staring at me. A musical blares from the TV in the corner.

"I'm so sorry, Louise. It's only me. I didn't mean to give you a fright. I just need to see your mother."

Camilla and Stuart both appear at the bottom of the stairs, no doubt summoned from wherever they were by Louise's reaction to my entrance.

"What are you doing?" Stuart asks me.

"I'm here to ask you both the same thing," I say.

They look at each other, like parents silently acknowledging the best way to deal with a difficult child.

"What about the children?" says Stuart, like I'm the one wholly responsible for their brief stint home alone.

"Goldie's there."

"Goldie is a dog, Marie."

"Thanks for pointing that out."

"Mum?" says Louise.

"Everything's fine," says Camilla to her daughter.

"Yes, it is," says Stuart. "Your mum and I were just clearing something up." To me, he says, "Let's go."

We leave, the cold of the night air only now hitting me.

I've never seen Stuart angry before, but I refuse to feel like I've done anything wrong. He strides toward the house. I don't even try to keep up with him.

Inside, he makes a show—in my opinion—of going upstairs to check on the children as if they'd likely have been kidnapped in the short space of time they've been alone.

When he returns, he appears to have regained his more usual Stuart-like composure. "I don't like being spied on."

"I don't like telling someone that I'm pregnant, then having them bugger off to have a cozy chat with another woman."

"I wasn't going to burden you with this, but you may as well know that I've received more unsavory cards in the mail. It wasn't a one-off. I didn't want you to know. I thought that Camilla was behind it, that's why I went over there now, but she's assured me she isn't. I want to put a stop to it, especially now."

"Do you believe her?"

"Yes, I do."

My stomach knots. "Then, who? If it's someone local…"

"Nina was well-liked in the village," Stuart says. "It could be a number of people who are judging our lifestyle."

"I know."

Nina embraced local causes, supported local businesses, raised money for charity—including the hospice where she spent her final days—even before she was diagnosed. Although I've tried my best, I've tended to focus my good deeds around school-based activities. Maybe I should cast my net further, show that I'm here to stay, put down real, long-term and well-intentioned roots.

"There was a strange photo, too…"

I unpin the photo from the corkboard and hand it to Stuart, grateful that we're now united in a common goal as we dissect and discuss if not Camilla, then who? I insist that he show me the cards, which are not dissimilar to the one pushed through the letter box the night we slept together.

You're wicked and immoral. No good can come from making a life off the ter-
rible misfortune of another.

I hate it when things I fear actually do come true. It makes
it more likely to happen again in the future.

"And falling pregnant so swiftly will only make things worse.
I am sorry," I say. "You and the children, you don't need this."

"We'll protect them," he says. "We didn't plan this."

I wish my conscience was as clear as his.

Every therapy room is different. The common themes, however, are usually two chairs opposite each other or a small sofa,
a box of tissues, glasses of water (not a given). Those who work
in a home environment tend to have books (with carefully chosen, relevant titles, never anything frivolous or that gives away
their fiction-reading tastes) lining wooden bookshelves, and for
some reason, there is always a vase. Some empty, some with fake
flowers. There are never any personal photos.

Christian has a filing cabinet in the corner of his room, with
a key. Sometimes, when the words don't flow and the quiet-
ness is unbearable, I distract my mind by trying to guess some
of the secrets hidden inside.

Christian congratulates me on my baby news.

Silence.

I tell him about Camilla and the fact that her daughter is my
ex-boyfriend's.

"The thing that annoys me the most—well, actually, there's
a lot that annoys me—but it's that she lied. When I confronted
them about it, they said that it was all in my imagination. Yet,
it wasn't. Louise is that proof. Camilla calls her Lulu." I roll
my eyes.

Christian smiles, and because he appears to agree with me
that it's a ridiculous nickname, it motivates me to continue.

"Nina knew," I said. "That hurts, too. I can understand why

she didn't want to tell me, especially as Camilla moved away, but she just buried it, didn't tell anyone, not even Stuart." I pause. "Which strikes me as odd."

Saying the words out loud forces me to consider and properly analyze what I've just said.

"In what way?"

"As soon as we returned from our Ibizan holiday, Nina and Stuart were together. She was *that* into him, which was strange, too, as although she liked him enough on holiday, I really didn't see enough there to think that it would continue in the way that it did. Nina wasn't that traditional either. She was only twenty-one. Yet it was engagement, marriage, babies. Bish, bosh, bash. She and Stuart must've talked to each other about their shared holiday together and the people they were with, especially after the end to our holiday was so brutally abrupt."

"How?"

I hesitate. I'm not sure I want to tell him. I never tell anybody because I'm afraid that I will confess to the tiny part I played in the catastrophic chain of events. Charlie was my first love, Camilla my nemesis, dramatic sounding as it is. I'm not sure I would know where to even begin.

I change the subject.

"Nina and I had time to talk. There was no reason for her to hide anything from me. One time that stands out in my mind is an afternoon out—just the two of us—at a nearby well-known garden to see the rhododendrons and azaleas. We both photo-graphed them. We ordered afternoon tea in the café—scones, Earl Grey, cupcakes decorated in sickly icing, the full works. Nina painted me a picture of the flowers and had it framed, which she gave to me as a—well, I wouldn't call it a goodbye gift—but in essence, that's what it was. She called it a forget-me-not present. That's something Nina has robbed me of. Rightful grieving. Was she a true friend or not? I don't know how to feel."

I reach for the tissues.

"Stuart is the father of my baby," I tell him (as if he wouldn't have guessed) and now that I'm confessing the words pour out. "I mean, what kind of a person does that make me? Here I am, moaning about the secrets Nina kept, yet what I've done is worse."

"Why do you say that? From everything you've told me, it seems that Stuart has encouraged your presence, welcomed and requested your help. I don't see how you could've entered a relationship alone."

"I fell pregnant."

"Not without his assistance, I imagine."

My turn to smile. "I guess we can be happy enough. We're both willing to make a go of the situation."

Funny how expressing things out loud makes anything seem not quite so…mysterious or as daunting. I relax a little. I fear I've not allowed myself to enjoy my pregnancy so far because I don't deserve happiness.

I take a deep breath as I study the book titles on Christian's shelf. Divorce, bereavement, sexual problems, illness, debt. The topics of human sadness and frailties are never ending.

"Stuart says that he thought it was Camilla who was writing the notes. He confronted her, but she denied it."

"Why did he suspect her?"

"I don't know. They've always seemed to have got on, generally. It soured my baby news. He dashed off to speak to her because she'd walked in on us hugging and guessed something was going on. I followed him and he was angry when I turned up. I've never seen him angry before. Ever. It was unsettling."

"Why was he angry?"

I don't want to tell him that I left the children alone, it makes me sound neglectful. Which I'm not. Obviously.

"He just was. We left together. He told me what he'd accused her of and then proceeded to tell me about the other notes, which he'd kept hidden from me."

I update Christian on the venomous comments, mostly directed my way, referring to me as wicked.

"Why did he keep them a secret from you?"

"He said he didn't want to burden me."

Silence.

"And do you believe that's the reason?"

The question is left hanging between us.

"I guess so," I finally say. "It's the sort of thing Stuart would do. I'm hoping it will all naturally die down once people accept us."

"Or there are practical ways to catch the culprit if it puts your mind at rest. Cameras aren't too difficult or expensive nowadays. That's one solution that springs to mind."

"True. Or perhaps I deserve it. At school, I shared false information about another girl who got too friendly with Nina. I didn't spread the rumors, I simply lit the fuse, so to speak, then watched as others were only too willing to fuel the flames of gossip. It worked. Now I'm on the receiving end of negative reactions and can fully appreciate what it feels like, it makes me feel even more remorseful. It's payback."

The fact that Christian doesn't look too shocked makes me feel slightly better.

"Take good care of yourself," he says at the end of our session.

It's not until I'm back home with Stuart that Christian's choice of words strike me as uncharacteristic. Rather than finding it comforting, it leaves a lingering sense of unease, which I'm unable to shake off all evening.

SEVENTEEN

Reality is not my friend. Near-constant nausea kicks in, forcing me to break the news sooner than I'd have ideally liked. I test the waters with my dad first, popping in to surprise him at his local.

He doesn't even try to hide his surprise.

"But aren't you pleased?" I have to ask him more than once.

"Cautiously pleased," he says. "I can't pretend that I'm delighted with your choice of child's father. He's taken advantage of you because he's lonely."

"Dad, this is the modern world. I had a say in it, too. Stuart and I have always got on, and now we don't have much choice but to make the best of things," I say.

"I would've thought you'd have got on in the way that friends should with their friends' partners," he says. It doesn't sit well with me. "I love you, and I'll always support you, but I had such hopes for you. They certainly didn't involve you being shackled to Nina for the rest of your days."

"Don't tell Mum yet," I say to him. "Please."

His reaction has tarnished the moment. I *know* she'll be happy, but not if she is influenced by Dad's negativity. She trusts his opinions.

He shakes his head.

"Promise?"

"Marie, love. All I've ever wanted is for you to be happy. All both of us wanted. I wish there was a way to make the right decisions for your child, to stop them making mistakes. You'll learn that soon enough, but it will be too late for you."

"Dad, please be happy for me."

"I will be. I just need time to come round to the idea."

His disappointment makes my chest ache. My mood shaken, I decide to tell my mother another day. I want to break it to her in the right way. I've waited this long, a while longer won't (I don't suppose) make much difference.

After several days, nausea becomes full-blown sickness. It's not just in the mornings, it continues until late in the afternoon, leaving me wrung out. Yet I don't have any choice but to cope.

Stuart and I take Deborah out for Sunday lunch to break the news.

It's a cautiously sunny March day. There is a slight turn in the temperature hinting at the possibility of a warm spring.

"Let's sit outside," I say. "It's too lovely a day to be cooped up inside."

I can't bear the darkness inside and the smell of roast pork and lamb emitting from the carvery.

While the children play on the slide and run up and down a bridge in the play area, Stuart, Deborah and I perch uncomfortably on a wooden bench.

"I know something's up," says Deborah as she sips her lime and soda, focusing on watching the children, not looking at us. "Look at those poor little people. It breaks my heart."

"Mine, too," says Stuart.

He visibly takes a deep breath.

"You're right, Deborah, something is up." His voice is gentle, his manner respectfully calm. In that moment, I feel the most affection I ever have for him. Relief. Our baby is not a mistake, it's meant to be.

My relief is short-lived.

"You two should be ashamed of yourselves," she says under her breath. "How am I going to break the news to Leonard?"

Nina's father's health has been fragile for years. I can't remember the last time I saw him.

"He's already heartbroken," Deborah continues. "This dreadful turn of events will just add to the devastation. Couldn't you have had the decency to wait for at least a couple of years or so? Or were you both carrying on behind Nina's back, waiting for my daughter to die?"

"I understand that this is extremely difficult," Stuart says. "I loved Nina. I miss her every day of my life. Yes, this is soon, but we came together through grief, not anything sordid or pre-planned. Given the choice, we'd both rather Nina was here."

Deborah wipes away her tears.

"I've always been fond of you, Stuart," she says. "But I wish you were stronger and could see through what *she's*—" she points at me "—done. Pregnancy! The oldest, most effective trick in the book."

"It does take two, Deborah," says Stuart.

"It's really not like that," I say. "You *know* I was with Ben. You *know* Ben left me. You *know* how much I wanted a baby with him."

Deborah stands up.

"I also *know* how envious you were of Nina. Ever since you were young. Everything that comes out of your mouth is a lie. Everything you do is to benefit you."

"That's not true. Yes, I made some mistakes, but who doesn't?"

She plows on. "I warned Nina before she left us. I warned her that you'd do this. Do you know what her response was?"

I shake my head.

"She said, 'Marie wouldn't stoop that low. Besides, she's not

Stuart's type, nor he hers. They wouldn't last five minutes together. They'd drive each other mad.' She trusted you because you loved her children. She gave you her blessing for the most precious of gifts and this is how you repay her! You're despicable— a scarlet woman!"

I inwardly flinch, yet *stoop that low* are likely to be Deborah's words, not Nina's.

Deborah walks over to Felix and Emily and bends down. Obviously, I can't hear what she's saying, but after she kisses and hugs them, she walks toward the car park.

"We can't let her drive in that state," I say to Stuart. "You go after her. She is clearly directing all her anger at me. I'll distract the children."

Stuart follows her. He is gone a good fifteen minutes. When he returns, he is quiet.

He sits down opposite me, rather than beside me. Our lunch was served in his absence and he reaches over for his. He breaks his cheese-and-tomato baguette in half and bites into it. The children have left most of their fish, having mainly picked at the chips.

I don't know what to say to make things better, to lift the atmosphere. Stuart is avoiding eye contact, and I can only begin to guess at some of the things Deborah's told him. Right or wrong, she's held me responsible for many a thing over the years. I feel sick, but I sit there picking at chips, too, slowly dipping them into ketchup, as if I, too, am reflecting. Which in a way, I am.

"Will Gran feel better soon?" Emily asks. "She said she had a stomachache."

"I'm sure she will," I say.

"Will she get sick like Mummy?"

"No, darling. Not sick like Mummy. It's just something small like when you have a tummy ache. She'll be fine, I promise."

The conversation with Deborah has made me realize that

I've put myself in the position of second best again, and now it's going to be increasingly hard to assert myself.

I do have moments of guilt—of course I do, I'm human—but never regret. When Nina asked me to surreptitiously vet Stuart's future partners, especially in relation to their suitability as mother figures, we wrote down a list of desired attributes. There were all the obvious things, of course, but by the time we'd finished, there was only one conclusion: the woman needed to be Nina's twin. Subconscious seeds were naturally sown—there only ever was one obvious candidate.

EIGHTEEN

We are outside a yacht club located at the end of a secluded road. Car ferries—comparative giants—slip past the marina heading for the Isle of Wight.

"The sea breeze will do you and the baby good," Stuart insists as he lifts out two orange life jackets from the trunk of his car and hands me one.

It's chilly, not the start of spring at all in my opinion, but Tamsin has offered to look after the children as long as we return the favor. She's "reembracing" (her word, not mine) the dating scene following a self-imposed break after giving up on "men who don't keep their promises" and there is someone she'd like to go out on a proper, grown-up date with.

I shiver as we walk along the jetty, past the signs warning us of deep water, submerged objects and sudden drops. To my right, stagnant water in between us and the grassy bank is thick with grease and litter. I turn away and try to ignore the smell of fuel, lest the sickness return.

Stuart is in his element, pointing out landmarks, educating me on the function of everything, issuing instructions.

"Hold this tightly, stand there—not there—to the left. Don't sit on that side," until, finally, we are off.

It's not the same exhilaration I remember from our younger years in Ibiza—you really can't compete with the weather, no matter how well you dress for it—but it is strangely exhilarating to be free from the constraints of my life. The sense of freedom and possibility initially feels the same as it used to, despite it being colder and a different type of boating experience. I feel my shoulders relax. My whole body has been storing tension.

It doesn't last. The motion gets to me as I clutch the metal on the side.

"Too fast," I yell at Stuart. "I want to go back!"

So much for me deciding that this was something I could do differently than Nina, that I would enjoy it. I'd thought about bringing the children, sailing off for jolly picnics, all-hands-on-deck type of atmosphere. My stomach lurches as we go faster, as if Stuart hasn't heard me.

I shout again, but my words are lost in the wind.

Oh God, I'm going to tip overboard. I clutch my life jacket and think of my baby being tossed around in my womb and hating me. We appear to be heading as far out to sea as possible. The *ting-ting* of something hitting the metal increases in sound and frequency.

When Stuart twists his head around, he looks shocked when I mime a slicing motion across my neck, but he at least gives a thumbs-up. We turn. It feels like a painfully slow process. As the shore gets closer, my heart rate slows.

When we reach the safety of the marina, I'm still furious. I anchor my feet to the ground with renewed gratitude.

"Why did you ignore me?"

"I didn't realize," he says. "I'm sorry. I remember you loving it."

"I did," I snap. "When I was young and not pregnant."

My legs shake as I step onto the walkway and head for solid land. The more I try not to be like Nina, the more I end up being exactly like her, mere footsteps behind. Relief at being safe, along with a sense of failure and futility intertwine.

Over lunch in the restaurant, artichoke soup and pasta, I calm down.

When various people pass by our table, Stuart almost seems to take pride in introducing me. He clearly loves it here and feels at home.

"I've been thinking," Stuart says. "But you need to hear me out."

"Why do I feel nervous?"

"Because what I'm going to suggest may sound hasty, so that's why I need you to listen carefully."

"Go on."

Despite my loyalty and dedication, if I could pause all of this for even another six months (while somehow obtaining magical seeing-into-the-future powers by knowing that I'd fall pregnant soon), maybe I would, but whenever I think of my own innocent baby, there is no way they will ever feel second best or born at the wrong time.

I tune back in to Stuart.

"We have four options." He counts them off on his right fingers, starting with his thumb.

"One—we give in to the haters and doubters. You move out, have our baby alone and we take things slowly. We could come to some arrangement. Two—you end this pregnancy, which I have to make very clear is something I don't want you to do."

"Me neither."

"Three." He pauses. "We get married. Let's prove to everyone that although it's quick, although it's not ideal circumstances, we have nothing to be ashamed of. That we intend to do the best for our children. Four," he slots in quickly, "we move away. Set up a new life elsewhere."

"Giving in to the haters and doubters," I say.

I know he doesn't want to move. I know the house was important to Nina. She wanted the children to be brought up in the place that she chose for them. There are really only two options. One, I go. Two, I stay.

"I don't want you to go," he says. "I didn't realize how lonely I was until you came. I hold back because of Nina, because I loved her, because of guilt and maybe shame that I have feelings for you, which perhaps I should or shouldn't." He stops. "I'm babbling, I know."

"I have feelings for you, too," I say. "Watching you with the children, seeing how gentle you were with Deborah, your parents, lots of things. Nina wanted you to be happy—she told me as much. She said that she knew that you'd move on, that it was natural, and her main concern was that it was someone who would love the children, put them first."

"It would have to be a very quiet wedding," he says. "Out of respect."

"I've been to enough flamboyant weddings in my time," I say. "I've seen it all. Quiet works for me."

Yet he takes out a blue jewelry box and slides it over the table.

"I was going to do this on the boat," he says. "I wanted it to be special, despite the circumstances."

Fresh guilt at my non-enjoyment of the boat trip hits.

I look around, hoping that no one is watching. The gesture feels off-kilter and I don't want any witnesses to my discomfort. I know that he proposed to Nina in Ibiza. At the time, she didn't take it seriously; it was just a holiday romance, an impulsive romantic gesture. But on her return, they flew to Verona and he proposed outside Juliet's balcony. Them and thousands of other tourists, I remember thinking uncharitably at the time.

As I open the box, Stuart starts speaking quickly.

"It's not an engagement ring. I wouldn't know your taste or be presumptuous, but it's something small, for now, to show my appreciation for all you've done."

It's a silver pendant, shaped in a teardrop and actually, I do love it. It's perfect.

I relax on the drive home, close my eyes and allow myself to think that maybe it will all be okay until the word *stability* I read in his phone notes pops into my head.

Is this what he's been planning all along? What if Nina planted a similar seed in him, one that pointed to me being an obvious replacement? No one enjoys feeling duped. Yet, the thought doesn't sit with what I knew of her or Deborah's angry outburst (her words hurt, which mean they hit a nerve, however much I try to deny it). Marriage is too drastic an option for mere convenience.

Still, it sends me down a negative mental path, one where I recall all the times Nina could be manipulative, and fresh anger toward her for dying (however mean and irrational) takes hold.

When we park outside the house, we kiss in the car, the most public thing we've ever done, despite the fact that no one can really see us. I put my arm around him as we walk toward the front door and reach for him before it properly closes.

"Let's go upstairs," he says.

"There's no one here, no one can see us," I say.

"I prefer it."

As I follow him upstairs, I wonder if I'm willing to accept that this may never be the most passionate of relationships or if things will gradually improve over time. I'm thankful that I don't feel sick anymore, that the worst of it seems to have eased off, so I want to make the most of the afternoon. But Stuart takes his time as I sit on the edge of my bed. He draws the curtains, takes off his jacket, pulls off his shoes. It's unnerving and off-putting.

"Aren't you going to get undressed?" he asks me.

"I thought you could help?"

He joins me on the bed. As he runs his hand across my naked stomach, with a hint of a bulge, the sickness returns.

Nina. I can't get her out of my head.

I sit up.

"Something wrong?"

"Please take off your wedding ring," I say. "I know it's a big thing, but…"

He looks distraught.

I sit up, put my dress back on over my head and lock myself in the bathroom. I sit on the edge of the bath.

Outside the bathroom door, it is quiet.

I wait. What did Stuart expect? Yes, our relationship has been on fast-forward, which really is not a bad thing after my relationship breakdown with Ben. People always say, "Things happen for a reason," usually when events are unfair.

However, in this case, perhaps the statement has a ring of truth to it. I had no control over Ben dumping me. Realistically, by the time I'd weeded out the decent, genuine men from various dating apps, it could've taken me years to get to the point of trying for a baby again. Impatience does not make me a bad person. All Stuart and I have done is skipped the insecure uncertainty of the early relationship stage and moved on to the more…settled and realistic, let's say. It's all about perspective.

When I emerge, there is no sign that Stuart was ever there. Other than his wedding ring on my bedside table.

I pick it up and place it in the palm of my hand. It's not mine.

I return it to his room and put inside his bedside drawer.

Out of sight, yet not out of mind.

Only I can change that.

NINETEEN

The respite from sickness was short-lived. I'm diagnosed with hyperemesis gravidarum—extreme morning sickness. In the short-term, it makes me feel better that what I'm experiencing is normal. I've canceled even more work as I try to make it through each day until midafternoon, when I seem to get a few hours of blessed respite. Nothing helps. Not the dry cookies, nor the toast and ginger recommended. Nothing.

I faint one morning, after a particularly bad bout of sickness. As I come round, I hear Stuart ringing for an ambulance. Consequently, I am hospitalized for forty-eight hours as a precaution, feeling the weakest I ever have.

Trapped in a hospital bed, alone with my thoughts, it is paranoia's gift. Unwelcome memories visit. When Nina was pregnant with Felix, I told her how lucky she was.

"It's more than I deserve," she said.

At the time, I interpreted it as a meaningless, throwaway comment. I assumed she felt bad because I wasn't in her position. Now, though, my mind keeps taking me back there. Around the same period she said, "Be careful what you wish for."

I can't help but feel that those words apply to me now. I should be planning our wedding. We've given notice to the register office. We had to prove that we were legally allowed to marry (of course) but because Stuart has been married before, he had to produce documentary evidence that his marriage had ended. In this case, Nina's death certificate. It's things like that that hit me hard, make me want to look at myself in the mirror and give myself a good talking-to.

My first ever therapist had her consulting room near Stuart's office. Whenever I hit a really low point, I'd sometimes walk past her building as it calmed me, thinking about old sessions, reminding me how far I'd come from my darkest days when suicidal thoughts could, at times, seep into my mind. I (eventually) came to believe that even though I had found my school years anxiety-inducing and needed Nina to feel safe, it didn't make me worthless. For a brief while, I even stopped endlessly reading fertility issues online.

On one occasion, I bumped into Stuart in a café. It was busy, and we ended up sharing a table, even though he'd asked for his brie-and-bacon baguette to be wrapped to go. I think he sensed my desperation or had noticed my red eyes. (I've always wished I could be the sort of person who can cry and still be able to venture out in public without giving myself away.) We ate our sandwiches and drank a coffee. We talked about Nina and how we'd all get a date in the calendar soon for dinner, the four of us.

It was never mentioned again. I don't know if Stuart told Nina. I didn't tell Ben, not for any reason. The moment never organically arose. I wonder now, was some kind of seed planted then? Did I subconsciously respond to Stuart's kindness, anchor a part of myself to him in the hope that someone like him would be able to save me from myself?

I can't read. I switch on the TV to try to drown out the endless hospital noises—cleaners, food carts, medical staff, visitors—but it's impossible. I drift. I hear the curtain being pulled back. I open my eyes, expecting to see a nurse, hoping it's Stuart, but it's Deborah. My stomach plummets.

She sits in the visitor's chair, her back straight, clutching her stiff, black handbag.

"It's not too late, you know, to end this charade," she says.

It sounds like something she's rehearsed.

"What do you mean?"

"Marie, do yourself the hugest favor. Don't marry him. No good will come of it. I know it's not what you want to hear, I know you're expecting, but there are other ways. You can co-parent—" it sounds like she's read a relevant article online the way she says it "—leave yourself free to meet someone else. There are many decent men."

"I love Stuart."

"No, you don't. You love the idea of him. Nina felt sorry for you, she wanted to give you hope. She felt desperately sorry that you couldn't conceive. But…this! She'd be horrified. It's bordering on incestuous."

"That's very dramatic, Deborah. I'm sorry for everything, but I'm here to stay. I loved Nina, too, I will do what's best for Felix and Emily. I promised her that and I promise you that. Please, try to trust me."

"I've known you too long," she says. "You lie compulsively."

"I'm different now. I wouldn't lie about something as serious as this."

I bet Deborah has told a fib or two in her life. I'd put money on the fact that everyone else on this ward who can overhear this pointless conversation has told many a lie between them, too. Honesty is only the best policy if it's beneficial.

"I so want to believe it, but the evidence is right before our very eyes that it's simply not true. Look at what happened with college. You could never leave Nina be, to just live her life."

Nina did want some healthy distance between us. She didn't tell me that she'd applied for art college, wanting to keep her future plans vague.

"Oh, I don't know," she said whenever we talked about the

future. "Art history maybe. Or I'll just travel. Visit Italy, study art there. The possibilities are endless."

So, yes, I snooped. I knew it wasn't ideal or right, but I didn't feel I had much choice. I searched her room when I visited. It wasn't hard, Nina was just so…careless. She was one of those people who believed that bad things only happened to other people. She assumed she could trust me. And she could, to a point.

I applied to the same college, acted and bluffed my way through the bizarre coincidence and in the end, Nina had no choice but to believe me. It wasn't malicious, it was fear, a lack of confidence in myself that I could thrive or manage without Nina. Pathetic, I know.

Yet, it worked out in her favor anyhow. Nina didn't make the type of friends she hoped she was going to. For a brief while, Nina was grateful that she had me there. Perhaps it even gave her an understanding of what life could be like for me. Until Camilla turned up, a few weeks into the new term.

So, although Deborah guessed what I'd done, she doesn't know or appreciate things like that, does she?

"You're a parasite!" she hisses (yes, really, her teeth clench, all the veins in her neck rise as the words escape).

That does hurt because it's so bloody unjust.

"This is going to come back and haunt you, Marie. Everyone knows what happens when you play with fire."

She gets up and walks away, leaving the curtain open behind her.

The woman in the bed next to me stares. I give her a *not sure what all that was about* smile, but she turns away from me.

People are so quick to judge, even when they only know one side of the story.

I still can't concentrate on reading, and when I tire of endless random TV shows, I turn to the internet for solace. I Google **widowers** and **length of time to remarry**. As always, it takes an enormous amount of time to sift through the information, sources and facts, but an overall pattern presents itself: men tend to remarry quicker to replicate the happiness they've lost. On the whole, they have fewer support systems and tend to deal with their grief in more practical ways. One article sums it up as, **women mourn; men replace.**

Rather than interpret this as negative (some of the comments are scathing), it makes sense when I think of how beautifully Stuart has tended to Nina's grave. He has way fewer friends than me, plus his family live far away. Rather than making me feel like a replacement, it brings out a protective surge of affection for Stuart. He has chosen (albeit relatively swiftly) to take a risk on a second chance at happiness. With me. It counts for something, surely?

When Stuart picks me up from hospital, I see evidence of spring in the form of daffodils pushing through the grass at the road edges, the sight of people without coats.

"So, I've arranged everything," he says. "The register office is booked for eleven o'clock a week from Tuesday with a lunch afterward at a highly recommended nearby restaurant."

"So soon?"

"Well, we both agreed there was no real benefit to hanging around, didn't we?"

"I guess."

Plus a weekday is safe. It affords people ample opportunity to give the *sorry, I can't get away from work* excuse and the short notice means no one has much time to stop us.

"I thought you'd be pleased? We've given notice to the registrar, filled in, signed and paid for all we need to. There are no other formalities."

"I am. It's a lot to take in."

"It's just a formality," he says. "You'll find that not much changes afterward."

I don't know how I feel about that either. Yet, despite my initial reaction at feeling a bit left out of the main arrangements, it is a relief that my life is moving on. It's a nicely rewarding feeling to have come this far.

Somehow, Stuart has managed to persuade Deborah to come in some days after school to help with the children. When she's around, I lie on my bed but it's not always possible to drown out the noise and I feel lazy not getting involved, plus there's Goldie to walk when I'm able to.

One Wednesday—Thursday?—afternoon, as I doze on and off, gratefully giving in to the gentle drifting in and out of consciousness, the sound of a lawnmower outside my window intrudes. It weaves its way into my dreams and everything is rewound. Nina is in bed, and I am sitting in the wicker chair beside her, just the way it was only a year ago. I open my eyes, dribbling, disoriented. I'm horrified when I focus properly to see Deborah standing in the doorway.

She looks as though she's going to say something, but manages to stop herself. She leaves, but not before I saw the look of utter hatred in her eyes. It's acutely shocking to be on the receiving end of such a clear death wish.

I force myself up, the urge to tell her that I'm not bad is so strong, but she's no longer upstairs. In the distance, I hear the front door slam shut. I should get the locks changed.

Thank God, when the big day arrives, I feel better, but from the moment I open my eyes, it's surreal, like drinking too much. Naturally, I've photographed a lot of weddings, and as a result, I've inevitably imagined mine from time to time. What I would or wouldn't do, have or not have. I'm not against living with someone indefinitely, but I could never have predicted how today would turn out. It's definitely a low-key day for a low-key event.

Prewedding doubts are normal for any bride. I did consider

talking to Stuart, thinking of alternative ways, until I considered our baby's future and their half brother and sister.

Felix has regular nightmares, he misses Nina dreadfully, and Stuart and I take turns to comfort him, often into the early hours. He needs stability and someone he can trust. There is a stubborn part of me that feels I shouldn't give in to the haters and doubters who are stacking up: Camilla, Deborah, Tamsin (she said it put her in a very awkward position), Ben, my own father.

To hell with what people think. They don't know me or appreciate my good intentions. This is my choice and it feels good to stand up to everyone. Stuart isn't exactly the man of my dreams, but Charlie was unfaithful before he died, Ben left me and from what I've generally discovered, gradual disillusionment eventually chips away at a lot of marriages, regardless of how optimistically they start out. I only have to consider the high divorce rate to trust that there must be some collective truth. My mum seems happy, but in all honesty, who knows. Stuart's parents are the only ones to have said anything positive.

Suzanne asked to speak to me on the phone moments after Stuart broke the news.

"I couldn't be happier," she said. "Honestly. You'll be the best daughter-in-law, I just know it. A wonderful mother, too, you're such a natural!"

It's hard to imagine what Nina did to annoy cheerful Suzanne quite so much, but it's pleasing for me, nonetheless. I can't deny it.

Stuart and I stand opposite each other, both self-conscious, in front of the registrar. I try to force some contentment into my mind. In the ways that count, I am happy, but the ghost of Nina is ever-present and my growing bump feels conspicuous. I'm wearing a loose, plain cream dress. My bouquet is simple. I've gone for understated and respectable. I am wearing the silver pendant he gave me.

As the registrar welcomes everyone, nerves well and truly kick in.

"You are here today to witness the joining in matrimony of…"

The solemnity and importance of the words hit me like never before. I'm very fond of Stuart—I do not love him.

Two of Stuart's closest friends are here, but only one of their wives. "It didn't feel right" to her apparently. She had nothing against me personally, "but…"

We had no choice but to have a quiet, almost apologetic wedding. Tamsin is here, but I'm sure it's only so she can report back on how subdued the event was. I can almost hear her voice as she holds court at school, at the book group, in the pub. She'll dine out on the story for as long as possible.

"Nina would be turning in her grave," I imagine she'll say. "Stuart didn't look happy. The poor man is still in shock. She swooped in, took advantage…"

I dream up lots of conversations such as these, along with my responses, things like, "But I didn't take advantage. Stuart's life is so much better with me in it, and the same goes for the children."

Camilla kind of invited herself. I didn't have the energy to deal with the misunderstanding. Tamsin told Camilla, who sent me a text expressing her concerns, saying that she still didn't agree, but as it was too late, she had no choice but to accept it for the sake of Nina's children.

Big of her.

"The purpose of marriage is that you always love, care for and support each other…"

I stare forward as I try to focus on the words. Sadness and disappointment creeps back in as my father is here alone, without my mother.

"She's not well enough at the moment, love," he said to me on the phone only yesterday. I glance behind. He has dressed up for the occasion. His suit is a little loose, and he looks as though he'd rather be anywhere but here. Bless him, he's trying. I smile my thanks at him and he smiles back. Fresh sadness threatens to take hold. If this were a normal wedding, he would have perhaps walked me down the aisle.

The children are at school and will be collected by Deborah.

"If you take them there and make them witness you professing love for *that woman*, I don't feel that I can be responsible for my actions," Deborah had threatened Stuart. "I refuse to play a part in this!"

And that's just the part he felt able to tell me about.

Stuart caved. Of course he did.

Felix and Emily will be having dinner out with Deborah and Leonard, at a burger place. Deborah's going to bring them home afterward, of course she is. Heaven forbid that Stuart and I be allowed a peaceful wedding night. My illness has pushed everything back but I will start the adoption ball rolling as soon as I can.

"Marie?"

Stuart is looking at me as if I've done something wrong.

"Sorry," I mouth.

I concentrate on the registrar's words, which I assume she's had to repeat.

"I give you this ring as a token of my love and friendship."

I spot Camilla. She must've slipped in late. Her arms are folded and she looks resigned.

"I declare that I know of no legal reason why Marie Langham may not be joined in marriage to Stuart Thompson."

There is none of the flowery language used at Stuart's first marriage. This is what it is: functional and legal. I am my own worst enemy, I always have been. I've allowed myself—and with Camilla as a witness, too—to be second best again. My stomach flutters as if my baby is reminding me that I need to be strong, to make sure that he or she is not sidelined. I stand a bit straighter.

I've chosen to wear a ring, but Stuart has not. As he slides it onto my finger, I regret not being more insistent. Every gesture, every action, appears to point to me as being the one who has led Stuart astray. Which is ridiculous.

Nina's rings (engagement and wedding) have been kept in the home safe for the children. I ensured that mine is very different, it's platinum, for a start, not gold. I'm not sure I will continue to wear it, but part of me wants something visible to outwardly prove that I'm not ashamed, that I'm not doing anything wrong.

"…you have both made the declarations prescribed by law and have made a solemn and binding contract in the presence of your witnesses here today."

Stuart has admitted that things weren't always ideal between him and Nina. That they were very different people. He craves security, she longed for travel and adventure.

"Her wings were well and truly clipped when the children started school," he said. "It was the end of being able to take off on mini breaks around the country whenever she liked. That's why she poured so much energy into starting her own business. I encouraged it because I thought that if she was happier in her home environment, she'd naturally feel happier in herself."

Every tidbit gives me secret hope because we are starting from such a practical angle. Every clue at her discontent helps me to adjust my own behavior. What Stuart and I have is unique and special in its own way.

"It therefore gives me great pleasure to declare that you are now legally married."

Stuart and I both grin and give each other a brief kiss. Relief. There's no going back now. The show will go on, but on my terms. I've made the right decision.

Tamsin takes photos on her phone. I clutch my small bouquet of pastel-colored peonies close to me and smile. I chose to wear my hair up, but still, my ever-annoying fringe threatens to escape. I'm grateful the hardest part of the ceremony is over as it's hot and I can't wait to get out of the register office.

We stand on the steps as Stuart's friends snap a few more obligatory pictures before we head to the pub next door.

"It's got decent-enough reviews on Trip Advisor," he said when he updated me on all the wedding plans.

"Well, that's all right then," I said.

I don't think he got it as he smiled blandly in response.

Strangely, that bothered me more than a lot of other things that genuinely should concern me. Denial is useful.

"Goodbye, my love," my dad says. "Sorry I can't stay for the meal, but I want to get back to your mum."

I pretend to understand. "Tell Mum I love her."

I stand at the door of the pub and wave his taxi off, swallowing the lump in my throat.

I accept a glass of champagne when a waiter offers it. I've done my research—a small one won't harm my baby.

Everyone, including Tamsin and Camilla, chorus, "Congratulations," as we all raise our glasses.

Stuart undoes his top shirt button. Relief that he appears more relaxed ups my optimism. Sun pours through the window highlighting the dust particles on the dark, wood-paneled walls.

My appetite has returned, so much so, that I don't care that Camilla has chosen to sit opposite me. I tuck into my stuffed mushroom starter and dip some white chunky bread into the sauce.

"How long did you plan it?" Camilla says to me after the starters are cleared.

I glance discreetly to the left. Stuart is involved in a lengthy conversation with a friend about a work client.

"Plan what?" I say. I lower my voice. "I hope you aren't implying that I had something to do with Nina's illness, are you? Because it's not possible. Nina died of melanoma."

"Sadly, I wouldn't put it past you, but no. I mean, the moment the news was bad, really bad, did you start planning this then? Were you somehow secretly delighted that Nina was never going to escape you again?"

"You're sick."

It's as if Camilla can read my thoughts. It's unnerving. Of course I didn't plan it, but it did plant a subtle seed of an idea that there would be...not so much a vacancy, but a plan B.

I will not let Camilla ruin this for me, too.

"And you're a fine one to talk," I continue.

I look at Tamsin, who has remained silent throughout the exchange, concentrating on her food.

"We went on a girly holiday just after we left college," I say to her. "Nina and I arranged it and Camilla decided that she wanted to be a part of it, too. My boyfriend joined us near the end and Camilla stole him."

Camilla looks mortified.

Good.

We are interrupted by the waiter placing down our main courses. I chose risotto, but regret it the moment the steam wafts my face. I look over at Camilla's salad and wish I could swap.

"You can't *steal* someone," Camilla says. "Besides, Charlie wasn't *yours*."

"Charlie?" Tamsin says.

"Yes," I say.

"Wasn't he the guy Nina told me died on holiday?"

Buried emotions threaten to choke me. Charlie was easily led, but he could also be a gentle soul, so alive, and that made his horrible death so much harder to stomach.

TWENTY

Our wedding night is as subdued as the end of the meal turned out to be. I did a brilliant job of acting fine, but the paranoid part of my brain wonders if Tamsin and Camilla planned to dampen the mood somehow. I don't like thinking about Charlie.

"It's partly my fault Charlie died," I say to Stuart when we're back in the blessed privacy of home.

"In what way?"

"I should've tried harder to make things work between us."

"You were young."

"Yes, twenty."

"Well, there you go."

It's easy for someone to tell you it's not your fault, all very nice and well-meaning of them, but it doesn't erase guilt. Nothing ever does.

"I'd rather talk about something a bit more cheerful," says Stuart as he selects a bottle of wine.

He opens a drawer and takes out a corkscrew. He refuses to buy screw tops, as he refers to them, no matter what anyone tells him.

"Just one small glass?" he says to me.

"No, thanks. I don't want to take even the slightest risk. I had a sip of champagne earlier."

"Nina had the odd few sips here and there. Felix and Emily are fine."

"I'm not Nina."

"True, I'm sorry. You're right."

He puts the bottle down, unopened, and pulls me in for a hug. I feel like I should say "I love you," or he to me.

"Thank you," I whisper instead, into his chest.

Weird as it is, I don't know what else to say. And I genuinely feel like I should thank him because his characteristic compliancy has given me a baby, the thing I want the most.

Stuart pulls away first. Behind him, two bouquets of guilt flowers (presumably from people who made up flimsy excuses as to why they couldn't join us, but still wish us well) lie on the side. Several wrapped gifts rest beside them. Some were handed to us today, others have been sent from Stuart's family in Australia. For something to do, I grab a pair of scissors and snip away at the cellophane covering the flowers. I stop. Their smell is cloying. I put them to one side.

"Shall we unwrap these?" I say, pointing to the presents.

"Why not?"

There are no kitchen utensils, nothing that assumes we are setting up home together. Everything about the gifts screams (to me) second marriage. There is a set of his-and-hers dressing gowns and slippers, a *Cooking for Your Family*–type recipe book, and the strangest one is an unlabeled, homemade gift: a badly engraved plaque-type thing. I'm not sure if it's an ornament or something to hang on the wall, with words declaring that love is wonderful but difficult.

"What shall we do with this?" I say to Stuart.

"Up to you," he says. "I really need that glass of wine now."

I don't blame him.

As he uncorks the bottle, I fill up some vases with water. I lift up the flowers from the kitchen counter and shove them in, not bothering to neaten or straighten the arrangements. I open the first small card attached to the cellophane and read the congratulations and good wishes out loud to Stuart. I don't recognize the names of the couple who sent them, but Stuart assures me that they're old friends of his.

As I open the second envelope, I notice that the white carnations in the second vase are already wilting and browning around the edges. That should have been enough of a clue for me, I realize, annoyed at my lack of awareness as I read out loud yet another spite-filled message, which ends with the line:

"Hope your marriage lasts as long as these flowers."

As Stuart dumps them in the bin, I pour him another large glass of red and take a sip myself.

"Just put it out of your mind," he says, taking a gulp. "No amount of misplaced, anonymous disapproval can alter that we're husband and wife now."

True. However much it secretly offends someone, nothing can change the fact that everything that was Nina's is now mine.

Stuart has left a lot of decisions up to me. He's "easy."

The first decision is my surname. I've decided to take his purely because of the children. I don't want my name to make me stand out as not being their real mother.

Another elephant in the room decision which has been left to me is Where We Sleep.

I thought about it long and hard and came to the only decision I could. I decided to move into his. It *is* the master bedroom, after all. It makes the most sense. I ordered new bedroom furniture, paid for express delivery and to have the old bed, chairs and drawers removed. I will no longer refer to it as Nina's old room. It is not. It is mine and Stuart's.

Yet, something I never considered (or fully appreciated) is that despite my familiarity with the house, I had never used

Nina's shower, never hung a towel on the heated rail, never negotiated my way around her bathroom or sat in front of the dressing table as I dry my hair, put on my makeup or whatever. Even though the furniture is new, it's mostly arranged in the same positions because of the location of the fitted wardrobes, doors and windows.

And despite the overriding smell of newness (even the bed linen is new, the colors opposite to the ones Nina chose), I cannot shake the feeling that she is watching. I imagine Stuart feels the same as we both change in the bathroom and slip under the covers. We switch off the light, lie in each other's arms and talk. We grab at neutral, pleasant, nonthreatening subjects until I feel myself drifting off to sleep, almost too scared to move. I must get over it. I can make more physical changes, yet perhaps— like lots of things in life—it's only time that will truly make a real difference.

When I wake up, it is quiet and late.

There is a note.

Morning, Mrs. Thompson...

I cringe at his cloying attempt at jollity.

I do not feel like a Mrs. Thompson. I feel weird. It's almost like homesickness, a strange combination of feeling crushed, suffocated or trapped. I don't understand this feeling.

Nina didn't change her name, she remained Nina Beaufort, although she agreed that the children could have Stuart's name. I had long conversations with her about the decision. She felt it was important that she didn't lose any sense of herself or her identity.

I'm glad that I have chosen something she didn't.

I am not the second Mrs. Thompson. I am the first.

My optimism is short-lived as I read on.

*Thought I'd let you get a well-deserved rest. F and E at school. Got something
to sort out work-wise so head for the hospital and I'll meet you there.
Love, Stuart x*

Today is such an incredible milestone: my twenty-week scan.
I've dreamed of this day and every step we make along the way
to meeting my child. We've decided not to find out the sex.
Nina found out during both her pregnancies, and Stuart has
confessed that he felt robbed of the surprise.

"Surely it doesn't matter as long as they're healthy, clichéd
as it sounds?" he'd said when I raised the topic for discussion.
"I was so grateful that Felix and Emily were born without any
complications."

"As I will be," I say, although I really want a boy, if I'm honest.

Of course, I can't ever tell anyone this, but I still find Felix
so much more amenable than Em. It's like she goes out of her
way to remind me that I'm not her mother. She has a lot of
Nina in her.

Despite leaving plenty of time for the appointment, parking
is even more of a nightmare than usual. By the time I obtain a
space at the Park & Ride, wait for and catch the bus, I feel weak
and a bit tearful. I munch on a fruit bar as I call Stuart several
times, but he doesn't answer.

In the waiting room, I read the latest book club selection. It's
dreadful, I knew it would be. I tried to steer Greg away from
his choice but he insisted that this was an important book to
read. It's not. It's trying to ram a controversial point home and
it makes me uncomfortable.

There's no phone signal, so I go outside, half expecting to
bump into Stuart, to see him running in, bursting with apologies. He won't have trouble getting a parking spot; he's one of
the luckiest people I know.

He's not. Instead a voice mail, the gist of which is, he's "so sorry. Held up. Can they reschedule for later?"

Anger flares. As if they will be able to *reschedule for later*. Appointments are like gold dust. Plus, I don't want to. I've been waiting a very long time for this.

Stuart has been through this twice before, it simply doesn't mean as much to him. I try to recall if he made all Nina's scans. I can't. But it's not something I would've thought to ask her or something she would've told me. My lack of a much-wanted baby created an unacknowledged gulf between us. Guilt hits. I should've risen above my own pain and jealousy.

Back in the waiting room, everyone is in pairs except me. Mothers, partners, friends. Everyone has someone. I sit up straight in my plastic seat and pretend that I'm fine with my situation.

"Ms. Langham?" A nurse or midwife stands at the entrance to the room.

I smile, stand up and follow him along the corridor.

I lie down. I keep my eye on the screen as gel is smeared across my ever-bulging stomach. The sonographer runs a probe (looks like a wand in my opinion) over my skin, applying pressure, which doesn't hurt. She points out parts to me. I listen, in awe, to her running commentary. My baby—a real baby—is in front of me with fingers, toes, arms, legs and a head.

"Would you like to know the sex?" she says.

I don't hesitate. "Yes."

It will teach Stuart never to let me down again.

"It's a boy," she says.

Relief. Until her next sentence.

"He's slightly sleepy, though, so I can't complete all my checks. It's nothing to worry about, but I'm going to suggest that you nip to the canteen and have a Coke or a coffee, then I'll arrange for you to pop back in an hour or so."

I am worried.

I want to call Stuart and beg him to come over—what if something is wrong? But then, he'll in all likelihood discover that I've found out he's a boy. As I sip a cappuccino, I silently pray that he's all right.

Stuart's right. All that does matter is that our baby's healthy. I focus on my breathing. Outwardly earth-motherly calm, inside riddled with buried guilt.

Thankfully, caffeine does the trick.

The technician is able to complete all her checks, and I'm told that the baby is perfectly healthy. (I must stop thinking of him as a "he" or I'll give myself away.) I can't stop looking at the black-and-white scan pictures of my baby as I catch the return bus to the parking lot. He's perfect. He's real.

There are several messages from Stuart. I ignore them all.

Emboldened in my new role, I set about making bigger changes. I replace two of Nina's smaller paintings with ones painted by local artists. I don't change the largest one in the main hall; I don't mind keeping that particular one as a reminder of Nina. To remind me of what was. In truth, it's not the only reason. Due to its size, it would be blatantly noticeable to remove it.

I swap several photos so that the bulk of the children's are ones I took of them when they were small. I indulge in a bit of creative editing, as I like to think of it, so it appears as though I've been more involved in their early lives than I was. In them, they are having lots of fun with me, walking, dancing, cycling, creating, baking. I'm a true earth mother. I seem to have more of Felix than Emily, but she's the only one who notices. I tell her that she's mistaken.

"You have to remember, sweetie, that Felix is a few years older than you. This means that he will naturally always have more. It's normal, it can't be helped."

She still sulked.

Now that the house is mine, I'm not sure I'm that keen on it anymore. The main living areas are actually quite small; there's little natural light. Even when the kids play hide-and-seek, it's not exactly hard to find them. It's claustrophobic. The house, I realize, is all about the grounds: the fantasy, the illusion of an idyllic childhood haven. The reality, like so many things in life, is completely different. Living within it naturally exposes its flaws. The things I used to find romantic about the property are not.

It dawns on me that perhaps Nina was unhappy, that somehow the house absorbed some of the misery and that Stuart knew but chose to ride it out. I've suspected all sorts—an affair, marriage too young, disillusionment—but there's nothing. If Stuart knows (which I don't think he does), if Tamsin knows, if Camilla knows, in fact, if anyone knows, they're not telling me. I've lost track of what's real and what isn't anymore; what matters and what doesn't.

Now that I feel so much better and most of the sickness has dissipated—I'm so grateful, I'm one of the lucky ones apparently—I continue to dig. I accept work for a few hours here and there, mainly on family portraits. It's tricky to get someone to look after Goldie during the day and a spate of negative reviews have appeared on my website. I leave a notice to say that I'm on maternity leave and try to remain confident that by the time I return, everything will have blown over. Photography, after all, is what I do, one of the few things I'm naturally good at.

I decorate the nursery, turning my old room into a magical space. It is bigger than Felix and Emily's, a fact that doesn't go unnoticed by Emily, despite their apparent nonchalance at the news that they are getting a little brother or sister when Stuart finally agreed that they needed to be told.

"Why does a baby need a room that's bigger than mine?" says Em.

"Because it's a very special baby," I say. "It's not about room size, it's about making your new brother or sister welcome."

"Mum said we weren't going to have any more brothers or sisters."

"This one will be a half one," says Felix.

He's such an adorable peacemaker.

"But just as loved as you two are," I say.

"Does my dad love you?" asks Emily.

I decide to tell the truth.

"Not as much as he loved your mum," I say. "But we both love you very much and we want us to be one big, happy family."

"I wish she was still here," says Felix.

"So do I," I assure him.

It's only half a lie; the truth is too complex and cruel.

I take a deep breath.

"Your mum made me promise to look after you. She loved you very much, as do I. So, that's why I'm here. It's for you two, so that you have someone else—as well as your dad—to look out for you." I take another deep breath; it's a gamble, Stuart may not like me mentioning it to them first, but I'll make up a feasible reason why it felt natural to do so.

"I'm thinking that maybe, to help me keep my promise to your mummy in the best way possible, that I should adopt you."

"What does that mean?" asks Felix.

"It means that I will be your new mummy."

"Maybe Mummy wrote about the word *adopt* in her notebooks," says Emily. "I can check."

"What notebooks?"

"The ones in the secret place where she kept things for me for when I'm older."

"Have you got them?"

"Yes," says Emily. "I took one because I am older now."

"May I see it, please?"

Em hesitates before she pulls a beautifully decorated notebook from beneath her bed and hands it to me.

I sit down next to her on the floor and gently go through the pages, my jaw aching. I stop reading—these are private messages from Nina to her daughter. Emily is advanced for her age when it comes to reading, but these are precious words that need to be kept safe for when she's much older.

"I'll look after it very carefully for you," I say. "Where did Mummy hide this, Em?"

There's no way she could have climbed into the loft on her own, regardless of how wise and capable she is for her age.

"I'll show you."

She goes into our room and into the en suite. She removes a chair from the bathroom and pulls it into the dressing room. I watch, speechless, as Emily first pulls open the door to Nina's old wardrobe (now mine, of course, like everything else in this house that was hers), stands on the chair, then pulls my sweaters off one of the shelves. She drops them on the floor, then points.

On the gray-painted wall at the back is an inconspicuous safe, the same color as the wall. It's like an optical illusion; I'd never have noticed it.

"Do you remember the code, Emily darling?"

"No."

My heart sinks.

"But I watched where Mummy hid the key..."

"Good girl, Em. Excellent."

I herd her and Felix downstairs. I start making dinner for them: veggie sausages which Emily says taste funny. I wish Nina had at least given some of my suggestions a go, it would've made life so much easier for me. I don't believe in fussy eaters; my baby will eat everything.

"I'll make you beans on toast," I say. "Just this once, though. I would like you to try to eat different foods. It's good not to eat meat."

"Is that because of not killing animals?" says Felix.

"Yes, exactly that," I say.

"Mum said that it's wrong to kill things."

"Your mum was wise. Why don't you go and stick the TV on," I say. "I'll be back down in a minute."

I put the beans in the microwave and press two minutes.

I don't intend to nip upstairs for long, but I am curious. I slide the key into the safe and pull out a small box. I relock the safe and hide the box beneath my side of the bed, fighting the urge to tip the contents out immediately. I return the key to its hiding spot.

The sound of smashing glass coming from the downstairs, followed by a scream, makes me run.

Baked beans ooze across the kitchen tiles. Goldie sniffs them as Felix holds up his right hand covered in blood. Emily won't stop screaming.

"Move," I shout at Goldie, trying to save her from getting glass in her paws.

"Stay still," I yell at Felix as I rush for a clean tea towel and wrap it around his fingers.

"Be quiet, Emily!"

The baby kicks.

"I just wanted to help," says Felix. "I heard the beep, so I knew it was finished."

Thankfully, we are saved a trip to the emergency room, but by the time Stuart is home, I'm a complete mess. He says all the right things, but the unsaid is clear: Felix never got burned or cut when Nina was in charge. The non-honeymoon really is over. I am a failure as a protector before I've even begun. It only makes me more determined to prove everyone wrong.

Something I read has always stuck in my mind: we can choose truth or happiness. I have always chosen the latter. Perhaps it's time to change my whole outlook. Starting with whatever is hidden inside Nina's mystery box.

TWENTY-ONE

Stuart takes an absolute age to go to sleep. The box lies beneath me. I had a peek while he was in the bathroom; it contains Nina's journals. When I'm certain he's been asleep for a good ten minutes, I lock myself in the baby's nursery.

There are two five-year diaries, four lines for each day, starting from when we were both ten, until she switches to plain notebooks with more sporadic entries. I skim, but can't help stopping every few pages or so when something funny or poignant catches my eye. Nina changed pen colors: green, red, blue, black depending on her mood. (Black, of course, is sad. Red for things she wants to remember. I know this because she underlines them.) It's strange seeing memorable events written from her point of view. It distorts my own memory.

Realizing that this will take me weeks, I skip to the last diaries. It's compelling and fascinating, this insight into Nina's mind. I justify this by telling myself that I may find useful things that will help with Felix and Emily. There's a lot of mother-guilt: deep, unsettling, contradictory emotions, the remorseful kind.

In the months leading up to her death, Nina rewrote parts of her old diaries. She's named the rewriting process Hindsight.

It's fascinating, as I flick back and forth through the befores and afters, the different viewpoints, I read faster as if to trying reach the end of a book.

I'm back in Ibiza. Naturally, Charlie's disappearance and death clouds the end. Except, it's more than that. Another chapter has been inserted. I know I should stop reading, that if I continue, something big will shift, but I can't. I open my eyes wider, read faster. Nina's voice from the grave is dominant, she is back here with me.

Original: *Spending time at the villa, it was almost like Stuart and his friends hadn't left. Dan said we could use his villa during the daytime. After lunch, I lay on the tube, my feet dangling over the edge in the pool. Bliss. I'm so going to be rich! But now, lying on the sun lounger, I feel restless. If Stuart was here, we'd be having a cheeky so-called siesta or heading out on his friend's boat. Perhaps I'll take the key…ha ha. I am good at handling it. Stuart said I am a natural, said I hardly need any lessons.*

Hindsight: *Reading these words makes me want to cry. I want to go back and stop my younger self at this point. We were living the dream, until we weren't.*

Why? I remember that day. I was glad Stuart had gone because it had meant that I could bend Nina's ear about my concerns regarding Charlie and Camilla.

We *did* take the key to the boat. Well, Nina did, but the rest of us encouraged her. We went out a lot with Stuart and his friends; we'd hang out with others who owned boats or yachts, too, jumping off the edge every now and then to cool off. Sipping sundowners. Snacking on olives and bread. Drinking beer straight from the ice, condensation dripping down the edge of the cans.

We packed the cooler, promising out loud that we'd replenish what we borrowed. But before we reached the jetty, loud music beckoned. There was a party at a nearby bar. The DJ was out on a platform on the beach and had already drawn in quite a crowd.

We dumped the supplies on the boat, Nina removed her heels from her small backpack and swapped them with her trainers. I untied my hair so that it hung loose rather than wearing it scraped back in a ponytail, the three of us put on some lipstick, and then, with those minor party preparations complete, we went to join in.

I was happy because Charlie and I were back on track. That afternoon, Camilla had been tired after finishing off her last contracted shift at the club the previous night and had dozed by the pool. When Nina had done the same, we crept off to the day bed, which was swathed in netting, to have sex. Twice. This memory felt relevant then and for ages afterward because it had given me a fresh confidence that he wasn't being unfaithful with Camilla, too. My suspicions had briefly dissipated. I cringe at my naivete.

Nina's original version is similar to my memories of the beach party:

We all danced, smiling at each other now and then. We felt alive.

She's added in *ironic* in a different-colored ink as one of her hindsight comments.

Camilla bought some pills. She was always the best at getting us stuff. Dealers sniffed her out.

Like that's a good thing, I think. Nina must've written this when she got back to the holiday apartment. They thought I was asleep (I wasn't, I was sulking, I saw them come in) but I heard them up for ages afterward, whispering. It was nearly light—they couldn't have got more than an hour's sleep—yet they hung out by the hotel pool all the next day as though everything was fine.

Marie and Camilla had an argument about Charlie (again) and Marie stormed off before I could reassure her. By the time I ran after her, she'd gone. I was torn. I really wanted to go back to the party, it was fun being without Stuart. Because he is older, he doesn't fit in the same way that Charlie and Camilla do. It was nice to feel free, off guard. We never took the boat out. We lost Charlie at the party. I guess he went after Marie, so that's eased my conscience.

Hindsight: *We took the boat out, me, C and C. We shouldn't have.*

I race through to the end; the details are scant.

Afterward we both agreed on a pact of silence, despite our matching stories. Dramatic as it sounded, it was the only thing that gave us hope that maybe our dreadful mistake would never come to light.

When I'm finished, my hands are shaking, my head full of disbelief and rage. No one—but me and Camilla—would've understood the significance of what I've just read. They told me they'd last seen Charlie at the party. Nina's mention of a conspiracy of silence has sent my mind reeling, coming up with all sorts of scenarios. But I now have a suspicion as to why her guilt was overwhelming. My closest friend was a liar (at best), and so is Camilla. However, reading between the lines, I've got a bad feeling that the lies are not the worst of it.

I don't know how I'm going to keep this to myself. It's lunchtime. I cancel my appointment with Christian. I don't trust myself not to tell him what I've just discovered. I can't divulge this to anyone, not yet. But there is one person I can confront: Camilla.

Everything slots further into place. *Of course* that's why she's returned. She must've been terrified when Nina got in touch.

She's here to find evidence and destroy it. My being here has thwarted that.

I can't sit. I can't concentrate. I take Goldie on her longest ever walk while I come up with a plan.

I phone Deborah and ask her to pick Felix and Emily up from school and cook them dinner. I don't give her the chance to say no, I simply insist that it's an emergency. I walk to the guest-house, let myself in and wait for Camilla.

She walks in with Louise. She stops.

"Hi, Louise," I say. "Deborah and the children are expecting you at the house for a bite to eat."

Camilla looks as if she's about to object, but she's not stupid. After all, she's been half expecting and dreading this moment for so long.

"That's right, sweetie."

Louise looks confused—of course—but acquiesces, none-theless.

We both wait until the door shuts behind her.

"I guess you know why I'm here," I say.

She doesn't question me.

"Let's go for a walk."

Camilla opens the door. I follow her out. We walk along the track to the forest at the back in silence. When we reach a se-cluded clearing, she takes a cigarette packet out of her bag, pulls one out and lights it.

I could do with one, too.

"Well?" she says.

"You and Nina—you killed Charlie."

For a brief moment, her expression is one of barely percep-tible terror.

"Of course we didn't. It wasn't like that."

Hearing her confirming the words is freshly shocking, yet it's an equal relief to hear her almost dismiss it. I thought she'd deny everything outright, but it's unreal that she's so quick to admit defeat.

"How was it then?"

"It was an accident. Really, it was."

"You've lied about so much."

"You'll know what it's like, the moment you give birth. You'll do whatever it takes to protect your child. I can't ruin Louise's life any more than Nina could ruin Felix and Emily's."

"Tell me what happened."

"How did you find out?"

"Nina wrote an update to her diary."

Camilla gives a wry smile. "I knew she would do something." She pauses. "Well, I imagine that's a good thing, in a way. I guess she described how everything was an accident?"

I ignore her question. "Is that the real reason you came back? Have you been looking for something?"

"Yes. I didn't know what I was looking for. I knew it wouldn't be an outright confession, she wouldn't take the risk of Felix and Emily finding it. Can I see what she wrote?"

"No."

I'm not going to give her the chance to read it so that she can match her story with Nina's so-called accounts. I've also made copies in case she gets hold of them.

"Did you try to get in before?" I need to know.

"Yes. It turns out it's more difficult to do than I thought. Nina mentioned in conversation that Stuart was really bad at locking the interconnecting door to the garage. Turns out he wasn't. And you nearly caught me in the guesthouse, you and Deborah. I knew it was highly unlikely that there would be anything incriminating hidden in the cottage, but I felt I had to do something when I couldn't find a spare key to the main house. I'd focused my attention around the front door area when the one by the back door was in such an obvious place. Stupid me."

She grinds her cigarette into the ground.

"Nina sensed that someone was out to get her," I say.

"Well, I wasn't out to get her. I merely didn't want her to drop me in it, leaving me to face the consequences on my own. She swore to me that she wouldn't leave anything incriminating, but I knew what she was like. She needed to confess, however cryptically. I suggested she talk to a priest. She said she had, but it hadn't helped. That's when I knew I was in trouble."

"I thought that whoever-it-was was after me now instead, so it's a relief to know that it was you." I tell her about the messages, the plaque, the photo, the wedding flowers.

"Those were definitely not me." She sighs. "I'm happy enough to be rude to your face. I don't need to hide behind snide notes and actions. But, Marie, what did you expect? Really? Of course people will naturally judge. How can they not?"

"How can you stand there and say that after what you've done?"

"I don't make the rules. What are you going to do?"

"I don't know. I really don't. It doesn't sit right with me. I loved Charlie. You—but Nina especially—knew how much I blamed myself because of the argument that night. I initially thought that he was upset, that he'd wandered off after you'd left him at the party."

"I'm sorry," she says. "If I could change anything, I would. It was horrific. A real-live nightmare that never left us. It will never leave *me*."

"What happened?"

She sighs. "We took the boat out. We lost control. Charlie fell overboard, nothing to do with us."

"And you just left him?"

"There was no way he wasn't dead."

"What do you mean?"

"We looked for him. He was gone. I'm not going into any more details. It's too painful. Anything we did, we had no choice."

"Really? Why did you use the words *incriminating* and *confess* when you said that you didn't want Nina to drop you in it? And why did you cover it up if was totally a tragic accident?"

"Really, Marie. I'm telling the truth. They are just words, I didn't mean anything in particular by them. We were so young—teenagers still, really—we were in a foreign country, scared that we could get accused of all sorts of things. We panicked. Please, get rid of what she wrote, for all our sakes. You won't want your child tainted with this either, and they will be, trust me. Nothing stays secret anymore. Nothing."

"This has."

"Only if we keep it that way. Look, if it helps in any small way, Nina was saving up money to donate anonymously to his extended family. Only, there is hardly anyone apart from an aunt and a cousin, apparently. I don't have any details about them, though. She was unable to track them down so she said I was to use it for charity. I'll pass it on to you."

At least that's one mystery fully solved: where the money Nina hid went to.

Camilla names a charity that helps people whose family members go missing abroad as Nina's preferred choice.

I want to cry. Nina cared for me, even at the end. If she cared about Charlie, she cared for me. I've made such a huge mistake in resenting her, hiding away her things, taking over completely.

"Nina was frightened, understandably. She wanted a comforting voice, a listening ear. I provided that," Camilla says. "I gave her lots of reassurance."

Meaning that she bullied or manipulated Nina into not airing her version of events.

A rustle startles us both: Stuart, with Goldie.

"I wondered where you'd got to," he says. "Lulu directed me this way, although I was worried. Deborah said it was an emergency, so naturally, I feared for you and the baby."

"Sorry," I say automatically. "I needed some air, a break from all the responsibilities. I'm ready to go back."

"All okay?" he says.

Camilla doesn't reply.

"Yes," I say.

What else can I do? To break the news to him that his wife was responsible for a death (or covering one up) is going to take a great deal of preparation and diplomacy. There's no way I can keep this kind of thing to myself and no way can Stuart have proof sitting in his safe like a time bomb.

Deborah eyes my stomach suspiciously as we return.

"Everything is okay, I presume?" she says.

"Yes. Thank you for helping out," I say.

As I open the front door to see her off, my mind still elsewhere, I nearly trip over a bouquet of flowers. Lilies.

"From a fancy man?" says Deborah as I pick them up.

"Must be a mistake," I say.

Yet the envelope is addressed to The Husband Stealer.

She watches as I slide out the card.

Roses are red,
Violets are blue,
This life isn't yours,
And everyone knows it, too!

A part of me wants to laugh. Who, over school age, makes up *Roses Are Red* poems? Still, anger overtakes because it's not funny, not at all.

"They're not for me," I say to Deborah. "I'll let Stuart deal with them."

I stand and wave, clutching the flowers to me. I hope whoever delivered them is watching. I hope they can see how blatantly unaffected I appear to be. Who has time for this kind of crap? Who?

Yet I watch, rooted to the spot as she drives off, as though if I can stand still, everything else will stop spinning.

TWENTY-TWO

I tell Stuart that we need to talk, so he organizes a babysitter for the following evening. It will be good to get away from the house. I'm desperate to escape for a bit. As we walk to the local pub, I can't shake off the sense that I'm being watched. I crave a drink for the first time in a long time. I choose a corner table for two, so we won't be overheard too easily.

I order a tonic water with an extra lemon slice. As I sip it, I pretend it's a G&T. I've plenty of time to allow my mind to wander as Stuart spends an absolute age studying the food choices.

I've learned not to interrupt when he's concentrating. It's counterproductive as he will only start from the beginning of the menu all over again because he'll have forgotten.

Nina and Stuart came round for tapas at our place once. Nina was in a niggly mood because Stuart likes to be on time. Nina was always late.

Stuart and I loved drinking games.

Ben and Nina did not.

By the time we were on our third cocktail, Ben and Nina had bonded like indulgent parents humoring difficult children.

Nonetheless, it was all good-natured until Nina, out of the

blue, staring at my photos I had framed all over one wall, made a strange comment.

"You have more pictures of the children than even I do," she said. "Although there's more of Felix than Em."

"He's older. And he's my godson," I said.

"Yes, but…there are so many."

She shook her head a couple of times, as if there was something odd about it, as though she was trying to figure out what she didn't like about them.

"I told her that, too," said Ben.

I glared at him.

"You should see her photo albums," he added, dropping me in it—whatever *it* was—even further.

I did have pictures of Nina and Stuart, too, plus ones of Stuart on his own or with the children. Some people are rewarding to photograph, some aren't. It's that simple.

"You can turn anything into something sinister if you try hard enough," I said.

"Sinister," Nina had repeated as though she was trying the word out.

"Are you going to have a starter?" asks Stuart. "There is a cheese soufflé or garlic mushrooms?"

Food doesn't appeal, but I feel like he's waiting for me to say yes, so that he will have one. I've got better at reading him.

"I'll have the soufflé," I say. "But I need to Google it first to make sure it's okay for me to eat."

"Nina ignored all the advice and ate what she wanted," says Stuart, not looking up from the menu. "We were both of the opinion that as long as diet was balanced and varied enough, our babies couldn't come to any long-term harm."

"I'm not Nina," I say.

"I know you're not." He reaches over and takes my hand. For a moment I think he's going to say that he's pleased.

"Nina was a risk-taker," I say.

"And you're not," he says. "It's a good thing."

"I agree," I say. "I've got something to tell you. Something really difficult and shocking and I'm not sure how to say it."

"I don't like the sound of this. You're worrying me. Let me get another drink in first," he says. "I like to receive any bad news a little numbed nowadays."

He goes to the bar to order and I notice an elderly couple staring over at me as though I'm someone to be studied. I feel like giving them a wave as if to highlight *this is what a scarlet woman looks like*, because they look like the sort of people who would be friends with Deborah.

Stuart returns with a pint of Guinness and a watered-down G&T.

"It's not even a unit, I promise," he says. "I got them to tip some of it out."

"Marie?"

A woman interrupts us. She's smiling and looks friendly, but I just can't place her.

I smile back, she must be someone from the school.

"I can't believe it has been five years!" she says. "How's your little one doing?"

Sickening dread, the worst kind, hits as I realize who she is. I need to get her away from Stuart.

"Darling, do you think you could order me a peppermint tea please?" I say to him. I pat my stomach when he doesn't react quickly enough. "I'm feeling a bit sick all of a sudden."

"Of course," says Stuart, smiling what can only be an apology at the woman, seeing as I've not even tried to introduce them.

As he stands up, she points to my stomach. How rude! Admittedly, I did start wearing maternity clothes as soon as I could.

"You're brave going for another one!" she says. "We stopped at one. It's so hard juggling work and—"

"It's lovely to see you," I say. "And I really don't mean to be impolite, but I must find the ladies'."

She does look hurt, but I really had no choice.

I lock myself in the end cubicle, praying she doesn't follow me. I lean against the tiled wall. Shit, shit, shit.

It was such a stupid thing to do. I knew it, even at the time, but I felt utterly compelled to do it. I was beyond desperate. Nothing seemed to work; I just couldn't fall pregnant. I even spent over two hundred pounds on some supposed fertility herbs: a brown paper bag full of twigs and leaves, which I had to boil twice a day into a liquid that looked like tar. The noxious smell permeated the house.

I'd found an article on infertility that suggested that if I immersed myself in the world of babies I would automatically draw children into my life. In desperation, I went to a prenatal meeting—that's where I know her from. Only twice. I wore baggy clothes and pretended I was earlier on in my pregnancy than the other attendees. It backfired. It was torturous because I wanted to be there for real and I felt even more wretched than I did already. The worst was when someone asked me to hold their one-year-old baby while they went to the toilet. I felt murderous, rather than maternal, that she was having a second shot at motherhood so soon.

I left the group, made up some excuse about moving away from the area (it *was* in a town on the other side of the forest, I wasn't that careless) or lied about being too busy with work, I forget the exact details.

I can't hang about for too long because Stuart will worry. He may even ask the woman—I still can't remember her name—to check up on me. The thought of them talking about me, of her telling Stuart where she met me, me having to come up with yet another lie on the spot, is enough to drive me out of the toilets. I wish lies had a shelf life.

I emerge, still feeling sick. There is no sign of her.

I sit down opposite Stuart and sip the tea.

"Are you all right?" he says.

"No."

I check that no one is in earshot, maybe a little too obviously, but nonetheless, I lower my voice and blurt out all I've discovered about Nina, a lot more crudely than I'd intended.

He listens. He doesn't interrupt. He doesn't ask questions. He doesn't doubt me. But most strangely of all, he isn't shocked. It dawns on me why. I'm not telling him anything he doesn't know.

He knew. All along.

TWENTY-THREE

"So, Camilla cracked," he says. "She's been avoiding my calls."

"You've both been keeping this from me?"

"I didn't know if you knew or not," he says. "I didn't think so, but you can be a bit of a dark horse. But when I saw the two of you yesterday acting suspiciously in the woods, well, it wasn't hard to figure it out."

"Of course I didn't know. As if I'd keep quiet about something as monumental as this!"

He shrugs. "You'd be surprised."

"I can't keep this to myself, I just can't. It's too...big. It makes me feel complicit, like one day someone who knew Charlie will come knocking and hold me responsible."

He leans over the table and grips my arm.

"You've no choice but to keep quiet," he says. "Just like I've had to. Emily and Felix will not be known as the children of a murderer."

"You're hurting me."

He eases his grip.

"What do you mean, a murderer?"

"Sorry, a dramatic choice of words. You know what I mean."

"But—"

"But nothing. You're in shock. It dies down, believe me. It becomes normalized, something you can eventually push to the back of your mind. It may sound unpalatable now, but sadly, it's true."

I take a large gulp. The unfamiliar sensation of alcohol slides down the back of my throat, hits me hard. Or is it just wishful thinking? I want to drink it all. I crave the welcoming pull of drunken oblivion. I want to write down my thoughts, one by one and untangle them. I want to see my mum, my dad, Christian.

His tone softens. "Think of the future, Marie. Our future. Our children's future. Nina paid a high enough price, believe me. Sometimes I wonder if it was the guilt that made her ill. I appreciate that's not how it works, but it does cross my mind from time to time."

I almost forget to breathe as I struggle to take it all in, for my mind to play catch-up.

"When I found out, I was angry. I felt duped. Nina hadn't been as into me as I was her—we all know that. But she came back from Ibiza different. More grown up. More sure of what she wanted. And I allowed myself to believe that it was because she'd missed me, decided that I was who she wanted. Except that it wasn't the case at all. She'd been horrified by what happened, craved stability and a shot at normal life."

"Did she tell you exactly how it happened?"

"I believe so."

"What did she tell you?"

"I thought you'd read her diaries? I'd like to see them, too, when we get home, please."

"I don't want the diary version, I'd like yours."

"Charlie and Camilla had an argument. Camilla reacted badly, so Charlie attacked them and fell overboard in the process. A terrible tragedy. Just awful. Poor guy."

"So you knew, all along, why Camilla came back?"

"Yes."

I revisit all my paranoia, all the secret little chats. The time he suggested to Camilla that they go boating, which seemed so out of context at the time. Oh my God, he was testing her. It seems...cruel and taunting. I remember his interest when I first mentioned Camilla's surprise return. It seems that we weren't having a normal conversation as I'd thought at the time; he was also fishing for information.

"No good, Marie, can come from speaking out. Camilla and I have come to an understanding. We think it's best if she leaves the area at some point. You and I, we can move on from this. I'm glad that you know. It's been a weight on my mind."

I can't see Camilla moving away. Especially not now that she knows I know. She'll want to keep an even closer eye on me.

"But you lied. The night I told you that I was pregnant, you said that you'd gone over to accuse her of being the mystery-note sender!"

"What was I supposed to say? I panicked, I was afraid that once Camilla knew about us that she'd crack, fear that I was going to tell you. Don't you get it—the more people who know, the more dangerous it is."

I truly don't know what to do, but the weight that Stuart talked about is now sitting heavy with me. I don't know what to believe.

"Promise me?" he says.

I nod, knowing that by doing so, I'm implicating myself ever more deeply in this tragedy now, too. Right now, I don't feel as if I have a choice. I'm buying time to give myself space to think.

On our walk home with flashlights, I ask something else that's been playing on my mind. "Do you know who is behind the notes and flowers?"

"No, I don't."

I search his face for clues that he's lying, but his expression and demeanor give nothing away. But then, it hasn't before, has it?

Back at home, as I'm removing my makeup in front of the bathroom mirror, Stuart comes up behind me.

"I have a gift," he says. "A wedding one."

I stare at him in the mirror. "It feels inappropriate, like you're trying to buy my silence somehow."

"Open it."

I can tell by the shape of the box that it's jewelry.

It's a silver charm bracelet.

The same thing he bought Nina as a wedding gift, and not too different from the one nestled among her precious things to pass on to the children.

I hold my breath as he clasps it around my wrist.

"I'll add to it each anniversary. I appreciate Nina had one similar, but yours has different charms."

"It makes me feel uncomfortable," I say.

"Only if you let it," he says. "Now, where are those diaries? I assumed that she had only written notebooks full of advice for the children to read when they're older."

I hand over the latest one only.

I wake up in the early hours, briefly disoriented. My son kicks.

Stuart is asleep beside me. Clearly, he didn't find Nina's journal that riveting.

My wrist aches. I fell asleep with the bracelet on, and it's made disfiguring red welts deep into my skin.

I remove it and place it in the bedside table. I feel hot. I take several sips of water. At first I wonder if I'm ill, if the minute amount of gin I drank has had an adverse effect, but no, something else is wrong on top of everything else.

It's a Tuesday night.

Is Stuart trying to mold me into his old routines?

Wide-awake, I study his face for clues that something isn't right. Of course, there's nothing. But what I must face up to is that I don't truly know the man I've married. Any more than I thought I knew my closest friend. They both kept secrets from me, big ones. It makes me fearful for what I've let myself in for and what else I've missed.

Meanwhile, I've been left with a bitter choice: justice for Charlie or keeping my longed-for family intact. One or the other, but clearly not both.

TWENTY-FOUR

I can't deny that I have secrets, too.

Thankfully I have an appointment with Christian the following morning. Exhausted, I drive over to his office, oblivious to my surroundings. When I walk into his consulting room, it's an instant relief. I've bottled too much up.

Usually, the things I tell him are so random and inane, sometimes they lead somewhere, but even then I'm never sure if what I'm talking about is what I *want* to talk about. I never come out of a session feeling like I've achieved or learned something useful, yet I must have. Surely? Most of the research I've undertaken suggests that it is beneficial, retelling stories to a stranger, but I have moments when I look at Christian and think, *can I really trust you?* I mean, who is he really when he's off duty? Responsible? Kind? Law-abiding? Does he gossip? Sometimes, I think in advance about what I'm going to say, but then I always veer off topic.

But not today.

"I think I've made a huge mistake," I tell him. "Stuart's been lying to me about various things. But worst of all, I let him do it. Do you remember the holiday I've mentioned before, the one the three of us girls went on?"

"Ibiza, yes."

God, he has a good memory, I like to flatter myself that it's because I'm memorable, but really, I know it's because he's clearly a good note-taker.

"Looking back from the position I'm in now, I'm frustrated at how much I adapted myself to fit in with Nina by default and always went along with what she wanted me to do. I never thought about myself and what I wanted. My first thought whenever arrangements—like which bar, club or restaurant—were discussed was to first consider what the others would like to do or how they'd like me to respond, then try to pretend that's what I wanted to do, too."

"Why do you think you did that?"

"Because I was scared that Nina wouldn't like me anymore if I didn't go along with what she wanted, and also I knew that whatever she and Camilla wanted to do, they would. So, by pretending to agree with them, to go where they wanted to go, it saved me having to deal with the embarrassment or face up to the knowledge that I was at the bottom of the food chain."

I pause.

"I'm annoyed with my younger self. Camilla and I had a drunken argument over her flirting with Charlie and I stormed off. But all that happened was that I ended up being on my own in our shared apartment. They stayed out, had fun and I was left simmering in envious bitterness. Or so I thought. The night they had didn't turn out that well in the end."

Sometimes, I play things down for Christian. He looks like such a gentleman that I don't want to shock him, which I know is silly and pointless. I decide to explain it better.

"It was more than a drunken argument, actually. It was quite brutal, nasty and ugly. It got physically violent when Charlie became embroiled in the conflict."

I slapped Charlie. He grabbed my arm to stop me doing it a second time.

And then…I remember waking up on the sofa to the smell of the ashtray lying on the coffee table. Lipstick on my beer glass. My makeup bag. (I don't recall why I had decided to get that out.) All the sad, hopeful debris of me staying up alone, hoping that Charlie would return.

Old wounds reignite, pain burns acid-like inside my chest.

"The thing that really gets me and is the beginning in a long line of punches to the gut," I say, "is that I wasn't wrong. I've recently found out that Camilla had Charlie's baby. Nina knew, Stuart knew more than he let on, and I don't know who to trust anymore."

"Can you talk to them about it?"

"I have. I fear I'm only a little the wiser. Another thing I've been blaming myself for is that all this time I thought it was *me* who pursued Stuart. I promised Nina that I'd look out for him and the kids, but also that I'd make sure that any women he formed relationships with were, you know, suitable. I understood that. I mean, you don't want just anyone around influencing your children, do you? And I let my desperation for a child cloud my judgment, too."

"Are you saying that you think Stuart took advantage of the situation?"

"In a way. It was mutually beneficial. But Ben was right to be pissed off." I glance up. "I mean, angry…"

Christian smiles. "You can speak candidly. You'd be surprised what I hear in here. If you're pissed off, you're pissed off. That's okay."

I grin.

"Ben was right. I did put Stuart ahead of my relationship with him. If he called, I ran. I thought it was a good thing, but now…I'm not sure. He called me once to say that there had been an attempted burglary…yet, I also feel it was just another good enough reason or excuse to get me round. To make me feel like he needed my help. It's my weakness."

"Have you spoken to Stuart about how you feel?"

"Kind of."

Christian waits for me to say more.

"I fear I've rocked the boat enough. I have a child on the way, Nina's children to look out for, financially I've been a bit careless, turning down work. I know the worst of his secrets now."

"Do you?"

"Well, I believe I do."

"Do you love Stuart?"

"I thought I did. Maybe I even convinced myself I did. Now... Well, I thought I loved someone I didn't know. I do enjoy his company, he's an excellent listener, a good father." I pause. "Whatever way I look at it, I'm embedded in the situation."

"Not necessarily."

"There are children involved. They've lost their mother and I need to find a way to make the best of the situation. We've pooled our resources and I don't mean financially or practically. I'm talking about emotionally when I factor in Felix and Emily and our baby. Investments of the emotional kind are the most difficult to get out of."

I want to tell him how I've read up on Rebecca syndrome: when the second wife or partner feels they can't match up to the image of the first. Not in this instance. My situation is completely different. But I don't get the chance to untangle my thoughts any more.

"We're running out of time, I'm afraid," says Christian. "But we can continue this thread in our next session if you'd like to."

I wasn't going to tell him how it ends anyway.

Regardless, I leave Christian's with more questions than answers. On the drive back, memories, good and bad, are dredged up.

At home, I sift through the few photos I have of Charlie. I haven't looked at them in ages.

Charlie and Stuart are so different. Stuart is a creature of habit; Charlie was a free spirit. Charlie's funeral was relatively quiet, but a blur. Mainly coworkers and friends attended. Still… Camilla said he had an aunt and a cousin. I wonder why they weren't at the funeral? Perhaps they were, maybe we didn't notice. I was so absorbed in myself, I wasn't thinking clearly. Although he was my first proper love, I realize that I didn't really know him as well as I thought. He was brought up in care—he said he'd never known his parents. When I pushed, he never gave a proper answer why. It still doesn't make any difference. He didn't deserve what Nina and Camilla did.

If I want to know the full story, I have to read Nina's words over and over until I can piece it all together. She was cautious. The words alone don't really mean anything without further knowledge, but they're probably the best version I've got until I can prize more out of Camilla. However, I'm not sure I'm quite ready. Forgiveness is a great idea in theory, harder in reality.

For now, I'll let the sleeping dogs lie very quiet.

The days are long. The nights longer. Stuart and I are forming our own rituals—like right now, I'm drinking a coffee at breakfast to keep him company instead of a tea (just a weak one; every time I eat or drink anything I think of my baby).

"Stuart…" I say.

God, it sounds forced. Nina used to call him honey. It's too cringey. I must Google terms of endearment and pick out a non-syrupy, natural-sounding one. "Stuart" feels too formal.

Despite hating the words *date night* for the purpose of this conversation, I can't think of a better description right now.

"The other night… The bracelet and everything… Well, it was a Tuesday night. It made it feel like it was a," I say it, "a date night."

Stuart looks surprised that I've even raised the subject. "Well, yes."

Now I feel stupid. There are only seven days in a week after all, it's hardly impossible that we go out on a Tuesday.

"Well, it's just I'd like us to do things differently."

"Okay. Like what?"

He sips his coffee and acts like he's interested, but I feel humored. It's irritating.

"Nothing springs to mind right now, it's just that it bothered me a bit when I woke up in the night and realized it was a Tuesday date night."

"Point taken. But it was you who said you wanted to talk. I thought it would be easier on neutral territory. The gift was something I've been meaning to give you for ages and then felt appropriate. I could hardly give it to you in the pub after your revelation."

"Daddy, can you take us to school today, please?" Emily interrupts.

She always interrupts.

I wait, hoping that Stuart will ask her to wait. Of course he doesn't. He never will, and each time it happens, it reminds me of my place. Once our baby is born, I will feel more secure. It will cement my place in the family.

It's quieter than ever once Stuart has taken the children to school. I sit at the kitchen table and reply to client queries. I must get working again properly, but I can't concentrate.

I distract myself by looking up pregnancy facts during the second trimester. Just reading about swollen ankles and tiredness makes me yawn and twist my wedding ring around my finger as though my fingers might swell any moment. I'm not used to wearing one. I study it. He's promised that later on down the line we can buy something bigger, if it's more to my taste, and an engagement ring, too, if I'd like one. It sums up our relationship perfectly: everything is backward.

I stand up and walk around the house.

Nina's presence is fading, but never her memory. I forget that

I am living her old life for days at a time now. I've tried so hard for the children's sake to replace Nina that I don't even think like myself at times, until something happens, like a random caller phones the landline and asks to speak to Ms Beaufort. It grates as I have to explain—yet again—that Nina has gone.

In my more paranoid or low moments, when I question my actions, I wonder if Nina *knows* somehow what I've done (I appreciate it's irrational). Deborah knows and judges, as do anonymous people. The more I think about it, the more I wouldn't put it past her to send the flowers and cards. Nina's unpredictable moods and selfishness came from somewhere. I wonder if Deborah would change her mind about me if she knew what her precious daughter was capable of?

What I crave, more than anything, is a good dose of my mother's sensible, no-nonsense advice. Usually, I ring my dad and let him know that I'm coming, but the urge to visit is so overwhelming that I just pick up my bag, get in my Mini and drive to my childhood home.

Their neighbor answers the door.

"Hi, Pam," I say. "Dad not in?"

"He's gone to the supermarket. I've educated him about online deliveries, but I think he enjoys the outing between you and me."

"How's Mum?"

"She's quiet today."

"Where is she?"

"She's at the back, in the conservatory."

My mother is in a straw-colored wicker chair facing the garden. I pull up a chair beside her. Mum's frailness gets to me every time. Her hair is neatly brushed, but the parting is wrong. She doesn't look herself. I sit beside her.

"Hi, Mum," I say.

I take her hand. She looks at me as if she's expecting me to say more. Now that the moment's here, now that the time feels right, I'm scared. I've imagined this for so long. I waffle, skirt around the subject because I know that once I get into the more natural swing of it, it's easier talking to my mother than it is to Christian because there's no expectation. I find I speak the most I have in a long time. My mother looks interested, makes the odd random comment and she does seem to enjoy the sound of my voice, so it gives me confidence to continue.

I tell her about Camilla's surprise return.

Silence.

"I wish Nina was still here," I say.

Mum used to say that there are many people who will enter our lives, Nina was just one of them. But I enjoyed hanging out with her. With Nina I felt like a better version of myself, that anything was possible. I would never explain it that bluntly to anyone else, especially not Christian, it sounds pathetic. I consider how I'd describe Nina to someone who didn't know her, who'd never met her. I think about the questions Christian has asked me about her. I mull over my dad's, Ben's, Camilla's frustration at my building my life around one friendship. I'd describe Nina as beguiling. Someone whose faults people tended to overlook because just being in her company made life feel better. More open to possibilities. I guess it's called charisma. It doesn't mean I didn't hate or resent her at times.

"I got married, Mum. To Stuart. I mean, a man named Stuart."

"No, you did not!" she says.

"I did. Dad came. You weren't well."

"Who are you?"

"I'm your daughter, Marie."

Pam walks up behind us. "Would you like a cup of tea?"

"No, thanks," I say.

"Didn't want to marry him," my mum says.

"It's all right, Mum," I say. "Everything worked out in the end. I'm happy. We're all okay."

"Nina," Mum says.

"No, I'm Marie," I say.

I wait until Pam's out of earshot.

"I've made so many mistakes."

When my mother first started forgetting things, I grew scared of her. Which is silly, I know, and it's another thing to hate myself for. When Nina was first diagnosed, I was relieved that at least I could still talk to her about what was wrong.

I'm not afraid anymore. I say what I've really come here to say.

"Mum," I say. "You're going to be a grandmother."

She smiles, but it is not one of recognition. It's one of incomprehension.

"I did it for you," I tell her. "I remembered. You wanted a big family." Everyone told me that it won't make a difference. That no matter what I do or say, she'll never know. But I had to try. It was worth a shot.

She smiles as though she feels that it's the right reaction, but there is definitely no sign of comprehension.

I swallow. Hard.

I can't trust my own judgment, and it's a horrible feeling. I can't even begin to imagine what it's like for my mother. I feel like I'm in a dream and there's an answer, so obvious, yet so elusive and out of reach.

I just need to figure out what it is.

TWENTY-FIVE

My insomnia worsens. I spend most nights keeping Goldie company, wondering how on earth Stuart manages to sleep. I keep a record of everything.

Things Stuart likes: Sunday roasts, clean sheets on a Monday, a pub visit at least once a month, a supermarket delivery every week, curry on a Friday night, at least two loaves of bread and one carton of full-fat milk in the freezer at any one time. Green grapes, not purple. He wears suits at the beginning of the week, more casual clothes on a Thursday and Friday. And date nights on a Tuesday.

Things that unsettle Stuart: Alternative suggestions to the above.

I make a chamomile tea.

My thoughts switch from Stuart to Nina and her lies.

"I was surprised to see you on the sofa," Nina had said to me the morning after the fateful night before. "I thought that you and he had made up."

"Hardly," I said. "He made it quite clear that it was Camilla he was interested in."

Nina had glanced over to the bar where Camilla had gone to get a bloody Mary: hair of the dog.

"In fairness, he almost didn't have a say in the matter once Camilla decided that..."

"Why didn't you stick up for me, why didn't you say something to her?"

"It's hard for me always being in the middle..."

Recalling that particular conversation is sickening because by then she knew that Charlie, the man I loved, was dead. Because of her. And Camilla.

They told me that they'd read loads of Ibiza stories online about people going missing, only to show up a day or so later. I had to pack up his belongings and leave them with the hotel's front desk, telling the concierge that I couldn't find Charlie and was extremely worried.

"Very common," was the response. "People get drunk, make new friends, wake up somewhere on the other side of the island, hungover, sometimes minus their wallet or handbag. You'll see him later and he'll be sorry about everything."

We caught a taxi to the airport. Camilla paid. (I should've suspected something then, really.) Charlie was booked on a flight several hours later than us because he'd arranged his trip with a different airline. I thought we were over and he hadn't had the guts to tell me. I sent him several texts, but (of course) he didn't reply. I assumed, or even hoped, it was because of the cost; he had said that he wasn't going to use his phone abroad. I was so angry and hurt when I returned, I could barely think straight.

When we heard that someone's body had been found drowned, I prayed. I thought Nina did, too, but clearly she was praying for something different. There was no mention of a Saint Christopher; it had been given to him by his birth grandmother before she died and he wore it on a chain around his neck all the time. It had given me brief hope that it wasn't him. Nina knew that.

She came to the funeral. Nina comforted me. She listened to me. Or did she? Perhaps I only thought she did. Maybe that's why she distanced herself from me as she threw herself into her new life.

I'm not sure I can carry a secret around with me as heavy as this. I need to talk to Camilla, talk to her properly, prize every wretched detail from her and how she copes with the knowledge.

I can't wait, even though it's 2:00 a.m. Enough is enough. An element of surprise may shock her into divulging more than she intended.

I tell Goldie to "shhh." Her eyes follow me as I go, reluctantly.

Coolness envelops, despite it being an early summer night. I am not dressed to be outside, in maternity tracksuit bottoms and a thin top, flip-flops on my feet. The thwacking noise of rubber as I walk is heightened by the silence. Shivering, I keep looking behind as though I expect to see someone emerge from the darkness. I speed up, fighting my natural instinct to be cautious. Camilla always leaves at least one downstairs light on.

I slide my key in the door but am thwarted by the chain. I'm not giving in. I try the back door—yes!

I stand still. The fridge hums. On a counter is a pile of papers, school forms (instantly recognizable by the logo) and a set of keys. A blast of air slams the door shut behind me. I freeze. I think I've got away with it for a moment or two, but no, footsteps thud down the stairs.

I flood the kitchen with light so that Camilla can see it's me. But it's not her. It's Greg.

Camilla appears at the bottom of the stairs, hair all over the place, eyes wide, her phone in one hand, a tennis racquet in the other.

"For fuck's sake, what the hell are you doing? I've already rung the police, you stupid cow!" She calls them back. "A mistake. So sorry."

When she ends the call, she turns her attention back to me.

"What are you doing, Marie? Do you even know what time it is?"

I look at Greg.

He shrugs.

"You and Greg?"

"It's none of your bloody business," Camilla says.

He gives me an awkward wave. "Hi, Marie. Hope everything's all right. Pretend you haven't seen me. I'll leave you two to it," he says, disappearing up the stairs.

"Thank God you didn't wake Lulu!"

"The door slammed. I didn't mean to wake you."

"Well, what then? Burgle? Breaking and entering? You can't just walk in here on a whim."

"Why not? You do what you like. I need to know. Exactly how it happened," I whisper, as if Greg and/or Louise are listening in.

"At two in the morning?" I notice she whispers back.

"Yes, at two in the morning. I can't sleep. It's haunting me."

"Bloody hell, Marie. Just try. Imagine what it's like for me."

"I don't know what to do."

"Speak to Deborah."

"Deborah? She can't stand me."

"Try her. She knows. And Marie...?"

I stop.

"Keep anything she says to yourself."

The walk back feels longer. As I approach the back door, I scream when someone grabs my wrist and shines a flashlight in my face.

"Oh my God, it's you!" Stuart's voice.

I can't breathe. I haven't had a panic attack since I was a teenager. He switches off the light, but I'm still blinded. I inhale. Breath, blessed breath.

He holds me around the waist and helps me up the back steps like I'm an old lady.

"Why did you grab me like that?"

"I thought you were a prowler."

"But you must've seen that I wasn't in bed? Dear God, the baby! I hope the baby's all right after a fright like that."

"I didn't know you'd be outside," he says. "Sit down. I'll make you a tea."

He reels out a list of flavors—jasmine, ginger, peppermint—and so forth, as if that will make amends for the fright he just gave me.

"Anything. I'll drink anything."

"What were you doing outside?" he asks.

"I needed air. I needed to think."

"Half naked?"

I shrug.

"For God's sake, Marie. Anything could've happened! Someone has been leaving threatening notes. We've had two attempted break-ins."

"I wondered if you'd made the second one up," I say. "To get me to come over and help you."

"Why on earth would you think that?"

Put like that, why did I? I'm having real trouble making sense of everything.

"Camilla tried to break in, before she let it be known she'd moved back. I don't think there is a someone other than the poison-pen author and flower-sender. Regardless, though, let's tell the police," I say. "What if someone *was* after Nina? What if they're after me now instead? What if I've made a mistake in believing that it was Camilla? What if it's all linked?"

"That's a lot of speculation. I'm reluctant for obvious reasons," he says. "But sadly, we can't rule it out indefinitely. However, logically, if 'they'—" he mimes quotation marks "—were after Nina, then surely they'd be after Camilla now, too?"

"Who knows, she's never mentioned anything," I say. "She's hooked up with Greg from the book group, so she's not alone at the moment."

"Greg? Really?"

"Yes."

"Well, if this is something to do with the past, they wouldn't be after you."

"Unless...Camilla *is* behind all this? She's desperate for me to keep quiet. Perhaps she thought that Nina had already told me. Perhaps she's got Greg in on it, too. He's a private investigator and a security guard, and Lord knows what else. He could be a hit man on the side."

"Now you're being ridiculous. Camilla wouldn't want to harm your baby," he says. "If anything, it's the best thing that could have happened. The chances of you speaking out now are so much less. You stand to lose out, too."

He's right.

And in a really perverse, childish, twisted way, I feel moments of jealousy that I was left out of the secret. Like I was a child to be managed, someone who couldn't handle the truth.

I don't want my child tainted with a history of murder, manslaughter or whatever it is. Or Nina's. Or Camilla's and therefore Charlie's. Yet as distasteful as it is, I have to embrace the secret and find a way to live with it. I'm a part of it now. Just like Nina, Camilla and Stuart. And I will find a way. Once I've spoken to Deborah. I need to piece everything together in my own way, in my own time if I'm to take such a monumental burden on board.

A tiredness like I haven't known in a long time hits. I let Stuart lead me upstairs by the hand and help me lie down on the bed before I give in to the blackness.

When I awaken, it's still dark. I am alone in bed.

TWENTY-SIX

Deborah is on holiday in the Lake District until Saturday.

I left her a voice mail, insisting that I needed to speak to her urgently, so she called me back. As soon as she ascertained that the children were all right, she asked me to leave her in peace until she returned.

"I need this break," she says. "The pain is so raw."

I feel terrible. Perhaps she has felt pushed out; her grandchildren are all she has left of Nina. I'll try harder to heal the rift, to ensure she's more involved in their day-to-day lives.

I manage to fit in some work, taking pictures of a local horror author who needs some up-to-date promotional photos. She wants them shot in the woods. I suggest that we use the abandoned barn in our garden as a backdrop, too. It's fun working again. It alleviates the stress and surreality of the previous week.

I can't just sit around waiting for Deborah, though. I must find other ways to keep occupied. I contact Greg through his private investigator website, using an email address under the name of Samantha Brown, and book an appointment. I receive an automatic response that says that I need to arrange a telephone conversation first to "discuss my requirements and see if his methods could work for me." Sounds ominous rather than hopeful. I compose an email lie, something along the lines of not wanting my partner (who works from home) to overhear our conversation.

When he emails back, we arrange to meet in two days' time.

If I didn't know Greg, I'm not sure how I'd feel about meeting him alone, in an anonymous place, but the building where he is based is staffed by several receptionists and gives a good overall appearance of being safe. The signs for multiple businesses adorn the walls, including advertisements for temporary office spaces. It's busy. All the same, I sign in under the same fake name I used to book the appointment.

I wait.

At four minutes past my appointment, I remember that Greg is rarely on time.

A phone rings in reception. The woman who answers it looks at me as she puts it back down.

"Upstairs, second floor."

"Thanks."

As I walk up, I don't feel quite so sure of myself and my online detecting.

His office is next door to the ladies' toilets.

I take a deep breath and walk into his office as confidently as I can. He rises from behind a desk littered with pens, mugs and paperwork, ready to greet me—his client. He stares at me as though it's all a mistake.

"Hi, Greg."

An element of surprise can't do any harm.

He does his very best to hide his shock by acting like he was half expecting me.

"Hello, Marie. What are you doing here? Is everything okay?"

"Sorry about the false name. Clearly, I'm not Samantha Brown. Shall I take a seat?"

"Please do."

He sits back down behind his desk and I sit on a plastic chair opposite.

"Look, if this is about me and Camilla, please save your breath. We're not doing anyone any harm. I'm guessing it was you who sent Stuart round to Camilla's the morning after your night visit under some rubbish guise to talk to her?"

"No."

Unsettling news to me.

"Camilla put him in his place. He would have received a slap on the face, too, if I hadn't been there to stop her. She's a fiery one."

"That all sounds very over-the-top but who you sleep with is none of my business, I agree. This is about Nina. You were her friend. I need to know if she confided in you about her fears that someone was following her."

I fold my arms in an attempt to look as though I mean business. My heart thuds. I feel stupid. The baby kicks. I feel like we're acting in a TV advertisement for a loan company or some kind of insurance.

"No."

To be fair, he looks genuinely quite baffled. I half expect him to scratch his head.

"Did she ever seem scared or distracted?" I ask.

"Not particularly."

"But there was something?" I push.

"It was something very general, unrelated to you or her children, and confidential. You were her friend, too, so you'll respect her privacy," he says. "No matter how well you think you know someone, no one can know everything about everyone all the time. Some of the things I see and experience, they could potentially make me doubt everyone I know, if I chose to let it happen."

I stay silent, pondering my next move. I try, without making it obvious, to study the room, wondering where he keeps his client records. They must be digital or kept at his house because there's no obvious filing cabinet with the key conveniently left in.

"As a friend, I really need to know exactly what you found. I recently discovered that Nina was looking for someone's relatives and I feel compelled by grief to continue her search," I say.

"I can't tell you anything, especially as I didn't find out that much. It happens occasionally, even in this day and age. Besides, it's too late now. Initially, I assumed that she was looking for people to inform them of her situation. I couldn't make it happen, otherwise they'd have been at her funeral."

I redden. Greg attended the funeral. He must remember what a fool I made of myself.

Nina had tried to dissuade me from making a speech. "I don't want too much overemotion," she said. "It will add to the upset."

I didn't reply. How could *I* ever add to the upset, the raw devastation?

As I made my way to the pulpit, I swallowed hard and took a few seconds checking that the microphone was at the right level to buy enough time to try to regain full composure. As I opened my mouth to speak, I felt a sense of *knowing* exactly what the right thing was to do. It was a pivotal moment, an opportunity to make true my promises to Nina, to myself, to Felix, to Emily.

I felt disconnected, like everyone else had faded away and it was just me. I heard (well, I didn't, obviously, but I felt extremely close to) those who weren't there. My future children, too, not just Nina.

I heard a cough, but it came from the distance. Briefly, I caught sight of rows of expectant faces. Greg's, come to think of it now, among them. There were all these expressions: Ben's concern, Stuart's fear, Deborah's look of *I knew this wouldn't be a good idea*... It gave me fresh impetus.

As I spoke, my voice filled the church, and although it was clear, it didn't sound like me.

"Nina was the best friend anyone could ask for. She was always there for me and it saddens me that I couldn't be there for her in the same way. I made her a solemn promise, though." I looked up when I said this and stared directly at Stuart. "That I would look after her family. That I would remind her children of what she was like as a child, the things we did, and always be there to answer any questions, to fill in the gaps."

I was briefly yanked out of my mission by a memory. Jealousy. I was jealous when I wasn't made Emily's godmother as well as Felix's. I felt excluded and I showed my anger by making an excuse not to come to Emily's christening, citing some ridiculous reason that was clearly made up. Nina was disappointed, but not as disappointed as I was in myself. I vowed then and there, no matter what cost to myself, that I would make amends. I don't know what came over me—my behavior was unacceptable.

However, the pressure of well, *everything*... It suddenly dawned on me, right there in front of everyone, that Nina was gone. And then...it was all a blur as I broke down. I will never forget the collective looks of concern while I was guided outside by Ben, sobbing.

But that was then. Greg can't possibly be thinking back to that time. Nina and I used to discuss how things could be worse in my mind, things that other people didn't give a moment's thought to. Although, it's not always the case. I take a breath.

"Greg," I say with a smile. "It's admirable that you're trying to protect her. But what is there to protect her from? Sadly, she's gone. I'm her children's stepmother in every practical sense. They have a sibling on the way and it's my job to protect my family."

"If I thought there was anything that would help you, I'd tell you. But there isn't."

I use Christian's technique. Silence is an extremely power-ful weapon.

He gives in.

"Marie...you've got what you clearly wanted. You were en-vious of Nina. It was obvious to anyone who saw you together. You were so grateful to be a part of her life. It's not a bad thing. People feel jealousy, rage, envy, all sorts. It's natural to feel the negative and the positive. I've yet to encounter a person who doesn't, but the speed at which you gleefully took over has left a few of us a bit shell-shocked. It will take time for people to accept the situation."

Could he be any more patronizing and pompous?

"Thanks for sharing your wisdom, but it takes two. I did not *take over*—what a ridiculous description—and even if I did, Stu-art is capable of making his own decisions." I pause. "We love each other," I lie. "We can offer each other comfort. What Nina's death taught us is that we can never know what is around the proverbial corner of life. We're grabbing onto a second chance with both hands, and in the process, those children have some-one—me—in their lives who loves them like no other woman ever will. If that makes me a bad person then..."

My mind goes blank.

Greg stares. Oh my God, it's him.

"You're the person behind the threatening messages."

I didn't mean to blurt it out loud.

"What messages?"

I briefly tell the story, all the while studying his expression.

Again, he looks baffled, yet my instinct is telling me to be wary. I don't trust people who say they're transparent and can't put on an act. They're either lying, deluded or plain sneaky. Any one of us, under the right circumstances, is capable of putting on an Oscar-worthy performance. I think that in order to find out what someone is *really* like, it's best to talk to the people they don't have to impress.

I lose patience.

"Forget it. You're hardly likely to admit that you've been creeping around the village at night trying to intimidate a pregnant woman. It's not something to be proud of."

I stand up and hoist my bag over my shoulder.

He shakes his head. "I've no idea what you're on about. But be careful, Marie. I know it's already too late, but keep your mind open. Nina did say one thing that always struck me as strange, and I never got the opportunity to fully work out what she meant by it."

"What did she say?" I ask before I step out of his office.

"She said that Stuart was her penance and that she could never leave him."

TWENTY-SEVEN

My mother's words come back to me.

Didn't want to marry him.

Doubt slithers into memories. Did she have suspicions, too?

I scroll through all the pictures I took of Nina and Stuart's wedding. I study every expression, all the special moments, and it's like an optical illusion. Where I saw happiness, I'm pretty sure I now see wistfulness. It's like pulling off daisy petals: she loved him, she loved him not. She was happy, she was not. Yes, no, no, yes.

Goldie's barks cut through my confusion; she needs a walk. I shove a tennis ball and some poop bags in a small handbag.

We have barely entered the woods when Stuart calls. This is a rare occurrence. We communicate by messages. Sometimes, at night, when he's asleep and I'm lying awake in Nina's old bedroom, I get up, open the curtains and stare up at the dark sky and think about our messages crisscrossing the networks and wonder if it's the only way we'll ever properly connect.

"Hi, Stu," I say.

I've still not been able to come up with anything more original, despite trying. Most words stick.

"Deborah's been on the phone," he says. "She wants to mark the occasion with the children on Monday."

I am a terrible person. How could I forget the anniversary of Nina's death? How?

"Good idea."

I'm not sure how much I'll be able to chat to her privately, but with a bit of persistence, I'm sure I'll manage. I feel a surge of fresh determination to build bridges with her.

"She wants me and the children to visit Nina's grave and spend the day together."

Silence alerts me to my misunderstanding.

"Without me."

"Without you."

The average time for a widower to start a relationship with another woman is a year, which I recall from my patchy on-line research and blog-reading. So, according to the average, I should no longer be treated as though I'm some sort of panto-mime homewrecker. Right now, I despise Stuart's weakness for not standing up for us just because I fit with some negative nar-rative. He's ashamed, however much he won't admit it.

It suits him, I realize, that I get the blame for leading him astray. Most of the horrible messages and cards refer to me in some derogatory way. For Stuart, it's casseroles, offers to take his suits to the dry cleaner's and to walk the kids to school. For me, it's death threats and requests for favors. No wonder he isn't bothered about dealing with it. He's ashamed, and I've allowed him to dump all his shame on me, too. No more! Rage hits.

"No! You, the children and Deborah can have an hour or two together alone. After that, we do something together. I'm your wife. I'm carrying our child. It's about time I'm treated better than someone who has to hide in the shadows and only be allowed to step out when it's deemed socially acceptable by someone else. I haven't done anything wrong."

It's the brief silence at the end of the phone before he launches into his Stuart-type platitudes that tips me over the edge. Spite pours from my mouth before I can stop.

"We all know that she was far from bloody perfect. Is this how it's going to be for the rest of our lives?"

"Watch what you say."

His voice is harsh. All traces of kind, amenable Stuart have gone.

God, I can't face a drawn-out row. As I struggle to come up with a response I won't regret, icy dread grips. I can't see or hear Goldie.

"Goldie!" I yell. "Goldie!"

I listen for sounds of her rustling through the undergrowth. Silence.

A plane passes above.

"Goldie! I can't see her. I have to go."

I hang up. Panic. I know my motivation in getting a dog to join my family was misguided, but I adore her now. None of us can take any more loss.

I hear barking. I can't tell if it's Goldie's or not. I stride forward until I reach a clearing near the river.

Stuart calls me back. I press Ignore.

Goldie is beside someone who is patting her. As I rush up, I realize it's Tamsin.

"Is this Goldie?"

"Yes. She ran off," I say. "Thank you. Goldie, you naughty girl! You gave me such a fright!"

"I thought so, I was just about to ring you."

As I bend down to ruffle her fur and attach her lead, she shakes muddy water all over me.

"What are you doing here?"

Tamsin is firmly in the *it's too much responsibility* camp of non-dog-ownership.

"I quite often take a walk on my day off. Fancy joining me?"

Does she, really? Do her walks just happen to take her on detours past my front door?

"Another time, maybe. Thanks."

I need space to sift through my thoughts.

Back home, having ignored several of his calls, I message Stuart the good news. After a milky tea and a sandwich, I focus on how I'm going to get Deborah alone. I'll grant her her wish and let her mark the anniversary with Stuart and the children. I'll visit Nina's grave in private. Deborah and I used to be so much closer (when she thought I wasn't suffocating Nina). It's sad that it seems so long ago. She was chill; from a young age, Nina and I were allowed to walk to the local convenience store and buy sweets and play out in the street unsupervised until dusk.

Stuart texts an apology, relieved, too, that Goldie is safe.

I send one back.

Peace is restored, yet restless, I Google the word penance, despite knowing what it means and why she said it. Some descriptions are harsher than others. There's everything from: it's an act to show that you feel sorry about something to definitions like self-inflicted punishment.

A surge of protectiveness toward Nina hits. Her promises take on new meaning. I vowed to look out for her family, and I will. How much was she willing to sacrifice and suffer to try to make the only amends left humanly possible? It's sad that she couldn't track down any of Charlie's relatives.

Nina and I were one of three Catholics in our class. At Easter and other religious occasions, we boarded a minibus (along with children from other years) to different church services. Camilla said that Nina had confessed. Which priest? Which church? It's not as if I can track the person down and force Nina's confession out of them.

I always felt vulnerable and exposed after confession (maybe that's where I first developed my taste for therapy) because the desire to share *something* is powerful. I've made up my mind, I'm not going to confess to anything. The secret stops here, with me.

I'll say the words out loud when I visit her grave tomorrow. (As long as no one is in earshot, of course.) Nina must be left to rest in peace.

Stuart is out for a run when the doorbell chimes. I'm cooking, the children are watching their allotted one hour per day of TV. (No longer as strictly enforced as it used to be, if I'm honest.) I hesitate. It doesn't ring again so I ignore it.

"Marie!" Felix's voice calls out. "There's a box for you!"

Heart pounding, images of all the nasty things I've seen in horror films, such as dead pets, birds or other such gruesome warnings, makes me drop my chopping knife and rush to him.

The front door is wide-open.

"Why did you unlock the door? Don't ever do that!"

Tears fill his eyes. "I wanted to be helpful—you're busy."

My conscience pricks immediately. "I'm sorry, darling."

I hate the person who is doing this to me even more for making me live in fight-or-flight mode every time something that should be perfectly innocuous occurs.

Resting on the step is a cardboard box, a standard one used for deliveries. A message is scrawled on top.

Thought you could do with this. Greg.

I lift it up; it's not too heavy.

"Did you see a man leave this?"

Felix shakes his head.

"Okay, thanks, sweetie, go back and finish watching your show."

I carry it through to the kitchen and place it on the counter. Curiosity takes over. I pull the sharpest pair of kitchen scissors out of their holder and slice through the beige packing tape.

After my adrenaline spike, the contents are oddly anticlimactic. Home CCTV security equipment. It doesn't eliminate Greg as a suspect completely, not yet, but I can't deny it's thoughtful of him after my accusations and outburst earlier.

My back aches. It's been a long day. Yet, it's win-win, I think as I study the instructions. If the mystery person is Greg, the messages will stop. If not, I'll finally get proof of who is behind everything.

TWENTY-EIGHT

I wake up early, bursting with excited anticipation. I had fixed up the CCTV after a fashion the night before. Downstairs, disappointment kicks me twice in short succession: once when I see the mat is devoid of any suspicious envelopes (what's wrong with me?!), and again when the footage is blank. Frustration hits as I try to figure out what I've done wrong.

Stuart and the children appear in the kitchen before I'm any the wiser. Caught up in the morning rush, my day begins before I feel properly ready. My new toy will have to wait.

I write Deborah a heartfelt card, which I drive over and pop through her letterbox. I hope it does the trick. As I emerge from my prenatal class, my phone rings. It's the school; they've not been able to contact Stuart. I'm summoned in because, Felix, of all children, kicked another child. It's not until I'm in the headteacher's office, defending Nina and Stuart's son, that she drops a second bombshell. The child Felix allegedly kicked is Tamsin's. It would be.

"Why did you kick Harry?" I ask as we walk home.

"Because he said that his mum said you were wicked. I know what wicked means and I didn't like it."

My blood runs cold. *Wicked* is a word frequently used in the threatening cards and it's not a word I hear commonly used outside of children's stories. How dare she say such a thing to a friend of Felix's.

"Thank you, darling," I say. "You were quite right."

I'll let Stuart decide what is the best thing to say overall, because, quite frankly, I feel immense pride at Felix's defense of me.

Stuart thanks me for dealing with it over a late dinner once the children are in bed.

"There's something I've been meaning to bring up for a while..." I say.

I've had to put off the adoption conversation (surprisingly, neither child has dropped me in it by raising the subject in front of Stuart) because something else unsettling has cropped up. Finances. Mine. It's my own fault that I've put myself in such an awkward position, but still...it places me at a disadvantage. I don't like feeling reliant on him.

However, I have to live with it for the time being because it doesn't take away from the obvious fact that I need more say. Once the children are adopted and I have much more control over everything without Nina's unsaid presence hanging over us, we're all in for a better chance at our collective new lives. The children must have lived with us both for at least six months before we can begin the adoption process—well, that's one hurdle out of the way already.

"I'd like to adopt Felix and Emily," I continue. "Formally, of course. I've been looking into it, and it's relatively straightforward with your cooperation. They weren't a part of our wedding, and I don't want them to feel left out after our baby is born. This could be the best thing for us all, a total fresh start."

Stuart looks at me. Not in a good way.

"Did you say something to the kids about it? Emily mentioned the word the other day."

Trust Emily.

"Briefly. But I didn't make any promises. They were asking if I was their new mummy now and...it slipped out as a potential option."

Stuart looks...traumatized. It's annoying. He recovers well, throws me a weak smile.

"That's a lovely gesture, but it feels too soon after Nina. I'm not ready to take such a big step just yet. I'd need to think about it."

"So, I'm good enough to look after them twenty-four-seven, take them to the dentist and doctor, throw birthday parties, get up in the night, change their bedding, help with homework, to name a few things, but not good enough to be a real mother, to make proper decisions about their welfare?"

"That's not what I meant. It's just that you've suddenly sprung this on me and—"

"You mean you've never thought about it?"

He doesn't reply.

Rage and regret simmer.

I've never felt more alone.

Felix is invited to play in a friendly football match as a one-off. I agree without consulting Stuart.

"Nina wasn't keen on him playing football," he says. "Neither am I. Maybe when he's a little older. But before we know it, he'll be signed up for a team and our weekends will involve little else but football."

"I doubt it," I say. "He's not a natural. This is just a bit of fun, a chance to kick about with his friends. I'll take him. And," I can't help adding, "it wasn't football she didn't want him to play, it was rugby."

He doesn't know everything.

I'm pointing my lens, snapping pictures of Felix as he proudly tries to save goals, when I capture him falling down. I want to run and save him, but I freeze, powerless to act quickly enough, to do anything but watch as a group of seven- and eight-year-olds kick their studded boots right near his head. I brace myself for the seemingly inevitable, but instead, something marvelous happens. He saves it! Still clutching it to his chest, he stands up—completely fine—with a massive grin on his face. I capture his image of happiness. All the parents on our side cheer and several shout, "Well done, Felix!" but I am the loudest.

I belong! It's wonderful to feel quite so full of genuine pride because I never thought I ever truly would. I feared that I would always feel like a bit of a fraud, a thief, accepting the stolen crumbs of Nina's life.

Greg is there, snapping pictures for the school website again. He is smiling and joking with some of the parents in between shots. He looks benign, like book-group Greg. I walk over to him and hold out my hand.

"Friends?" I say. "Thanks for the gift."

"Friends," he responds. "You're welcome. Caught the culprit yet?"

"I haven't installed it properly. I need to read the instructions more thoroughly. I think I was too overkeen when I first tried to set it up."

"Let me know if you need a hand. I can go through all the security options."

"Thanks, I will."

"Felix is really coming along nicely as a player," he adds.

"Thank you. Sorry for—"

He holds out a hand, palm upward.

"No need. Water under the bridge. I'd feel the same in your position. Sorry for my accusations. I let myself get caught up in general opinion. It was wrong. Clearly, I'm not busy enough."

"Photography's coming along well, then?"

"Yes, fingers crossed. As well as this, I've been asked to take some pictures for a local angling magazine."

Professional jealousy hits. I was stupid to let my business

slide as much as I have. I miss my old life more than I thought I would.

"I can't think of anything I'd like less than hanging out by a river or a lake with a fishing rod, especially, waiting for something to happen. And surely, it's cruel?"

He conveniently ignores my *cruel* comment.

"It's surprisingly addictive and peaceful. I try to go at least once a week. I'm embracing the whole work-life balance ethos now ever since the doc broke the news that I have high blood pressure. I even go night-fishing sometimes."

"Definitely not my sort of thing," I say as he names a nearby river where a friend has a lodge.

My heart sinks as he continues with the inevitable enthusiasm of a recent convert.

"It's bloody expensive, I need to choose a cheaper hobby next time. By the time you've bought or hired the equipment, paid for a license…"

"Must dash," I interrupt as I spot Tamsin. "Bye," I say to him over my shoulder, striding over to catch up with her.

"Excuse me, Tamsin. Felix, go and kick a ball with Harry for a few minutes."

"We're in a bit of a rush," Tamsin says.

"Go on," I say to the boys.

They don't need any further encouragement.

"I understand that Harry told Felix you called me wicked."

She laughs. Nervously.

I hold her gaze.

"It was a misunderstanding. It was something taken completely out of context. Felix really shouldn't have kicked Harry."

She gives me that annoying *boys will be boys* grin that infuriates me so much.

I wonder whether to mention that the police may be interested in the use of the word, *wicked*, but decide against it. Let her dig her own grave and get caught doing it.

"Actually," she says, "it's great that we're having this little chat, as it has been decided that I'll take over hosting the book group."

I haven't been imagining that I can sense the hatred coming from outside and my paranoia isn't helped by this unwelcome news. I glance over to see if Greg is watching. I wonder why, now we're such great pals, he didn't think to mention this?

There is no sign of him.

"We all decided you'd be too busy preparing for your new arrival," she said with a generous smile.

I can't wait for her to be caught out, arrested and forced to confess.

"Thoughtful of you," I say.

"Thanks, I knew you'd be fine about it. Greg is going to take some photos at the next meeting, raise our profile a bit."

"It's our local book group. There are ten members."

Well, nine now if you exclude me.

"Yes, but it will be fun to share our views on social media, that way, more people can join in! What's the point in living in this century if you can't use it to your advantage?"

I honestly don't know how she expects me to answer that.

"There's just one more thing…"

What now? I half listen. Apparently, I broke some unspoken rule when I hosted a recent birthday party for Felix.

"The general feeling was that it was a little over-the-top, Marie. People can't compete, and it isn't fair to put that kind of pressure on others."

Tamsin is lying. So many parents (well, two) messaged me afterward to say that their little ones had the best time! I didn't have the confidence to have parties as a child. I couldn't cope with being the main focus of attention. Felix and Emily will always have whatever kind of parties they like.

"It was his first birthday without Nina," I say. "Honestly, you can't begrudge the poor child that."

"Nina didn't want them to be spoiled," she says, igniting fierce defensiveness deep within me. "You only did a small one for little Em."

"She got exactly what she wanted, a pirates-and-princesses one!"

I spent hours online organizing Felix's party after Stuart suggested we take a load of kids swimming! As if I'd want to leap about in a swimsuit in public, notwithstanding the sheer responsibility of all those children in water.

I call Felix back over before I can give in to the strong urge to follow Felix's lead and give her a good kick in the shins. My hands are clenched.

It's fortunate that I have my own friends now, too, made through the baby groups I used to mock and be so envious of. I get it now, that Nina wasn't excluding me intentionally (not then, anyway), that it's natural to gravitate toward people with whom you have something in common. I have embraced my new world, and I love the delicious secretiveness that no one but me knows the sex of my future child. It is one of the few things that I have all to myself. I cling to anything positive because so much else feels off-kilter.

Greg is waiting for me in his car when I arrive home. He eases his large frame out of the driver's seat as I pull up.

"What are you doing here?"

"You can say no, but I'm here to install the camera," he says. "It's simple enough for me to do and it sounded like you were having difficulties. I know you can do it, but thought it would cross another thing off the to-do list."

I hesitate.

He shrugs. "I have sprung it on you, I know. No worries— it's an open offer. I can come back another time."

I don't like to admit defeat. Despite that, I agree. He's right about the to-do list, it's too tempting.

"Did you know I was being kicked out of the book club?"

Maybe *kicked out* is a bit strong, but it feels like it to me.

Greg opens the trunk of his car and removes a tool bag. "What? No!"

"Yes."

I brew us a coffee while he sets to work and moan about Tamsin. I can't help it, he's a good listener.

"Thanks for this," I say, as he runs through how the equipment works.

"It's a pleasure. I always wanted to be a policeman. I don't like 'the bad guys'—" he mimes quotation marks "—getting away with it."

"Why did you go into private investigator work instead?"

"Long story. My jobs have been pretty diverse over the years."

My response is silence, to encourage him to spill some (potentially interesting) beans. Perhaps I should retrain to be a therapist.

He half bites at the opportunity.

"Like I said, it's a long story, which I don't bore people with, but the outcome meant I had to kiss goodbye my career dreams."

My face must give away my unease because he rushes to reassure me.

"Don't worry, it's not as if I murdered anyone!"

"Well, of course."

"I wish you'd confided in me sooner. Usually, a camera alone is a good enough deterrent. Spread the word that you've installed one if you're convinced it's someone you know. That also usually does the trick."

"How well do you know people in the village?"

"I moved here over five years ago, so I don't have a long-term history with anyone local."

I note that it was the year Emily was born, a year in which I felt almost permanently despondent at my inability to conceive. Conscious that I've gone silent for too long, I come up with something polite to move the conversation on and so as not to dwell on now redundant, sad times.

"Where did you move from?"

"Devon. And, before you ask, it was for love."

We both smile.

"It didn't work out in the way I thought it would," he continues. He sounds mournful? Bitter? Wistful? I can't quite put my finger on it. "But I like the area, so I've settled, made it my home."

I type his name into a search engine after he's left. Nothing immediately untoward leaps out. It's funny how I've sat next to him so many times in book meetings and never given him or his background a moment's thought. Until recently, in my mind, he has always been just book-group Greg.

I distract myself instead by staring at the images of our house entrance and immediate surroundings, watching cars, cyclists, ponies and pedestrians pass by. It's reassuring, and I'm grateful for the fresh focus it has given me; a practical approach to divert my fears.

Yet, come morning, impatience and disappointment strikes again with more uneventful footage. Whoever it is, they aren't going to make it easy for me to unmask them.

TWENTY-NINE

I will soon be forced to take a break from therapy because the countdown to my due date is turning into weeks, no longer months. The thought of losing my emotional crutch is disconcerting. When I sit down opposite Christian for one of our last sessions, I can't get comfortable. It's not just my size, it's the unsettling atmosphere at home, Nina's shadow and the secret.

"I haven't just made one mistake, I've made loads because one invariably leads to another."

Saying it out loud makes it real and true.

"I don't know why I ever thought I wanted what I've now got," I say. "The kids are beginning to pick up on the atmosphere because they're playing up. The place is a mess. We don't have a cleaner at the moment." I realize how that must sound. "I know that this isn't a problem in itself, that I'm very lucky," I say. "But all the little things keep adding up. For example, Ben, my ex, had a baby girl a few weeks ago." I pause. "I saw pictures—online, of course. There's no escape, however hard I try to avoid them." That is the truth, we still have mutual friends. I continue, "He looked overjoyed and proud. When my baby is born, Stuart won't feel the same."

"Why do you think that?"

"Because he's done it twice before."

"In my experience, that's not how it works. This is a new life, one you chose to create together."

"Only, he didn't choose, not really." I take a breath. "I chose. I knew what I wanted and I went for it. I was angry with Nina, fed up with always feeling like she'd got one over on me. I appreciate how that sounds, but it's how I felt. I thought that if I had her life, I'd understand things more, that I'd feel better. Whole. No, that's not what I mean either."

I stop. This is hard, really hard, because I'm balancing the truth with my less-decent motivations. It wasn't my fault that Nina fell ill and died. I do love her children. Those are true. Everything else blurs into grabbed, sometimes slightly murky, opportunities.

"I thought that if I led her life, I'd have her confidence," I say. "And by confidence, I mean that sense of feeling like I'm living the right sort of life."

I give up. I'm even confusing myself.

"You've talked about the holiday you had together a fair amount here," Christian prompts.

I look up in surprise. He rarely does that. He lets me meander until something of potential interest manifests and then I sense that we both grab it in gratitude and go with it. I must have done a good job of boring him, too.

"There's nothing left to say about it. I've told you everything," I lie.

"I got the impression that you also held Nina, as well as Camilla, responsible for the loss of a man you fell deeply and quickly for."

"Do you write notes?" I say.

Paranoia at some of my innermost thoughts and secrets being held in Christian's cloud somewhere sends a wave of panic right through me. I clutch my stomach and smooth it down to calm my baby in case he's sensed my fear.

"Very basic ones, like we've discussed," he says. "There's nothing in them that would be able to identify you in any way."

It doesn't reassure me. I reel back, trying to recall everything I've ever told him, told Judy, told all the therapists over the years. I can't remember all the details.

"Did I tell you that Charlie died?"

"I assumed as much. I am sorry."

"No, I'm sorry." I stand up. "I don't want to do this anymore. I'll be in touch…after the baby. If I can."

"We can arrange to talk on the phone any time, if it helps," he says.

"I'll bear that in mind," I say.

I mean it.

On the way home, I make a detour. I want to explain out loud what I couldn't bring myself to go over with Christian. My mother is the best person to talk to, but I don't want Pam or my dad overhearing.

I do something I'm ashamed to say I've never done. I offer to look after her. Alone. I should've done it many times, offered to give Dad a break. But something stopped me, I couldn't bring myself to do it. Her diagnosis was such a shock, such a drawn-out loss, that I couldn't deal with it head-on.

"What's the catch?" my dad says.

I don't blame him.

Alone, just me and Mum, I go back *there*. To ten years ago. I need to go through the past in detail, to take myself back, to remind me why I made the decision I did. Even though hindsight isn't necessarily useful; it makes me want to kick myself in frustration.

She smiles in a way that I choose to interpret as encouragement. I take out my journal, which I've rewritten in an attempt to make it sound more like a story for her, and read aloud.

It was the final day of our holiday and if I didn't make a decision soon, it would

be too late. Our flights home were booked for the early hours of the next morn-
ing. On sunbeds on either side of me, the others were lying flat, asleep.

The smell of sun cream, cigarettes and chlorine lingered. I glanced to my
right. Camilla's pale pink sarong matched her bikini and towel. I turned to my
left. Nina was lying on her stomach, an arm dropped to the side, her fingers
curved awkwardly against the concrete.

I picked up my camera, but the memory card was full. I put it down again. I
couldn't settle. Burgeoning dread had returned. I needed a distraction. I hadn't
planned on having a drink, yet I stood up and walked to the water's edge and
eased myself in.

I swam over to the pool bar and ordered a fruit cocktail. As vodka and
pineapple chunks were mixed and chopped in a too-screechy blender, I looked
ahead, past the bar. A man, his back to me, placed a towel on his sunbed
and smoothed it down. For a hopeful second, I thought it was Charlie. But it
wasn't. Too tall, too broad. He still hadn't turned up after our row and it was
no wonder after what I said.

I stop. Mum has closed her eyes. Unsure, I sit and watch her.
She looks at peace. Maybe she likes the sound of my voice? Perhaps it offers small comfort? There's not much more left to read.

After drinking my cocktail, I swam back to our spot. The other two were
awake. Camilla was sitting next to Nina. They stopped talking as I approached.

"Hi, Marie, we wondered where you'd got to."

"I went for a swim," I said, picking up my towel and wrapping it around me.
"What were you two talking about?"

Paranoia isn't paranoia if you know, rather than suspect, that people are
talking about you.

They fobbed me off with dismissive smiles. "Just comparing hangovers, such
a comedown," Camilla said as she went off to buy drinks. "Hair of the dog."

It should have felt nicely familiar, just the two of us. Me and Nina. Instead,
a horrible sense of foreboding mushroomed. I took a deep, audible breath. Nina
clearly sensed that I needed comforting.

"I'm sorry," she said, taking my hand and giving it a squeeze.

She so rarely apologized. It wasn't her thing.

Reassurance replaced some of my anxiety. There was no dilemma, not really, because there could only be one reasonable conclusion. Charlie and I were over. There was no point in looking for him. Where would I even start? His phone wasn't switched on. He'd only be even more annoyed when he did show up, and his lack of interest in me was plain. I got the message. My place was here, with my friends. I needed to draw a line under the previous night and take a leaf out of their book: be cool and nonchalant.

Homesickness kicked in badly. A yearning to get away from the island grew. I pushed away my instinct that Nina and Camilla's smiles were too bright, their reassurances too OTT. Because, deep down, I still hoped that Charlie would at least come back to say goodbye, but Nina (especially) and Camilla were so full of care and concern.

"He doesn't deserve you," they said. "If you still feel the same way when you get back, you can have it out with him at home. We can't miss our flights just because he's being selfish and inconsiderate."

I should have been stronger and ignored them. I hate that I allowed myself to be so easily manipulated. And I wish I'd known what I know now back then. It would've saved me—and others—so much angst.

Mum opens her eyes and stares at me. Briefly, I think she recognizes me. But seconds later, the slight recognition I hoped I saw has gone again. I really am on my own with this.

Nina bequeathed me her share of the problem. I'd love to tell Mum lots more, like how they lied to me about what time they got in after their night out. They claimed it was earlier. I thought it was because Nina was trying to give the impression that the party hadn't been that amazing after all, to stop me from feeling so bad about myself and the situation with Charlie. How I hate that I thought so well of her. I don't say any more. All this guilt and regret won't change a thing.

"Be safe," Mum says.

She used to say that to me every time I went out. She said it before I went to Ibiza and "that it was a dangerous world out there." It was stifling. One of my therapists suggested that it sounded like she had struggled a lot when I reached the teenage years and craved freedom. "You're precious to me," was another phrase she used a lot.

We sit in silence. I hope that whatever her thoughts or memories are, they're happier than mine.

Upon my dad's return, he is very keen to know how we got on. His barely disguised hope—that maybe it could become a regular thing—brings a lump to my throat. I am a bad daughter to have never offered before.

I arrive home to a postcard faceup on the mat. It depicts our village during bluebell season. Spiteful words litter the back, the ridiculously bad handwriting clearly a disguise.

What goes around, comes around. You will get your comeuppance because bad luck will haunt you until your dying days.

I scroll through the CCTV, but no one comes to our front door apart from the postman. It's only later, after hours of wasted time, that I take proper note of our address and the second-class stamp. It's the first time a message hasn't been hand delivered.

Enraged and discouraged, I sift through all of the old messages and cards apart from the first one burned in the fire. I've logged everything else.

"I'm handing my evidence over to the police," I tell Stuart. "It's irresponsible not to. What if they attack me or hurt our baby?"

"I'll do it," he says. "I don't want you to have to deal with the stress of it."

"Okay. But if you don't do it ASAP, or if they don't take it seriously, I'm going to deal with it. Enough is enough."

"I'll phone them now," he says.

He explains the situation with more urgency than I thought he would, to be fair. He takes out a pen and jots down notes.

Social media—contact individual companies
Phone provider
Notes, calendar, dates, times
Update
Call if escalates

He disconnects after writing down a number.

"I've done most of that," I point to his list.

"Yes, and we've got to continue to keep a record," he says.

"No one has said anything on social media or phoned. Everything is mainly through the letterbox, which points to someone local. In all likelihood, someone we know well."

"I've got a crime reference number," he says.

"Well, that solves everything," I say. "Forget it, I'll visit a police station and take in the evidence myself."

A horrible thought crosses my mind. "Do you *really* not know who is doing this?"

"Marie," he says in a tone of voice that I've grown to dread. "Everything's fine. I won't let anything happen to you or the children. Of course I don't know who it is! What are you accusing me of?"

"I don't like being told that everything is fine when it is so far from fine."

I comfort myself by dreaming of all the wine I'm going to knock back after the baby's born.

My phone rings. Deborah's number shows up.

"I'm going out," I say, resisting the urge to slam the door behind me, and take her call.

As I walk toward the café where she's agreed to meet me, it is the greatest feeling to have escaped my own life, however briefly.

I can breathe again.

THIRTY

"Thank you for agreeing to see me. I appreciate that it's been really tough. I'd be the same, probably, if the roles were reversed."

Actually, I'd be nicer, I hope, but I really want to build bridges. We sit in a local café in the window. I notice that the sugar pot in the center of the table needs filling while we wait for our order. We both sit in silence as a waiter puts down our cups and saucers, a teapot and a jug of milk, decorated in pale pink roses.

As I pour, keeping my eyes focused on the steaming tea (I can't do much eye contact with Deborah, it's too disconcerting), I get on with it.

"Camilla suggested I talk to you."

She takes a sip, her face guarded.

"I *know*," I say, taking her hand. "As in *know*, know. About Nina. About the accident. But it's fine, I'm not going to do anything about it. I will continue to protect Nina, and of course the children, but I must know exactly what happened. Charlie was my first love, my boyfriend. I need the truth about how he died."

Tears stream down her face. She makes no attempt to wipe them away as I reach for my bag and fumble around for a pack of tissues.

"I'm sorry," she says. "I miss her so much. She had children. It was so unfair. I took it out on you and blamed you for being alive when she wasn't. I knew it wasn't right, but I couldn't stop myself. But…"

With Deborah there is always a *but*, she can't help herself. She accepts a tissue from me.

"Why would I trust you?" she asks.

"Good question." I place my hand on my stomach. "Because this child will be the half sibling of your grandchildren. I know you don't agree with me and Stuart, and I do understand why, but my intentions are good."

She doesn't look convinced.

"Stuart knows, Camilla knows, I know. But I would like to have heard it from Nina, so you are the next best thing. I should've known right from the beginning that she'd have confided in you."

She wipes her cheeks and beneath her eyes. "How are things with Stuart?"

The tone she chooses to use alerts me to the fact that she knew something else, too. Something about Nina and Stuart's relationship.

"Stuart's Stuart," I say.

"What did he tell you?"

"Not much. I was shocked that he knew."

I tell her all that has happened. It feels nice to have Deborah back in my life, a second mum. I hate how badly our relationship has deteriorated.

"Stuart covered it up," she says.

"He couldn't have. Stuart wasn't there. His holiday ended sooner, so he left before it all happened."

"He flew back, inviting an unsuspecting friend for a long weekend away as a guise. Nina and Camilla had forgotten a cooler on the boat and Nina was afraid that when it was discovered on the boat by the owner, another friend of Stuart's, that he'd realize it had been taken out, that it might then lead to further investigations. Stuart and his friend took a day trip. Afterward he gave the boat a thorough clean."

"Does Camilla know?"

"No, as far as I know, I imagine Stuart assumes his secret died with Nina." She pauses. "I'd keep it that way if I were you."

"Why?"

"Knowledge is power," she says in a rehearsed-sounding way.

"I will keep it to myself, but still, I need more than that."

"It's how he got her to marry him so quickly, so young. He did this massive thing for her and Nina cared for him. He loved her. He knew the truth. She felt indebted, greatly so. I didn't know at the time—she didn't tell me until years later."

"He told me he'd felt duped, that—"

"Stuart doesn't like being single. When he met Nina, he was married. Estranged, but married, nonetheless. Meeting Nina encouraged him to rush through with the divorce."

"Oh my God. How can I not know that?"

"Nina didn't like to make it common knowledge."

I don't know why it never occurred to me to ask Stuart about his romantic history. I realize that I've always merely assumed that I knew him inside out. Of course, I don't.

"What happened to his ex-wife?"

"I don't know."

Could it be her behind the threatening cards? Perhaps it wasn't her choice to split up from him, perhaps, deep down she realized that she still loved or missed him and hoped they'd reunite until I was on the scene.

My tea has gone cold. I feel numb, like nothing will ever be normal anymore. I don't know how I'm going to go home and play happy families. How can I not know the man I've known for so long, my...*husband*.

I pay the bill and we leave, walking toward the open area of the village where the ponies roam freely.

"I'm not surprised that Camilla won't tell you," Deborah says, "it was hard enough for Nina to divulge the details. If you really want to know, I'll tell you."

"Fair enough. Thank you."

The anticipation of finding out what happened to Charlie, to really discover the horrible truth, fills me with both fear and relief. When Deborah starts speaking, I almost want to stop her, find some kind of way of hearing but not hearing, like peeking at a horror film through fingers partially covering my eyes.

"Nina said that they decided to take the boat out. It was her idea. She said she was showing off to Camilla, it was *her* boyfriend's connections that gave them access to a boat, *her* newly acquired skill."

Sounds about right, I think.

"But once they set off, she wasn't as confident as she thought. It's one thing doing it when you have an experienced person alongside you on board, obviously quite another when you're wholly responsible. She said that as soon as she realized that, she should've turned back. But she got distracted."

Deborah pauses and glances at me as if she's still unsure whether or not to trust me. I don't blame her, to be fair.

"I want to know," I say. "But I understand this is hard for you."

"It was Camilla and Charlie who distracted her. They were all over each other. Guilt hit her hard. She'd let you walk off by yourself, no doubt thinking that you'd made a fuss over nothing, had overreacted.

"They anchored, I think the word she used was, at Stuart's favorite spot because their original plan was to watch the sunset, but Nina was frightened when reality dawned that it would soon be dark and she wasn't even sure where the lights were or how to turn them on or which one was for what situation. She obviously didn't want to get pulled over by the coast guard or the police. Or worse, cause an accident."

I remember when I first passed my driving test, how it felt totally unbelievable that I was legally allowed out on the roads on my own. How the first time I hit fog unexpectedly on a tiny, country lane, I couldn't recall where the fog light was. I remember the panic that someone was going to smash into the back of my car and tensing my whole body, already braced for impact.

Another memory: Stuart had mentioned that there were rules about lights on boats at night and that he avoided going out too late so that he wouldn't have to return in the dark.

"They argued. All three of them. About leaving, about you."

Sorrow for all our younger selves filters through my happier memories of us being out at sea, huddling in the tiny patches of shade beneath the small canopy in the dazzling afternoon sun. The smell of beer, sun cream and salty air. We really did have our whole lives ahead of us.

Deborah's voice interrupts. Now she's started, she seems unable to stop.

"Nina just wanted to get back, but as she tried to pull away, Charlie grabbed the helm. He was drunk, he wanted to argue his case, he didn't want Nina to tell you."

Why? I wonder. Clearly, he didn't love me as much as I, him.

"But he overbalanced, fell back and hit his head on the side of the cooler or the bottom of the boat, she wasn't sure, she was trying to keep control. Camilla helped him back up, but he just…swayed. Nina turned the boat round toward the shore. At that point, she was going to head back, alight anywhere, ask for help. Camilla took over the steering so that Nina could help steady Charlie, but she realized he was only pretending to be hurt as he lunged at her, begging her not to tell you."

"He was really quite out of it before I even left," I say. "Charlie didn't really have an off switch when it came to drink, drugs, food, life, anything. He always was an all-or-nothing type of person."

"He was furious with Nina—she said it was all a bit of a blur as I can well imagine—and then…Camilla cut the engine to help her and somehow, Charlie got pushed overboard."

"Somehow?"

"It was both of them. They didn't mean to, he was out of control, yelling, they said he was going to punch them both, they were utterly convinced that they'd be knocked out or badly hurt. There was a struggle, they looked over the edge, expecting to see him climb back but there was no sign of him. Nina said it was like a horror film in slow motion, the sky was beginning to dim, even the sea was starting to look black. The boat was rocking badly. Nina almost went overboard herself as she felt dreadfully seasick."

She pauses as a couple walks past.

I'm trying to take it all in, trying to picture the Nina I knew in this scenario.

"I'm very sorry, Marie, but Nina said when they spotted him using the boat's lights—she'd frantically pressed or flicked everything until *something* worked—he was clearly dead. He was facedown and had been in the water for a considerable time by then. He was being dragged away from them, drifting toward the rocks. There was nothing they could do."

"Didn't they even try to get help?"

Charlie's body was eventually found several kilometers away from the area where the boat was kept.

"Yes, of course they wanted to get help. They managed to steer the boat back, but by then they were freezing and in shock. The severity of what had happened dawned on them. They'd effectively stolen the boat, taken 'drugs'—" Deborah mimes quotation marks "—I don't know the names for all the different ones nowadays. Back in the day, we hardly came across anything. There was nothing like the variety on offer today."

"But they might have been able to save him—"

"Nina was adamant that there was absolutely no way. She said that you could just *tell*, they both could, that he was…gone.

There was no one there, they'd got away with it, and so they walked away from the boat. Nina said to me, 'It was one step at a time, Mum.' With each footstep she expected a hand on her shoulder from *someone* but nothing happened. They just... got away with it."

"I've beaten myself up over it for so long. I was so hurt. I loved Charlie. Nina was my friend. I trusted her."

Deborah's characteristic defensiveness returns. "It was self-defense. Them or Charlie. He was a strong lad, according to her."

"Nina and Camilla sat by the pool with me the next day and acted like nothing was wrong. How does anyone do that? It was a horrible feeling. We had to leave not knowing where he was, everyone told me it was normal for people to disappear, especially after a drunken argument. I thought he'd dumped me. People, including Nina and Camilla, implied that he'd probably met someone, or gone on a bender, but no matter what anyone said, there was stupid, naive me thinking it was my fault."

"Shock. Denial. You name it, there are lots of reasons why she kept quiet. What would you have done if she'd told you, burdened you with the secret? She did you a favor, in a way. She protected you."

Fresh anger takes hold, but I don't show it. I don't want to stop Deborah or make her regret telling me.

"Look, I didn't agree with what they did. Of course not. If she'd confided in me before the children...earlier... And Charlie, if he'd had parents, siblings or anyone looking for answers..." She stops. Loses momentum. "If, if, if. Excuses, excuses. The truth is that you protect your family, you do what you have to. Not even Leonard knows. I never thought I'd say these words out loud." She stops and grips my hand, hard. "Don't let me down, Marie. And please, no matter what, don't let those children down."

"I won't, I promise."

"You were a good friend to her, Marie. Continue to give the children, and your baby when he or she is born, the absolute best of you."

"Thank you, Deborah, that means everything to me. I am doing my best and I always will."

"To be honest, it's a relief to talk about it. Keeping it to myself, it makes me feel rotten."

I feel bad for her. Her daughter made one bad decision leading to another years ago, just one monumental fuckup that led to such tragedy, and it is still impacting us now.

"One final thing," I say. "Charlie's backpack, it was never found. He carried it with him most of the time. Did she mention that?"

"They threw it into the sea when they realized...that he wasn't alive. I've no idea why it never reappeared."

Somehow, that feels more calculated than anything else I've heard. It makes things sound even worse. If that's possible. There's so much to take in. As Deborah's revelations properly begin to digest, they twist around in my mind. The word *shock* doesn't even begin to describe the sick feeling permeating my entire body as images of Charlie's last moments torment me, scene by scene, as I picture his body sinking beneath the water into darkness.

Back home, I tell Stuart that I don't feel well. I lock the bathroom door and cry until it physically hurts.

Stuart coaxes me out.

"I understand your grief," he says. "Nothing seems to make it better."

"It is overwhelming," I say. "But there's so much, I really don't know where to start. For one, why didn't you tell me you were married before Nina?"

"I assumed you knew, that she'd have mentioned it?"

"No."

"I was young. We both were, it was a mistake. When I fall, I fall hard."

"Could it be her behind the hatred and mistrust of me? Was she jealous of Nina? Would she have somehow been hoping for a reconciliation?"

"Definitely not."

"How can you be so sure?"

"She lives in Australia."

"Still, are you certain?"

"I never check. We didn't part on good terms."

"Can I have her name, please? I need to check for myself."

"If you must."

I must.

While Stuart sleeps—deeply, how can he do that—I lie as close to the edge of the bed as I dare. My baby moves all the time as though he can sense my underlying, growing fear. Sleep remains elusive. I shiver with cold. I can't get warm. It frightens me that something will go wrong with the pregnancy, that I'll be punished somehow for all the mistakes I've made.

I get up. My search for his ex-wife reveals that there really is nothing to worry about. She is a travel journalist and does still live in Australia. From her stunning social media pictures, she most definitely does not appear to be mourning the loss of Stuart. I was barking up the wrong suspect tree with that theory.

Sleep eludes me as I go over past conversations and memories, coupled with my newfound knowledge, desperate for clues. Listening to Deborah, I got so caught up in her story, so convinced she had all the answers, that I didn't think to question anything thoroughly.

Because, would Nina *really* have told her mother the absolute truth about Charlie's demise? Nina was a natural editor; she regularly painted herself in a favorable light. Realistically, anyone would alter the story to make it palatable. Who would willingly incriminate themselves or tell their mother the raw, brutal facts rather than protect her? It's a valid thought. Which means I can't really trust Deborah's version of events because the more I rerun through her words, the more they sound like a rehearsed, half story.

Camilla sent me to Deborah to hear a soft version. If I add up all the versions (Deborah's, Stuart's, Camilla's and Nina's), they are much the same. I still don't feel as if everything adds up. Not only that, when Charlie's body was found, he had a head injury. It was assumed he hit a rock (foul play was not mentioned), but Deborah said he hit his head on the deck or the cooler. Why on earth would Stuart fly back to Ibiza for Nina? The cooler doesn't seem like a good enough reason. A thought forms and grows until I can't keep it to myself.

"Stuart! Wake up!"

He sits up. "What?"

"You flew back to Ibiza, why?"

He looks utterly flummoxed.

"Was it to find Charlie's Saint Christopher?" I prompt.

He nods.

"Did you?"

"No."

"But you would've got rid of it, even if you had?"

He doesn't reply.

I must get away. I need space to clear my head, sort out facts from imagination before I snap. I deserve the complete truth. There is only one person who can help with that.

THIRTY-ONE

"A holiday? With you?" Camilla frowns. It doesn't suit her. "Are you even allowed to fly?"

"No, of course not. I'm thinking of somewhere closer to home. I'll check out last-minute offers. A seaside cottage in Cornwall, perhaps."

"I appreciate that I haven't lived in this country for years, but even I know you'll have a hard time booking anywhere midsummer holidays at a decent price. Anyway, I can't take a week off work."

"Louise can come with us. You can join in for a long weekend. I'll sort something."

She hesitates, but I can tell that she's itching to say yes so that Louise is entertained. Louise is bored; she spends her days hanging around with me most of the time anyway. Camilla leaves her to fend for herself while she's at work. If it wasn't for me, Louise would be a proper latchkey kid. The poor girl has taken to spending nights at ours more frequently when Camilla invites Greg over. Louise and I have lovely long chats, and it's tempting to share snippets of Charlie's views on life and his funny ways. It is so maddening (and quite sad) that I have this rich insider knowledge of her biological father, and yet it's not my place to tell her or share my memories.

Annoyingly, Camilla is right about the lack of holiday options. I start off with optimistic expectations: private pools or giant glass doors that concertina open, leading straight onto the beach, and end up depressing myself by even considering a dingy place on the outskirts of a large city I don't wish to visit. Images of perfect holiday snaps with joyful #blendedfamilyfun captions (just to publicly prove that I'm doing a good job) dissolve. Stuart isn't keen either.

"I've been on enough wet-weather holidays to last me. I'd rather we go to Disneyland sometime next year, perhaps."

"I need a break now."

He agrees that if I succeed in finding somewhere decent, he'll join us for the week, taking the children home at the weekend to give me time alone.

It strengthens my resolve—how hard can it be—yet, I'm still struggling when Camilla pops round.

"Good news, I've found a place and it's free!"

"Really?"

I wait for the catch and of course, there is one.

"Greg's old house—his parents' originally—is lying empty on Dartmoor. They used to run a small B&B and he hasn't got round to selling it yet." She smiles. "He's much more sentimental than he lets on, that man. Anyway, he says we're welcome to use it if we are happy to ignore the old decor and the steep, death-trap stairs."

"Sounds ideal...not," I say.

"Oh, Marie, you're such a bloody misery all the time. Just tell the children to be careful, it's not as if they're preschoolers." She pauses as she looks at my stomach. "Mind you, you'll have to be wary, too, in your current state. Just resist the temptation to push Stuart down them," she adds with a grin, "and everything will be fine."

If she's noticed my irritation with him, it must be bad.

I grin, too, I can't help it. "I'll try not to."

It's probably the most genuine moment we've shared.

"Isn't Dartmoor a bit bleak?" I can't help saying.

"Only if you choose to see it like that, and I wouldn't imagine so in summer. There will be gorgeous walks and beaches not too far away. Also, there's llama trekking, cycling, all kinds of fabulous, wholesome activities for the children! They'll love it. I'll join in on Friday for the weekend."

I agree to it. If Camilla's on board, that's the whole point. Just me and her, with plenty of time to bond. I'm going to get my answers, even if I have to threaten to throw Camilla down the dodgy staircase myself to get them.

I do my own research and discover waterfalls, climbing and horse riding. Idyllic. Camilla's right, we will have loads to keep us occupied. The children will love the time away, which is an added, positive benefit, despite my underhanded motive.

Before we go away the following week (it can't come soon enough), the urge to visit my mother again is strong.

"She's in the conservatory, love," says my dad when I arrive.

"You go out for a walk or something."

"Thanks. I'll be back in an hour or so," he says.

I wait until I hear the front door close before I speak.

"I knew when I slept with Stuart that it was the right time. I have this thing called an app, you see. I mean, it wasn't guaranteed, it had never worked with Ben. But that night, I knew. I hoped that I had a chance. And it happened. After just one time. I couldn't believe it, but it goes to show that despite what I did, it was surely meant to be, don't you think?"

I wish my mum could say yes.

"I suspect that I couldn't conceive with Ben through guilt," I say. "I know it sounds stupid, but I lied to him not long after we first met. I pretended I was pregnant. I thought I was doing

the right thing, moving us along. Ben could be so bloody indecisive. But I was wrong."

I can't bring myself to confess everything, but it's enough for
now. I brush her hair and straighten her cardigan, then worry
that I'm overfussing before I leave. Still, I do feel slightly lighter
afterward, like I've been given permission to enjoy some of the
August holidays.

Even so, the week drags. I take the children strawberry picking and on one particularly wet day, to an indoor play center.
Still, not-so-distant, inexplicable dread lurks.

I visit the midwife, attend prenatal classes and it's freeing to
get out of the house, which has shrunk around me. Stuart doesn't
like me going out for too long "in case something happens."

"Like what?" I say. I don't need any fuel for my fears and
paranoia.

He shrugs. "I like to know where you are."

"I can look after myself."

"I'm not saying you can't."

Nonetheless, it's suffocating and oppressive.

He's particularly stressed about being in the middle of nowhere when we're in Dartmoor (it's not that cutoff if the situation arises), but still, it was much harder to win him round to
the idea than I thought it would be.

The threatening cards dry up. Maybe it was Deborah and
now that we've had a little heart-to-heart, she's decided to back
off. Until now, my money was definitely on Tamsin. It could
even have been more than one person, which is a horrible
thought. I hate not knowing and being suspicious of everyone,
from people in the book group to my neighbors. Whoever it
is has decided that it's not worth the risk because of the camera, which records nothing but genuine visitors, post and delivery people. I waste hours of my life viewing endless film,

staring at the gravel on the driveway, scanning for suspicious passersby on the lane.

Perhaps there really is nothing to fear.

The night before we go away, having packed and completed all the necessary tasks, I pace downstairs, desperate to feel comfortable. I'm forced to give up and pour all my energy into my photo project: the one to celebrate Nina's memory. I turn the pages. There's something so rewarding about capturing a moment that will never be repeated. Even now, I still enjoy catching people unawares. It drove Nina mad, but only when she didn't like the picture.

"I look too fat, too miserable, my hair looks crap..." she'd moan.

But when she liked them, it was different. She'd get me to print extra copies, and we'd experiment together with black-and-white and color effects. Any money I earned from my Saturday job was spent, not on clothes or stuff, but my photo-taking hobby. I told Nina I'd destroy any photos that she didn't like, but I didn't. However much people say they hate pictures of themselves, they're a part of history.

Our faces naturally altered as we grew up, attended art college and went on our Ibizan holiday. Our collective expressions were unencumbered by worry, guilt or regret, despite my resentment simmering beneath the surface. People underestimate the innate desire to belong. It can be all-consuming, given the right cocktail of vulnerability and desperation.

I want to correct people when they refer to Ibiza as "the party place" because although it undeniably is, the soft sandy beaches are its best kept secret. (I sometimes wonder if the island hugs the knowledge of its beautiful landscape to itself as tourists flock to the clubs and bars.)

Of course, I have included images of the sea and landscape, the blues and greens, but among these are the hippy markets,

Nina and me on the disco bus on our way to a club, the reds, oranges, golds and pinks of sunsets.

I stop. The next images include Charlie. I remove them and pile them to one side. Yet I can't stop myself from looking at his eyes. Louise's eyes. Would our future children have had green eyes, too, if things had turned out differently?

The floorboards upstairs creak. One of the children? Please let it not be Stuart, I want to be alone. It goes silent. I exhale, until then not even realizing I'd been holding my breath.

I've inserted more happy-looking wedding photos than I'd initially intended, for the children's sake. I study Nina's expressions again with my benefit of knowledge. Yet again, I hate that Nina deceived us all. She does not betray a hint of concern or doubt. I've always prided myself on my ability to photograph the truth. If I'm wrong, where does it leave me workwise in the future? I want to come out from the shadows, show people what I'm capable of.

I have great plans for when I get back into the swing of work. I intend to build on my previous good name. The thought cheers me. I've been feeling lost. I've allowed what happened to Nina to have an impact on me, too. I got caught up in her problems and dramas when I didn't need to. Nina was always good at tugging me into her world, despite not trusting me when it mattered most.

In between the pictures of the wedding and the arrival of first Felix, then Emily, I could have added one or two of their honeymoon. But I couldn't. I thought of passing them off by saying that Nina had given them to me, that they'd been taken by a stranger, but Stuart isn't stupid. The shame of admitting that I spent a night on the same island as them in the Whitsundays because I felt left out is too great. It would be too implausible to pass off as a mere "one of those things."

I do have limits. Lies have to contain an element of believable-enough truth. I did spot Nina and Stuart when I was in the same hotel for one night. I watched as Nina sat at the breakfast buffet and Stuart got up to get her coffee, piled her plate with food, was generally there to do her bidding. I admit, I was jealous. Not because I necessarily wanted that, but because she was clearly his world.

Nina loved parties. She'd throw one on her birthday every year. There were way too many to include, so I've picked out a few of the best: highlights of her looking her most radiant and happy.

One in particular stands out as a clear winner. She'd held a barbecue (but splashed out on caterers) during an uncharacteristic early autumn heatwave. She is wearing a pale pink dress and a cowboy hat. Her favorite necklaces (obviously she couldn't decide on just the one that night) adorn her neck. I remember that party well because it was the first time I didn't personally know all of Nina's friends.

It's impossible not to pick up on the change in fashions (and hairstyles!) over the years, the hard-to-miss transitions from flares to skinny jeans or short skirts to long. I glance at some of the partygoers—it's so much easier now I'm not the outsider and it doesn't hurt so much. I recognize people I didn't know then—there's Tamsin wearing the same style of cowboy hat as Nina. (Was *that* the theme? I don't recall.) There are also shots of Sharon, Greg and Miriam, plus lots more people from the school and village who are now my friends, too.

The last pictures taken were after Nina's diagnosis. I worked incredibly hard at not making these shots staged while I took pictures of them all at home, going about their day-to-day lives. Nina wanted them to have ordinary memories recorded, too, not just the obvious celebrations and milestones. She and Stuart baked with them, played board games, went cycling, "messed around" in the garden in the paddling pool, played hide-and-seek. Happy family moments, all immortalized. By me.

The final pictures are of us: me, Stuart, Felix, Emily and Goldie. My bump is clearly visible.

I hear footsteps.

Stuart appears and floods the kitchen with light.

"Can't sleep either?" he says.

"No, too uncomfortable."

"What are you doing?" Stuart points to the remaining few photos that didn't make the album.

"Finishing off Nina's memory album. I want everything in order before the baby's born."

"Nesting," he says. "Nina was—"

"Please don't tell me that Nina was the same."

"Sorry." He smiles. "And you're right. About Felix and Em. About the adoption. It's just that everything has happened so fast. If someone had told me a few years ago that this would be my life now, it wouldn't have seemed possible."

"Join the club. Some days I lie there when I first wake up and really can't quite believe it either."

Stuart picks up the pile of photos I've removed. "What are these?"

I want to snatch them from him. They're mine. They're personal.

"Pictures that include Charlie."

He glances through them.

I hold my breath.

He puts them back down.

The one on the top is the one I found in the attic, the one I love of Charlie, despite Nina and Camilla on either side of him. Boat masts are visible in the distance behind them (which I can easily remove), farther beyond is the sea. He is wearing a blue T-shirt with an image of a shark on the front. He loved that T-shirt almost as much as Nina loved the leopard print shoes she broke that night. I'll get some more copies printed. I will cut Camilla out of mine completely, yet I realize that if she ever decides to tell Louise the truth about her father, the poor girl may appreciate this one of her father and mother together. I'm sure that Christian would approve of me accepting things and moving on, if I ever decide to tell him.

Stuart pulls me close, kisses my neck. "Come back to bed."

"In a bit, I'm in the middle of something."

He persists.

I try to reciprocate, I really do, I don't wish to ruin this moment. I follow him upstairs, as slowly as I can, my mind desperately searching for the right way to convey my reluctance in a tactful way.

The right words don't come to me in time even though I want to stay downstairs, alone, in peace, and study the photos some more. There's something about the image of Charlie, Camilla and Nina that feels unsettling but my mind can't quite home in on what I think is wrong.

In bed, I mentally study the background: the sea, the boats, the horizon. But like an elusive Spot the Difference image, there's nothing tangible that I can latch on to.

Perhaps I'm looking to the past to find answers when really, my life is here now. Somehow, right now, just the thought of the permanence of everything makes me flick back through all the pivotal moments to try to pinpoint exactly where I may have made a bad decision. The conclusion I come to is that there may have been many. It is not a comforting thought.

THIRTY-TWO

Most murders are committed by someone the victim is connected to. Mainly their spouses. Everyone knows that. Stuart is a middle-lane driver and it takes all of my self-control not to insist that I do all the driving. Thankfully, our route is predominantly non-motorway and the children are delighted because we stop at a burger place for lunch that offers free ice-cream desserts on the kids' menu.

As we enter the open landscape of Dartmoor National Park, I relax. Following the quiet road leading to Greg's address, I take in the scenery. Granite tors are visible against the green moorland. Occasional paths snake through the flatness, marking out potential walkways. My dad recently told me that we camped somewhere in the area when I was young, but nothing feels familiar.

When we pull up outside the stone cottage, I'm both apprehensive and delighted at its remote location. Inside, it is fairly dark. Some of the stone floor tiles are uneven, and there's little natural light, but at least it's fresh-smelling. (According to Camilla, Greg has someone who cleans, does a spot of gardening and keeps an eye.)

The stairs aren't quite as horrendous as Camilla made out, but overall it's the type of place that could be described as in need of improvement. There are five bedrooms. I let Felix, Emily and Louise choose their own. I have to hide the old-fashioned keys from the bedroom locks inside a chest of drawers in our room because the kids take immediate delight in locking each other (and themselves) in their rooms. The main bathroom is in definite need of immediate refurbishment, but the room we've picked has a fairly modern en suite. Stuart busies himself making up the beds with our own linen.

The worst room, a smallish one at the end of the corridor, with a view over the dilapidated garden shed and an unkempt section of the back garden, will be Camilla's.

I help Louise unpack. I've never spent quite this much time alone with her (without the inevitable distractions of home life), and it's strangely disconcerting in a I'm-not-sure-how-to-make-conversation kind of way. I desperately want her to feel welcome. She's neat, likes her things just so. Like her father. I suggest we head downstairs where she can help unpack the groceries in the kitchen.

Later, Stuart takes them out for a walk to explore while I have a doze on the sofa. I wake up with a start, dripping with sweat and utterly disoriented. When everyone returns, their faces red asking for snacks and drinks and full of questions about what they're going to do next, Stuart takes one look at me, makes me some tea and orders me to go and lie on the bed upstairs.

Listening to the muffled sounds of excited chatter beneath me, I plan what I'm going to say to Camilla. Spending time with Louise has renewed my resolve. Before too long, she does deserve to know the truth about who her father was.

I opt out of most activities, leaving Stuart to get on with it. Louise is a delight; she's slotted in with us as though she belongs. I sit in cafés and read. It's bliss.

As he's preparing dinner on our final evening before Camilla arrives, I take a cool shower. Stepping out into the bedroom, it strikes me that I can't imagine Greg living here, even though he comes across as quite a loner. Camilla aside, I've never heard him mention a special anyone, apart from moving to our village a while ago "for love," as he described it. Dressed in a loose tracksuit, I wander around all the rooms. In Camilla's, there is a writing desk in the corner. I open the drawers. They are empty, as is the wardrobe.

Downstairs, I make myself a chamomile tea.

"Smells nice," I say to Stuart, indicating the pasta sauce simmering on the gas stove. "I'll lay the table."

Still unfamiliar with the location of everything (there's an abundance of crockery, place mats, glasses and just stuff, presumably from the B&B days), I open most drawers and cupboards. One is crammed full of paperwork. I try to shut it again, but it jams. I pull out the top layers and retry. It works, but I drop the pile. They fan out on the kitchen tiles.

"I'll get them," Stuart says.

As he does so, dumping them on the table, a bold font catches my eye. As I read, I hear Stuart say, "Fancy a small wine?"

I stop reading and smile. He's been great company this week. Perhaps he's not as bad as I've feared lately. "I'll have a spritzer with dinner."

I glance back down and continue reading an invoice for a photography course. The name of the company is familiar, and it eventually dawns on me why. It's the same course Nina took. I remember seeing it when I sorted out her files.

I check the date: the year after Felix was born. Something niggles. I'd assumed that the course they did had been more recent, more local to us, for some reason. But the four-day residential course was nearby, here, in Dartmoor.

I do the math as I think back to the photos I recently viewed. Greg had been at the barbecue to celebrate Nina's birthday, a year before he moved to the area. I access the copies of Nina's album on my phone. I scroll, then enlarge Greg's face. I don't think I'm imagining it: he's staring in Nina's direction with what I can only perceive as admiration or longing. It's unnerving.

My appetite disappears as I sit down opposite Stuart at dinner. I go through the motions of conversation with the children, but it's hard. I can't stop thinking about Greg and Nina, because no matter how I try to look at it, I can't shake off the feeling that Nina was Greg's mystery love. If that's true, then I've missed even more than I realized.

Camilla's arrival the following lunchtime brings further unsettlement. I'd forgotten that it somehow takes a few days to get into a holiday rhythm, more so, I now realize, when you're a family. A late guest shakes up the routine. Her arrival makes me doubt the wisdom of my plan. I'm unsure how to be with her: is she a genuine guest, a fellow holiday companion, an unlikely friend or an enemy I need to be wary of? Our relationship is more blurred than ever.

We opt for a waterfall visit. I'll walk as far as feels comfortable, then chill in the café nearby. I may even suggest that Camilla accompany me back down. Perhaps I can get her to talk candidly then, rather than force it out of her somehow.

Lush green foliage borders the lakes. We select one of the easier walks, supposedly for me, but really it's for Emily, and meander through fern gardens. It's the coolest I've felt all week, and caught up in nature's beauty, it briefly dulls my ever-gnawing need to push Camilla for the truth. But every time I catch sight of Louise's smile or hear her laugh, it reminds me that I owe this to Charlie.

Random dark thoughts ping into my mind. Like, how easy it would be to push Camilla over and onto the rocks. Bye bye, Camilla. I even conduct the imaginary aftermath conversation in my head: *It was an accident, she slipped right in front of me. So shocking. So terrible.* I'd adopt Louise as well as Felix and Em.

I stop myself. I'm glad no one can read my thoughts.

★ ★ ★

While Stuart and the children are packing up in the morning (he is going to drop Louise at her grandparents' for the weekend), my resolve is tested when Louise asks if she can stay with us instead. Everyone looks at me. Camilla doesn't want to admit to Louise that she's invited Greg to join us. "We'll go out, leave you in peace," Camilla had said. "Greg wants to show me his home area, so sweet, don't you think?"

I am the one forced to break the silence. "We'd love you to, sweetie, but your mum and I have things to talk about."

Camilla throws me a grateful look. She has no idea that I'm telling the truth.

"Plus, Granny and Grandad are looking forward to seeing you," Camilla says.

She's a good liar and she does it well by focusing on a true fact (her parents adore Louise) and omitting the truth, which is that she is putting spending time with her lover before her daughter's wishes. I will never be a selfish mother. That's one of the problems with people like Camilla; because she fell pregnant with such ease, she has assumed that being a mother is a right, not a gift. She'll learn.

I give Louise an understanding look. She and I have grown even closer these past few days. I hope she understands that I have no choice in this instance. She gives me a trusting smile, which is no doubt helped by Emily insisting that she won't get in the car unless Louise comes, too.

"She's my new big sister," she says.

I give Emily a huge smile of encouragement. Louise has been such a positive influence, not just on Emily, but on the whole family dynamic.

For a freaky moment, I think that Emily winks at me, but of course she didn't. It's just my nerves at how far I may need to go to force the truth out about what really happened on board that boat in Ibiza.

I kiss everyone goodbye and let Camilla wave them off. As she does so, I message Greg and ask him if there's any way he could delay his arrival until tomorrow.

I'd rather you didn't let on to Camilla that I've asked. I feel we need some girlie

(I can't think of a better word right now.)

time alone. I think it's what we need to sort out our past differences. However, I do completely understand if it's not possible.

He responds almost immediately with a thumbs-up emoji. It makes me think that he wasn't that fussed about coming anyway.

Camilla's phone beeps not a minute later. Greg's name flashes up on her screen before disappearing. I can't read it all, it disappears too quickly, but he's gone along with my request, no questions asked.

I go upstairs and wait for Camilla to digest the news that she and I have the next twenty-four hours with only each other for company. The quiet of the house without the others is already beginning to unnerve me. Yet, I must see this through. I silently work through my options.

THIRTY-THREE

As I walk downstairs, clutching the metal railing attached to the wall, I re-rehearse what I'm going to say. Camilla is on the sofa, feet curled up beneath her thighs, flicking through a magazine she clearly has zero interest in.

"Greg is delayed," she says.

"I know. It's my fault," I say.

She puts down the magazine and looks up. "What do you mean?"

"I explained that we needed time alone to talk."

She frowns, a bit too theatrically. "What about?"

"I'd like the truth about what happened to Charlie. Deborah spun a good story, but I know it's not the whole truth. Please tell me exactly what happened that night."

She looks around the sitting room as though expecting a camera crew to appear from somewhere, or the police. I understand how she feels. It's hard nowadays not to fear that every move is being captured, ready to be held in future evidence against you.

I try to put her at ease. "It's just you and me," I say. "No cameras, no one else listening."

She gives a little laugh. "It's nothing like that. It's just that Nina told me that she'd told Deborah everything."

"She gave Deborah a PG version. It was entertaining, it had me hooked while I was listening, until I twigged that there has to be an X-rated version that's being kept from me."

"For God's sake, Marie. Charlie fell off a boat. It was an accident. End of. You have a baby on the way. Move on."

"I can't. I need to know. I thought my future was with Charlie. I thought that he and I would have children. We talked about it."

"I'm sorry. For what I did. It was wrong, but you have to let it go. I'm not discussing this anymore. If I'd known you'd planned a confessional session, I'd never have come. I thought you merely wanted a change of scene or a break from the kids." She stands up. "I'm calling Greg to tell him that you made a mistake. If you don't want to stay here with us, and really, why would you, I'm happy to give you a lift to the station."

"What do you know about Greg's ex?"

"Which one?"

"The one he moved to the village for."

"Nothing much. I'm not that fussed about who he was with before me. We enjoy each other's company. It's early days. Why are *you* so interested in his exes?"

"Because I think he and Nina had a fling or something."

She sits back down.

Now, I've got her attention.

She dismisses my theory instantly. "Why would he have pursued me so intently if that were the case? Wouldn't it be a little creepy?"

"Has he ever asked you about your past, anything to do with Nina, the holiday?"

"No…" She stops. "Actually, yes. I have a picture of the three of us on an Ibizan party boat. He asked about where and when it was taken."

My pulse quickens.

"Anything else?"

"Just…you know, the random stuff you talk about when you first meet someone. I didn't think anything of it."

"You didn't think anything of what?"

"He questioned me about any stupid things I'd regretted, but I thought he was referring to dodgy exes. The holiday with Nina came up because she was, apart from you, our common link. I even told him about my stint in the ridiculous fake champagne glass."

We both laugh.

"But he did seem interested in Charlie's death. Which, thinking about it now, considering he'd never met the guy…" She stands up again and paces the living room. "This is screwing with my head way too much."

I up the pressure; I need her to crack.

"He *is* a PI. Being inquisitive and curious is his job. He likes to unmask the bad guy."

"I'm going for a drive."

She picks up her bag and leaves before I can persuade her otherwise.

This wasn't in my plan.

I'm trapped, unless I give up completely on the weekend and my plans. Camilla's belongings are still here; it gives me confidence she'll return. She's already moved her stuff into Louise's much nicer old room, and to while away the time, I have a good look around. What I'm hoping to find, I don't know. She has two pairs of sneakers, a pair of heels (for the countryside! It reminds me of Nina), no books and three cosmetic bags bursting with makeup. I place a bottle of water on her bedside table, it makes me feel less guilty about coming in here. All it needs is a chocolate on the pillow and it would look really quite professional.

Still restless, I go through the pile of Greg's paperwork, hoping to find hotel receipts or gifts I'd recognize as belonging to

Nina, but there is nothing. Having run out of entertainment options, I open the fridge door, briefly mulling over dinner choices, then close it again. I pace the kitchen and living areas, all the unanswered questions building up further in my mind. I sit at the dining table, nursing a cup of ginger tea, and come up with potential solutions to prevent me from driving myself into unbearable frustration. An idea forms. It's not ideal, but I have to work within the constraints of a real situation, not my fantasy or preferred one.

Tiredness hits. I lie down on the bed, but I can't settle. I feel exposed and vulnerable, alone in the middle of nowhere. I go and bolt the front and back doors before going back upstairs. Again.

Heavy banging pierces my dream about being on holiday in a desert. For several seconds I have no clue where I am. I sit up and take a large sip of water. The knocking continues. Groggy, I clutch the rail and walk slowly downstairs.

"Marie! Marie! Answer the bloody door!"

Camilla.

She pushes the door open wider as soon as I open it. "You had me worried."

"Where did you go? Did you get in touch with Greg?"

She holds up some shopping bags. "No, I did this instead. Retail therapy. I even bought you a gift."

She hands over a bag. I accept, but hesitate to look inside. Gifts are tricky things—they make me feel beholden.

I give in. "Thanks."

I peek inside. Layered among flimsy blue tissue are lemon and raspberry bath bombs. The smell is cloying.

I escape to the bathroom to wash my face and to properly waken up. And that's when it hits me what has been bothering me about the photo of Charlie, Nina and Camilla: a memory.

Nina hadn't been keen for me to sift through her photos when I asked for ones of Charlie. She wanted to select them herself.

No wonder. She knew I had a keen eye for detail. I thought it was because she was being sensitive, perhaps by protecting me from potentially unsettling memories. How stupid and naive of me. Despite knowing what I know now, the sense of betrayal hits me afresh as my mind reruns the story.

They said they left Charlie behind at the party. By the time I left, Nina had already broken her shoe and had changed back into sneakers. In the photo, she is not wearing her heels. Yet, I clearly remember her changing into them beforehand because we all laughed at her as we walked in the direction of the loud music while she struggled along a narrow, uneven beach pavement.

I take out the picture. The coloring of the sky reveals that it is later than I initially appreciated. The party was slightly away from the harbor, so if it had been taken there, the boats would not be visible in the background. This is physical proof that they lied—it proves that they all left at the same time.

I shudder. This is surely the last photo ever taken of Charlie alive and it's a macabre thought. So many niggling things that didn't quite make sense at the time are coming together. Fresh waves of grief, pain, rage and humiliation hit because it's as if by having something tangible, it makes it even more real somehow.

Back downstairs, Camilla is microwaving a ready-made lasagna.

I slide out a bottle of white wine from the fridge and offer her a glass.

"Hoping to get me drunk to prize out a better story than Deborah's?" she says.

"Yes," I admit, pouring her a large glass.

I'm not going to tell her about the photo evidence yet. I want to hear the truth from her first.

"You'll have a long wait," she says.

The evening is not the bonding, confessional one I planned. Camilla has clearly decided on several safe topics for discussion and won't allow me to veer off her preplanned course. All she'll say is that she's not going to mention anything about what we discussed to Greg.

"It's not as if it will lead to anything serious anyway. We're too different."

She takes a large gulp of wine as she tries to convince herself that her words are true. I discreetly check the bottle; it's almost empty. My agitation grows as I watch the hands of the kitchen clock move ever later. I open another bottle while she loads the dishwasher and top up her glass.

She catches me.

"Nice try, Marie. But luckily for you, I'm in the mood to get pissed enough to get through tonight."

Good, she's going to need anaesthetizing.

I run the kitchen tap and pour myself a large glass of water.

Finally (thank you, God) she heads upstairs.

"I'm going to change into my PJs. Don't top up my glass any more just yet," she says. "And by the way, I know how much is left in the bottle. I'm not that far gone!"

"Don't worry, I promise not to get you drunk enough to push you down the stairs."

Shut up, I tell myself. I'm waffling. I'm going to give myself away.

I wait for a few seconds before I follow her up. It isn't easy doing it quietly—the stairs creak. My heart hammers. I remove the key from the pocket of my maternity jeans and turn her bedroom door lock.

I spent far too long overthinking the whole situation. When, in the end, it's usually the simple solutions that work best.

THIRTY-FOUR

Camilla wastes no time in pulling on the doorknob.

"Marie, this isn't funny."

I pull a chair out of Felix's old room and make myself as comfortable as is possible, given the circumstances. "I agree. Tell me what really happened to Charlie, and I'll let you go."

"I have told you." She yanks some more. The door shakes.

"I don't believe you."

"Marie! This is bloody ridiculous. Really, what do you think you're going to achieve?"

"I want the truth."

She kicks the door next, the pounding echoes. My poor baby kicks, too. I stand up.

"Desperate measures," I say when she gets bored of trying to smash the door down. "This is your fault. We can do this quickly or slowly."

"Aaaaah!" she screams.

Her phone rings downstairs. It's still ringing by the time I reach it. I snatch it up off the counter.

Greg.

I open the back door and walk outside. The bashing noises subside.

"Hi, Greg. It's Marie. How are you?"

The sun is setting. How can it not be dark yet? This day has gone on forever and if Camilla remains stubborn, it's only going to get longer. Golds, yellows and oranges streak the horizon. It reminds me of Ibiza. It's a sign; it strengthens my resolve.

"Where's Camilla?"

"Getting into her pajamas."

"Can I speak to her?"

"I get the impression she's going to be a while. Shall I get her to call you back?"

"Tell her I'll be there by tomorrow lunchtime. Are you two having the catch-up you wanted?"

"Kind of. Thanks, Greg. I appreciate you giving us the time."

"Bye then."

I nearly ask him about Nina, but now is not the time. I want to see his face when I do pick my moment.

I hang up, slide the phone into my pocket and as I return to Camilla, a strange resolve descends. I have to do this. For my own sanity and for Charlie's memory. And for the baby we didn't have. It motivates me to keep going. I crouch down (it's not easy given my size) and peer through the keyhole. It's dark. Realization dawns that it's because her eye is peering back. It's freaky. I yank my face away and sit back down on the chair.

"Greg sends his love."

"Are you two in this together?"

I reassure her that the answer is no. However, if she's banking on the thought that he's going to rescue her—worst-case scenario—tomorrow, she may well try to hold out until he arrives, so I mention that he's not sure of his latest arrival time.

"Camilla. Please. So we can both get some sleep tonight, just tell me what I need to know."

"If you think I'm spending the night under the same roof as you, you really have lost it. What the hell is wrong with you, Marie?"

"I was pregnant. With Charlie's baby. You stole the child that I should've had. Imagine what it feels like for me seeing Louise. You have no sensitivity, no awareness, no conscience."

It goes silent.

"Now, will you tell me?" I say.

"I am sorry, Marie. Let me out first and I'll tell you whatever you want to know."

"No."

The kicking starts up again. I've had enough for now. My back aches, my legs ache. I ease up out of the chair and walk to our bathroom. I run a bath. The water further muffles the sounds of Camilla's escape attempts. She needs time to reflect and I need a break. The bathroom mirror mists. I wipe it and stare at myself. What have I done? How did I turn into this person? Why am I not at home, in my own bed?

I ease into the water and close my eyes. It lifts some of the tension immediately. I almost give into the tiredness until I hear the creaking sound of the bathroom doorknob twisting. Oh my God!

I jolt up and grab a towel to cover myself. The door opens but no one appears.

"Who's there?" My voice cracks.

Silence, apart from the loud, rhythmic thudding of my heart. "Camilla?" I call out.

I hear someone breathing. I freeze until I hear Camilla's curt voice. Relief floods my entire body.

"You're lucky you're heavily pregnant," says Camilla, still hidden from sight behind the wooden door. "Otherwise I'd do a lot worse. Where is my phone?"

My legs are still shaking as I clamber out, dripping water all over the bath mat as I rush to dry myself.

"Who let you out?"

"The lock broke. You're paying for Greg to get the whole door fixed because I'm not. Now where is my phone?"

It's still in the pocket of my jeans, which are crumpled on the bathroom floor. I pull her phone out, turn it off and slide it beneath the bath mat.

"Um..."

The door flings open and Camilla stands there. Her face is flushed, her expression is demonic. "Get dressed and give me my phone before I pull the whole place to pieces!"

She looks around, sees my clothes on the floor, picks them up and gives them a shake before slamming the door.

I dry myself too quickly. As I pull on the same jeans, they stick to my legs. I nearly fall over. I can hear Camilla in my bedroom, pulling open drawers and slamming them shut. I open the door.

"Listen, Camilla—"

"Don't 'listen Camilla' me, give me my phone, you thieving cow! I should've known better than to let myself be talked into this ridiculous break. To think it was me who persuaded Greg that you were a reasonable, rational person who could be trusted to rent his property. Never again."

"I've hidden your phone outside, you won't find it in here. I'll return it when you've told me what I want to hear."

She screams and storms out the bedroom, slamming the door behind her.

I open it and follow her downstairs. The door to her bedroom is wide-open. The chair I was sitting on lies on the floor.

Camilla is clutching her car keys. "If you won't give me my phone, I'm still getting far away from you."

"You're drunk," I say.

"I don't care," she says.

"Do you want to hurt someone or worse, potentially kill another person? Are you trying to get yourself sent to prison? Think of Louise, think of someone else other than yourself for a change."

"I need to get away from here."

"Let's go for a drive. I'm insured to drive other cars. You tell me what I want to hear. I'll give you back your phone as soon as we're done."

She stares. She really is quite drunk.

"You gave me such a fright creeping into the bathroom like that," I say. "I might need to be close to a hospital to get the baby checked out. I'm feeling a bit panicky, suddenly a bit too cutoff from everywhere."

It's not a complete lie, I did feel a twinge of pain as I walked downstairs.

It does the trick.

"Let's get in the bloody car then. But I want my phone."

"As soon as we get back, I promise."

We both climb into her car. I have to adjust the seat and move it quite far back so that I can fit in behind the steering wheel. Luckily, her car isn't dissimilar to Stuart's, which I've driven on occasion. I press Record on my phone (for what it's worth) and place it down by the side of the driver's door, out of her reach, then adjust the rearview mirror.

It's now dark. I drive down the empty lane, properly aware for the first time just how isolated the moor is and how easy it would be to get lost.

"I'm listening," I say, to give Camilla a prompt.

She looks as if she might pass out asleep. It's definitely not what I need her to do.

It's eerie, surrounded by darkness, apart from the headlights. I reach a crossroads. Left or right? I opt for right. Camilla stares out of the passenger window into nothingness.

"All right. We killed Charlie accidentally on purpose. Is that what you want to hear?"

My legs go weak. "Go on."

She tells the same leaving-the-party story I've now heard before, followed by the taking-of-the-boat one.

"Charlie and I had a fight." She speaks in a monotone. "Over you. He wanted to go back and find you. He said lots of vile things to me, he had a real mean streak. We fought. He wanted to turn the boat around, he threatened to jump overboard and swim back to shore. He wanted to tell you the truth about us, tell you he was sorry. I mean, who did Charlie think he was? He let me believe that I was special, that you and he were all but over. Then, out in the middle of the bloody ocean when we're off to romantically watch a sunset, after he'd let you storm off as if he didn't have a care in the bloody world *and* after I'd risked our friendship, he does a complete about-face. I didn't deserve to be treated like that! Nina started yelling at me, too, saying that she'd been put in a shitty position. Like it was all about her! Charlie stood really close to the edge. Nina yelled at him to step back."

She stops.

She pushed him in on purpose, I know she did.

"And you pushed him."

She doesn't reply.

I'm prepared to take her silence as a yes until she says, so softly it's hard to hear, "We both did."

Oh. My. God.

"We fought some more. I tried to stop him, but then he got really nasty. We were both really scared of him, Marie. You've heard what you wanted to hear."

I'm filled with renewed rage, that she killed not only Charlie, but my future—our future—along with him. I remain silent, focusing on the road ahead. I'm not certain how long we've been driving. I see a sign for a village six miles away.

"Okay," she continues. "I hit him on the head first, with some kind of metal pole thing. He picked it up first. I panicked. We managed to wrestle it off him. Nina threw it into the sea afterward. But it was an accident. I didn't mean to hit him and I didn't mean for him to fall. If we hadn't got him under control, we all could've died. We were out at sea, for God's sake! Now are you happy?"

Oh my God. It's worse than I feared. Charlie's head injury wasn't from the boat or the deck.

"What did you do afterward? You and Nina didn't get back until it was nearly morning."

"We were in shock. Terrified. We returned some things to the villa, including the boat key. We talked and figured out our story. We even briefly went back to the beach, pointlessly, to see if a miracle was going to occur and that Charlie would magically reappear from the darkness, safe and well."

I don't want to hear any more. It sounds more like murder than manslaughter. I need proper distance between us.

We drive in silence. I thought we'd have reached the village by now. I check—we've been driving for over eight miles. I must've missed a turn somewhere. There are no lights, no signs of life close by. I don't want to be anywhere near her. I've never hated her more. I want to push her out and leave her to find her own way home. Let her be frightened. Let her feel helpless.

Poor Charlie. I feel winded. I pull over to the side of the road, open the window and take some deep breaths.

Camilla watches me but doesn't say anything. Even she seems to realize that she's said enough. Surrounded by darkness, I can hear her breathing. Is she frightened? I reach down with my fingers and check my phone. No signal.

Camilla, swift and predatory in her realization, lean overs me and tries to grab it. I am faster. I drop it back down to my side, release the hand brake and pull away from our secluded spot, relieved when the white signpost (only one more mile) to the next village is illuminated by our headlights.

As we pull into the village, I see a pub. The lights are on and there is a board outside offering bed and breakfast. Perfect. For Camilla. I pull into the parking lot.

"Get out," I say.

"I'm not getting out of my own car in the middle of nowhere."

"Fine. I'll call the police and tell them that I had to stop you drunk driving. I want you out. You have your handbag, stay the night here, order a cab, I don't care. But I'm not driving you back."

"You can't do this."

"Watch me," I say, as a surge of rage gives me strength when she makes no effort to get out.

I unclip her seat belt, open my door, stride around the back of the car and yank open the passenger door. She tries to pull it shut again but isn't quick enough. She leans away from me as if she's planning on climbing over to the driver's side, so I pull hard on her arm.

I realize just quite how drunk Camilla still is as she loses her balance and half stumbles, half falls out of the car. She staggers slightly before putting out her arms and reaching for the side of a nearby truck, leaning against it for support. I reach inside for her bag, throw it down on the ground beside her and slam the door.

I rush back round, slide into my seat and shift the gear to Reverse. I pull away, driving slowly enough to check the rear-view mirror and see Camilla pick up her bag, briefly rummage through it, then disappear through the entrance to the pub. I pick up as much speed as possible, given my surroundings. The growing distance between us is a welcome relief.

I grip the steering wheel. I've no idea where I'm going, only that it will do Camilla good to have some more time to reflect. The area is unrecognizable in the darkness, of course it is. I must go back, this is madness. I am directionless in the middle of nowhere.

I pull over to set the GPS, when a wave of pain knifes my stomach. Feeling sick, I open the door and lean out. Cold, harsh realization hits as the second pain forces me to get out and pace up and down the deserted road.

As soon as it eases, I call Stuart. It goes to voice mail. Icy fear ups my indecision a notch. Do I try to drive back to the house? Call an ambulance? Camilla. God, why did I think it was such a good idea to leave her behind? Even her drunken, horrible company is better than being alone right now. I take some deep breaths.

I feel better, much more in control, as I restart the car. Think. I must come up with a proper plan: return to Camilla, tell her we're even (we're not, but now is definitely not the time). She can drive me to a hospital if the pains worsen to get checked out; it's too early for the baby to come. I turn the car around until I remember that Camilla is in no fit state to drive.

I'm on my own.

THIRTY-FIVE

The decision is made for me. The pains subside long enough for me to drive myself to the nearest hospital twenty miles away. Stuart was right to be concerned, for once. I can't take any risks with my baby's health, not after all I've been through. Camilla will be all right. Worst-case scenario, she'll have to pay an expensive cab fare back to the property. Greg will be with her by lunchtime.

Fresh pain hits and distracts as I leave the car in the hospital parking lot. I follow the signs to the maternity unit as I try to call Stuart again. Thank God he answers, albeit in a sleepy, hoarse voice.

My plight spills out in a torrent of jumbled words.

"What? Slow down, Marie. Where are you?"

I name the hospital. "Please, call Deborah to look after Felix and Em. Get here quickly. Just in case."

As I walk through the automatic doors, sickness swamps. I'm terrified. I thought I was a strong person, could take anything. I'm not. Everything I thought I'd learned or prepared for doesn't happen. There is no order, only sickness, pain and desperately busy staff. I want to die.

My baby is putting in an early appearance.

Time passes in changes of medical staff. I take every drug I'm offered and give in to the surreality. I didn't think I'd be able to stay still long enough to have an injection in my spine, but I can't wait for it to work its magic powers once the anesthesiologist has been located. I think I see my dead grandmother. I even see Nina at one point.

I drift in and out of reality. I'm told to push. To not push. I'm sick. I'm hot, I'm cold. I'm terrified yet resigned simultaneously. The baby is back-to-back, meaning that he is pressing against my spine. There is talk of forceps, of a cesarean. I don't care as long as my baby comes out alive and all this is over. Time is suspended and distorted, yet the end comes in sight swiftly.

"Your baby's heart is in distress," I'm told. "We need to take you into the operating room and deliver the baby quickly."

I sign a consent form while the risks are read out loud to me. "Is my husband here yet?"

A midwife squeezes my hand. "He's on his way. He won't be long."

She has no way of knowing, but I'm grateful for the lie, nonetheless. I stare at the ceiling as I'm wheeled to the operating room. I look up at the largest round lights I've ever seen, like UFOs. I hold out my right arm to be injected. Then, nothing.

I open my eyes.

Ice-cold fear floods.

"Where is my baby?"

Stuart is sleeping in a plastic chair in the corner. I try to sit up, but there is a burning pain, like fire, where my bump used to be.

I am not pregnant any more.

"You've had a beautiful, healthy boy," says a midwife.

Thank God.

"Would you like to hold him?"

She helps me into an upright position before she hands him to me.

"Make sure you hold his head," she says.

I know, but I don't mind her telling me.

He is dressed in the little white onesie I chose for him, decorated in teddies. Someone has put a blue hat on his head. There is a white plastic name tag around his wrist. He has the smallest eyelashes. Every now and then he jerks suddenly as if he's realizing that he's out in the real world and has space.

"You're perfect," I say to him.

Stuart opens his eyes, leans forward, stands up and comes over to us. He looks tired but happy.

"You're awake," he says. "Isn't he gorgeous?"

"He's early. Is he all right?"

"Yes, he's fine. He wasn't that early."

I want to cry with happiness. Finally. I am a real mother. I did do the right thing.

I'm only given a few precious moments holding him before my blood pressure is taken and I'm told I'll be prescribed liquid morphine for the pain. After all the years I've spent eating as organically as possible, trying to limit toxins, I'm a rapid convert to drugs.

I'm offered a cup of tea and some toast. To my astonishment, I'm hungry. The tea is the nicest I've ever tasted.

"I'd like to call him Jack," I say to Stuart. "I think he looks like a Jack."

Stuart smiles. "It sounds like a good name."

I knew he wouldn't disagree. After all, he can't. As he keeps telling me, he's "done this all before."

When I'm feeling up to it, I ask Stuart to pass me my phone so I can let my dad know the good news.

I freeze.

There's a missed call from Greg asking why Camilla hasn't answered her phone, followed by a couple of messages. He's been delayed by an unexpected, money's-too-good-to-turn-down job.

I check the time. I abandoned Camilla in almost the middle of nowhere and took her car.

My whole body feels like jelly. I hope nothing awful has happened to her. I don't want to be like Camilla and Nina. I don't want to be responsible for something bad happening to someone else. I do the only thing I can: confess to Stuart.

I give him Camilla's car keys.

"Be quick," I say as he leaves me and our son alone.

I'm wheeled through to a bed in the middle of the main ward. It's busy and noisy. Jack is attached to my bed in a plastic cot. Navy curtains are drawn around us to give an illusion of privacy, but they can't block out sounds.

My first hours as a new mother are the worst of my life. I cannot feed Jack, and when he cries, I press the call bell as I'm not allowed to lift him due to my surgery, but the midwives are overworked and cannot get to me quickly. Babies cry.

Every time the doors to the ward open, I pray to see Stuart and not the police. I ring him every twenty minutes. Panic at being trapped and so helpless is utterly surreal and petrifying. When I see a message from Stuart, I want to cry with relief.

Camilla's fine. She's back at the house. She got a taxi, which she says you owe her for by the way. She's furious, but relieved. Especially when I told her where her phone was hidden. Without her contacts, she couldn't remember any phone numbers.

Did she say anything else? I message back.

What I mean is, is she going to call the police and tell them I locked her in her room, then stole her car? I doubt it—she's hardly likely to want to get them involved after confessing to murdering my old boyfriend—but being helpless creates powerful paranoia.

I'm going to drive her to the hospital to get her car, then she's heading home. She's not going to say anything, but she's as mad as a snake. I'll check into a hotel, get some sleep. I'll see you both as soon as poss in the morning.

The woman next to me sobs relentlessly, yet I'm unable to move to go and comfort her. The pain, the spaced-out feeling, the sheer sense of powerlessness is overwhelming again. This is not what I had in mind when I craved being a mother, not at all. When I look at my baby, rather than being in awe, I pray that he doesn't start crying again.

I'm wrung-out by the time Stuart visits. I can't feed Jack. Formula is a totally frowned-upon no-no. I learned this in prenatal classes, where everything sounded so straightforward and simple. I'm desperate and exhausted.

"I'll sort this," Stuart says.

It's such a relief to hear those words. He arranges a single room for me, reserved mainly for women who need longer hospital stays. Once I've been assisted upright and proved I can stand, then walk, unaided, I'm wheelchaired to the relative sanctuary of the private room. Finally, Jack feeds. He feels calmer in my arms. I cry in gratitude. When he falls asleep, Stuart lifts him from me and places him in his Perspex cot attached to my bed.

From where I'm lying, all I can see are windows. Yet, my world exists here, in this room. It's tricky to imagine that life really is going on outside.

Yet it is. A message from Camilla among the many good wishes (there's even one from Ben) bursts my bubble.

Greg's dumped me. But that's not the problem. We need to talk as soon as you get back. (And not through a bloody door this time or on some drive in the middle of nowhere.) Don't think I won't hold that against you forever. Btw, I know I'm supposed to say "congratulations" and ask how you are, etc. But this is important otherwise I'd be ignoring you.

I message back. OK. Sorry.

Me too.

It doesn't let her off murder—not by a long way.

I no longer think of Greg as benign "Greg from the book group." I'm certain he has had a hidden agenda for a long time. If I'm right, then he's dangerous to us both. Who'd have thought that after all this time, Camilla and I would have to join forces for both our sakes.

Nina's legacy is becoming increasingly twisted in ways I don't think even she could have foreseen.

THIRTY-SIX

Everything at home looks the same, yet my whole life and out-look is different. One of the first things to catch my eye is the camera. It strikes me as odd how so very recently I was obsessed with watching the footage. The shift in my priorities is stark. Actually, thinking about it...

"We need to dismantle that one," I say to Stuart, pointing at it. "I don't want to use Greg's stuff anymore. We can buy and install our own."

I can't be too careful. I don't need to feel paranoid in my own environment.

While Jack lies asleep (thank goodness) in his car seat, I read congratulations cards, admire flowers and open gifts. Exhaustion hits at the same time that Camilla opens the back door and lets herself in.

Strange to think that I haven't seen her since that night. Time has distorted, like it could have happened weeks or months ago. The memories are dreamlike, almost as if they never happened.

She makes a show of oohing and aahing over Jack, but I can tell that she's desperate to speak to me.

"He's gorgeous."

"Thanks. Please don't stand too close to him," I can't help saying.

She throws me a look.

What does she expect? She confessed to murdering my ex-boyfriend.

"Coffee?" Stuart asks.

Camilla shakes her head.

Stuart gives me an *are you all right to be left alone with her?* look behind her back.

I reply with a discreet nod.

He retreats to his study, closing the door behind him.

"It wasn't true, what I said," she begins. "I was angry, I wanted you to stop questioning me. I thought that if I told you what you wanted to hear, I could sort it out later."

Photo evidence aside, I don't believe her. Charlie's body had a head injury. It's like some sort of sick game, was it a rock, a cooler or a metal pole? For now, I'll let her deny away. It's not as if I don't have enough on my plate, and Nina isn't here—as we all well know—to corroborate or dispute her story. I go along with the polite chitchat.

"Sorry about..." I say.

"It was a ridiculous stunt, but I understand now why it's been so hard for you having me and Louise back here. Do you want to talk about it?"

"No."

Jack makes a sound. We both turn and stare at him. He remains asleep.

"So... Greg," she says. "Guess why he dumped me?"

I shrug.

She lowers her voice. "I asked him if he'd had a fling with Nina."

I glance at the closed study door as if Stuart could be on the other side, listening.

"Talk about an OTT reaction! He was furious. I'm scared."

"I'll find out what Greg knows. It sounds as if he's just put two and two together and come up with—"

"Exactly four," says Camilla.

"He can't have proof," I say.

"What if Nina gave him some, even if she didn't realize it?"

"I have an idea..."

Camilla throws me a look of such hopeful gratitude, that—briefly—I forget how much I detest her.

I phone Greg.

"I have a favor to ask," I say.

He agrees.

I will keep my plans a secret until Sunday. Meanwhile, Stuart fusses. He opens and closes windows, drapes blankets on and off Jack. He cooks healthy stir-fries when I just want to eat a pack of cookies or a bowl of cereal. The children show intermittent interest in their half sibling. It takes all my willpower not to shoo them away from Jack. He looks so fragile in comparison.

Deborah comes in and takes over for hours at a time. I let her.

Stuart keeps trying to tell me "how to do it."

Midwives visit and give me forms to fill in to ascertain whether or not I am at risk of postnatal depression. I am not. I know what depression feels like and this isn't it.

But something isn't right.

There's an expectation to be happy after having a baby. I am not over the moon. I am anchorless, fearful and in a constant state of fight-or-flight.

I write charts, religiously figuring out how much sleep I haven't had. Naturally, it's unhelpful, but I can't stop myself. When painkillers ease off between doses, barely controllable anger flares, which I know is wrong because I have a healthy baby. I must be more grateful. Flashbacks start one night and increase in intensity.

The agony.

The shortage of midwives.

Being alone with no clue what was happening, I think my baby and I are dying but no one has told me.

Seemingly insignificant little things all seem to add up, one on top of the other.

Young trainees are sent in each evening to ease the burden of the exhausted staff, one of whom picked up Jack when he started to cry, held him upright and, staring at him, said, "Not on my watch!" gripping him as though she were about to give him a shake.

Why didn't I tell her to put my baby down?

The casual cruelty and lack of empathy still leaves me reeling.

Why didn't I speak up, stand up for myself more?

Other women manage to give birth without drugs, without fuss, breastfeed without being curtly told, "It's not that difficult."

I become obsessed with thoughts of old, vulnerable and sick people and other pregnant women, wondering what I can do to save them.

I encourage the steady stream of visitors at home because without distractions, my thoughts threaten to tip me over the edge. I consider calling Christian for an emergency phone consultation, but no one can help me but me. I must keep busy.

On Sunday, I announce that I have a surprise. I bought Felix and Em new outfits online in colors that suit their complexions and Stuart a new T-shirt, which I ask them all to wear.

"Let's go outside, guys!"

It's a beautiful afternoon, a good sign. It's so nice to feel in control of something, I feel almost manic with joy. I prepare a picnic with all the children's favorites. I even buy some meat sausage rolls to show that I'm being open and happy to compromise.

I lay the table outside, creating a magazine-perfect picture. The crockery and napkins match (peach, Emily's favorite color at the moment). I fill two jugs of water, one plain for the children, adding freshly cut slices of limes to the other. The table-cloth edges waft gently every time a slight breeze picks up.

My phone rings: Greg.

"I'm outside your front door," he says.

I let him in with all his camera equipment and show him out to the back.

"Right, everyone, Greg has come to take some informal portraits of us all," I say with a grin I've seen so many times on children's TV presenters. "The sooner it's done, the sooner we can have our yummy picnic with lots of special treats!"

"What's all this about?" says Stuart.

The T-shirt is too tight on him; having me looking after him has made him regain all the weight he lost after Nina's death.

"I've asked Greg to take some new family portraits," I say. "They're overdue. We need Jack and Goldie in them."

"I'm not keen on the guy," Stuart says under his breath.

"Well, he's here now," I say. "It's too late to send him away."

Perhaps Stuart did suspect or sense that there was something going on between him and Nina.

Greg has a surprisingly authoritative voice while he's work-ing and does not come across as the sort of person that anyone would want to disagree with, which is a relief as neither Stu-art, Felix, Emily, Jack or Goldie are acting thrilled with the impromptu photo shoot. Their sulky expressions (not Jack or Goldie, of course) grate.

By the time it's over, even I'm glad. It's hard being on the other side of the camera—I don't think I've ever fully appreci-ated that. It will make me a better, more patient photographer when I return to work. The children are hungry. They pile a random assortment of food onto their plates. Goldie hangs around, ever-hopeful that the children will feed her something under the table.

Greg declines my offer to eat with us, thankfully (Stuart invented an excuse to escape almost as soon as the final picture had been taken), so I accompany him back to his car.

"Thanks, Greg. Any chance you could get these to me as soon as possible, please?"

"I'll do my best."

He loads his bags into the trunk. This is my opportunity to talk to him.

"I know it's none of my business, but..."

"You want to know why Camilla and I broke up?"

"Yes."

"You're right, it is none of your business. I thought I could make it work with her, but I have too much baggage. I do have something to tell you, though. I've been trying to hold it in or time it properly, but I've realized that there's no perfect time or way."

My heart thuds.

"I'm all ears."

"There really is no easy way to say this, but, Marie, Nina was a murderer."

THIRTY-SEVEN

"What on earth makes you say such a thing? Who, exactly, did Nina murder?"

"Because it's true." He doesn't answer my second question.

"Why do you think Nina was a murderer?"

"She told me."

"I don't believe you."

"Not in so many words. But who goes looking for the relatives of some guy they hardly knew when you've had a terminal medical diagnosis? Something didn't add up. She spun some story, but failed to convince me."

"What was the story?"

"That she was on holiday with you and Camilla and a bloke went missing. She felt bad for his family and it was something that had always preyed on her mind."

"Yes, that's true. But it doesn't sound like much to me. What good would it do raking over it? Think of her children."

"That's what she said to me when I started probing."

"Well, then. You definitely told me in your office that you did some work for her but hadn't reached a conclusion."

"I wasn't sure of all my facts then, hadn't quite put everything together."

"As you know, I was on that holiday as well, and believe me, it was a tragic accident. If that wasn't the case, it would've been investigated more thoroughly at the time."

He falls silent.

"Do you know how long I've waited to have a family? I love Felix and Emily as if they were my own. I promised Nina I'd look out for them."

The look he gives me isn't pleasant. "I thought you'd be on my side. But it seems you've known all along and worst of all, you seem to find it acceptable. I had you down as a person of integrity."

"We do need to talk. There's a lot I can maybe help you understand. Charlie, the man whose relatives she was looking for, was my boyfriend. I loved him. She was trying to help me."

"I know what I know," he says. "I wasn't one hundred percent sure, but then Camilla filled in the blanks. Inadvertently, admittedly. There was just too much that was a coincidence. She said that the two of you had fallen out over a man. I was curious as to why she showed up at your house that time and joined the book group. I could sense a story straightaway. Maybe I should've pursued a career in journalism—I have a sixth sense when people are trying to hide things. I did consider it before I became a PI."

"Are you trying to tell me that you targeted Camilla deliberately?"

"No. But it helped that she provided the missing pieces of the information."

"Did you and Nina…? What I'm trying to say, was she the woman you loved?"

"Yes. We clicked immediately. But…she was married, unhappily, but she said that her husband had a hold over her. And the only way she could make amends for a mistake she'd made was to stick it out with him. She didn't love him."

"Yet you moved here to be close to her?"

"She wasn't happy about it at first, but she came round. We only slept together once more after I moved. It happened so naturally and unexpectedly. We went out for a walk together. I intended to take photos of the bluebells. Nina longed to paint them. There were carpets of blue—we both agreed that we'd never seen them look so stunning. We got carried away, we couldn't stop."

"I get the overall picture, thanks. Think about what you've just told me. Can't you see, Greg, when you talk about integrity, sometimes it's not that simple?"

He ignores me. "We knew it was wrong, that she'd never leave Stuart, but I hoped. And then it was too late. She came to me for help, so I gave it, willingly, because I respected her and had feelings for her. But I didn't know the real her, it turns out. It made me feel like I'd been lied to or misled."

For someone who gave me such a *live and let live* lecture in his office, he is very judgmental.

Greg hates books where the villain gets away with it. He likes bad people to get their just deserts. He believes in an eye for an eye. He believes in vengeance.

"This isn't a novel, Greg. You've got conspiracy theories about actual people with real lives who could be gravely impacted. Children, I'm talking about."

He doesn't budge. If I don't accompany him to a police station ("which will, long-term-wise, help you, Marie. You really don't need to be an accessory by keeping silent"), he'll go alone.

"I'm being cruel to be kind, Marie. One day you'll thank me. The longer you ignore this, the worse it will get."

"You've got this all wrong, Greg. You're going to get fined for wasting police time. I'm sure there's nothing they can do about an alleged historic crime abroad, possibly caused by someone who has passed away. It will just cause grief for her family. And me. I thought we were friends."

"If you knew she'd done absolutely nothing wrong, you

wouldn't be trying to buy time. Do the right thing. I can't keep such damaging knowledge inside my own head for much longer. It's unhealthy and stressful. On top of that, her accomplice, or silent witness, whichever you'd prefer, is Camilla."

Good Lord. Who does he think he is?

"There's guilt in silence," he says. "It gives away more than people realize."

He's not wrong. If Charlie's accident had been genuine, I believe that Camilla and Nina would've tried to get help and spoken up about what happened. Their guilt was most definitely in their silence.

I try a change of subject.

"Greg, did you put all those horrible notes through the door? Was it to scare me off? Was the camera a ploy to throw me off your scent?"

"No, but I do know that it was Tamsin."

"How do you know?"

"I saw her putting something through your letterbox one evening."

"That's it?"

"That's it. Believe me or don't believe me. It doesn't bother me either way. I thought you'd like to have it confirmed on camera, proper proof and all that. I'm sorry that hasn't been the case so far. One more thing before I go...Tamsin did voice her disgust to me, and others, on more than one occasion regarding you and Stuart moving on so swiftly."

I watch him drive away, wishing he was leaving our lives for good.

Holding Jack in my arms, I say good-night to Emily and switch off her light.

"Marie?" she says into the darkness.

"Yes, darling?"

"Are the photos Greg took going to be better than the last ones?"

"What do you mean?"

"He took pictures of me, Mummy and Felix when he was still practicing, but Mum said they weren't his best."

Goose bumps snake down my arms. "When was this, darling?"

"A long time ago. He had a beard then. He made us say 'pizza,' not 'cheese.'"

"Can you remember what you were wearing?"

She shrugs.

"How about if I show you a photo?"

"Okay."

My legs are weak as I walk down the stairs and remove the first ever anonymous picture I received through the letterbox (of Nina and the children) from my evidence collection. Back upstairs, I show it to Em.

"Yeah, that's the one he took."

"Thanks, darling. You've been a great help."

I feel such a surge of affection for her. I've been too harsh in judging her. She'll go far, she has a natural energy and curiosity about her that I must nurture and appreciate more.

Why is Greg trying to frame Tamsin for something he's done?

THIRTY-EIGHT

I'm trapped by all my unwise past choices. As much as I hate what Camilla (and Nina) did, Greg doesn't have the right to make that decision. One thing makes perfect sense: I cannot allow Greg to break my promise to Nina. She trusted *me* to protect her reputation for the sake of her (now my) family. If Camilla is investigated for this, she'll pin all the blame onto Nina because she isn't here to defend herself. Clearly, she's spun Greg a version where Nina played a greater role than she did.

An accomplice indeed! Jack does not need to be connected (however loosely) to something so negative and potentially harmful so early on in his life.

I take several walks a day, sometimes with Jack in his buggy, but mostly in his baby-sling, which slows me down as I stop every few minutes to check that he's breathing. This morning, after school drop-off (it's wonderful to be back into some kind of routine), I'm braving a longer walk with Goldie by my side. As I head toward the main part of the village, a bird thrashes in a beech tree, making me jump as I exit the pathway.

I bump into Clare and Ellie from my prenatal classes pushing a designer buggy with a beige canopy. They both look tired, yet so normal. They had a boy, too, also named Jack.

It's the first time I've met their Jack and vice versa, so we are all obliged to go through the baby introductions and the obligatory sharing of sympathy when it comes to sleep deprivation.

"Let's catch up properly next week," says Ellie. "Florence from the group is going to organize a picnic in the park."

"Sounds good," I say automatically.

Ellie looks completely fine, serene, even. She does not look traumatized by something as natural as giving birth. Which means that there's definitely something wrong with me. I turn back.

Camilla is sitting on our back doorstep, waiting for me, clearly desperate for yet another furtive chat.

"I feel like a sitting duck," she says.

I open the door and we walk into the kitchen. "We do need to do something. He blamed Tamsin for the creepy messages, but something Emily said makes me think it was him all along."

I outline my plan.

"Have you gone out of your mind?" Camilla says. "This will make things worse! We'll never get away with it."

I quite like the fact that she doesn't watch what she says around me. Everyone else avoids certain words which may imply that I'm not coping as well as Nina did. Camilla does no such thing. It's strangely refreshing and comforting to be around someone with no filter, someone who doesn't treat me as if I'm fragile.

"All we have to do is threaten him, make him see that he really has no choice but to shut up."

"It's blackmail," she says.

"Well, come up with a better idea. I'm trying to help. Surely you can think of a reason you need to go round to his office? How hard can it be? I'll come out of this situation mostly all right. You, on the other hand…"

"Yes, I know. He's trying to have me investigated for murder."

"Well then, even better. You have a perfectly valid reason

to visit him. Persuade him he's got it wrong. Use your imagination."

"Okay, I'll do it," she says. "I don't have a choice. What am
I looking for?"

"Client records we could threaten to leak to make his business
lose credibility or, better still, proof that he was behind all the
threatening cards. We received a ridiculous plaque-type thing
as an anonymous wedding gift. While not threatening, it may
help prove something."

"Greg is not stupid," she says. "If he's gone to all the trouble
of executing some malicious campaign to scare you, he's not
going to use a traceable debit card to buy them or nip down
to the local convenience store to be served—and remembered
by—Mrs. Miller, is he?"

"Fair point, but he'll have slipped up somewhere."

I hope.

"I doubt it. He wouldn't be so keen to run off to the police
if he thought he'd get caught, too. He's a private investigator.
He must have loads of nifty techniques."

"Didn't he ever share any information with you?"

"No. And why would he want to scare you?"

"I think he was more in love with Nina than he admitted
to and he felt betrayed by her. I think he is getting back at me
because he can't and couldn't with her. Or he felt that he was
looking out for her by frightening me away."

Camilla shakes her head but doesn't tell me that I'm wrong.

"It's creepy to think that I slept beside that man and didn't
suspect a thing."

"It is."

But not as creepy as Camilla admitting that she has no choice
but to carry out the plan. There's no way she'd be this desperate if she'd made it all up as she now claims.

We agree to meet the following afternoon.

"We can surprise him at his mate's fishing lodge with our

findings. He goes nearly every Thursday," says Camilla. "We can talk to him without interruptions or being overseen."

"Well, it's either that, or we set the place on fire with him in it."

"Sometimes, Marie, I can't tell whether you're serious or not."

Mess with my family, mess with me.

It's another day for visitors, as no sooner does Camilla leave than the doorbell rings. I spy through the camera (the one I insisted in installing myself) and spot Tamsin clutching an actual mini olive tree in a cream plant pot.

"Congratulations," she says as we politely sip Assam tea. (Another gift, from whom, I can't remember.) It crosses my mind that I've never drunk as much tea in my life as I have since I've had a baby.

"Jack's gorgeous," she continues.

Everyone tells me that my baby is gorgeous before they can move on to what they really want to talk about. It's the rules. I'm not complaining. Jack is gorgeous. I realize that my mind has drifted. Tamsin is speaking.

"I'm sorry that I haven't got round to visiting until now. Please let's start again. I'm sorry I lashed out. It was just brutally unfair that Nina died so young. My sister had a health scare around the same time and it frightened me. I took some of it out on you. We miss you at the book group."

"Thank you," I say. "How's the online dating going?"

She pulls a face. "You wouldn't believe some of the creeps on there! Do you know, one of them asked me to pay him back for the meal he *insisted* on paying for because I wouldn't go back to his place! The cheek!"

I pull a sympathetic face.

"I have something awkward to ask you," I say. "It's very awkward, which is hard because we've only just made up and you know…" I nod at the olive tree standing on the kitchen counter.

She looks nervous.

"The nasty cards you've been sending…"

She frowns and tilts her head. "Cards?"

"Yes, and the creepy flowers?"

She looks over at the olive plant as if she's made an error and brought flowers instead without realizing. The thing about lies is that if you're not a bloody good actor, it's deceivingly hard to act surprised. She doesn't ask for any details, which is another giveaway. Perhaps I should give her lessons in how to lie.

"Why are you asking me?"

I take a risk, run with my hunch. I need to know, was it Greg or Tamsin?

"Just something we caught on camera," I say, keeping it vague. "But I don't want to report it to the police because I'd hate to do that to a friend. I just want them to stop," I say. "I understand if people initially disapproved, but it's time to move on, live and let live, don't you think?"

"Very wise," she says.

"I'm prepared to leave it at that," I continue. "Although I will keep the footage. I hope I won't need to use it."

Tamsin holds a smile in place, clearly trying not to give away her relief, but it's visible to me nonetheless.

So, Greg wasn't lying.

I'm happy to play the let's-pretend-it-never-happened game. I've bigger things to worry about as long as she behaves in a less *Midsomer Murders*-like fashion in future. If I hadn't thrown out the wedding gift plaque, I'd return it to her now. I should feel angrier, but I'm too tired, and it's quite fun watching her discomfort as she sips her cold tea, then glances at Jack, asleep in his baby chair as if willing him to wail. He remains chill. Well done, Jack!

She opts for another tactic by rummaging around in her bag.

"I also came round to invite you to this," she says, handing over a leaflet, which opens out into three sections. "It's to raise money for new sports equipment for the school."

I study it. It's an art exhibition with small photo samples of some of the exhibits. Greg (no surprise there) is taking part, and there are pictures of his photos.

"Did you decide which photos he'd use, or did he?"

"We selected them together, actually. He said he's going to help me sort out my own collection. They're all just saved to my laptop and I never look at them."

"How long have you been friends?"

I'm trying to figure out if she had access to the photo he took of Nina and the children. Tamsin appears oblivious, seemingly grateful that she's off the hook.

"Oh, ages! We matched on a dating app a long while ago— don't tell anyone, *please*—but we both agreed that there was no way. I mean…Greg. He's just, well…Greg, don't you think?"

I don't trust myself to reply. Instead I give the leaflet further attention. The samples of Greg's photos are of a bluebell wood in among shades of mauve, blue, green, purple and brown. An easel holding a canvas stands among the bluebells. A woman with long, dark hair, her back to the camera, is painting the woodland scene, capturing it perfectly. It is Nina's unmistakable style.

I shiver. Is Greg about to go public with his affair with Nina? If so, it means he's beyond caring and his threats are real.

The urge to see Christian is overwhelming. I tell Stuart that I need him to watch Jack while I go to a medical appointment alone. I catch a bus, which takes an age, but I enjoy staring out the window at the passing forest scenes with nothing to do and only myself to think of.

All therapy rooms are the same but different, I know that, yet Christian's should feel familiar by now. It doesn't. Something has changed. I look around the room, at the throws over the chairs, the jade cushions, the books on the shelves. Same titles, same human problems. I half considered going to seek the help of a new therapist, start afresh. But I can't face repeating the bland facts detailing my early life.

So, here I am, back with Christian. It's comforting. I'm out of sorts and I can't seem to find the right words, despite his familiar presence making me feel safe. I'm vulnerable, so much so, that if someone is too nice to me, I will crack. He isn't the overly sympathetic type, and I need that right now.

I tell Christian about the helplessness I felt during Jack's birth, the anger at losing control, the avoidable indignities, the rage that won't go away, the pregnant women I want to warn, yet can't because I don't want to frighten anyone. How I feel duped by the classes I went to prebirth that misled by discussing calming playlists and aromatic oils. There was no mention that some women will have no choice but to accept drugs and medical intervention. No balance, however well intended. How I'm amazed that the human race continues, how any woman has more than one child.

"But," I say, desperate to lift my mood, "my dad visibly melted the moment he met Jack, despite his reservations about the father. The best thing out of all of this, the actual moment that has totally erased my doubts, is that the day I placed Jack in my mother's arms, she smiled. She lit up. It was genuine joy and recognition. I won't have anyone tell me that it was anything different. Everything I did to have my baby was worth it."

He smiles. We drift into silence, and for once, I don't rush to fill it. He does.

"It sounds as if you may have suffered from post-traumatic stress disorder or birth trauma. It's not uncommon, apparently. There is more understanding and recognition surrounding it now," he says. "I've encountered a few cases. The guilt is silencing because everyone knows someone who hasn't been fortunate enough to have their own child or has lost one, so naturally, they keep quiet out of consideration, out of fear of appearing ungrateful, making a fuss or even the fear that social services will deem them an unfit mother and remove their child."

He must've felt passionately about it as he breaks one of his own unspoken rules by sharing a rare snippet of personal information: that it affected his wife after their third child.

When there are mere minutes left of the session, during the usual time when Christian disengages and wraps up our conversation as best as he can, the urge to confess that's been building all session, the desire for release, is so overwhelming that I blurt out, "I aborted Charlie's baby."

Apart from what I shared with Camilla, I've never said these exact words out loud to anyone. Deciding to trust Christian has (at times) felt like being given a key to unlock my subconscious. Although painful, telling the truth, the real story, isn't as frightening or as exposing as I feared. Strangely. I already feel better than I do when I lie or mislead.

I recall an ex-friend telling me that people feel as if they are wasting their time and energy on a liar. I understand a little better now what she meant, although I was furious with her at the time because clearly she was having a go at me.

Discovering who Louise was—it was such a monumental punch in the gut. I was hurt when Charlie started to distance himself from me, even before the holiday. I thought that he—we—were too young, unprepared, too everything-wrong or not-ideal-circumstances. I thought he'd feel trapped, pull away further. I'd read this article in a magazine about attraction that stated that people could sense neediness, that it acted as a subconscious repellent. A part of me felt I'd done the right thing, or so I thought. But, of course, afterward, during the horrendously shocking aftermath and the months that followed, it dawned that I'd killed a part of him, too.

If only I'd known about Camilla's pregnancy, I'd still have felt pain, of course, but it wouldn't have been as all-consuming.

It's not until after I leave that I realize it wasn't the room that was different. It was me.

★ ★ ★

The session leaves me feeling disconnected, my mind crammed full of disturbing thoughts. A part of me had hoped before the session that Christian would somehow sense that I'm on the edge of doing something dangerous and desperate. I wanted him to intuitively see beneath the chitchat, to push and probe beneath the *look how well I'm coping* veneer and save me from myself.

In my darkest moments, I regress to a childlike state and want someone to give me permission to silence Greg.

There's a side of me emerging that scares me; the desire to protect what I've given so much up to attain is so overwhelming, so powerfully strong that I feel frightened of what I might do and how easy it would be to lose sight of what's right and what's wrong.

THIRTY-NINE

Stuart hovers in the kitchen as I zip up my jacket and fill a water bottle.

"Are you sure you're all right? As in, all right, all right? You've been quiet."

"Fine. I just need a long walk."

He doesn't look convinced. "What route are you walking and how long will it take?"

Stuart has developed an annoying sixth sense when I'm up to something. It's disturbing and ups my anxiety level another notch.

I make up a route and mutter something about being "a few hours" and "stunning early autumn leaves." He doesn't question me further because Jack saves me from more interrogation by wailing through the baby monitor. Stuart goes upstairs to console him.

I hesitate before I shut the back door behind me. I want to cocoon myself away, snuggle up with Jack. I could tell Stuart the truth and get him involved. But Nina trusted *me* with her dying wishes. She wouldn't have wanted Stuart to find out about her fling with Greg either; she trusted me to hide her secrets. Just like she trusted me to protect her family. Me, not him.

★ ★ ★

Camilla opens the guesthouse door with a cup of coffee in her hand.

"Want one?"

"Go on, then."

As I watch her brew it, I already know what she's going to say.

"I'm sorry, it was impossible to get into his office, let alone sniff around and hunt down potential blackmail information undisturbed."

"So, we are left with no choice but to visit him at the fishing lodge and appeal to his better nature or make him see sense."

"I'm going to reason with him," says Camilla, as if my disappointment has spurred her on. "Let's go. Two against one."

I mull it over. "No, I think it's best if I go alone. I haven't done anything wrong. He thinks you deserve to pay for what you did, along with Nina's family, too. I'll be firm, emotionally blackmail him. I'll tell him about Felix and Emily's nightmares and force him to understand."

"I can't let you go and see him alone."

"Why not? He's hardly likely to turn violent when he's utterly convinced by the notion that he's way up on the moral high ground. Plus, he won't be expecting me there, he'll be caught off guard."

"I'll babysit, get Stuart to go with you." "No, don't. He doesn't need to hear about the affair. I can handle this, really."

"He can't stake a claim too high up the morality mountain if he terrorized you with the notes and creepy flowers."

"It was Tamsin, not Greg."

I update her on my discoveries. Afterward, still seemingly fearfully reluctant, she gives me directions to the lodge and watches through the upstairs window as I walk in the direction of the river. It starts to drizzle.

It takes a good forty minutes because I'm mindful not to push myself too hard. I have to rely solely on Camilla's description;

there's no hope of using any phone maps in the woods. As I approach what must be the correct property—because it's the only one in the right spot—I notice the rain has stopped. It was impossible to tell beneath the dense trees. I spot a rainbow. Such an auspicious sign buoys me up.

The lodge is more of a large wooden shed with a raised outside porch. There's a sign near the open gate stating that it's private, but the flimsy fence around the perimeter of the grounds is in bad need of repairs and not conducive to blocking out unauthorized access.

I hang back by the trees. The place is deserted. No way is Greg here. His car is not in the drive and the desolation is freaking me out. Perhaps I'm not quite right, as Deborah is fond of suggesting lately.

A couple of hikers walk past the lodge, soon followed by someone on horseback along the nearby bridleway. It is comforting, especially when I notice that kids have tried to build a den a few meters away, which means that I'm not a million miles away from civilization. I inhale the coolness of the approaching evening, feeling the best I have in a long time, in fact. Almost myself again. It gives me hope.

It's time to leave, to admit defeat. I feel strangely at peace with the decision until I hear the sound of a car approaching, growing louder. I stay put, out of sight.

A smallish black truck drives past, flattening the wild grass in the center of the track as it does so and parks by the gate. It's not Greg's, which is bloody disappointing. Yet a part of me feels relieved. This was clearly a crap idea of mine. I've tried my best. My conscience is clear.

Yet it is him. Either he's bought a new vehicle or he's borrowed one. I watch as he unloads bags and equipment, losing my nerve. I manage to convince myself that it's not my problem after all. Yet really, it is, because Nina isn't here and I am. My hands start to feel numb. The sun is disappearing and the rainbow has dissipated. I pull on my gloves and a woolly hat, before walking alongside the grounds to warm up.

Greg is setting up by the river to the far right of the grounds where there is a gap in the lush foliage. He looks as if he's settling in for the evening or night. He is erecting a proper, sturdy-looking tent, not like some of the more flimsy ones I've noticed fishermen use by the local rivers and lakes over the years. He sets up a camping stove, a canvas stool, various kinds of fishing equipment, a box and rods.

Barely dormant anger returns at the sight of him getting on with his life so calmly, not a care in the world, while he has the power to upend mine.

I open my mouth to call out to him, a cheery *Hi, Greg, I was just out walking and fancy seeing you here…*type of thing, but I remain mute.

I walk back in the direction of the woods. Go or stay? Stay or go?

Camilla's fear of violence comes to mind. It's one thing encountering someone in a civilized environment, like our book group, quite another out here in the comparative wilderness. I tease out a branch from the random kids' makeshift den, taking time to make my selection, like playing Jenga.

A mistake. The whole structure tumbles down, echoing loudly. Afterward, silence. No one but me was disturbed by the noise. I come to a decision. Taking the branch with me as a protection (if need be), I'll make one final attempt to talk to him. If that fails, well, so be it.

The wind picks up slightly again; I hope Greg packed his winter woollies. He has been fast, efficient and has wasted no time in my brief absence. He's comfortably sitting down as if he's drinking in the view, exuding an air of calm and contentment. He hasn't set up a rod yet; he must be taking a breather.

"Hey, Greg!" I call out.

"What are you doing here?" he asks as I approach.

"I wanted a chat in private."

"There's a surprise."

"Please listen to me, Greg. My baby is related to Nina's children, he's their half brother. Please don't humiliate her memory in public. For my sake and Jack's, if not hers. I understand that you're angry."

He shrugs. "Marie, I don't have anything against you personally, but I'll do whatever I feel is right. Please don't tell me that you came all the way out here just to try to make me change my mind? I'm a man of my word."

"Can we at least talk a bit more?"

He shrugs, as if my feelings are inconsequential, and picks up a rod. He points to the branch I'd almost forgotten I was still clutching.

"Planning on tying a piece of string to the end of that and joining me in a spot of fishing?" he says, as if he thinks it is some sort of suitable response.

He sits down on his stool again, picks up his rod all the while chuckling—actually laughing to himself—as if my feelings and fears are inconsequential.

I don't know at what point I make the decision, or if I ever actually consciously do, because something possesses me, propels me forward. A rush of rage floods as I recall all the hours of angst, and each terrifying moment hurtles back in short, sharp, brutally clear images. I rerun through all the fear he's caused and all that he can make me lose.

I'm convinced that I must've have gained Nina's strength, too, because I lift the branch up above my head.

He swings round and looks up at me, his expression a picture of uncomprehending horror as he topples to the side when the branch strikes his right cheek. The fallen camping stool lands and rests against his calves. A pair of small, black binoculars drops into the water with a plop.

Greg doesn't reach out for them—he doesn't do anything. He

just lies there, silent. His face is tilted away from me. I lean over slightly to examine him closer. I force myself to look, to see if he's hit his head on something, but there is no obvious rock or stone and without me moving him to check, I can't tell.

Oh my God. This isn't right. Yes, I'm angry but I only wanted to give him a fright and perhaps demonstrate how desperate and helpless I'm feeling. Of course, there's no way he could have appreciated just how much I've been through to have a child of my own and attain the family life I now have.

My legs start shaking uncontrollably; I fear I might collapse. Jack is a young, helpless baby. I've wanted him for so long. What if I'm arrested? Sent to prison? I couldn't bear being separated from Jack. Stupid, I've been so stupid.

"Greg! Greg! Get up! You're giving me a fright. I'm sorry."

A slight breeze rushes through the trees. I wait. Nothing happens. Greg does not get up. I don't know what to do. I just wanted to make him understand what lengths he'd driven me to. A small plane flies overhead. Greg's face is mere inches from the water's edge. I gently nudge his head slightly forward with the branch. Water snakes past, lapping the bank, splashing his face.

I'm going to have to get help and explain that it was all an accident.

Something grabs my foot. I scream and drop the branch. Greg is holding on to my right ankle, it is unsteadying. He turns and stares at me.

I can't stand it, I can't cope with it, I have to make him stop. It's freaky, like dead, staring fish eyes, and he won't let go. He sits up. With his free hand, he reaches over and I see him pick up a serrated knife from his fishing box. I kick his arm. He drops the knife and tries to grab it. I lunge for it with my free hand and pick it up to threaten him, but he grabs my other foot, the knife is pulled from my grip and a pain rips through my recently healed cesarean scar.

As I fall back, Greg sits up. My pain vanishes as I focus on his eyes—he's staring, but unfocused, as though he can't recognize me. His right arm lifts, still clutching the knife as he leans toward me. I roll over onto my side to pull myself up, but no sooner am I on my knees, I feel hands around my calves as Greg pulls me toward him.

"Let me go!" I twist around to kick him but my aim is completely off. "Greg, it's me, Marie! What are you doing?"

I reach for a large stone, grab it and throw as hard as I can. It hits the side of his head with a dull thud. His eyes bulge and—still—they stare at me but his arm drops and the knife slides to the ground. Thank God!

"Greg!" I say.

It's the wrong thing to do, it snaps him out of his trance and he lunges forward, his hands grasp my neck. I can't speak. I grab his fingers—they slacken as I pull them off. I scream. I see someone else… Camilla!

Greg turns around. Camilla picks up the knife as I back farther away. At first, I think she's going to throw it in the river and try to run away with me, but a look of utter rage twists her features, her jaw clenches and she grits her teeth. Camilla raises the knife and aims for Greg's throat. She stabs. He slumps back onto the bank, the knife sticking out. She clasps it tightly with her right hand as if she's trying to yank it out, to have a fresh go.

"Stop!"

We both stare as blood oozes onto the soil. A horrible, gasping sound fills my ears. Oh God. It's horrible. His eyes! I can't look at his eyes anymore. One hand is slumped on his chest as if he was going to try to pull the knife out himself, but gave up.

"What are you doing?" I yell.

Camilla's words tumble out as she struggles to catch her breath. "I couldn't let you come here alone. Louise went to a friend's for tea, you took so long, I was afraid, I saw you, and him…"

We both stand and stare. Birds flutter in the branches, making us both jump. Camilla bends down and picks up the large stone as if she thinks Greg (or someone) is going to attack her. I hold my breath as she holds it above him. There is silence and stillness apart from the running water and a breeze in the trees. She throws the stone into the river.

"We don't have long," she says.

I still expect Greg to sit back up, splutter, come after us, do something. Nothing. Through the flowing water, I see green moss being tugged downstream, dancing in the current. Stones and debris rest on the sandy bottom. It's...mesmerizingly beautiful.

I pick up the fallen branch and chuck it into the water, watching it float away as innocently as a Pooh stick.

I wish I'd watched more true crime. There's something more we should be doing to cover our tracks, I know there is. Theft.

"We have to steal something," I say out loud.

Camilla ignores me, remains standing still, eyes wide, staring at Greg. She's looking at him in hatred, not fear. I grab her by the shoulders and give her a shake.

"Steal something! We've got to take something."

We both look around.

"His wallet?" she says.

I don't want to go through his pockets because I'll be sick— I can't touch him. It comes to me: his camera. It's easy to find, just inside the entrance to his tent. I shove it in my backpack and we both turn and walk away as fast as we dare.

The pain in my abdomen is gnawing, viselike.

Camilla stops. "The knife!"

I look down at her bare hands, half expecting to see them covered in blood.

"You'll have to go back and get it," I say.

"I don't want to."

"You have to. I'm not."

I bend over and clutch my stomach as I wait.

★ ★ ★

Halfway back, there is a rushing noise in my ears. I stop to be sick, but nothing comes up.

As we approach the guesthouse, I can't stop shivering. I've read so many stories where this type of thing happens, just one mistake, one wrong turn, and a whole life, or lives, can be completely upended. It can't be happening to me. I won't let it.

We go in through the back door.

I pull off Nina's old wellies. They were too big anyway, I must destroy these, get some new ones of my own, the right size next time. It's funny how, despite the trauma, my mind is quick to figure out ways to self-preserve.

Still, I throw up into the sink.

Camilla puts the kettle on. My teeth chatter. She gets a throw off the sofa and wraps it around both of us. We both sit there, shivering.

I force myself to look at my scar. It doesn't look split, but the pain remains.

"It was the lesser of two evils," says Camilla. "We had no choice. He was threatening us. He was going to destroy me, Louise, damage Nina's memory for Felix and Emily. He grabbed the knife, not you. It was self-defense, Marie. I had to save you."

"It was history repeating itself."

Everything I found so abhorrent about Charlie's death, I've mimicked.

"Where's the knife?" I ask.

"In my bag."

"Get rid of it!"

"Where?"

"I don't know." My mind is all over the place. I don't want to know. "Somewhere not overlooked by CCTV. I'll wait here, be your alibi, but don't take forever. Disguised in something in a public bin? Water? One of the lakes, maybe?"

My silence is now in exchange for Camilla's, and vice versa.

We've formed an irreversible, macabre bond. Yet, perversely, I believe that Nina would approve of us becoming—if not exactly friends—then companions or partners in crime, at last.

FORTY

I awaken to Jack's cries, the shouts of the elder two fighting over something—I can't ascertain what—and the reality of yesterday's horror. Rain, so heavy it sounds like hail, hits the windows. My abdomen aches. My head throbs. My stomach is a ball of pure dread. The doorbell rings and I rush to the toilet to throw up. Nothing happens.

I hear Stuart go downstairs. I stand by the bedroom door, listening. I wait, anticipating the thump of police boots on the stairs. It's our online grocery delivery. I'd forgotten all about it. I hear Stuart exchanging pleasantries with the driver. After several minutes, my breathing still hasn't returned to normal but my legs stop shaking. I call the doctor's surgery.

"How did you do it?" asks the GP as she rolls down some blue paper onto the examination bed.

"I don't know," I say, clambering up. I lie down.

"Does it hurt when I do this?" Prod.

"No."

Another prod. "This?"

"No."

There's no permanent damage, thankfully. I'm prescribed painkillers and told to be careful.

Back home, there is no way I can take it easy. I go to Camilla's. We sip hot chocolate and talk in polite code because Louise is in the room. It's impossible to articulate what I really want to say, and Camilla clearly feels as agitated as me.

"Lulu, sweetie, seeing as it's such a rubbish day, why don't you go and watch a movie in my room?" says Camilla. "As a one-off. You can even take your drink up with you."

We remain silent for several moments, even once we're alone.

"How did you manage to act so normally after Charlie died?" I say. "I remember you sitting by the pool in a pink sarong, sipping a cocktail as if nothing had happened. Like we're doing now."

"We had no choice but to behave as normal or go down the confessional route. One or the other. We made a decision and stuck with it. Shock is numbing. It insulates you from the true horror."

Camilla is a cold fish. She would've stabbed Greg a second time. Maybe more, I'm convinced of it. Perhaps she was more furious at being dumped than she let on. Did she feel the same toward Charlie when she realized it wasn't her he wanted, but me?

"Why did it end with your partner in Canada?"

It suddenly feels important that I know.

"He met someone else. We had a lot of bust-ups, which got physical. I had to get away."

I feel cold, despite the second hot chocolate Camilla makes us.

I lie on the sofa back home with Jack in his chair beside me. Intermittently, he jerks awake before dozing off again. Felix and Emily watch *Finding Nemo*.

After Camilla's revelations, when I discovered that the money

Nina had been putting away was for a charity dedicated to help-ing the families of people missing abroad, I'd felt—just for a moment—so utterly, pathetically, *grateful* that she'd cared enough about me. Stupid of me to react like that because of course, it never was about me. It was about her guilt.

A memory resurfaces: Camilla lost her temper with an on/off boyfriend at art college. We were in the canteen one lunch-time and he wouldn't immediately agree to the plans she was trying to make with him that night. She yanked the tray from his hands and dropped it. As we all stared at the congealed mess of food and the smashed white plate on the floor, she insisted it had been an accident. I can't remember his name. Jake? Luke? They split up for good after that.

I doze. Snagged to a rock is silky, emerald moss, which frames Greg's face as he stares up at me, incomprehension and utter be-trayal written all over his features. I run, but my body doesn't move. I hear Jack screaming, but when I rush to his cot, it's empty.

I sit up so quickly that Felix and Emily gape. I must look frightening—my hair is all over the place and my hands are shaking.

Jack is perfectly quiet. His little chest rises and falls. The elder two are absorbed in clownfish, shrimp and turtles. Everything is calm.

Guilt festers, churning my insides, making me raw with fear and self-hatred. Every rattle of the letterbox, every ring of the doorbell, reinforces that I have no idea if I'm on borrowed time or not.

The news is delivered the following afternoon by Tamsin. Of course.

Snippets of (mostly false) news filter through over the days, reminding me, yet again, of Charlie. News, old and new, in-tertwines.

Back then it was the talk of the island. Apparently. There were various rumors when it was known that someone had drowned. It wasn't clear initially whether it was a man or a woman.

Now it is: *He slipped and fell, an accident, a robbery gone wrong, an ex out to get him, a heart attack, a stroke, a branch fell from a tree and hit his head. Stabbed, brutally murdered.*

I listen to all the local discussions and dissections with an expression of *No? How awful* plastered to my face, when inside, my stomach is knotted in panic and my mind is full of remorse and fearful regret.

Dreadful. Apparently he was alone. Wasn't noticed for days because of bad weather. A tragic accident. Cowardly attack on a lone fisherman.

Stuart doesn't seem as upset or shocked as everyone else is.

This seems harsh, despite him telling me that he didn't like Greg.

I keep repeating the words *it was an accident* over and over until I believe them myself.

Which it was, really, on my part. I wish I'd never gone to make him see sense. I wish I'd spoken up at the time.

It's amazing how many noises can sound like police sirens if you have a guilty conscience. Images of being cuffed, being guided into the back seat by a police officer, won't leave me alone. I wouldn't be tough like the characters I see in soaps, defiantly saying, "No comment." I'd crack within the first five minutes and confess, probably even to crimes I didn't commit.

Every day I have a better understanding of Nina and how she must've felt. Strange, really, that I know her better after her death than when she was here. If she could be involved in murder, so it seems can I. The metamorphosis is complete.

I donate the money Nina collected in Charlie's memory to the charity of her choice. I tick it off my mental list of good things I must do to make amends, however small.

Nothing helps take my mind off things for long. I go for endless walks in the forest with Jack and force myself to walk along the river, but never as far as the exact spot of Greg's death. Guilt gnaws. Fear grows. My mind tosses around endless scenarios. I thank God for the heavy rains that followed; it must have helped destroy some evidence. I force myself to think of every worst possible outcome so that I can mentally prepare.

I recall reading that it's not just what you leave at a crime scene, it's also what you can take away: mud, plants and seeds. The list could be endless. I throw away the gloves and hat I wore on the morning of on bin collection day, then wait and watch as our garbage is crushed in the truck. The backpack I used on that fateful day I wash many times and I use it regularly on outings with the kids so it's filled with all kinds of crap.

When I'm not tending to Jack or Goldie or the children, I finish Nina's memory album with increased urgency. I have the photo evidence of Nina, Camilla and Charlie, hidden in plain sight, yet buried within the Ibizan pictures. It's a part of Nina's history—our history. It felt disingenuous to leave Charlie out, somehow, thinking about it. You'd have to know the story to realize that it's incriminating.

Yet I made a mistake, too.

If I'd opened my mouth and told anyone who'd listen that Charlie was missing, regardless of how common it was, I could have extracted myself from them. I should've insisted that we went to the police or at least tried to find him. They'd have had to face up to what they'd done, however accidental (or not).

I'd have got on with my life, but by allowing myself to be guided by Nina, I remained immersed in her world. That's the thing when you don't fit in—you'll be surprised at what you'll do to make yourself more popular. I used to lie to make my life appear better. Back then, I lied through my inaction and a failure to act in the right way. It's hard to forgive myself.

Now I'm stuck with yet another dilemma. And poor Charlie has faded away from collective consciousness. No one truly cares anymore. It gives me an idea. Perhaps I'll create a small album for Camilla, too. Everyone hopes they're safe, that they can slip through life with various misdemeanors or more serious crimes unseen, but the camera can always see.

When I photographed weddings or parties, the purest details were revealed in the images I snatched during the final hours. The same applies to that photo of the three of them. A random stranger snapped that image while momentarily hidden behind Nina's camera, unseen in the picture, yet they were a witness to Charlie's final hours. It can't do any harm for Camilla to have a reminder of that.

I close the album's cover; it's done. In pictures, Nina's old life flows into the new: me, Jack, Goldie. The last picture is one of all the children in age order: Louise, Felix, Emily and Jack. Two boys, two girls. #happyblendedfamily. We have plenty of digital memories. It was important to have a physical one, too.

I phone Christian. There must be something in my voice, because he agrees to see me the following morning.

I am openly wistful, raw, with nothing left to hide. Strange, really, that I used to carry around with me this (yet another) irrational fear that if all my therapists somehow got together, they'd get a fuller, more accurate picture of me. For the first time, I speak from the heart, unfiltered.

"Be careful what you wish for," I say. "It's one of those things that you think you get but I didn't, not until I wished for something for so hard and so long, then I got it. And it wasn't what I wanted, or what I thought it would be. I *did* set out to steal Nina's life."

"In what way?"

"I thought if I had what Nina had, I'd be happy. She and I… We were friends, but I felt like her assistant or yes-person rather than us being in an equal friendship, especially as we got older. Love, hate. Envy, desire. It's hard to explain what keeping quiet, or always guessing at what is the right thing to say or do, does to someone. I was never fully myself because I thought we wouldn't stand a chance of being friends if I was. She was full of life, full of confidence in herself."

I stop. I feel pathetic even saying that out loud. I don't want Christian to think that our work together has been a complete waste of time, that I don't get that I am responsible for my own actions, feelings and thoughts. I do—now—but it doesn't take away the fact that, deep down, I have to admit to myself that I always wanted what she had.

I believed that Nina had it all: a family (and no question about whether or not to keep her first baby), work she adored, a life partner I assumed she loved, too. I really did believe that the grass was greener. Now, here I am. And it's not nearly as green as I imagined. I try to explain it differently.

"When I was with Ben," I say, "I always carried with me a sense of feeling like the outsider looking in. I especially hated bank holidays, all those families crowded everywhere having *fun*."

We both laugh.

"If we were out having lunch, I'd stare at my plate of olives, artisan bread or whatever, and I never fully appreciated what a luxury it was because I wanted to be with the *other* people, the ones who were having a nicer time than me. I assumed that they were the ones who had got it right, who understood life's rules. I truly had no idea, did I? I was wrong."

Christian smiles in understanding.

"I thought I'd be happy, that I had one chance to grab at life and everything would slot into place, that it would all suddenly make sense...yet it hasn't happened that way." I take a deep breath. If I'm in the mood for being honest, I may as well continue. "I wanted a baby to replace the one I didn't have, plus the future family I didn't have with Charlie."

"It's normal to mourn a loss," he says. "You made the right choices for you at the time."

"A friend of mine died recently in horrible circumstances," I blurt out.

I drop tiny hints at my guilt at falling out with him not long before his death. It's tempting fate (a tiny bit) but I trust Christian to keep anything he guesses to himself. From my patchy online research—I'm cautious with my searches—it seems that therapists don't have a legal duty to report a crime; it's an ethical decision based on their beliefs. I think Greg would approve of these small clues. He loved figuring out if the bad guy was going to get caught.

My mind flits. I want to get everything off my chest. I have a feeling that it's time to say goodbye to Christian for good.

"I'm trapped," I say. "By my own choices."

"You do have options, Marie," he says gently.

I nod as if I do. "I know," I lie. "Thank you."

When it's time to say goodbye, I want to tell him how sorry I am that there are some people who are beyond help and that I am one of them. Christian is one of the good guys, he tried his best with me. I'm going to miss him and his understated wisdom.

I wait outside on the street in the rain for Stuart to pick me up. I'm too emotional and tired to drive. I told Stuart that Christian is my grief counselor. It's true, really.

Stuart is late.

I don't take out my umbrella. I enjoy the sensation of getting wet, the fresh drops on my face. I've always found it hard after a therapy session to switch off. This time is no different. I can't erase the image of Greg's eyes, the sound of the stone hitting his skull or Camilla's hardened expression and the knife penetrating Greg's throat.

Was it the exhaustion, was it anger, fear? What was it that made me so determined to get involved, to silence him? I'm still shocked by my own rage. The desire came from somewhere deep within. I genuinely felt such a rush of protection toward my family, that it was inevitable. If not then, if not that way, then maybe another. It's hard to know. I'd love to debate it—properly debate it—with Christian, rather than hint "at something bad, something irreversible, feeling enormous guilt at being the last person to see my friend alive," but I have to work within the only safe boundary I've got. Which is myself.

When Stuart pulls up, I open the passenger door, sit down and twist around to face the back and give Jack a smile. His car seat is empty.

"Where's Jack?"

"Deborah is looking after him. She's going to pick the children up from school, too. We're not expected back for a while."

Stuart doesn't take the expected route home. Instead he drives toward a different part of the forest.

"Where are we going?"

"We need to talk."

I don't like the sound of this at all. Yet, I can't think of the right things to ask or say.

It's only as he starts driving up a track, that I realize where he's headed. The lodge. My insides knot.

He pulls over.

My heart beats faster.

"I think this is the spot. It looks like the place from the news," he says before he switches off the ignition and twists around in the driver's seat so that he can fully look at me. His expression is intense. "You're going to need me, in a perverse kind of a way, just like Nina did. To be your alibi."

Oh. My. God.

"You've been acting strangely," he continues. "I recognize the signs. Guilt. I appreciate what you've done, Marie. Greg was a bad man. He targeted Nina when she was vulnerable."

"How did you know?"

"She told me about him. She didn't want me finding anything out after she was gone that she couldn't atone or apologize for."

"But you've never said anything—"

"I didn't blame her. I blamed him. Then, I was so grief-stricken after she died that in the grand scheme of things, it didn't seem important anymore. But he kept coming to the book group, getting friendly with Camilla, then you, as if he thought I didn't know. When you told me he was with Camilla that one night, I was concerned. Yet things have worked out. After all, give someone enough rope..."

I don't know Stuart at all, any more than I suspect Nina did. Sickening thoughts race, one after the other, twisting and re-forming. Did I take an unnecessary risk? Have I tried to protect him when he didn't need me to? Perhaps he would've taken action himself. Have I been played?

Yet, he looks so calm, so innocent, so grateful, even. I can't trust my own mind to figure it out.

The rain beats down on the car roof. It's oddly soothing. It's nicely isolating being temporarily cut off from the outside world. Drops snake down the windows.

"As for you and what you've done for this family...it's amazing, Marie." He takes my hand. Both our hands are cold and mine are shivering. "There's something I've never told you. Kevin is my stepfather. I found out during my teenage years that my real father had run off, left my mother as soon as he found out she was pregnant. It's hard to explain, but I wanted my children to have a perfect-as-possible life, free from the negative actions of others. It's very important to me."

"I see."

I'm not sure I do. I'm genuinely surprised and hurt that Suzanne never let it slip. I assumed we were close.

"Everyone has secrets. I loved Nina. I had to do whatever it took to make things work for all our sakes. Listen carefully to me." He cups my face in his hands. "It's too much of a burden for you to keep this to yourself. It ate Nina up. I'm not going to let that happen to you."

"It wasn't me," I say, releasing his hands from my face as gently as I can. "I didn't kill Greg."

"No," he says. "But you're culpable. You and me, we're a proper team now. Just like Nina and I were. You can rely on me, I promise. I won't let you down."

Tears fall. It wasn't supposed to be like this. The faint taste of salt dissolves on my lips.

"Don't be sad," he says.

I need to get away from this place. "Drive us home, please. It was a horrible choice of place to bring me."

However, something becomes clear: if Stuart is my alibi, then I can't be Camilla's.

FORTY-ONE

Greg's camera has remained hidden and camouflaged among my own equipment. Until now.

It needs a new home. I remove it from its hiding place.

I hesitate outside Camilla's front door—listening—before I slide in my key, even though Camilla's car isn't in the drive. She's showing no signs of moving out.

I befriended her ex-partner on social media. He accepted my friend request within days. It amazes me that people still do that—I could be anyone. He appears to have moved on, as he is expecting a child with a new partner. After lots of painstaking digging and reading of endless inane comments, as well as figuring out that he had disagreed with Camilla moving away with Louise, I discovered that he was married when he and Camilla met. Although, I'm hardly in a great position to judge. What I can judge, though, is Louise's welfare.

The police investigation is ongoing. The rumors don't die down and every time an article or someone's comment sails close to the truth, it strengthens my resolve that I will not pay for Camilla's—or Nina's—mistakes any longer. I hide the camera in the top of Camilla's wardrobe, beneath some scarves I've never seen her wear.

As I go downstairs, removing my new gloves (paid for in cash and which I will dispose of), I nearly trip down the last two stairs in shock when Louise's bedroom door opens.

"Louise! Why aren't you at school?"

"I thought you were my mum! Please don't tell her."

She doesn't ask what I am doing in her home. Full of tears, she is desperate to share how she hates her new school, is being bullied, how Camilla doesn't want to hear it.

"I want to live with my grandparents, but they say that they're too old to have me living there full time."

I hug her and promise that I'm going to make everything all right. I'm going to fix this. I often hear Christian's voice in my head: *Control the things you can.*

I'm invited to rejoin the book group, and there's no choice but to return because everything I do or say has to be about behaving normally. I walk into Tamsin's living room and scan the faces. Miriam, Abigail, Sharon, Camilla, they are all there. I genuinely half expect to see Greg. It's weird how quickly I've adapted and managed to convince myself that he's alive and well.

I think, not seeing him there, that's when everything really hits me.

Afterward, we both walk home together. She has forgotten to bring a flashlight and her phone battery is low, so I light the way with mine. She collects Louise from our place and I walk them both back to the cottage. As she opens the door, I rummage inside my bag and hand her the photo album I've created especially for her.

"A gift," I say.

"What for?"

I say goodbye to Louise and wait until she is well inside the cottage before I reply.

"A little reminder," I say. "Pay particular attention to the first photo. It's the last one ever taken of Charlie. Physical proof that you lied about leaving him at the party, along with the confession you made to me which I recorded." (It's very bad quality, but I don't need to mention that.) "All the little things add up."

She is silent.

"I've always had this little theory that the purest photos, the truth, if you like, are taken near the end of any event," I say.

"This is all very unnecessary," she eventually says.

"Maybe," I say. "But you can't blame me for having an insurance policy. I must think of my family. I know if it ever comes up, you'll try to pin all the blame on Nina because she's not here to defend herself. I also know that you'll try to pin Greg on me, too, if it ever comes to it. Yet it seems you're the one with a history of violence, not me. It wouldn't look good for any potential future defense of yours if you were also being investigated for an earlier murder. You would be the common factor, the link between the two. Not Nina. Not me."

I leave her with that thought as I walk slowly back to the main house.

Stuart has truly embraced our marriage. He has chosen to see what I did to Greg as evidence of my loyalty. Suddenly, despite everything I've worked for, it feels like living with a python, the life squeezed out of me in a torturous, slow fashion. When I read to the children from *The Jungle Book*, I am morbidly fascinated by the picture of the grinning snake coiled around the main character.

But I can't leave Stuart, for so many reasons. He might say he wouldn't drop me in it for the kids' sake, but who is to say that he won't? There are no guarantees that there wouldn't be any drunken pillow talk with a future person or that the urge to come clean won't strengthen over time. People change. I learned that from Christian.

Stuart insists that he wanted to protect Nina, but it's undeniably creepy how almost gleeful he was to be able to do the same for me. As if he knew it would trap me, make me stay. Because I can never risk being separated from my son. Greg's observation that Stuart was Nina's penance makes more sense to me now. And now it seems he is mine. While no one has been arrested for Greg's murder—yet—I suddenly almost feel as though I'm serving a sentence of my own; if I stay with Stuart until Jack is eighteen, that's roughly six thousand, five hundred and seventy days.

Kevin and Suzanne are due to fly over to spend Christmas with us. Even my brother with the eternal itchy feet is apparently going to return before the new year. Life goes on.

Meanwhile, we'll all carry on pretending. If we get up each day, get dressed, eat breakfast, check our calendars and go through the motions, we'll all get through this. In a few more years, the children's memory of Nina will have diminished further, and it will be me who they turn to for advice. I'll try not to overprotect them, however hard it may be. I want their upbringing to be different than mine even though I now realize that every parent does their best. I will teach them to be strong, to not rely on other people for their own self-worth, to make friends or keep friends who want to be with them because they genuinely like them. Also, to choose a partner wisely.

I frequently dream of the knife that killed Greg: the sharpness of the blade, the serrations, the easy-grip handle enabling Camilla to hold it so tightly as she plunged it into his neck.

I start to believe that nothing will ever happen, Greg-wise. But I promised Louise that I'd help her. Sometimes, things need a push.

I invite her over to stay one evening and we watch movies, talk about her problems, make pancakes (sweet and savory), which are a big hit with everyone. I pretend not to notice when she feeds Goldie a small piece of one.

We laugh. There is a genuine, happy family atmosphere, full of camaraderie and love. Perhaps I'm not so bad after all.

Camilla is arrested at dawn.

An anonymous tip-off. Apparently.

FORTY-TWO

So much makes sense now. Nina tried desperately to cling to the respectability of normality, hide behind society's cruelly deceptive structures. Foundations can be ripped away. Marriage, mortgages, children. No matter how much she clung to the rules, she couldn't shake off her guilt.

Strangely (or not?), Stuart and I get along well at times. When he's a caring dad, when he and I have to make joint decisions for the benefit of our family, I can mentally push away the downsides. We ebb and flow, a perpetual work in progress involving endless compromises. Just like a real marriage, I guess.

Despite my own deliberate yet subtle targeting of Stuart, and his of me, I really can't see how it could've worked out any other way. Did Nina deliberately plant the idea in his head? Mine, too? We'll never know, and I'm surprisingly all right with that. Perhaps it was her way of protecting her children. On some level, I can now understand. I do honestly believe that Nina would approve of most of my actions.

I may have taken over Nina's life, but in doing so, I've fulfilled my main promise to her: to protect her family. Because there was one thing that Nina knew she could rely on: my loyalty, however misplaced. Yet she was right to trust me, at the time.

Nina wanted Stuart to concentrate solely on the children for as long as possible.

Stuart means well, but if he makes noises about selling, Marie, move in! Make a mess to put off any potential buyers, get the kids on board, they'll love it!

I smile at the memory.

I've had to make up my own version of what really happened on that fateful boat trip. I like and choose to believe that Camilla probably made a bitchy comment about me and it awoke some kind of buried loyalty in Charlie, which is then what motivated him to turn on her while they were on the boat. Nina knew how guilty I felt about Charlie and how I held my drunken jealousy (however provoked) partly responsible for the path that ultimately led to his death. I'd told him that he wasn't good enough for me or whatever I could think of in my rage that would hurt him as much as possible. Nina heard every vicious word, knew how shameful my last words to him had made me feel, yet she never gave me even a hint that I wasn't to blame for what happened. In her blind confidence of me in the end, Nina overlooked the fact that everyone has a breaking point.

Yet, still my feelings toward her ebb and flow. Affection, resentment, love, hate. But, right now, strangely, I miss her more than ever.

Four months later...

I retrace Nina's footsteps for one of the last ever times. Winter cold clings to my coat as I walk round the garden with my camera, the strap slung around my neck. Goldie is sniffing and exploring. Jack is asleep in his buggy. I take photos of him, of Goldie, of the grounds. I snap the final pictures, memories for the children.

"Say goodbye to this place," I say out loud. "We're moving to a much better home."

We are. It's a cottage with a thatched roof and a smaller, more manageable garden filled with rhododendrons. It's not so far away, Deborah can still visit. We'll be away from the bad memories, as well as Tamsin and her constant comments:

Did you really not suspect a thing, Marie? I've never known a murderer before. I wouldn't admit this to just anyone, but it's really quite morbidly exciting! Not for Greg, obviously, that's just awful. She pulled a sad face. *Do you know I've had offers to sell my story? I've said no, of course, but when you think about it, she just used to sit there, in our book group as if butter wouldn't melt!*

If only she knew...

We are still awaiting Camilla's trial.

Stuart stuck to his word. So far, he has been utterly convincing as my alibi. I'll give him that.

I've promised Camilla that I will look after Louise to the utmost of my ability, despite her threats to drag me down, too, until I reminded her of our conversation, that she is the one with a violent history, not me.

It's a shame I don't know where she hid the knife. She'll never tell me now.

"I'll love Louise as my own," I said. "She'll want for nothing. I'll treat her as if she was the daughter Charlie and I would've had."

She gave me a strange look when I said that. I think it was then that the penny really dropped, that she knew or suspected what I'd done, but visiting hours came to an end. She had to return to her cell.

Really, what did she expect me to do? I'll have to watch my back if and when she's released. I can't erase the look on her face during the moments she stabbed Greg or forget what she did to Charlie when he rejected her. Her ex in Canada had a lucky escape, it seems to me.

★ ★ ★

I walk around to the front of the house and lift Jack out of his buggy. Goldie barges ahead, pushing the front door open. I survey the empty rooms, full of cardboard boxes. Stuart took a lot of persuading to put the house on the market but eventually agreed to the ever-hopeful fresh start we all crave and need to believe exists.

All the boxes are, of course, labeled. Inside one marked Louise's Bedroom is a gift, a framed picture. It is of me, Charlie and Camilla. I now have the power to reveal his true identity. I won't be cruel, I won't completely destroy the tale Camilla spun about her father: *a whirlwind holiday romance.* However, I can take charge of the narrative now.

I hear tires on the gravel. Still holding my precious Jack tightly, I open the door.

A woman in a trouser suit emerges from a black Audi.

"Mrs. Thompson?" she calls out.

"Please, call me Marie," I call back. "You must be Jennifer, from the real estate agency?"

"Yes."

I watch as she walks toward the entrance gate and replaces the For Sale sign with a Sold one.

Nina was right to rely on my loyalty because I never let her down. I promised her three things: I swore that I'd look out for her family and however possible, sabotage any new relationships and ensure that Stuart held on to their family home.

But I have no qualms about breaking one of my promises and selling the house—it's just not the one I thought I'd break. After all, the house was her dream, not mine. I'm entitled to something of my own. This is my story now.

★ ★ ★ ★ ★

ACKNOWLEDGMENTS

As always, there are many people to thank. I'm very fortunate to have the support and encouragement of my brilliant agent, Sophie Lambert. Her patience, insight and wisdom are limitless. The same can be said of the wonderful Wildfire team: Alex Clarke, Kate Stephenson and Ella Gordon; and at Graydon House, Brittany Lavery and the team in North America. Definitely included in this list are Hillary Jacobsen at ICM, Katie Greenstreet and Emma Finn. Grateful thanks also go to the wider teams at C&W Agency: Jake Smith Bosanquet, Kate Burton, Alexander Cochran and Matilda Ayris. Also to Dorcas Rogers and Tracy England for all their help. I appreciate your tireless hard work, dedication and passion. An enormous amount of teamwork goes into publishing a book, and I am grateful to everyone, including eagle-eyed copy editors Julia Bruce and Chris Wolfgang, and proofreaders Sarah Bance and Terra Arnone. Huge thanks to the fantastic team at Headline: Rosie Margesson, Jo Liddiard, Siobhan Hooper, Tina Paul and Rebecca Bader. And to the fantastic team at HarperCollins Canada: Leo MacDonald, Karen Ma, Cory Beatty and Kaitlyn Vincent.

Thanks are extended to the wider writing community: booksellers, librarians, readers, bloggers, reviewers, authors. Thank you for being so generous with your time. Thanks to my writing friends: my fabulous Faber group (five years since we first met!) and to the Ladykillers for the support and many laughs. Thank you to all the readers from around the world who take the time to get in touch.

A huge thank-you to Nicci Cloke (Phoebe Locke) for her patience, kind support and for the endless tech help (especially the time I sent photos of my laptop in a panic!). Thanks also to Nicci for introducing me to Arabel Charlaff, a psychotherapist who offers a service called Characters on the Couch. The therapy scenes in this book are partly a result of attending psychotherapy sessions in character and attending Arabel's course at the Faber Academy. Thank you to Arabel for taking the time to answer my questions. Huge thanks also to Amanda Reynolds for all your help (another excellent listening ear).

Some more thank-yous: Graham for your photography advice and Susan for answering dog-related questions (and Amanda, too). To my mum and in-laws and to my wonderfully kind friends who helped out during the summer holidays childcarewise: Henri, Lindsay and Nicolette.

A mention and hello to my local book group: Danielle, Jemma, Jo, Linda, Lindsay, Steph and Vicki.

A friend of mine, Sharon, wanted "to be in the book," so her name features as part of the novel's book club.

To all my friends who make me laugh and spread the word, too many to list individually, I want you to know that I appreciate it. I hope I tell you.

Thank you, of course, to my mum, dad and sister, my in-laws, and my wider extended family. Finally, thank you to my husband and sons, who have to live in the same house as me when I'm in my own thoughts and inhabiting a different world. Their love and pride in what I do mean everything.

THE LAST
WIFE

KAREN HAMILTON

Reader's Guide

GRAYDON
HOUSE

1. What did you make of Marie? Hero, victim or villain? Or somewhere in between? Did you have sympathy for her? Why or why not?

2. Marie and Nina both keep secrets from each other—with disastrous results. Think of a time you kept a secret from a friend. How did it impact your relationship?

3. Many people have ambivalent feelings about family. Why do you think Marie feels so trapped by how her relationship with Stuart has unfolded?

4. This novel takes place in a small village, and everyone seems to know everyone else's business. What is the role of community in this novel?

5. Think of a time you wanted something very badly. How did it make you feel, and how did it affect your life?

6. Do you think that Nina was right to keep the truth about Charlie from Marie? Why or why not?

7. Reflect on Marie's career as a photographer. At the beginning of the story, she says, "The camera does lie." What does this mean, and how does this sentiment play into the story?

8. Marie is desperate for children of her own, and this desire drives her to extreme ends. Can you think of other stories in which the desire for children and/or family leads someone to disregard their own moral compass?

9. What do you make of Camilla's decision to return to the UK? Do you think she made the right decision? Why or why not?

10. How does envy function in this story?